New York Times Bestselling Author

Elaine Barbieri
and
Allie Pleiter

The Redemption
of Jake Scully
&
Masked by Moonlight

HARLEQUIN® LOVE INSPIRED®CLASSICS

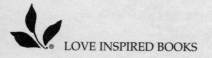 LOVE INSPIRED BOOKS

Recycling programs for this product may not exist in your area.

ISBN-13: 978-1-335-00755-1

The Redemption of Jake Scully & Masked by Moonlight

Copyright © 2018 by Harlequin Books S.A.

The publisher acknowledges the copyright holders of the individual works as follows:

The Redemption of Jake Scully
Copyright © 2008 by Elaine Barbieri

Masked by Moonlight
Copyright © 2008 by Alyse Stanko Pleiter

www.Harlequin.com

Printed in U.S.A.

CONTENTS

Elaine Barbieri was born in a historic New Jersey city. She has written more than forty novels and has been published by Berkley/Jove, Leisure, Harlequin, Harper, Avon and Zebra Books. Her titles have hit *USA TODAY*, the *New York Times* extended list and other major bestseller lists across the country, and are published worldwide. Ms. Barbieri has received many awards for her work, including Storyteller of the Year, Awards of Excellence and Best Saga Awards from *RT Book Reviews*. Her novels have been Doubleday and Rhapsody Book Club selections, and her book *More Precious Than Gold* was a launch novel for Romance Alive Audio. Ms. Barbieri lives in West Milford, New Jersey, with her husband and family.

Books by Elaine Barbieri

Love Inspired Historical

The Redemption of Jake Scully

Harlequin Intrigue

Silent Awakening

Visit the Author Profile page at Harlequin.com.

THE REDEMPTION OF JAKE SCULLY

Elaine Barbieri

Rise up and help us;
redeem us because of your unfailing love.
—*Psalms* 44:26

To my brother, Andrew Favati,
whose life was a celebration of God's love,
and who left us with the memory of his smile.

Prologue

Weaver, Arizona
1872

The heat of midafternoon scorched Weaver's main street as Lacey Stewart walked wearily toward the Gold Nugget Saloon, pulling a limping burro behind her. Her platinum pigtails were in disarray, her face and clothes smoke-stained and the wound on her forehead was grotesquely swollen. She was feverish and more tired than she had ever been in her eight years of life, but she forced herself on.

Dizzy and disoriented, unaware of the sudden silence her appearance elicited, she pushed open the saloon doors and started toward the bar. Fragmented sounds and images raced across her mind. She heard again the gunshot that had awakened her at dawn in her grandfather's isolated cabin. She heard the crackle and hiss of fire, felt the intense heat and choking smoke of the blaze suddenly surrounding her. She saw her grandfather appear beside her bunk to guide their frantic escape through the flames and falling beams.

Flashing even more brightly before her eyes was the image of her grandfather slumping to the ground when she thought they were safe at last, the same moment when she noticed the bloody wound on his chest.

Her grandfather's final words resounded in her ears as Lacey reached the saloon bar—words he had spoken as he pressed the small, family Bible he had also saved from the flames into her hand...

Go to town...to the saloon. Ask for Jake Scully. Tell him who you are. He'll take care of you, Lacey. Take the Bible. Depend on it. Let it guide your way. It's yours now, darlin'. Go...hurry...

Lacey nodded in response to the voice so vividly real in her mind. She had been too numb to cry when she covered her grandfather's still body with Careful's blanket and placed a bunch of drooping wildflowers beside it. His instructions had reverberated in her mind as she left the charred remains of the cabin behind her and turned the burro toward town.

She couldn't remember when Careful started limping, or when she started walking.

The sound of her name penetrated Lacey's confused haze. She turned and looked at the big man standing behind her in the silent saloon.

The big man reached for her as darkness abruptly consumed her.

Lacey came slowly awake in a large, shadowed bedroom. Her head hurt, and her limbs felt too heavy to lift. She shifted in bed and moaned slightly at the pain. She became belatedly aware that the tall man was sitting close by.

She strained to focus as he moved closer. She heard him say, "My name is Jake Scully, Lacey."

She rasped in response, "My grandpa's d-dead."

"I know."

"The cabin burned down."

"I know that, too."

"My grandpa said—"

"I know what he said." Interrupting her, the gentleness in his deep voice a comfort despite his emotionless demeanor, Scully continued softly, "Charlie Pratt was a good man. He staked me when I needed help. He did right when he told you to come to me. Don't think about anything but getting well, Lacey. I'll take care of the rest."

The single tear that slipped out the corner of Lacey's eye somehow scorched her skin as it slid across her temple, but Scully brushed it away with his hand.

His deep voice soothed her fears as her consciousness began slipping away and he repeated, "Don't worry. I'll take care of everything."

A bright afternoon sun lit the large, masculine bedroom as Lacey slowly awakened. She glanced at the unfamiliar surroundings, gradually recalling the numbing events of the past few days: long, confused hours as she lay in bed recuperating from her wounds; the doctor's gentle words; encouraging female voices; Jake Scully's reassuring presence.

Lacey's throat choked tight and she threw back her coverlet. She stood up slowly, hardly aware of the oversize man's shirt and rolled-up trousers that hung loosely on her childish frame as her attention was caught by the muted notes of a song coming from the saloon below.

She stepped down onto the barroom floor and walked toward the piano, where a gray-haired, heavily mustached fellow continued his enthusiastic playing.

Unconscious of the attention she drew from the saloon patrons, Lacey joined in, singing hoarsely, "Oh, Susannah, don't you cry for me..."

So intense was her recollection of the many times she had sung that song to raise her grandfather's spirits after another day's fruitless prospecting, that she did not notice the two men at the end of the bar who exchanged anxious glances at the sight of her. She did not see them slip out the doorway into the alley, nor did she see them meet up with the fellow obviously waiting for them there. She had no way of knowing that fellow harangued the two men for their ineptitude before slapping money into their hands and giving them new orders that they dared not ignore.

Lacey remained beside the piano as the old fellow banged out another boisterous tune. She was unaware of the danger that still threatened her until Scully slid a protective arm around her shoulders and turned her back toward the safety of the upstairs room.

Chapter One

New York City
1882

Yes, her hands *were* trembling.

Lacey stared at her hands, at the long slender fingers with well-tended nails, and at the smooth skin and soft palms reflecting the total absence of physical labor. They were "a lady's hands," which she realized was part of the reason for their shaking.

Lacey did not need to look at her reflection in the dressing table mirror to know that the image there further perpetuated that description of herself. She was no longer eight years old. The neat pigtails she had worn when she first arrived at Mrs. Grivens's Finishing School had given way to a graceful upsweep of hair that was still a brilliant platinum in color; her childish features had matured into a finely sculpted countenance in which clear, blue eyes hid uncertainty behind a downward sweep of surprisingly dark lashes; and her slender, adolescent proportions had developed feminine curves that went undisguised by the ladylike cut of her simple, gray traveling dress.

Lacey glanced toward the hallway door at the sound of a soft knocking. It opened at her response to reveal a small, dark-haired girl who rushed sobbing into her arms.

"I don't want you to go, Lacey." Tears streamed from her eyes as fourteen-year-old Marjorie Parsons drew back and rasped, "I'll be so lonesome here when you're gone."

Her reassuring smile aimed as much at boosting her own confidence as it did comforting the motherless girl who had become almost a sister to her, Lacey replied, "I can't stay in school forever, Marjorie. Everyone graduates when they're eighteen years old—even me."

"Maybe so." Marjorie brushed away her tears and continued almost pleadingly, "But Mrs. Grivens would gladly let you stay on as an instructor if you wanted to. Everybody knows that."

An instructor.

Lacey was almost amused by those words. She could read, write and cipher. She could "play the piano with considerable finesse," "embroider beautifully," was well versed in the rules of etiquette, knew the proper protocol and manner to address any member of a titled aristocracy and had committed to memory the correct placement of every piece of silverware that could possibly be needed at a formal dinner party. Those accomplishments aside, she was at a complete loss when it came to cooking or maintaining a household without a battery of servants. She was also totally ignorant as to how a "young lady" was supposed to earn a decent living in a society where the only choices open to her were a good marriage or sensible spinsterhood.

Yes, she'd be good at teaching young women to be as clueless as she.

"Please tell Mrs. Grivens you'll stay."

"I can't do that. Uncle Scully sent me tickets for my transportation home. He's expecting me, and I owe him that."

She did not bother to tell Marjorie she had decided that the chaperone Uncle Scully had arranged to accompany her was unnecessary, or that she had cancelled the arrangements he had made and cashed in the extra ticket he had provided so she might return the funds to him when she arrived. Yes, she owed him that…and so much more.

Lacey blinked back unexpected tears, then continued kindly, "I'm not like you, Marjorie. I have…obligations. I don't have a wealthy father ready to introduce me to society so I can get properly married after I graduate."

"Pooh! Papa would introduce you to society, too, if you wanted. I'd make him do it. And you're so pretty that you'd find a husband in no time."

"That wouldn't work for me, Marjorie."

Marjorie stared at her, uncomprehending.

"It's time for me to pay Uncle Scully back for financing my schooling and supporting me all these years." She smiled sadly. "He must be pretty old by now. I know he never married. He probably needs somebody to take care of him."

"But he never came out to see you—not once!"

"He wrote to me faithfully and made sure I always had whatever I needed." Lacey felt no need to explain that Uncle Scully's letters had rarely arrived more often than six months apart, or that while being friendly and expressing concern that her needs were met when he wrote, Uncle Scully had shared little of the private information that would have made him seem more like family.

"He didn't visit you on your birthday, or at Christmas."

"But he never forgot me." Lacey did not feel she needed to add that she would have preferred a visit to the sometimes elaborate presents that had arrived without exception on the holidays.

"He didn't even send you a likeness of him to remember him by!"

"That's because I didn't need a likeness." She did not choose to clarify that her actual memory of Jake Scully had dimmed over the years—that all she could truly remember was that he had been tall and well dressed, and that with a single glance of his sober, gray eyes, he had made her feel safe from the gunshots that had robbed her of the life she had known.

Lacey added solemnly, "I owe Uncle Scully more than I can ever repay."

"But you shouldn't waste your life caring for an old man when you're so young."

"I owe it to him, Marjorie." Lacey silently added that she owed her grandfather a debt, too—to return to the place that gentle, decent man had loved so she could clarify memories that had become confused and distorted by the violence of that night long ago and put an end to the nightmares that still haunted her.

Lacey turned at the sound of a summons at the door. She pulled it open to see little Amy Harding standing solemnly in the hallway.

"The carriage is here, Lacey." Amy's eyes were moist. "Mrs. Grivens said to hurry or you'll miss your train."

Lacey was conscious of the footsteps following her as she carried her suitcase down the staircase toward the front doorway.

Tears, hugs and sincere, loving words behind her, Lacey stepped up into the waiting carriage. She looked back as the conveyance jerked into motion and she waved at the solemn group gathered in the doorway of the boarding school.

The carriage turned the street corner, and Lacey took a breath, wiped away a tear and determinedly faced forward. She had told Marjorie the truth. She needed to go "home" because she had obligations she could not ignore.

Lacey withdrew her grandfather's worn Bible from her reticule. She scanned the text, taking comfort from the familiar passages and the small illustrations her grandfather had drawn on the page corners when they had read together.

Her attention shifted back to her well-tended hands.

Yes, her hands were trembling—because she had no idea what the future held in store.

Weaver, Arizona
1882

Lacey looked out the window of the stagecoach as it bumped and swayed along the rutted trail. She glanced at the harsh, dry land bordering both sides of the narrow expanse, then at the rise of mountains in the distance outlined against a brilliant blue sky devoid of a single cloud. She breathed deeply, aware the heat of the day was climbing.

She recalled the carriage ride to the train station in New York, through streets that were neatly cobbled, where well-dressed pedestrians hurried to meet their needs in a city that bustled with activity. Somehow, she had not expected that that uneventful ride would initiate an endless, uncomfortable journey that had not yet come to an end.

Lacey did not choose to recall the countless times along the way that she had doubted the wisdom of making the journey alone. She had not taken into consideration that the passing years would have dimmed the memory of a wild country where civilization was held partially at bay by long-haired, thickly bearded and heavily armed men—a place where she stirred surprised attention and whispered comments wherever she went.

Despite the tedium and discomfort of the journey, however, Lacey found herself somehow shaken at the thought of her arrival in Weaver, where she would meet up with a past she suddenly realized she hardly remembered.

Lacey looked at the unpaved trail ahead, then glanced up at the shadowed mountain peaks in the distance. Why was it that everything looked so unfamiliar to her? Why had the ten years she had been away dimmed all clear memory of this place?

The sound of a crackling blaze echoed unexpectedly in her ears. She felt the heat...the flames...the smoke... *the fear.* She saw the faded image of her grandfather's body.

Yes, all clear memories had dimmed...except one.

Lacey closed her eyes. She clutched her small Bible tightly in her hand.

"Are you all right, ma'am?"

Lacey looked up, focusing for the first time on the disreputable-looking fellow seated across from her. Like the two other rough-and-tumble male passengers presently sleeping, his hat was stained, his beard was overly long, his clothes were worn and the gun at his side was *exceptionally* large—but the concern in his bloodshot eyes was obviously sincere.

She replied, "I'm fine. I'm just tired, I guess."

"We'll be getting to Weaver, soon." The fellow frowned and added, "If you don't mind my saying so, ma'am, Weaver is a fine little town, but it's not accustomed to ladies like you."

Lacey almost smiled. "I was born in Weaver—or thereabouts."

"Oh."

"I'm going home."

The fellow nodded. "Been gone long, ma'am?"

"Awhile."

He nodded again. He looked at the Bible in her hand. "Going to join Reverend Sykes, are you?"

"Reverend Sykes?"

"I hear he's a fine man and real dedicated to his work in the church."

"I'm sure he is, but I don't know him."

The fellow's frown deepened. "You'll be having somebody meet you in Weaver, I hope." He stammered, "I mean, it's a fine little town, but...well..."

Lacey stared at the unkempt fellow more closely. Because of his questionable appearance, she had done her best to ignore him and the other two occupants of their coach when she boarded. Now, glimpsing the man inside his unappealing exterior, she was oddly warmed by what she saw.

Lacey replied with a smile, "Someone will be meeting me. His name is Jake Scully. Do you know him?"

"Jake Scully." The fellow blinked. "He's...you... I..."

He took a breath, then continued with a tip of his soiled hat meant as an introduction, "My name's Pete Loughlin, ma'am. I'll be spending some time in Weaver, and I want you to know I'll be at your disposal if things don't turn out the way you expected." He paused, adding, "I hope you'll remember that, ma'am."

"I'm pleased to meet you, Mr. Loughlin. My name is Lacey Stewart, and I thank you for your concern."

"Everybody calls me Pete, ma'am."

"Thank you. I'll certainly remember your offer, Pete."

His face reddening unexpectedly, Pete averted his gaze toward the window and ended the conversation as abruptly as it had begun. With no recourse but to follow his lead, Lacey turned to the Bible in her hand, silently embarrassed that she had been so harsh in her first assessment of the dear fellow. She looked down at the page to which she had inadvertently turned.

Judge not, lest ye be judged.

Somehow startled by the familiar passage, Lacey glanced back up at Pete Loughlin, whose bloodshot eyes had fallen closed.

A timely lesson, gently served.

Lacey's spirits lightened.

The stagecoach rounded a turn in the trail and Weaver came into view. Lacey reached up nervously

to adjust her hat and smooth back a few pale wisps that
had strayed from her upswept coiffure. She then slipped
her Bible into her reticule and gripped the handle anxiously. Her three fellow passengers had somehow awakened the moment Weaver appeared on the horizon. They
appeared as eager as she to see the end of their journey.

Lacey did her best to ignore Pete's frown as they
entered town and she searched the street in vain for a
familiar face. She struggled against an expanding anxiety as the conveyance rumbled farther down the dusty
main thoroughfare, passing a livery stable, a blacksmith's shop, a bank, a hotel. She scanned the street
more closely, seeing what appeared to be a jail, a barber
shop and several other stores. Her gaze halted. Memory
stirred when she viewed the establishment that took up
the major portion of the street at the far end.

The Gold Nugget Saloon.

Lacey took a shaky breath, then searched the street
again. She was expecting too much, she knew, to expect Uncle Scully to be waiting for the stage as she had
hoped. The exact date of her arrival had been uncertain when they had last communicated. She certainly
couldn't expect that he would meet every stage the week
she was expected to arrive.

The stage shuddered to a halt in front of the mercantile store and Lacey's heart began pounding. She
silently scolded herself for her rising apprehension as
she waited for her fellow passengers to alight. She reminded herself that she had just traveled hundreds of
miles alone, that she had walked through the Gold Nugget's swinging doors by herself once before, and she
certainly could do it again.

"Ma'am..." Lacey took the hand Pete offered her.

She stepped down onto the street as he continued politely, "If you're needing any help…"

Lacey skimmed the street again with her gaze. She saw a tall, gray-haired gentleman step out onto the boardwalk a distance away. Her heart leaped when he turned in her direction.

"Lacey?"

She went still at the sound of the deep, familiar male voice behind her. She turned toward the big man who started toward her from the shadow of a store's overhang.

Lacey's throat went dry as the well-dressed, dark-haired man approached. This fellow wasn't old at all. Actually, he appeared to be a man in his prime, with strongly cut features and dark brows over eyes that were a soft, sober gray.

Lacey caught her breath. She remembered those eyes.

The man stopped in front of her. He said, "Welcome home, Lacey."

"U-Uncle Scully?"

"If that's what you want to call me."

Lacey looked over at Pete, who remained stiffly solemn beside her. Uncertain why he stood rooted to the spot, she said, "I'd like you to meet one of my fellow passengers on the stage, Uncle Scully. His name is Mr. Pete Loughlin, and he's been very kind."

Scully's expression remained unchanged as he replied, "Pete and I are old acquaintances." He addressed Pete directly, adding, "I appreciate your looking after Lacey, Pete, but she's in good hands now."

Scully turned again to Lacey. "I'll get your bag."

Dismissing the introduction and Pete with that statement, Scully strode toward the rear of the wagon to catch Lacey's suitcase as it was tossed down from the stage.

"Ma'am…"

Lacey's attention jumped back to Pete.

His voice lowered, Pete whispered, "I hope you'll remember what I said."

"Thank you, but you don't have to worry about me. As Uncle Scully told you, I'm in good hands now."

"Like I said, if things don't turn out the way you expected and you're needing any help, I'll be around."

"Well, thank you again, Pete."

Glancing back at Scully as he approached, Pete added, "I guess that's all I got to say." He walked away without waiting for her response.

Scully was frowning when he reached her side. "What did Pete say?"

"Pete just offered me his support. It was very kind of him."

"Kind…right." Scully's frown deepened. "Let's get going. I told Helen to make up a room for you upstairs from the saloon."

"Helen?"

"Helen's the woman who cleans the second floor for me at the Gold Nugget. She's a nice old lady whose husband died a while back. She agreed to move into the spare room and serve as a chaperone while you're living there."

"Living there…like before." Lacey's throat choked tight as memories began flooding back. "I'm glad."

"I'll find a more suitable place for you as soon as I can."

Struggling to keep up with Scully's long-legged stride as they started across the street, Lacey was not able to reply.

This was going to be harder than he thought.

Intensely aware of Lacey as she walked beside him, Jake Scully shoved open the swinging door and stepped back to allow her entrance into the saloon. His jaw ticked at the silence that came over the barroom as she walked in.

Well, what had he expected? Did he think Lacey would return the same little girl in pigtails that he had sent away to school years earlier?

Scully remembered that little girl clearly. Lost and alone, and so brave… Charlie's granddaughter. She had looked up at him with total trust in her eyes, and he had lost his heart to her the moment he saw her. He hadn't doubted for a moment what he would do.

Memories of Charlie were vivid. Scully had been in his teens when he met the old man. He'd been out on his own after the deaths of his parents—jobless, homeless, without funds and unsure where his next meal was coming from. He couldn't remember exactly how he met Charlie and struck up a conversation with him, but he did remember that Charlie bought him the first good meal he'd had in days, and that he'd never tasted anything better. He had ending up working with Charlie at his claim for almost a year before starting back out on his own with a stake that Charlie had insisted on providing. He had made good use of that stake, and he had never gone hungry again.

Nor had he forgotten Charlie. Years passed, however, before the old man walked into Scully's saloon one day and told him he was prospecting in the area, then mentioned during their extended conversation that he had taken in his granddaughter after his daughter's death.

The next time he saw Charlie, the affable old man was lying dead outside his burned-out cabin.

There hadn't been a moment during the years following that Scully had doubted providing for Lacey, the poor, wounded little girl in pigtails who had needed him. But the child in pigtails was now a woman—and everything had changed.

Scully remembered the look in Pete's eyes as he had stood protectively at Lacey's side. He recalled the stunned silence when Lacey and he had walked through the saloon doors moments earlier.

It had started already.

The truth was, he hadn't been ready for Lacey Stewart, the beautiful woman who had stepped down from the stagecoach, and the shock of it was with him still. Charlie Pratt had been a rare man, indeed: sincere, generous, God-fearing and God-loving, and the truest friend he'd ever had. But he had also been a scrawny little fella with a crooked smile and bowed legs. Somehow, Scully hadn't considered for a moment that Charlie's granddaughter would turn out to be a beauty.

And not only was Lacey beautiful, but she was also a lady, and the combination of the two had set his mind spinning.

His hand on her elbow, Scully ushered Lacey directly toward the staircase to the second floor. Barely acknowledging the greetings of a few customers in passing, he urged her up the stairs. He introduced Lacey briefly to Helen when the old woman appeared at the top of the stairs, then pushed open the door of her room to allow Lacey to enter and followed her inside, making certain to leave the door open behind them. He deposited her case on the bed and turned to face her expectant expression fully.

Lacey looked up at him, waiting for him to speak, and Scully went suddenly still. There she was...the child he had seen ten years earlier. She was visible in the trusting blue eyes Lacey turned up to his, in the shadows of uncertainty he saw there, in the faint glaze of tears gradually overwhelming them. On the outside, Lacey was a mature, beautiful woman, but on the inside she was still the little lost girl who had looked up to him...to whom she had come "home."

And she was waiting.

His slow smile sincere, Scully said again, "Welcome home, Lacey."

With a single, spontaneous step, Lacey stepped into his welcoming hug. With that step, the past dropped away. Lacey was again his brave little girl, and he was her protector, provider and guide for her future.

And he was glad.

The hum of curious conversation and leering snickers following Scully and Lacey's entrance into the Gold Nugget had gradually faded. No one noticed that the swarthy fellow at the bar glanced back surreptitiously over his shoulder to scan the upstairs landing where the couple had disappeared from sight. Nor did anyone hear the angry curse he muttered under his breath before exiting the saloon as inconspicuously as he could manage.

Chapter Two

"I like the Gold Nugget. I don't want to 'find a more suitable place to stay.'"

Scully looked at Lacey, who sat across the small table from him in Sadie Wilson's restaurant, the town's only eating establishment. They had taken to having breakfast together there each morning, and in the few days since her return, an indefinable bond had developed between them that somehow erased their years of separation and dismissed the reality that they were virtual strangers. Lacey had grown into a woman whose stunning beauty left Scully a bit breathless—yet she was still the determined little girl who had walked miles in a deadening heat, injured and feverish, in order to follow through on her grandfather's last wishes.

"Scully…"

Lacey had automatically dropped the "uncle" prefix from his name when she saw it was turning heads, and Scully was glad. He didn't need it to remember he was still responsible for her safety and for the direction of her future.

"Scully…"

Responding with an unconscious furrowing of his brow, Scully said, "The Gold Nugget isn't the right place for you to live."

"*You* live there."

"That's different."

"Why?"

"I own the place."

"So?"

He could not believe she could be so dense. As determined as she, Scully asserted, "Helen can't stay indefinitely. She'll want to go home, and your grandfather wouldn't approve."

"Grandpa sent me to the Gold Nugget."

"He sent you to me, not to the Gold Nugget."

"He sent me to the Gold Nugget to see you because he knew I'd be safe with you. I *am* safe with you there."

Scully took an impatient breath. "You're a respectable young woman, Lacey."

"You're respectable, too."

"No, I'm not."

"Yes, you are!"

Scully stared at Lacey. He had angered her by refuting her statement, but he couldn't let her dodge the truth. "I own a saloon, Lacey," he explained. "You saw Pete Loughlin's reaction when I met you at the stage. Even he didn't think I'd be a good influence on you."

"He doesn't know you like I do."

"He probably knows me better."

The startling blue of Lacey's eyes linked with his. "I don't believe that."

"Lacey...things get pretty wild in the saloon at times. Drinking, gambling...and more."

"Oh..."

Scully remained conspicuously silent.

She shrugged. "I've read the Bible, you know. I know about those things. But Jewel and Rosie both told me you don't allow that kind of activity on your premises. They said they respect you for it, too."

Scully's frown darkened. How had Lacey become so friendly with the girls at the Gold Nugget in so short a time? And when had they begun talking so frankly? He didn't like it. He needed to get her out of there as soon as possible.

He replied, "Whatever the girls said is beside the point."

"No, it isn't."

"A room just became available in Mary McInnes's boarding house this morning. It's a fine place—clean and respectable."

"The Gold Nugget is clean."

"But not respectable."

"It's respectable enough for me."

"No, it isn't."

Lacey was beginning to smart at his insistence. She countered, "Besides, I don't have an income yet and I can't afford to pay the board at Mary McInnes's."

"Pay the board..."

"That's right. I don't intend to let you support me forever, you know. It won't cost you as much to keep me at the Gold Nugget until I find a position and can start paying my own way."

"A position...?"

Lacey's lips tightened.

"No."

"No what?"

"No *position*. And I'm not supporting you. I'm only returning a favor to your grandfather."

"Grandpa may have helped you, but in time, you went out on your own."

"In time. It's not time for you yet."

"When will it be time then?"

"I'll let you know."

"No."

"Yes."

Lacey continued resolutely, "I'm not going to move into the boarding house right now. The Gold Nugget is fine."

Scully didn't agree. Choosing to conclude the discussion for the present, he said, "Are you finished?"

"I'm not moving out of the Gold Nugget."

"With your breakfast."

"Oh...yes."

He stood up. "Let's go."

Lacey drew herself to her feet as Scully dropped a few coins on the table and nodded at Sadie. She felt the firm pressure of his hand on her elbow as she smiled a quick goodbye at the hardworking woman and Scully guided her toward the door. She knew she had made him angry, but she refused to let him say harsh things about himself in an effort to protect her.

Lacey raised her chin as they walked toward the restaurant doorway. A familiar passage rang in her mind.

Man looketh at the outward appearance, but the Lord looketh at the heart.

She didn't need anyone to tell her that Scully's heart was good. No matter how he looked, she knew the Lord could see that as well as her grandpa obviously had—and she had only to look into Scully's eyes to see that he wanted only the best for her. As for the *outward appearance* part...well, maybe it needed work, but she believed the hand of the Lord had played a part in directing her to Scully, she hoped for both their sakes.

Lacey glanced at Scully where he walked beside her. Whether he chose to accept it or not, he had proved to her in so many ways that he was a better man than he considered himself to be. Also, she *trusted* him. She felt *safe* with him. Those truths had become more desperately important to her since she had arrived back in Weaver and the vague shadows surrounding her past had begun shifting in her mind.

She was determined not to burden Scully with the lingering fears that haunted her. It was up to her to resolve them. She would, too, but she needed to assume responsibility for her future first.

However, Scully did not agree.

That thought in mind, Lacey stood stock-still as they emerged onto the boardwalk. Scully was still frowning when he looked down at her, and she asked simply, "Are you angry with me, Scully?"

"Angry? No."

"You look angry."

His gray eyes searched her face. His gaze softened. "The Gold Nugget isn't the place for you, Lacey. You know it, and I know it."

"No, I don't know that."

"All right." He was angry again. "Whatever you say."

She supposed there would never be a better time.

Dislodging her arm gently from Scully's grip, Lacey said, "I'm going to stop in at the mercantile store to see if they received any mail for me there. The girls back at the boarding school said they'd write to me the same day

I left. They're very dear. I know they'll follow through with their promise."

The anger in Scully's eyes mellowed. "All right. I'll be in my office. Come back there as soon as you're done. I have something to show you."

Scully did not see Lacey turn back to watch his departure after starting toward the mercantile store. Nor did he see her frown as the thought struck her that perhaps she was being unfair. Scully was a mature, powerfully masculine man. He might not consider himself respectable, but she had seen the way the *respectable* women in town looked at him. It wasn't much different from the way the girls at the Gold Nugget looked at him. Maybe she should give him the space he needed.

That thought somehow difficult to accept, Lacey shook her head. Maybe...but not now.

She raised her chin and quickened her step.

Definitely not yet.

Things weren't getting any easier.

Scully nodded automatically at the heads turning his way as he crossed Weaver's main street. Taller than most at a height well over six feet, and with broad muscular proportions that belied his supposedly sedentary lifestyle, he was aware that he stood out in a crowd. Dressed as he was in a well-tailored dark suit and fine linen shirt, with a brocaded vest and the dark Stetson he wore pulled low on his forehead, he was also unmistakable as the owner and operator of the Gold Nugget Saloon, the most successful business in town. He had always been proud of his success. He had dressed appropriately and behaved as suited him best, uncaring of fluctuating public opinion.

Scully paused to glance back at Lacey as she walked

toward the mercantile store. His jaw tightened at the assessing looks she drew from passing matrons. Those busybodies were already beginning to talk. Given a few more weeks, they would paint Lacey a scarlet woman simply because she lived in a room upstairs from the town's only saloon—two doors down the hallway from him, the town's most notorious bachelor.

Illustrating his concerns, Scully watched as a bearded cowboy turned with a sly remark to his friend when Lacey passed them on the street. Scully took an angry step in the man's direction, then checked himself in time. He'd just make matters worse by defending Lacey's honor when it needed no defense at all.

Galling him was the reality that Lacey seemed oblivious to the implications that living at the Gold Nugget raised. He was living proof that rumors—sometimes without a speck of truth—spread fast and functioned as gospel. He also knew that once damaged, a woman's reputation was never fully regained. Charlie had trusted him with both Lacey's reputation and her future. He owed it to the old man and to Lacey to see that she found a man who was worthy of her—a respectable man who would marry her and give her the good life she deserved.

Scully watched as Lacey neared the store entrance. It occurred to him not for the first time that Lacey dismissed her beauty as playing any part in the person she was, just as she dismissed her own purity of heart with the belief that everyone had the same spark of goodness inside them—including him. He knew that wasn't true. He had been on the wrong side of that equation for too many years as a youngster not to realize that the spark—if it ever existed in him—had long since been extinguished. He was determined Lacey would never experience that difficult truth firsthand. He was dedicated to that resolve…more than he had ever believed he could be.

Lacey disappeared through the mercantile store entrance, and Scully took a shaken breath. Whoever that *respectable* man who eventually won Lacey's hand turned out to be, he'd be lucky, indeed.

Still frowning, Scully pushed his way through the Gold Nugget's doors. He had started toward his office at the rear when a familiar, throaty voice turned him to the sultry redhead who stepped into his path.

"You don't have time for a good morning today, Scully?"

Scully's gaze swept over Charlotte briefly. He remembered the first time he saw her, when she came into the saloon looking for a job a year earlier. He had known at a glance she'd be an asset in his establishment.

Scully's smile softened. He and Charlotte had both been on their own long enough to be well versed in what the world had to offer people like them.

He responded, "You're in early today, aren't you?"

"Maybe." Charlotte smiled with a quirk of her arched brows. "I've got a lot of energy stored up, I guess."

"Charlotte…"

She said unexpectedly, "I like her, Scully. Lacey's a real nice girl…innocent, you know? Not like you and me, who've seen it all and made our choices." Charlotte took a step closer. "I expect she'll make some rancher a real good wife someday. She's suited to that life. She'll take to it like a duck to water."

Charlotte's heady perfume filled his nostrils as she added, "I'll see you around, Scully." She winked. "You know where to find me."

Charlotte walked back out through the saloon doors, disappearing as quickly as she had appeared, and Scully looked up to the expressive wiggling of Bill's hairy eyebrows as the rotund bartender stood behind the bar. Bill had the keenest eye in town, but Scully resented having it turned in his direction. He made a mental note to tell him so, too.

That thought firmly fixed, Scully turned toward his office, and within seconds he had slammed the door behind him.

"You're sure you don't know of any positions that might be open for a young woman in town...anything at all?"

Wilson Parker stared at Lacey Stewart from his customary position behind the mercantile store counter. He had been standing in this same spot ten years earlier when a bedraggled little girl walked down the town's main street dragging a scrawny burro behind her. Nobody had been more shocked than he to see how that pale little girl had turned out.

"Mr. Parker...?"

And no one was more incredulous than he as he responded, "Do you mean to say Scully thinks that you should...that he expects..."

"Scully has nothing to do with what I'm intending." Lacey's gaze pinned him as her smooth cheeks colored. "Is there something wrong with supporting oneself, may I ask? If I were a man, everyone would expect it of me. Certainly being a woman doesn't change things that much."

"But you're not a woman. You're a *lady*." Lacey snatched back her well-groomed hands as Mr. Parker said, "Scully wouldn't have to support you forever, just until the right fella comes along."

The right fella, Lacey thought. There it was again.

Lacey controlled a spark of impatience as she responded, "I have plans for the future that don't include waiting for the 'right fella' to turn up, and I'll need to earn some money in the meantime."

"Still, I don't think—"

"That's the trouble." Lacey turned toward Sadie Wilson as the matronly restaurant owner interrupted their conversation. Sadie continued, "You *don't* think, Parker. You just react, and this lady here is the kind who chooses to use the abilities God gave her to support herself instead of depending on others. I'd say that's admirable, wouldn't you?"

"Admirable?" Mr. Parker shrugged his narrow shoulders. "For a woman your age, I suppose it is, but Lacey—"

Sadie turned her back on the storekeeper, dismissing him with a roll of her eyes that said she had heard it all before. Addressing Lacey directly, she said, "I couldn't help hearing your conversation, and I'm thinking it might be lucky for both of us that I happened to come in here to get some things I ran out of in the restaurant this morning. The fact is, I'm going to be shorthanded at the restaurant soon. Millie—you know, the redhead with all the freckles—she's leaving to get married at the end of the week. I'm going to be needing somebody who's looking for good, honest work."

Lacey's heart jumped a beat.

Sadie searched her expression. "It's not easy work, mind you. There's a lot of running involved when things get busy."

"I'm not afraid of hard work."

Appearing pleased at her response, Sadie replied, "Well then, as far as I'm concerned, you're hired. The restaurant is busiest in the early morning and during the supper hours. I have a woman who helps at night, so I'll try you out in the morning. If you're agreeable, you can start at the end of the week when Millie leaves. I'll pay you what I was paying her." Sadie winked. "I'll be expecting to get more work out of you, though, because Millie's mind hasn't been on her job lately."

"That's fine with me." Lacey added, "And...thank you."

Lacey watched as Sadie walked to the back of the store to scout out her purchases. Her heart was pounding. She had a position and she'd start at the end of the week! She'd have money to pay for her board at the boarding house and she—

Lacey's high spirits plummeted as she bid the disapproving storekeeper goodbye and started back toward the Gold Nugget with the prospect of moving from the Gold Nugget suddenly looming closer. Also plaguing her was the prospect of informing Scully that she had agreed to take a job. He'd be angry, but she'd remind him that she'd be able to take the room at Mrs. McInnes's sooner than she thought. That would please him. Lacey pondered that thought. But how would *she* feel about moving to the boarding house? Mature...responsible...finally self-supporting?

Lonely.

She'd had enough of loneliness. She had thought her loneliness had come to an end when she came home and Scully had welcomed her with open arms.

It looked as if she was wrong.

* * *

Scully looked up at a knock on his office door. The knock was tentative...uncertain. It could be no one else.

"Come in, Lacey."

"How did you know it was me?"

Lacey stood framed in the doorway, platinum hair piled casually atop her head, intense blue eyes putting to shame the pale blue of her dress, delicate features composed in a half smile. A lovelier picture than Scully had ever expected would be his, even temporarily. The thought was disconcerting. He refrained from answering her question. Instead, he stood up, reached for his hat and said, "Come on with me. I have something to show you."

Around the desk in a moment, Scully took Lacey's arm. She hesitated momentarily, then said, "I suppose we can talk later."

Talk. Talk meant continuing the same argument they'd had earlier that morning. He'd had enough of it for the day.

He drew her out of the office with him toward the saloon's rear door.

"Where're we going, Scully?"

Again ignoring her inquiry, Scully ushered Lacey along with him, then pushed open the door of the back entrance and urged her out ahead of him into the narrow yard.

He felt the shock that rippled through her.

Lacey gulped. She took a deep breath. Tears brimmed in her eyes as she started toward the hitching post where the small burro was tethered.

It couldn't be...but it was!

"It's... *Careful!*"

The burro's name emerged from her lips with a sob as Lacey reached the animal in a few running steps. Careful turned his head toward her with a welcoming bray and tears streamed down her cheeks. She slid her arms around Careful's neck and hugged him tight....

She was a child again. The days were long and sun-filled, and Careful was her loyal playmate, helpmate and friend.

The choking stench of the fire hung on the air. Her grandfather lay dead in front of her and the charred remains of her home behind her. She was terrified and alone, but Careful stood steadfast nearby.

The road was long, the sun hot. Her head throbbed, her legs ached and her throat was parched. She was afraid. She couldn't walk any farther, but Careful trudged on beside her, limping every step of the way.

The Gold Nugget came into view at last. She couldn't make it. She couldn't walk another step, but Careful wouldn't give up, and neither could she.

She was sick. She didn't want to get better. She didn't want to remember...but Careful was alone, and he needed her.

She was fully recovered. She was leaving for boarding school to be educated as her grandpa always wanted. She was leaving Careful behind, and the emptiness inside her ached....

So many years in between. So many clouded memories and uncertainties, but she was home again at last. She knew that now, because Careful was with her again.

Uncertain how long it took to compose herself, Lacey turned back toward the big man who stood silently watchful behind her. Aware that words could not adequately express the full scope of her emotion, she said simply, "Thank you," then walked into Scully's embrace.

Enveloped in joyful tears as Scully held her comfortingly close, Lacey was not aware of the well-dressed man lurking in the shadows nearby. She had not seen him lingering in the mercantile, listening intently to her conversation at the counter. Nor had she noticed him following her at a safe distance when she left the store and started across the street.

Standing still unseen, Barret Gould paused to coldly assess the emotional scene unfolding. He had overheard the statement Lacey Stewart made in the store minutes earlier. She said she had returned to Weaver with plans for the future that had nothing to do with Jake Scully. She'd added that her plans didn't include waiting around for *the right man to come along.* Both were commendable statements that appeared innocent enough to the average person.

Yet the average person did not know Lacey's secret—a secret she did not know he shared.

A slow elation expanded inside Barret. He was being given a second chance for success in a plan that had met with devastating failure ten years earlier.

He would succeed this time, and the distinguished future that had escaped him—for which he was destined—would finally be his.

Lacey Stewart didn't stand a chance.

Chapter Three

"The answer is no!"

Lacey stood opposite Scully in the morning shadows of her room. The events of the previous day, when Careful was returned to her, had left her shaken. She hadn't had the heart for the argument she knew was certain to ensue when Scully learned she had accepted a job in Sadie's restaurant, but he had appeared at her door that morning for breakfast, and she had known it was now or never.

Never was not an option.

Lacey took a deep breath, then said, "Try to understand, Scully. I—"

"I said, the answer is no. You aren't going to do that kind of work."

Her reply was spontaneous. "I don't recall asking your permission."

Scully's gray eyes pinned her. Somehow, he had never looked bigger or more intimidating than he did at that moment as he towered over her in his anger, but Lacey did not back down when he replied, "No, you didn't ask my permission, but you should have."

"You forget. I'm eighteen years old—an adult. You're not my guardian anymore."

"I'm not, huh?"

Regretting her harsh statement, Lacey took a conciliatory step toward him and said, "Please… I don't want to argue with you, especially after yesterday. You've done so much for me, and taking care of Careful all those years while I was gone… I appreciate every bit of it, but I can't let it go on, don't you see? I have to start out on my own sometime."

"Sometime…but not now."

"When, Scully? Am I supposed to let you support me until I wither on the vine waiting for 'the right fella'?"

"You don't stand a chance of 'withering on the vine,' and you know it."

"No, I don't know it. And neither do I care. It's time for me to take responsibility for my own life."

"That's good thinking. It's premature, that's all. You need time to settle down here for a while so you can get reacquainted with the real world."

"The real world…" Lacey took a stabilizing breath. "You're right. The world I lived in these past ten years is far removed from Weaver. It wasn't a real world—not for me. I knew it then, and I know it now. Many of the memories of my life with my grandfather are unclear, but they aren't so dim that I wasn't able to see the differences. I belong *here*. This is my home, and the sooner I make myself fit back in, the better it will be."

"You're rushing things. You're not giving yourself a chance."

"I'm ready now to step back into my life, Scully. I need to, for so many reasons."

"None of those reasons are good enough. You need

time. You deserve better than you're asking for yourself."

"Do I, really?" Lacey took another step closer. "Do I deserve better than working in a place where hardworking men like my grandpa felt privileged to have a good, hot meal set down in front of them at the beginning of the day? Do I deserve better than getting to know them so I can share a part of their sometimes lonely lives?"

Lacey paused, forcing back a gradual thickening in her throat as she continued, "I miss Grandpa, you know? He loved me. With his dying breath, he gave me the best advice he knew when he placed his Bible in my hands and told me to depend on it and the Lord to guide my way, and then when he sent me to you. He taught me so many things that'll stay with me the rest of my life. But somehow, so many of my memories of him have become vague and cloudy in my mind. I was robbed of those memories that last day, and I want them back. I don't know any other way to get them except to make a place for myself here so they'll eventually become clear."

Lacey looked up at Scully's still, unemotional expression. She said, "Those memories are all I have left of the only family I knew. The blank spots nag at me. They give me no rest. I need to fill them in so I can be whole again, and I'm doing that the only way I know how."

Lacey saw the brief flicker of change in the gray eyes regarding her so closely, yet she was unprepared when Scully said, "Are you ready for breakfast?"

Taking a moment to recover, she responded, "Y-yes, I guess I am."

"Let's go, then."

Lacey halted abruptly when they stepped out into the hallway. When he looked down at her, she said, "You did hear what I said, didn't you, Scully?"

"I heard you."

"Then you understand."

Silence his only response, Scully ushered her toward the staircase.

The noisy hustle and bustle of Sadie's restaurant continued around him as Scully sat at the corner table he shared with Lacey. His empty plate in front of him, he sat silently as he had through the entire breakfast meal. Frowning, he glanced across the table at Lacey, who was picking at her food, then scanned the occupants of the crowded restaurant. They were a varied lot: transient wranglers obviously eager to be on their way, businessmen engaged in conversation, a few ranchers, some locals who looked to have spent a night on the town and a grizzly prospector or two in for their first good meal in months. He saw Doc Mayberry in deep conversation with Reverend Sykes at a table in the far corner. His frown darkened when he looked at the table occupied by three women from the Gold Nugget who looked to have remained active long after the Gold Nugget doors had closed for the night. Millie White, her plump, freckled face flushed and her hair in disarray, moved almost breathlessly between the tables.

Strangely, he hadn't given Millie much thought before this, except to wish her luck when he learned she had finally set the date for her wedding with her seemingly recalcitrant boyfriend. The thought that Lacey would assume her frantic pace between these same tables at the end of the week held little appeal.

Scully compared the two women. The result was no surprise. Lacey was slender, almost fragile in appearance. Her delicate features were faultless, almost mesmerizing. With her pale hair and vividly blue eyes, she drew speculation wherever she went. Conversely, Millie's only outstanding feature was her freckles. Although a pleasant enough girl, Millie could be easily lost in a crowd with her common appearance.

That could never be the case with Lacey. He had known the moment he saw Lacey that first time when she was a frightened, injured child that she was special in so many ways. The years had only served to confirm his opinion of her. She was lovely and sweet…and innocent. He needed to protect that innocence, to hold her safe. She was too friendly, too nice. The world held too many unnamed dangers for someone like her, and the mix of people she would meet in this place only increased the threat involved.

"Scully…" He hadn't realized he was staring at Lacey until she continued, "It's obvious that whatever you're thinking, it isn't good." She smiled…a glorious, apologetic smile as she added, "Don't worry so much. I'll be fine. Sadie's right behind the counter if I need her for anything, and you're across the street. What more could I ask?"

Scully was saved from a response to Lacey's question when Doc Mayberry appeared unexpectedly beside their table with an all-too-familiar man in a dark suit. He said, "Scully…nice to see you again."

Scully shook the hands extended to him and replied with limited courtesy, "Doc Mayberry… Reverend Sykes."

"And this must be the Lacey Stewart I've been hearing about all around town."

Doc's smile was too gracious. The old fellow had an agenda that went beyond a simple introduction. That thought was confirmed the moment he added, "Reverend Sykes and I haven't had the pleasure of meeting Lacey."

Enforced courtesy never his greatest strength, Scully said, "Lacey, it looks like these two fellas are determined to meet you."

Flushing slightly at Scully's brusque manner, Lacey replied, "I'm pleased to meet you both, gentlemen." She added without a moment's hesitation, "The girls at the Gold Nugget speak very highly of you, Doctor."

Scully's head jerked toward Lacey at the thought of what those conversations between Lacey and "the girls" had included.

Lacey continued, "And your name was one of the first I heard on my arrival in Weaver, Reverend Sykes—with an extremely favorable comment, of course."

"You're referring to Pete Loughlin, I'm sure." Reverend Sykes's smile broadened. "Pete told me you and he were passengers in the same stagecoach. He was very impressed with you, which is one of the reasons I wanted to meet you. Like you, my wife and I are recent arrivals in Weaver. Our church and the size of our congregation aren't very impressive yet, but we have great hopes for a change in the right direction. I'd like to extend an invitation for you to join us for worship." He added, "We'd appreciate any extra time you could spare for us, too. We need all the help we can get."

Appearing delighted at the invitation, Lacey replied, "Thank you. We'll both come, won't we, Scully?"

The brief silence that followed spoke volumes.

Scully stood up unexpectedly and said, "Lacey and I have some important business to tend to this morning. If you'll excuse us..."

Ignoring Lacey's shocked expression as he drew her to her feet, Scully dropped his coin on the table and turned her toward the door.

"I don't like seeing you taken advantage of."

"No one was taking *advantage* of me—except for you, that is."

Lacey was livid. Common courtesy had been thoroughly ingrained in her since childhood—common courtesy that had been severely abused when Scully dismissed both Reverend Sykes and Doc Mayberry so abruptly. Scully and she had arrived back in her room minutes earlier after their exit from the restaurant and a rush that had left her breathless. She continued with astonishment, "How could you be so *rude?*"

Scully did not smile. Without realizing it, Lacey proved his point. Of the many things he had been accused of in his lifetime, being rude ranked very low on the list—yet Lacey spoke as if he had committed one of the cardinal sins.

He hadn't, and he knew the difference.

"It should've been obvious to you what was happening, but it apparently wasn't, so I decided to save you from yourself."

"What are you talking about?"

"It was a ploy."

Lacey did not speak.

"Come on, Lacey, it's obvious what happened. Your *friend,* Pete Loughlin, went to see Reverend Sykes because he didn't like the idea that I was the man who was meeting you here—because he thought I'd be a bad influence on you."

"That's ridiculous! Why would he think that?"

"Because I threw Pete Loughlin out of the Gold Nugget a while back, and he obviously hasn't forgotten it."

"Why did you throw him out?"

"He claimed he had been cheated at one of the tables. He started a fight, and I stopped it."

"Anybody could make a mistake."

"Pete didn't make a mistake. He probably *was* cheated. I fired that dealer a week later when I found out he was dealing from the bottom of the deck so he could skim a profit off the top for himself."

"Oh...how terrible! You did make sure Pete got his money back, didn't you?"

"This is the West, Lacey. It's sometimes wild and sometimes unfair. I do the best I can."

"But, poor Pete—"

"I told you, I do the best I can, but that doesn't excuse Pete for going behind my back."

"Behind your back..."

"I told you, he doesn't approve of your association with me. He thinks Reverend Sykes can put an end to it."

"No!"

"Yes."

"I mean... I'd never let that happen! You believe that, don't you, Scully?"

Scully looked at Lacey. She was shocked and righteous. She didn't consider for a moment that Pete might be right, that maybe he *was* a bad influence on her.

Something inside Scully clenched tight. Doing his

best to ignore it, Scully said, "I meant what I told them, you know."

Confused, Lacey shook her head. "What are you talking about?"

"We have some important business to tend to this morning—before it gets too late."

"What business?"

His expression sober, Scully said, "Wait here. I'll be right back."

"But—"

Lacey's reply went unfinished as Scully pulled the hallway door closed behind him.

Lacey looked down at the package Scully had tossed onto her bed. He had returned within the half hour, true to his word, but it was obvious she wasn't that easily mollified. She asked, "What's that?"

"Open it up and see."

"I asked you—"

"It's riding clothes. They should fit. Mrs. Parker said she's had a lot of experience fitting women with ready-made outfits."

"I'm sure they will, but I still want to know what all this is about."

Scully's irritation at the conversation with Doc Mayberry and Reverend Sykes still smarted. He resented the implication that he wasn't fit to properly oversee Lacey's future. Didn't they realize that he recognized Lacey's special qualities as well as they did? Didn't they realize he'd always done his best to protect her, and he was committed to that course?

Obviously not, and that thought rankled.

But it wouldn't change anything. He had always

done the most he could for Lacey. His caretaking of old Careful was only a small part of it. He had known how much Lacey loved the animal, and how important a part the small burro had played in her survival on that last, desperate day. He had wanted to spare that beautiful, dear little girl as much grief as he could. He had instinctively sought to maintain her connection to Weaver any way he could.

He had made arrangements to have the burro stabled with his own horse over the years. He had taken Careful out with him on frequent overnight trips; and the truth was, he had grown as fond of the feisty little critter as he was of his own mount. Yet, the moment when Lacey and the burro were reunited had been more than he had ever hoped for.

He would never forget it, the way that reunion had made him feel.

Yes, he was committed to Lacey, with all that word entailed.

Aware that Lacey awaited a response to her question, he said, "What do I have in mind? Just put the riding clothes on. You'll see."

"I don't like mysteries."

Scully dismissed her reply with a glance. "Just put the clothes on. I'll be outside waiting."

The sun was hot and steady as the morning hours advanced. The terrain was flat as they traveled toward the distant mountains, and an inexplicable tension began assuming control of Lacey's senses.

Traces of her vexation still remaining, Lacey looked at Scully, who rode at her right. She had been upset at his attitude in the restaurant when Doc Mayberry and

Reverend Sykes introduced themselves earlier, but she had gotten truly angry when he explained the reasoning behind his behavior. The thought that he might've believed for a moment that anyone could influence her against him had stunned her. He was her lifeline to a past she hoped to reclaim, her stability in the present and a stalwart presence as she looked toward an uncertain future. She considered the bond between them to be impervious to assault of any kind. The thought that Scully possibly did not feel the same had shaken her.

Those thoughts had deluged her as she had dressed in the riding clothes he had brought. When she opened the door, she had found him waiting, his dark suit exchanged for more common Western wear. It had not escaped her notice that the ordinary shirt and trousers he wore somehow emphasized his superior height and breadth of shoulder, which set him apart from the average fellow on the street, or that the brim of the weathered hat he wore pulled down low on his forehead added a new element of determination to the strength of his compelling features. She had frowned at her certainty that the gun belt he wore strapped around his hips was not for adornment.

Scully did not smile when they reached the street and approached the two mounts waiting for them at the rail. He said, "You do remember how to ride astride, don't you? We don't have sidesaddles in Weaver, and the trails are a bit rough for a buggy."

She had responded by mounting up in a fluid movement that had surprised even herself—a prideful display for which she now silently suffered stiff, aching muscles.

Her eyes straight forward, Lacey heard Scully say,

"It's getting hot. You have water in your canteen if you're thirsty."

Lacey turned toward him, a tart response on her lips, only to have it fade at first contact with Scully's concerned gaze. In a flash of insight, it was suddenly clear to her that both she and Scully had gotten angry for the same reason—because, in one way or another, the bond between them had been questioned. She wondered why she hadn't realized that before, then silently thanked the Lord for relieving her distress by imparting a bit of wisdom that had escaped her.

Lacey responded, "I'm not thirsty, but I would like to know where we're going, Scully."

The shadows in Scully's eyes darkened with uncertainty as he replied, "Surely you realize where we're going by now."

A cold chill raced down Lacey's spine at his response. Her mounting tension exploded into breathlessness as she turned to scrutinize the terrain more closely.

Endless wilderness…a sunbaked trail…the mountains in the distance drawing ever closer…

Lacey gasped, "I-I'm not ready to go there yet!"

"Your grandfather's buried there."

"No, I don't want to go."

Suddenly trembling, Lacey shook her head. She couldn't go back to the site of her nightmares, not even to see her grandpa's final resting place. Not yet.

"Lacey, are you all right?"

The terrifying shadows began shifting in Lacey's mind.

The fire was all around her. Her skin was burning. She couldn't breathe. She tried to call for help.

She was afraid…afraid…

Lacey did not feel the strong arm that encircled her waist the moment before Scully swept her from her saddle and settled her on his horse in front of him. She was not aware of the sob that escaped her throat when his embrace closed around her. She felt his breath against her hair and heard Scully whisper, "It's all right, Lacey. It's over...in the past. You don't have to be frightened anymore. I'll take care of you."

Shuddering, Lacey burrowed closer against him. She knew it was true. She was safe with Scully. She'd always be safe with him.

Scully filled his canteen at the stream, then looked back at Lacey. She was sitting in the patch of shade where he had left her. Her skin was ashen, her eyes red-rimmed. Strands of pale hair hung loose at her hairline and trailed down the back of her neck, but she was unaware of her dishevelment as she leaned back and closed her eyes.

Crouched beside Lacey moments later, Scully untied the bandanna from around his neck and wetted it, then ran the damp cloth across Lacey's forehead.

Lacey opened her eyes, then looked away as she said, "I'm sorry, Scully. I don't know what happened to me. It was really thoughtful of you to think of taking me to see my grandfather's grave. I should want to see it, but somehow..."

"It was my fault." Scully's sober gaze met hers. "I did a lot of talking about it being too soon for you to do things, then I pushed you into something you weren't ready to face."

"It wasn't your fault."

"I should've realized how you'd feel."

"Scully, please..." Lacey gripped Scully's hand and held it tight. It was big and surprisingly callused, but she felt only its warmth as she rasped, "How could you realize how I'd feel if I didn't realize it myself? Besides, I haven't been completely honest with you. I wanted you to think of me as an adult ready to assume charge of her life, not as a frightened child still plagued by nightmares."

"Nightmares? What kind of nightmares?"

"Of that day...only they're all mixed up and unclear. They've been more frequent lately." A chill shook Lacey as she continued, "The heat and the fire are so vivid, but shadows surround everything else. The shadows move, Scully. They twist and turn. They advance toward Grandpa while we're outside the burning cabin, then they run away. And all the while, Grandpa is dying. He's trying to talk to me, but his voice is fading. I strain to hear him, but he can't talk any louder. He puts the Bible in my hand, and I hold it tight. It burns my skin, but I clutch it tighter and tighter, refusing to let it go, even when the shadows return and try to take it away from me. The shadows are suddenly chasing me. I run faster and faster, but they keep getting closer and closer. Suddenly I'm back at the fire again, and there's nowhere else to run but back into the flames."

"That's enough." Scully's voice was sharp. He clutched her close to halt her shuddering. "You don't have to tell me any more."

"There's no more to tell. I don't know how it all ends. It's all...shadows."

Scully stroked Lacey's fair hair as he held her in his comforting embrace. When he moved her away from him at last, he whispered, "You don't have to be afraid of the shadows anymore, Lacey. That's what I'm here for…to chase the shadows away." He smiled and wiped the dampness from her cheeks with his palms, "That's why your grandpa sent you to me, and there's no way I'd let that old man down."

"We share that, don't we, Scully?" Lacey's small smile was shaky. "We both loved him."

"Yeah…we share that."

"And he loved us both."

Scully appeared to consider Lacey's statement for a moment before he responded, "Yes, I suppose he did."

"He would never think you aren't *respectable* enough."

"Lacey…"

"I'm not moving from the Gold Nugget."

"Lacey…"

"Not yet."

Scully looked down into Lacey's resolute expression. He would pursue that argument another time.

It was happening again.

Barret Gould stood behind the carved mahogany desk in his impressive office, his expression tight as he faced his two hirelings. Blackie Oaks had been an itinerant wrangler who couldn't hold a job and Larry Hayes had been a waster too lazy to labor honestly to support himself when he'd run across them shortly after arriving in Weaver years earlier. He had used their services openly whenever their meager talents served his purposes as Weaver's best and only attorney, and as one of its best-respected citizens. His "generosity" in giving the two "good, honest work to do" had been commended by many. What Weaver's residents didn't

know, however, was that he had also used Larry and
Blackie's services covertly when opportunities to advance himself financially beyond the confines of the
law were presented.

In both situations, however, his contempt for the limited mentalities of the two men was boundless.

Barret struggled to control his ire. He had been raised
in San Francisco, the only child of wealthy parents. He
had made good use of his pleasing appearance—thick
brown hair, deceivingly warm brown eyes and even, patrician features—from an early age, and had employed
it to great advantage when attending the best schools.
Scholastically and socially successful, he had graduated
as a lawyer with a great future in store while enjoying
a clandestine lifestyle that went unsuspected.

But that was before his father was found to have par-
ticipated in illegal activities and the family wealth was
confiscated. That was also before his father was sent to
prison a broken man and his mother took whatever family funds could be salvaged and ran off with her lover.

When he'd discovered he was also being investigated
for participation in his father's illegal affairs and the
same fate might follow for him, he made a fast escape.
He had chosen the vast, wild interior of the country as
the best place for him to hide, yet Weaver, Arizona, had
been as far as he had been willing to run.

Barret would never forget his disgust when he arrived in the small, unimpressive town wearing hand-
tailored clothes and a deceptive smile. He had since
used his practiced facade to become a valued member
of the community while silently despising Weaver for
its ignorance, for its location in the middle of nowhere
and for its lack of proximity to any city of reasonable

refinement. He had sworn that he'd find a way to re-
store himself to the civilized world before his youth
was spent.

Eleven years had passed since then, eleven years of
silent frustration made bearable only by the sum accu-
mulating too slowly in his name to have made the lost
time worthwhile.

Barret struggled to suppress his disdain at Blackie's
undiscerning observances as he said, "You're telling
me Scully and Lacey Stewart rode out into the wilderness with no apparent destination in mind, then turned
around and came right back to Weaver. That doesn't
make any sense. Lacey has waited more than half her
lifetime to claim her grandfather's strike. There's only
one place she'd want to go if she went out riding."

Larry, the smaller of the two men, interjected,
"Scully and the lady didn't come right back. They
stopped at a stream for a while to cool off."

Barret glared with impatience. "'The lady…?' That
'lady' you're talking about is Lacey Stewart, you
know…the same Lacey Stewart who was a child at
her grandfather's cabin ten years ago. The same Lacey
Stewart who could've identified you and Blackie as the
men who shot her grandfather."

"Yeah, but she's all growed up and she's a lady now.
And she didn't blink an eye when she saw me and
Blackie on the street a few days ago."

"She saw you?"

"Yeah, and she didn't give us a second look."

Barret took a firm hold on his forbearance. "So
you're telling me, that's it…they just stopped at a stream
to cool off? They didn't get as much as halfway toward
the old man's cabin?"

"Right."

Silence.

"They did a little cuddling while they were at the stream, is all."

"Cuddling…"

"Yeah, it looked to me like the lady was crying for some reason, and Scully was trying to comfort her."

"They didn't…you know…?"

"No, they didn't even come close. They just stayed for a while until the lady got herself back together, and then they headed back."

"Was it Scully's idea to turn back, or was it the woman's?"

The two men exchanged glances before Blackie replied, "I'd say it was the lady's. She didn't want to go on."

Barret nodded. She didn't want to look anxious. The girl was smarter than he thought.

He said, "All right, that's all I need to know for now. Get out, and remember what I said. Don't let that 'lady' out of your sight."

Waiting until both men had left his office and closed the door behind them, Barret sat down at his desk and reached into his drawer for the small sack that was never far from his reach. He withdrew the gold nugget from inside the sack and held it tight in his hand as he had many times before. He recalled the moment when Charlie Pratt had walked into his office late that first day. Short, wiry, unkempt, Charlie had been indistinguishable from any other prospector he had ever seen, but when the old man smiled and put the nugget down on the desk in front of him, Barret knew his moment had come.

A man of few words, Charlie told him he'd struck it rich, that he wanted to register his claim in his own name and that of his granddaughter, and he wanted to do it "real legal like, so there'd be no problem afterward." Charlie left the nugget behind for a "retainer" without disclosing the location of the claim, and said he'd return to sign whatever papers were necessary in a couple of days.

Barret's heart pounded in vivid recall. He had immediately set Blackie and Larry on the old man's trail. His plan had been simple. Charlie had kept his strike a secret. He had been cautious enough not to tell anyone but Barret about it. Blackie and Larry would follow the old man, find his claim and report the location back to him so he could record it in his own name before the old man returned—"real legal like, so there'd be no problem afterward."

A familiar knot of frustration twisted tight inside Barret as memory returned the details of the debacle that followed.

Charlie also had been smarter than he thought. Charlie had evidently spotted Blackie and Larry following him and had led them on a circuitous trail obviously meant to confuse them before reaching his cabin in darkness. He had then tricked them into thinking he had gone to his bed, only to appear unexpectedly behind them with a gun, demanding to know what they were after.

According to Blackie, the situation deteriorated into chaos from that point, ending up with Charlie being shot and with Blackie and Larry determined to hide their crime by throwing Charlie's body into the cabin and setting the structure afire.

Furious when they returned with their story, Barret had still considered the situation salvageable. It had seemed a matter of simply scouting the area Charlie had been working to find the source of the gold.

Barret remembered his panic at the news that Charlie's eight-year-old granddaughter, Lacey Stewart, had arrived in town injured and bleeding, fresh from the scene of the burned-out cabin. He'd been sure she would tell someone about her grandfather's strike, that she might even know its exact location. He had been furious with both his men for having allowed her to survive.

Fearing Lacey would be able to identify his men and the identification would eventually lead back to him, he had paid them off and told them to leave town. They had obediently stayed away until Lacey was sent to a school back east and it was safe for them to return. The girl never spoke of her grandfather's strike. He had been overjoyed at that, but his dream of a return to the wealth and prosperity of his youth had died when all manner of prospecting and excavation in the area of Charlie's cabin had failed to locate Charlie's gold.

Now Charlie's granddaughter had returned to Weaver, and with her return, his dream had been revived.

Barret clutched the nugget tighter. Lacey Stewart may have fooled everyone else, but she didn't fool him. She wouldn't have traveled back from the big city to a town in the middle of nowhere if she didn't think it would be worth her while—if she didn't have some idea where to look for the strike her grandfather had made.

It appeared, however, that she wasn't about to share the strike with Jake Scully.

It also appeared that Jake Scully was totally taken in by her.

But Lacey Stewart didn't fool him. He would get that claim—one way or another.

Chapter Four

The sun had barely risen and Weaver had not yet fully awakened when Lacey crossed the empty main street and headed toward Sadie Wilson's restaurant. Against Scully's adamant protests, she had started working there a few days ago. She had made certain to rise at dawn so she would be at the restaurant before the first customer even thought of appearing at the door, and she now knew she would find Sadie already at work in the kitchen when she arrived.

Lacey smoothed the apron tied around her narrow waist. Sadie had provided it the first day of her employment and she wore it proudly. It was important to her that she do well in her new position. Scully had not mentioned again her near hysteria on the trail when he'd attempted to take her to her grandfather's gravesite, and she was grateful. His solicitude during those frightening moments, however, made her more determined than ever to become independent. Scully was too good, too caring of her welfare. She could not bear the thought of telling him that her nightmares had grown more vivid since that day, nor of becoming a burden to him that he did not deserve.

A smile touched Lacey's lips as she neared the restaurant. She had prayed, asking the Lord to help her do well so Sadie would be satisfied with her work, and her prayers had been answered. She hadn't made any major mistakes so far in serving the customers, she was adapting well to the restaurant routine and Sadie had complimented her on the job she was doing.

Her thoughts were interrupted at the sight of the person waiting outside the restaurant door. Lacey hastened her step. She tapped Rosie on the arm when she reached her side. She liked Rosie and her friend, Jewel. Unlike some of the other Gold Nugget women, they had been friendly to her, and she appreciated their openness.

Rosie turned hesitantly toward her, and Lacey gasped with surprise. Wearing a plain cotton dress that bore no resemblance to the gaudy satin she normally wore, and without the heavy makeup of her trade, Rosie looked so young—certainly no older than Lacey, herself—but it was not that thought that stunned her.

A large bruise marked Rosie's pale cheek.

Lacey asked spontaneously, "What happened to your face, Rosie? Did you fall?"

Rosie flashed a weak smile. "Yes…that's what I did. I fell. I'm just clumsy, I guess." She hastened to add, "But I'm all right. The mark won't show under my makeup tonight, so Scully won't have to worry about it when I work."

"I'm sure Scully will just be glad as I am that you're all right."

Rosie changed the subject, saying, "Sadie hasn't opened the door yet. I guess I'm early, but I didn't get a chance to eat supper last night, and breakfast at the boarding house won't be ready for hours yet. I couldn't sleep for the loud complaints my stomach was making, so here I am."

Somehow hesitant, Lacey replied, "I don't think Sadie has everything ready, but you can come inside with me and wait, if you like."

"No, I'll wait outside." Rosie took a backward step. "Some of the ladies in town don't approve of Gold Nugget women, and I don't want to cause any trouble."

"Sadie's not like that." Lacey took Rosie's arm. "Besides, you're hungry, and that's what the restaurant's here for."

"That's all right. I'll wait here."

"Rosie, please." Lacey smiled encouragingly and said, "It's no trouble if you come inside now...really."

Lacey drew Rosie reluctantly behind her as she entered. She called out to Sadie as the older woman worked at the stove, "Good morning, Sadie. I told Rosie it would be all right to wait at a table until you're ready to open up."

Sadie glanced over her shoulder. "That's fine. I'll be ready in a few minutes."

Standing beside Sadie moments later, Lacey whispered, "I hope you don't mind, Sadie. I didn't want Rosie to wait outside. She fell and hurt herself. She's kind of pale, and her face is bruised. I don't think she feels too well."

"Fell and hurt herself, huh? Is that what she told you?" Sadie looked back at Rosie, then shook her head. "It's that boyfriend of hers. That Riley fella uses his hands on her when he has too much to drink. Everybody knows it."

"You mean he *hits* her?" Lacey was stunned. "Why does she let him do that to her?"

"Life is sometimes hard for a woman out here, Lacey, especially somebody like Rosie who doesn't have much to fall back on. I guess she figures she's better off with Riley than without him."

"But—"

"I know. It's not right or fair."

"But—"

"But that's the way things are."

Voices at the door turned Sadie's attention to the four cowpokes who entered and sat down at a table. She said, "It looks like the restaurant's open whether I'm ready or not. You'd better get started with the customers, Lacey. We're going to fill up in here in a hurry."

Lacey looked at Rosie.

"But take care of Rosie first. Like you said, she looks like she doesn't feel too good."

Lacey nodded. She swallowed the thickness in her throat as she turned in Rosie's direction.

"You're looking very fine today, Lacey."

"Thank you, Mr. Gould. What can I get for you this morning?"

Barret smiled his practiced smile as Lacey awaited his reply. He had entered the busy restaurant for breakfast a few minutes earlier, as he had for the past few days since Lacey started working there. He knew he made a good appearance. He knew his clothes were impressive, and that the deference the customers of the restaurant showed him made him stand out favorably in Lacey's mind. He also knew gaining Lacey's confidence could be useful in so many ways.

He looked at Lacey as she smiled at him, showing even, white teeth with a candid, guileless expression.

He said softly, "You forgot to call me Barret, Lacey."

To her credit, Lacey managed a demure flush. "Of course. I'm sorry."

"No need to apologize. I'd like us to be friends." Responding to her initial inquiry, he said, "I'll have some of Sadie's fine hotcakes and eggs this morning, but I know they couldn't be any finer than the service."

Barret complimented himself on the inroads he was certain he had made into Lacey's esteem as she returned to work and he nodded at the familiar faces quickly filling the restaurant. Amused, he watched the cowhands at a nearby table scramble to retrieve a fork Lacey had dropped. He almost laughed. She had everyone fooled with her innocent appearance—everyone but him. He wondered what they would think if they knew how carefully she was guarding her real reason for returning to Weaver.

Those thoughts were still prominent in Barret's mind when Lacey returned with his breakfast in hand. He patted her slender, ladylike hand as she placed his plate on the table and he commented, "Reverend Sykes and I look forward to seeing you at Sunday services this weekend."

Withdrawing her hand, Lacey responded, "Yes, I'm looking forward to attending services, too."

She walked quickly back to the counter to retrieve another customer's breakfast. Barret turned under the weight of someone's stare to see Jake Scully looking at him from the doorway. Scully did not return his smile of acknowledgment and Barret turned his attention to his breakfast in an effort to conceal his anger at the slight.

Barret inwardly smarted. He had never liked Jake Scully. Scully had never shown him the same respect that other residents of Weaver displayed toward him. As unbelievable as it seemed, he had the feeling Jake Scully looked down on him.

On him!

Actually, he was astounded that a man of the world like Scully could possibly have deceived himself into believing Lacey had left the refinement of city life behind and returned to Weaver without having greater prospects in mind. Could he possibly believe Lacey had come "home" because of a sense of obligation to him?

If so, he was a fool.

Barret watched covertly as Scully settled himself at a corner table. Scully's gaze was fixed on Lacey with an intensity that appeared almost proprietary, and Barret's questions were answered.

Jake Scully—a man who had seen it all, taken in by the wiles of a cunning woman!

The thought was delicious.

He didn't like it…not one little bit.

Scully scrutinized the patrons who had filled Sadie's restaurant to capacity although the day had hardly begun. His breakfast lay untouched in front of him as Lacey moved between the tables serving customers.

He seethed.

He watched as Barret Gould again called Lacey to his table, as Barret looked up at her with his suave, cultivated smile. His stomach churned as Barret stood up and whispered into Lacey's ear before paying his bill, his hand lingering on hers a second too long.

He hadn't needed that display to realize Lacey was

out of her depth here. Lacey was too naive, too sincere. She wasn't experienced with the divergent personalities frequenting Sadie's establishment—just as Sadie's customers weren't accustomed to a person like Lacey.

Nor was Lacey accustomed to or deserving of the type of treatment she was subjected to by them. He had heard the occasional complaints if the food took too long in reaching the table, the demands that kept Lacey running. He had noted the assumptions about her instinctively friendly manner. One misguided cowhand had actually whistled to get her attention! True, Lacey seemed to handle it all gracefully, but it galled him.

As Scully watched, a young cowpoke summoned Lacey back to his table for the fourth time, smiling broadly. Obviously intent on impressing her, he joked and teased until Sadie called her away with a flimsy excuse. He saw the table of cowboys seated nearby whisper as Lacey passed, then laugh aloud. He noted the glances two matrons seated nearby exchanged when their husbands followed Lacey's progress across the room with more than common interest, and he observed with growing heat the drummer who called Lacey to his table, then pressed a coin into her hand with a wink. If that man thought he could buy his way into Lacey's affections—

"Say now, what does a fella have to do in here to get some service?" Scully's rioting thoughts were interrupted by the loud complaint of an unshaven cowpoke who stood up unsteadily at his table and slurred, "I've been waiting an hour in here, Sadie. Ain't your new girl going to wait on me? I'm a good customer!"

Scully tensed. Everyone in the restaurant knew Jud Hall had walked through the doorway only a few minutes previously, just as everyone knew Jud was trouble. He knew, because he had tossed the drunken cowpoke out of his saloon on too many occasions to count.

Tensing, Scully watched as Lacey approached Jud, her face hot. He saw Jud's face change as she drew closer. He didn't like what Jud was obviously thinking when Lacey said, "What would you like Sadie to make for you this morning?"

A leering Jud answered, "Maybe I don't want Sadie to make nothin' for me this morning, darlin'. Maybe I want *you* to cook me my breakfast."

Interrupting from her place beside the stove, Sadie called out, "I'm the cook in this restaurant, Jud. If you don't like it, you can leave."

"Maybe I don't want to leave." His leer turning aggressive, Jud continued, "Maybe I want this girlie here to—"

Scully was on his feet in a flash. Gripping Jud by the back of the neck, he paid no attention to the chairs that scraped out of his way and the customers who dodged Jud's flailing arms and legs as he propelled him toward the door. He waited deliberately until Jud hit the street with a thud before walking back into the restaurant and closing the door behind him. He did not look at Lacey as he slapped his coin down beside his uneaten breakfast, then walked over to her and said in a voice meant for her ears alone, "When you finish up work here today, tell Sadie you're not coming back."

Lacey looked up at him, her face red.

"Tell her."

He did not wait for Lacey's response as he walked out the door.

* * *

Barret observed the scene from the street.

A saloonkeeper protecting the virtue of a prospector's granddaughter.

How quaint.

How noble.

How *stupid.*

But it told him something. He had been right in everything he had been thinking. Scully was totally taken in by Lacey's pretended innocence.

Barret watched as Scully exited the restaurant. Scully's involvement with Lacey complicated an already difficult situation. He need tread lightly in dealing with Lacey because of Scully, and Lacey would need to tread just as lightly if she expected to claim her grandfather's strike without her unwanted protector following at her heels.

Barret considered that thought. It appeared he could be in for a long siege.

Unless...

Barret frowned.

Unless he could find a better way.

Lacey walked across the saloon floor toward the staircase to the second floor where her room awaited her. It had been a difficult morning at the restaurant—the most trying so far because of the incident with Jud Hall and Scully. She recalled the silence that had followed Scully's departure from the restaurant, then the gradual hum of speculative conversation that had ensued. She was glad it was over. She was anxious to reach the silence of her room, but she knew she would first meet another brief, revealing silence—the one her appearance always elicited when she walked through the saloon doors.

Lacey knew that silence was one of the reasons Scully was so adamant about her taking a room at Mary McInnes's boarding house. She also knew it was the reason he had arranged for the dilapidated outside entrance to the saloon's second floor, previously unusable, to be repaired.

Lacey nodded at a few familiar faces in passing, then climbed the staircase, head high. She would be glad when the outer staircase was finished, actually more for Scully's sake than her own. It would relieve some of his stress. Yet she knew Scully would not be truly satisfied until she had severed all connection with the saloon and its patrons.

Lacey considered that possibility seriously for the first time. Her room above the Gold Nugget was the only home that remained for her. It was her haven. It was the place where she had recuperated from the most traumatic experience of her life. In it, she had known she was safe because Scully was nearby. She felt the same way now, but she was becoming acutely aware of the disservice she did to Scully in insisting that she stay.

Gasping with surprise when Scully stepped unexpectedly into sight at the top of the stairs, Lacey did not protest when he took her arm and said with an expression that suffered no protest, "I need to talk to you."

Lacey turned toward Scully when he ushered her into her room, leaving the door ajar as he turned toward her to ask, "Did you tell Sadie you won't be back to work at the restaurant again?"

"No."

Scully did not look pleased.

"I'm not going to quit, Scully."

"Yes, you are."

"No, I'm not."

Scully's chest began an angry heaving. He said tightly, "You tried and did your best, but working at the restaurant was a bad idea in the first place."

"It isn't."

"You saw what happened this morning."

"I could've handled it, Scully."

"Really."

"I could have! Sadie warned me about Jud. He causes trouble every now and then, but he's always been manageable in the past."

"In the past…before you started working there."

"What's that supposed to mean?"

"You have a mirror, Lacey."

"I don't understand."

Scully paused a moment, then grasped Lacey by the shoulders and turned her toward the washstand mirror. He held her facing her reflection as he demanded, "What do you see when you look at yourself, Lacey?"

"Scully…"

"Tell me."

Lacey frowned as she studied her image, then said, "I see a young woman with blond hair and blue eyes whose hairdo needs repairing and who looks confused."

Standing behind her, Scully stared at her reflection as he said, "I'll tell you what I see…what every man in that restaurant saw this morning. I see a young woman whose fair hair and womanly figure catches a man's attention even before he gets a closer look that stops him in his tracks."

"Scully…" Lacey gave a short, embarrassed laugh. "That's ridiculous."

"Is it? Look at yourself more closely. Is there another woman in this town who looks as good as you do?"

"Of course there is!"

"Who?"

Momentarily taken aback, Lacey stuttered, "There's…ah-ah… Noelle Leach, the blacksmith's daughter. She's a natural beauty."

"Right, and she smells like horses."

"Scully!"

"Go ahead, name another."

"There's Rita Johnson, the apothecary's niece. I haven't met her personally, but I've seen her, and she's lovely."

"Lovely? She's also so snobbish and impressed with herself that she repulses any man who might think of looking her way."

"You're not being fair." Lacey shook off Scully's grip and turned back toward him with a touch of irritation. "What difference does that all make, anyway?"

"What I'm trying to tell you, Lacey, is that you're different from the women in this town. You're kind and innocent, and too friendly for your own good. You trust people too much. You don't seem to realize that some of the men who look at you in that restaurant don't have the best of intentions."

"Oh, pooh!"

Scully's expression darkened. "Take Gould, for instance."

"Barret?"

"He can't be trusted."

"How can you say that? He's a lawyer."

"Is that supposed to prove something?"

"He's educated, and dedicated to serving the law."

"Is he?"

"He's also a member in good standing of Reverend Sykes's church."

"Oh, so that's supposed to mean something?"

"Of course it does!"

"Lacey, Reverend Sykes arrived in town only a few weeks before you. He doesn't know the townsfolk any better than you do."

"Scully..."

"But even Reverend Sykes accepts that people aren't always what they represent themselves to be. And as far as our town lawyer is concerned, I've seen too many peculiar things happen over the years after some poor fellows wandered into town and went to Barret Gould for advice. He isn't to be trusted, Lacey."

"No one else in Weaver seems to feel that way."

"I'm in a unique position in Weaver, Lacey. I see people come and go that the respectable members of the community don't give a second glance."

"I can't believe that."

"You should, and the fact that you don't is just my point. You're too gullible to be exposed to the element that frequents the restaurant."

"You and I have eaten there every morning since I arrived!"

"That's right, but you weren't working there, where everybody feels you're at their beck and call."

"Everyone respects me there."

"Oh? What about Jud?"

"That was different. He got out of hand. One of the

customers in the restaurant would've stepped in to take care of him if you hadn't."

"Is that what you want…to be exposed to that kind of treatment, hoping somebody will step in to stop it?"

"It's not what I *want,* Scully."

"It's not what I want, either."

"But it's not the norm at the restaurant—and I don't want to discuss this with you anymore. Please understand. I won't quit my job there. Sadie needs me…and I need this job."

"Why, Lacey?"

"Why?" Lacey took a deep breath. She swallowed against the emotion that abruptly choked her throat as she attempted to continue. "You…you had a very pleasant life here before I came back, but since I arrived, you've done nothing but worry about me."

"That isn't the point I'm trying to make, Lacey."

"But it's the point *I'm* making. Please listen, and try to understand. You've been so good to me, Scully— and I've rewarded you with one problem after another." Lacey hesitated, dreading the words she was about to say before saying, "I've been wrong. I need to admit that to you. I need to move away from this room and give you some space so you won't feel so responsible for me."

"Lacey…"

"I'll go to see Mrs. McInnes today. If she still has that room, I'll take it and tell her I'll pay for my board at the end of the week, when Sadie pays me."

Scully's hands dropped back to his sides.

"That is what you wanted, isn't it?"

"Maybe."

"Maybe?"

"What I want is for you to be safe."

"I'll be safe there. You said so yourself."

"What about the nightmares?"

Lacey took a short breath. "I have to grow up some-time."

Scully looked at her for silent moments, then nod-ded. "All right. Mary is saving the empty room at the boarding house for you."

"How—"

"I told her you'd be taking it soon."

"So she held it for me…no charge?"

Scully did not reply.

"Thank you, Scully."

Expressionless, Scully said, "Let me know when you're ready to move."

Lacey stared at the door that closed behind Scully as she heard his footsteps retreat down the hallway. When she could hear him no longer, she frowned, sud-denly at a loss.

She had done it…broken a tie that she had not truly wanted to sever.

What had she done?

What had he done?

Scully walked down the hallway, entered his room, closed the door behind him, then stood still. He had wanted Lacey out of the Gold Nugget environment, hadn't he? He had insisted that she move into the board-ing house…had even paid the rent on the vacant room while Mary McInnes held it for Lacey. He had reasoned it was best for Lacey that way.

What he had not considered, however, was if it was best for him. He was, in effect, thrusting Lacey out on her own even more surely than she was with her job in the restaurant.

Scully shook his head. Her job in the restaurant... that was the problem. His respect for Sadie aside, Sadie was not prepared to handle the complications that having a beautiful, sincere young woman like Lacey working for her would entail.

Lacey needed to find a place that was more secure... more protected. The problem was, that place did not exist in Weaver, except in her room near his.

Yes, what had he done?

Chapter Five

"Are you sure you can't stop for breakfast, dear?" Mary McInnes's lined face moved into a frown of concern as Lacey passed through the boarding house kitchen on her way to the street. "You haven't been taking any of your meals here. I worry that you aren't eating right."

"I'm fine, Mary." Breathless with haste, Lacey continued, "Sadie will be waiting for me at the restaurant. I can eat there if I get hungry."

"But the restaurant is so busy…"

"I'm fine, thank you."

Outside moments later, Lacey walked quickly toward the main street. Mary was a dear woman. A widow with grown children who had made their homes away from Weaver, she looked after the residents of her boarding house with a surfeit of motherly love, which Lacey appreciated, and which she was certain Scully had taken into consideration when arranging for her room there.

Scully…

Lacey took a deep breath as she approached the corner of the street. Scully had helped her move her things when she had said goodbye to Helen and taken her room at the boarding house a few days earlier. Mary had had no problem with allowing Scully into her room to help her—a privilege that Lacey had learned Mary granted to few male visitors to her respectable establishment. She had been comforted by the warmth Mary displayed toward Scully and had been pleased to see Mary show insight into Scully's character.

As for herself...

Lacey's step faltered.

She missed Scully. Not that he had distanced himself from her since she had moved. He hadn't, but the physical distance between them had been as difficult for her as she had expected. She was lonely in her room with strangers on all sides—residents of the boarding house who were friendly, who said all the right things intended to make her feel at home, but with whom she had no connection that even approached the bond Scully and she shared.

She had been so cautious in staying out of Scully's way during the nighttime hours at the Gold Nugget. She had remained in her room and busied herself with countless necessary tasks. When they were completed, she had sat down with her Bible to reread the familiar words she had virtually committed to memory, while images of nights spent in that same way with her grandfather grew gradually clearer in her mind. She suspected that the sense of security she had felt knowing Scully was nearby had somehow facilitated the clarification of those memories. She had come to anticipate with true warmth Scully's knock on the door before she retired for the night, when they would spend unhurried time talking in the doorway, no matter how heavy the traffic in the saloon below had become.

Those moments with Scully had meant so much to her. Losing them had cost her dearly.

Even her nightmares…

A chill raced down Lacey's spine. The intensity of her nightmares continued to increase. When she awoke in her silent room after those nighttime terrors, the shadows seemed somehow darker still.

Lacey murmured a prayer for the strength she needed to combat her fears. She was an adult now. She had come home to Weaver to repay Scully for his generosity and his caring over the years, and to regain memories of her grandfather that eluded her. She couldn't accomplish either of those purposes if she allowed her fears to gain control.

In the meantime, she was anxious for Scully's morning visit to Sadie's restaurant, anxious to see in Scully's sober gray eyes a warmth that was meant for her alone. She—

Lacey stopped still as the sound of a slap turned her toward the less respectable boarding house on the opposite end of the side street, where most of the Gold Nugget women lived. Rosie was standing outside the door, holding her cheek and sobbing while an unfamiliar fellow turned and walked angrily away from her. He was gone in an instant, the same instant it took for Lacey to start in Rosie's direction.

Rosie had already slipped through her boarding house doorway when Lacey reached it. Determined, Lacey was about to follow when she heard a female voice say, "Don't do that. It won't help."

Lacey turned to see Jewel behind her. A tall cowboy

stood silently at her side. Not bothering with an introduction, Jewel turned toward him and said, "Go back to the ranch, Buddy. I'm all right. I can take care of Rosie."

Lacey noted the fellow's reluctance before he nodded. With a tip of his hat in her direction, he was on his way.

Jewel turned back toward Lacey. She still wore the satin dress and heavy makeup of her dancehall trade, but her expression was sober and concerned when she pushed back a straying strand of dark hair and said, "Rosie wouldn't like it if you saw her right now. She'd be embarrassed. She always is when Riley treats her like that, but she'd be especially embarrassed if she knew you saw him hit her."

"But she might be hurt. I only want to help."

"If you want to help her, don't let her know you know what happened. Rosie likes you. She likes to think you like her, too."

"I do like her."

"Then let her believe you don't know about the way Riley treats her. She thinks you'd lose respect for her. She doesn't have much, and that's important to her."

"But—"

Jewel's dark eyes grew suddenly moist and her voice hoarse. "Rosie's a good girl who's had a hard life, Lacey. Riley treats her pretty good for the most part. He just gets out of hand sometimes."

"But he hit her."

"And he'll come back tomorrow and tell her he loves her. To Rosie, that means a lot. Not too many people have told Rosie they love her in her life."

"That Riley fellow couldn't love her if he'd do that to her."

Jewel shook her head.

"What does that mean?"

"I know Riley doesn't really love Rosie. He just enjoys his power over her. You know it…and in my heart, I think Rosie knows it, too. But she's alone, and right now she figures he's the best she can do. I know how she feels because I've been there, too."

Lacey glanced spontaneously in the direction into which Jewel's quiet cowboy had ridden off, and Jewel responded, "No, not Buddy. He's all right." Her voice softened with suppressed emotion as she said, "Buddy's a fine fella, but he's not the first man in my life. I don't expect he'll be the last."

Sadness and frustration combined to tighten Lacey's throat as she whispered, "What can I do for you both, Jewel?"

"I'm all right. Rosie's the one who has trouble right now. If you want to help her, just be her friend. You're not like the other people in this town. You don't treat Rosie any different than anybody else just because she works at the Gold Nugget. She appreciates that." Jewel hesitated, then said, "I do, too."

Lacey still had not found the words to respond when Jewel turned away and slipped through the boarding house doorway.

"Can I have some more coffee here, Lacey?"

Lacey turned toward the young, curly-haired wrangler who had made the request. The restaurant had been filled since the door opened that morning. She had responded to the rush with instinctive haste, but her mind had not yet left the moments she had spent with Jewel in the doorway of her boarding house.

Lacey refilled Todd Fulton's cup, then felt his callused hand touch her forearm to stay her as he said, "Is something wrong, Lacey?"

The thought that if not for her grandfather's Christian teachings, his dying guidance and Scully's boundless generosity, she might now be standing in Rosie's or Jewel's shoes had lodged deep inside Lacey.

"Lacey…?"

Todd's hand tightened on her arm, bringing her back to the present, and Lacey replied, "I'm fine, Todd, just a little distracted this morning, I guess."

Todd's brown eyes searched hers before he said, "I was beginning to worry. I haven't seen you smile since I got here."

"Well…" Lacey forced her expression brighter. "I'm smiling now."

"You are all right, aren't you? You'd tell me if you weren't…."

Lacey replied sincerely, "It's nice of you to be concerned, but I'm fine."

"Good." Todd scrutinized her a moment longer, then said, "Because I came here this morning with a purpose in mind."

"A purpose?"

Lacey saw warm color creep up Todd's neck as he said, "Talk was that Jake Scully was looking after you, then somebody said you moved out into the boarding house to be on your own."

"You aren't another fellow who's going to say you're glad because Scully wasn't a good influence on me, or that my job here isn't right for me, either, are you?"

"No, ma'am. I'd never say that."

"Well, in that case, my response to you is, it's about

time I started out on my own, don't you think? Scully is family—all the family I've got, anyway. He'll always be my closest friend, even if I am living at the boarding house."

"Then he wouldn't mind if another friend asked you to have supper with him on Saturday."

"Another friend? Who?"

"Me."

"Oh…" Somehow startled, Lacey responded, "Why would you do that?"

Todd grinned. "Let me see…so we could get to know each other better, maybe?"

"That's so kind of you, Todd," Lacey responded, "but I've been eating my meals with Scully."

Lacey frowned at her own response, suddenly realizing how presumptuous she had been in taking for granted that Scully would always give her needs precedence. Determined to correct that mistake but somehow reluctant to commit to Todd, she continued, "I can't have dinner with you on Saturday, but if you'll ask me again sometime, it'll be my pleasure."

"Fine. That's fine. I'll do that…soon."

Gratified to see that Todd's response and his smile were genuine, Lacey hurried to answer Sadie's call. She was returning with another breakfast in hand when she saw Scully sitting in the corner and realized she had been so preoccupied that she hadn't seen him enter. Uncertain how long he had been sitting there, she met his gaze with a sense of relief inexplicably so great that it brought a rush of tears to her eyes.

At his table moments later, Lacey saw Scully's fists slowly clench as he asked, "What did Todd say to upset you?"

"He didn't upset me."

"No?"

"No. I just…before I came here this morning…" Lacey halted. Scully was Rosie's boss, and Jewel had asked her not to embarrass Rosie. She couldn't relieve her own distress by talking the situation out with Scully and asking his advice. Rosie would be mortified.

Scully was waiting for her to finish her statement.

Lacey said sincerely, "I was feeling a little lost this morning until you came. I feel better now."

Lacey had spoken those words automatically, and she suddenly realized how true they were. Just to know Scully was nearby made her feel better. What would she do without him?

Lacey was looking at him with her great blue eyes so open and earnest that Scully could barely restrain the impulse to hug her protectively close. If he were honest, he would say the same—that he'd been feeling a little lost until he saw her, and he felt better now.

Well, almost better.

Scully scrutinized Lacey's pale face more closely. She had been frowning as she worked, something she rarely did, and there were light shadows under her eyes, indicating a lack of sleep. Something was bothering her…and whatever bothered her, bothered him. He asked softly, "Are you all right, Lacey?"

"Yes, I suppose I will be when I learn to use the resources the Lord gave me to depend on myself a little more. You don't seem to have that problem, but I do."

Scully said flatly, "I wouldn't exactly say the Lord has much to do with my line of work."

With unexpected sobriety, Lacey replied, "It's more

clear to me today than ever before that whether you realize it or not, you've been doing the Lord's work in
caring for my needs over the years. And if that's clear
to me, I know it's clear to Him."

Scully pondered Lacey's response. He had been
doing the Lord's work? He was suddenly aware that,
before Lacey's return to Weaver, he would not have
given a thought to the gulf that lay between the Lord's
work and his.

He pondered that reality, then dismissed it.

Lacey seemed to have dismissed it as well when she
said, "You do want breakfast, don't you?"

He nodded. "The usual."

"Hotcakes and eggs." Lacey smiled into his eyes and
all was momentarily well. She was back with his breakfast within a few minutes, and he mentioned casually,
"Careful's due for some exercise. I take him with me
occasionally when I go riding. The little critter seems to
enjoy it. I'm going to take him out this afternoon after I
finish some work at the Gold Nugget." He paused, then
asked, "Do you want to come?"

Before she could respond, Scully stressed, "You
don't have to worry. I don't have any particular destination in mind."

"Oh, I'd like that, but I have to do something first.
It'll only take a few minutes. I could meet you at the
livery stable afterward." She hesitated. "Unless that'll
interfere with your plans."

Unless that'll interfere with your plans...

Didn't Lacey realize he wouldn't *let* it interfere with
his plans?

It occurred to him that she did not.

Scully nodded his assent and saw her relief. He

watched her walk away, wondering what was so important to Lacey that she'd chance missing a ride with Careful.

"How are you, Reverend Sykes?"

Lacey neared the small, dilapidated church situated in a less frequented area of town. She was uncertain exactly when that morning she had decided the visit was a necessity. She only knew it was.

Paintbrush in hand, Reverend Sykes turned at the sound of her voice. He had abandoned his customary dark suit for work clothes, and he seemed to be wearing more of the paint than he was successfully applying to the outside of the building. Yet the front portion of the church was already done, and he appeared determined to continue.

Reverend Sykes responded, "Well, I've been better. Painting isn't my specialty, but Leticia said we needed to do something to freshen up the church, and I've learned that she knows more about these things than I do. So, she's working on the inside, and I'm working on the outside."

"You're doing a fine job."

"You're a true diplomat, Lacey." Reverend Sykes's lean face moved into a smile. He searched her expression, then glanced at her riding apparel and said, "You're on your way somewhere, it seems. What can I do for you?"

"I wanted to stop by and tell you how much I enjoyed your sermon last Sunday." She had slipped into a back pew alone. She had wished Scully would offer to accompany her, but when he did not, she had left for Sunday services with a smile on her face and a strong hope for the future. She added, "I'll be there next Sunday, of course."

"I'm pleased to hear you enjoyed my sermon and we certainly look forward to seeing you again, but you needn't have made a special trip to tell me that."

Lacey hesitated. "I came for another reason, too, Reverend, but I can see this isn't a good time."

"Anytime is a good time, Lacey."

"I just…need some advice."

Reverend Sykes's expression sobered.

"About how to help someone who's in trouble without embarrassing that person with my concern."

Reverend Sykes responded bluntly, "Is this person in desperate need of help?"

"I think she is."

"She?"

"Yes."

Reverend Sykes nodded. "You might send her to me. I'm experienced in helping people, both socially and spiritually, and Leticia is especially good in dealing with women."

"No, Reverend, I can't do that. I don't want to embarrass her. It would damage our friendship."

"And if the friendship was damaged, you wouldn't be able to help her at all…is that it?"

Lacey's brief nod was her only reply, and Reverend Sykes's expression grew thoughtful. "You've caught me off guard here, Lacey. I don't know this person, so advice is difficult to give." He hesitated at her frown. "You want to hear my thoughts right now, is that it?"

Lacey nodded again.

"Well, I could tell you to pray for this woman. Prayer is powerful, but it's apparent you don't need me to tell you that. You obviously want to use the gifts God gave you to do more."

Reverend Sykes paused again to scrutinize Lacey's expression, then continued. "So, my advice is to do just that. You know this woman better than I. Use the gifts the Lord gave you, and use them well. I can see you have many. You're honest and concerned about someone who needs your help, yet with all your good intentions and determination, you are also conscientious enough to recognize this person's need to retain a sense of dignity, however limited it might be. From my observation, the particular gift you bring to this situation is your realization that God's work is sometimes a very delicate task, that we occasionally need to tread lightly in order to bring Christ into the lives of someone we wish to help. Pete mentioned to me that you spent a good portion of your journey toward Weaver reading the Bible. I would encourage you to use what you've learned there to guide you."

Searching Lacey's gaze a moment longer, Reverend Sykes quoted softly, "'Trust in the Lord with all your heart, and lean not unto your own understanding. In all your ways, acknowledge Him, and He will direct your path.'" He smiled. "I don't think I could give you better advice than that."

Of course. She should have known. The Lord would show her the way, just as He had shown her the need. She need only remain open to the opportunities he presented.

Intensely relieved, Lacey said sincerely, "Thank you so much, Reverend."

A few pleasantries then concluded the visit, and Lacey turned back toward Weaver's main street. She had come for advice and had received the best that could possibly be offered.

Lacey looked up at the position of the sun in the cloudless sky, then hastened her step. But for now, Scully was waiting.

Barret stood at his office window. He had walked away from his desk in exasperation a few minutes earlier. He was tired of the inane paperwork that seemed to comprise the sum total of his work as Weaver's only attorney. He looked out at the main thoroughfare, at the unfashionably dressed citizenry who trod the boardwalk, then at the traffic of bearded horsemen and broken-down wagons on the unpaved street. He remembered the gaiety and color of San Francisco...the excitement around every corner that awaited a man of imagination and means. His imagination had not faltered over the years. It was only the means that had made those wonders unavailable to him.

He had always known how to fix his situation with the law in San Francisco. All he had needed to erase any connection to his father's crimes was a sum sizable enough to convince a chosen few that he'd had no part in his father's illegal activities. Had not suspicious deaths been included in that list of illegal activities, he knew his situation could have been resolved more easily, but that recourse still was not available to him. An adequate incentive was the only answer to his problem.

An adequate incentive...

It galled him that his life was being wasted because of his inability to accumulate a large enough sum of money to erase the charges against him—and he had little patience for delay.

Barret's thoughts came to an abrupt halt with Lacey's unexpected appearance on the walk a distance away. She was dressed in riding clothes, and if he didn't miss his guess, she was presently hurrying toward the livery stable.

Barret's heart began a slow pounding. In this desolate country, she could have only one destination in mind.

Barret searched the street for a sign of Blackie or Larry. Where were they? He had given them instructions not to let Lacey out of their sights.

Panicking, Barret stepped out onto the boardwalk as Lacey neared. He stood boldly in her path as she approached, searching his mind for a way to delay her. If his hirelings didn't show their faces soon…

Barret smiled as Lacey approached. He said, "Riding clothes. Are you intending an extended foray into Weaver's countryside?"

"Yes, I suppose I am." Lacey's smile was tight. "Scully's waiting for me."

"I expect Scully's not a man to tolerate being kept waiting, but I'm sure he'd make an exception for you. He does seem to be concerned about you, although his behavior isn't exactly in your best interest."

Barret saw the flicker of displeasure that crossed Lacey's face at the casual negativity of his comment. He knew he had made a mistake even before she responded levelly, "I think you're mistaken in that observance, Barret. Scully's behavior *is* in my best interest, because he cares about me. He was responsible for my education and welfare. His concern for me has never lapsed, and he's now intent on helping me reestablish myself in Weaver."

"Of course, Lacey, dear. Scully's devotion to your well-being is obvious. It's just difficult sometimes when good intentions go astray."

"Astray?"

Barret took a conciliatory step toward her. "He means well, I know."

"He not only means well. He's *done* well."

"Yes, but, dear..." Barret made his handsome, patrician features sober. He glanced at the street behind Lacey and noted Larry's appearance in the doorway of the Gold Nugget. He saw Larry's momentary panic when he noticed Lacey on the street wearing riding attire.

Larry and Blackie stepped out onto the walk and began approaching as Barret continued casually, "Well, I don't expect we should be discussing these matters on the street when you're obviously pressed for time, Lacey. But I would like an opportunity to discuss your situation in Weaver with you in the near future. I knew your grandfather only casually, but I know he'd want the best for you."

"You're right. My grandfather wanted the best for me. That's why he sent me to Scully."

"But that was then, Lacey. This is now. Circumstances have changed since you've matured. Association with Scully could prove detrimental to your future."

"No."

Uncertain of the meaning of Lacey's response, Barret said, "What was that, dear?"

"I said, no. Association with Scully could never prove detrimental to me." Lacey paused, her gaze direct. "I hope I've made that point plainly enough."

"Of course you have, but inexperience sometimes

guides one falsely." Barret offered his most concerned smile. "You're a lovely young woman. I wouldn't want you to find yourself in embarrassing circumstances because of a situation that's not of your making."

"I'm sorry. I'm in a rush."

"Now you're angry with me."

"Yes."

Marveling at her boldness, Barret said earnestly, "Now it's my turn to be sorry. It wasn't my intention to offend you. I hope you'll accept my apology."

"Perhaps I will when my anger fades, but right now it's impossible for me to accept your apology since I consider your observations ignorant and untrue, and your intentions questionable."

"My intentions questionable?"

"You obviously don't like Scully."

"I admit to that."

"Well, he doesn't like you, either. That said, I bid you good day."

"Lacey, please…" Forcing himself to stay her with a touch on her arm and a conciliatory expression, Barret offered, "Please accept my apology. It is sincerely meant."

"I'll consider it." Lacey shook off his touch. "Good day."

Barely concealing his silent ire at Lacey's abrupt dismissal, Barret stepped back into his office as she continued on down the street. She would *consider* accepting his apology, would she? Who did she think she was talking to?

Barret took a firm grip on his temper. He had intended his conversation with Lacey to be a casual flirtation that would delay her long enough for his insipid hirelings to appear. She should have been flattered. After all, he was good-looking and still in his prime. There wasn't a young woman in town who wouldn't have been flattered to have a man of his stature show an interest in her. He had actually even briefly indulged the thought of a casual liaison with her.

That was a mistake.

Barret reviewed their conversation again in his mind. In retrospect, a simple, pernicious phrase had turned Lacey against him.

Although Scully's behavior isn't exactly in your best interest.

With those words, their conversation had taken a fast track toward disaster.

Barret waited until Blackie and Larry reached the walk outside his office. His anger erupted when they appeared intent on walking past. He opened the door and snapped, "Get in here!"

Waiting only until the door had closed behind them, he said, "Incompetent…that's what you both are!"

"You don't need to get upset, boss. Blackie and me was right behind her. She wasn't going nowhere without us."

"That isn't what it looked like to me."

"We was watching from the Gold Nugget window."

"You were, huh?"

Blackie chimed in, "You don't have nothing to worry about with me and Larry on the job. We aren't going to let nothing go wrong like it did last time."

"I suppose you know she's off to ride with Jake Scully."

"Sure…" Blackie attempted a smile. "That's what we figured when we saw her riding clothes."

"I don't want you to let them out of your sight...*out of your sight,* do you hear?"

"We hear you, boss. I told you—"

"I don't care what you told me. Mess this up, and you're on your own—both of you."

Barret watched as the frowning duo continued down the street, agitation twitching inside him. He had meant what he said to those two fools. What they didn't know, however, was that if they failed this time...if they lost him his opportunity to return to the life he had been born for, they wouldn't need to apologize—because they would not live to regret it.

Careful trotted briskly behind them as Scully and Lacey rode slowly along the narrow trail. Scully glanced around at the flat, broad valley spotted with cholla, prickly pear and barrel cactus, at the giant saguaros and the palo verde and mesquite trees outlined against rugged mountains in the distance. He was familiar with the trail. It would lead them to one of the occasional running streams where they would water their horses and where small trees would provide a measure of protection against the relentless sun as they spent a few leisurely moments.

Engrossed in her thoughts, however, Lacey seemed to be paying little attention to the passing terrain. She had apologized for keeping him waiting when she arrived at the livery stable for their ride, but the apology had been unnecessary. He knew whatever had been on her mind and had necessitated the delay was important to her, or she would not have kept him waiting. He wondered, however, if that important matter was the cause of her silence and preoccupation since the beginning of their ride.

"What's wrong, Lacey?"

Snapped from her reverie, Lacey turned toward him. Her expression still sober, she replied, "What makes you think something's wrong?"

"You're quiet. If there's one thing I've learned since you came home, silence is not one of your characteristics."

"Scully...are you saying I'm a chatterbox?"

"No, but you normally speak up when something's on your mind."

"Oh. Well, nothing's wrong."

Choosing not to reply, Scully turned his mount toward the distant stream. Careful made his way directly to the water when they dismounted beside it minutes later. The horses and the small burro were ankle deep in the refreshing stream when Scully joined Lacey in the limited shade. She was still frowning.

"You might as well tell me what's wrong, Lacey. You're not doing a very good job of hiding the fact that you're upset."

"I'm not upset."

"Really?"

She looked up at him, still sober. "I suppose I owe you an apology."

"Another one?"

His reply meant humorously, Scully was surprised when Lacey responded seriously, "Yes, another one. I guess I'm not as good a judge of people as I thought I was."

Scully felt a heat unrelated to the temperature rise

inside him. He snapped, "If that Todd Fulton can't take no for an answer—"

"Oh, it isn't Todd. He's a nice fellow."

Scully went silent.

"You were right. Barret Gould doesn't like you."

"Barret Gould." Scully paused to rein back an angry response, then said, "What did he say?"

"I talked to him briefly on the way to meet you. I think he intended to give me what he believed was some well-needed advice, but his dislike of you took over somewhere. It shone through bright and clear."

"What did he say?"

Lacey scrutinized Scully's tense expression, then said, "I'm only telling you this because I had said you were mistaken in judging Barret harshly. I don't want you to get angry."

"Too late."

"Scully…"

"Tell me what he said."

"It wasn't really bad. He just said your behavior wasn't exactly in my best interest."

Scully hardly breathed.

"Scully…"

"I'll take care of it."

"No!"

"I said—"

"Scully, please…" Suddenly so close to him that he could feel her sweet breath against his cheek and see the silver specks of agitation in her eyes, Lacey rasped, "Promise me you won't confront Barret. It's important to me. I don't want to stir up any trouble for you."

"You didn't stir anything up. Barret did."

"I'm sure he meant it for my own good."

"I'm not."

Somehow unwilling to concede that point, Lacey responded, "Whether he did or not doesn't matter. I didn't come back to cause you problems."

"You came back because Weaver is your home."

"I want Weaver to be my home, but it's *your* home first, Scully. You've made a life for yourself here. I don't intend for my presence to complicate things for you."

Lacey was so close. Scully took an unsteady breath before responding, "You aren't the one complicating things for me here."

"Yes, I am, and I don't want to. I'd rather go back east and take a position at the school than cause trouble for you."

"Back east…" He shook his head. "Not a chance."

"Then promise me," Lacey begged. "Please."

"Lacey…" Scully stared into Lacey's disturbed expression.

"Please."

Scully slid his arms around her and drew her against his chest. He hugged her tight, a myriad of emotions assaulting him as he said, "All right. I won't confront Barret about what he said this time. I promise, but if there's a next time—"

"You don't have to worry, there won't be a next time." Drawing back from his embrace, Lacey smiled sheepishly. "I got a little angry when he admitted he didn't like you, so I told him that was all right, because you didn't like him, either."

Scully gave a hard laugh.

"He did apologize for what he said, you know, but I told him I couldn't accept his apology because his remarks were ignorant and untrue, and his intentions questionable."

Scully listened intently.

"He asked me to reconsider accepting his apology, and I said maybe I would, but I didn't want to talk about it anymore." Lacey paused, then added, "Truthfully, I may accept Barret's *need* to apologize, but I won't ever accept what he said about you."

Scully stared at Lacey a moment longer, then offered, "Even if it's partially true?"

"It isn't."

"You're so sure of that?"

"Yes."

Scully had no words to reply as he scrutinized Lacey's sincere expression. She believed in him without exception. The thought was sobering.

At the sound of a soft bray, Scully looked up to see Careful approaching them. Lacey laughed as Careful nudged her head with a look that could only be called a half smile, and then grasped a lock of her fair hair with his teeth and pulled.

Scully was about to chastise the brazen burro when Lacey said, "No, don't. Careful pulled my hair in order to get my full attention. He always did that when I was a child." She stroked the animal's muzzle and added with a touch of seriousness in her tone, "See that, Scully? Time and circumstances don't change real friendships. If friendships are true, they're impervious to all assaults."

Scully watched as Lacey stood up unexpectedly. She drew Careful back with her to the stream, took off her boots, then waded into the water and splashed the burro playfully. He realized that what she had said was true. Time and circumstances didn't change true affection.

Or did they?

Succumbing to impulse, Scully pulled off his boots and walked toward the stream.

"They didn't do nothin', boss."

Blackie stood opposite Barret in the cool confines of his office, but the unkempt boor hadn't yet stopped sweating. Barret attempted to ignore Blackie's offensive odor as he replied, "What do you mean? They certainly didn't ride out just to pass some time. It's hot out there, in the event you didn't realize it."

"Me and Larry realized it, all right." Blackie pulled off his hat and ran his hand through hair stuck slickly to his scalp with perspiration, then wiped his arm across his forehead before continuing. "Larry and me was stuck out there in the sun, watching, while them two took off their boots and walked around in the stream to cool off."

"You're telling me—" Barret took a firmer grip on his agitation "—that Jake Scully rode out into the afternoon heat just to splash around in a stream?"

"It sure looked that way."

"Well, maybe you weren't looking hard enough!"

"Look, boss…" His bearded face growing unexpectedly menacing, Blackie snapped, "Me and Larry spent a long afternoon trying to cool off in the shade of a few, miserable bushes while them two was kicking up some fun in the stream. We was looking hard enough, all right, and it wasn't easy."

Barret gauged Blackie's reaction critically. The man was irritated because he had been sent out on a wild-goose chase in the heat of the day, but that was too bad. He snapped back, "Where's Larry?"

"He went straight to the Gold Nugget to get a drink."

"And he left you to carry the 'good news' to me."

"Like you said, it was hot out there."

Barret nodded. He pressed, "They didn't travel in the direction of Charlie Pratt's burned-out cabin?"

"I told you, they didn't go nowheres near it."

Barret paused to consider the situation. Lacey Stewart had waited ten years and it appeared she was content to wait a few more weeks until she was again familiar enough with the territory to be able to locate her grandfather's strike without Scully. That could be the only explanation, because if she intended sharing the claim with Scully, they would have headed directly for it that afternoon.

So he need wait a little longer.

Barret felt a hot flush suffuse his skin. But *he* had waited ten years, too, and he wasn't as patient as Lacey Stewart obviously was. It occurred to him that the way the situation presently stood, Lacey would find it difficult to ride off alone when she was ready to search, without Scully trailing behind her. He'd need to figure out a way to separate the two of them. He hadn't been successful in ingratiating himself with Lacey earlier that day, but he was no longer concerned about that failure.

An uncouth, barbaric adage commonly used by Weaver residents sprang into Barret's mind. He despised it, but the truth of the saying was so appropriate.

Yes, *there was more than one way to skin a cat.*

Chapter Six

Lacey took a deep breath as she walked down the hallway toward her boarding house room. The afternoon spent with Scully in the wild Arizona terrain had been exceedingly pleasant, even though the day had started out poorly in so many ways.

Lacey's mind returned to the scene between Rosie and her beau earlier that morning. The image of Rosie sobbing as a result of Riley's blow shook Lacey even in retrospect. She had not quite recovered from witnessing that devastating encounter or her revealing conversation with Jewel when she was stopped by Barret Gould. Lacey recalled the unpleasantries of the exchange that had followed. Barret's audacity in criticizing Scully so boldly had been infuriating. She wondered how he could believe for a moment that she would prefer his advice to Scully's about any portion of her life.

She supposed she shouldn't have told Scully about that conversation, but she had needed to let him know he was correct in his assessment of the haughty lawyer, and that she had been wrong.

But the remainder of the afternoon, while they had

stopped at the stream to cool off themselves and their mounts, had been one of the most pleasant times she could recall in recent years. Sitting so close to Scully and speaking to him so honestly from the heart, she had been even more conscious of the special intimacy they shared. Careful's affectionate bid for attention had interrupted their dialogue, but the display had warmed her heart and returned her briefly to a carefree period of her life that she cherished in memory.

She recalled her astonishment when Scully waded into the stream behind her, his feet as bare as hers. She remembered how they had both stomped around in the cool water. She recalled the moment when Scully laughed out loud in spontaneous enjoyment. Her heart had jumped a beat at the sheer beauty of the sound.

She truly was fond of Scully. There was no one whose affection was presently more dear to her. She whispered another brief prayer of gratitude, knowing she could never give enough thanks to the Lord for His having placed Scully in her life—although she wondered why she deserved such a precious gift.

Lacey closed the door behind her. Their visit to the stream had been invigorating, a relief from the intense heat of the day. Their damp clothing had cooled them for the greater portion of their ride home, but once their clothes had dried, the heat had become oppressive. She was presently looking forward to sponging herself with cool water from her washstand and refreshing herself with the delicate fragrance of the lilac-scented soap she favored.

Lacey looked at the clock on the mantle. She had a few hours until Scully and she would go to the restaurant for their evening meal. It occurred to her that Mary was right. She had yet to take advantage of the food the dear woman provided her guests—meals reputed to be consistently excellent. She knew, however, that even if she were given the choice, she would prefer Scully's company to a meal fit for royalty.

Lacey turned to the washstand. She was unbuttoning her shirtwaist when she looked at the soap dish and stopped cold. She had used up the last of her soap that morning.

Impatient with herself for having forgotten to stop at the mercantile to buy another bar, Lacey checked her small purse for change. Satisfied, she started for the door.

Lacey walked briskly toward the store. Her path lay past Barret Gould's office, but the possibility of a second encounter with him that day was more than she could presently face. Deciding to avoid it if she could, Lacey crossed the street and walked quickly along the crowded walk, hoping no one would notice her circuitous route when she crossed back again to the other side.

Lacey moved quickly between the last straggling shoppers of the day and the influx of wranglers just beginning to arrive for the weekend's entertainment. She approached a small boutique where it was rumored that many of the Gold Nugget women did their shopping. According to the whispers of two matrons standing behind her while she had waited for her order to be filled at the mercantile a few days earlier, the clothing at the boutique was fashionable, direct from Paris and well beyond the reach of the "decent" women in town.

He who guards his lips, guards his soul.

She had wondered if those two "decent" women were

familiar with that passage. Less important than that, she had then wondered if the clothing in the store was really direct from Paris.

That thought lingered as Lacey spotted a familiar figure standing in front of the boutique. She recognized the distinctive shopping basket Rosie carried. Rosie's surprising talent for weaving was well-known at the Gold Nugget, and her baskets were easy to pick out.

Lacey's step slowed as she approached the thin dancehall girl and said, "I thought it was you standing here, Rosie."

Rosie turned toward her, then glanced away—but not before Lacey saw the fresh bruise at the corner of her eye.

Rosie replied, "Marcella told me that Madame Lilly had reduced her prices on some dresses because she expects new stock to arrive on the stage at the end of the week." Referring to the voluptuous brunette rumored to be so popular in the Gold Nugget, Rosie continued, "Marcella bought herself a beautiful dress. I thought I might be able to find something. My old gold satin got ripped somehow."

Lacey paused in her response. She knew how Rosie's dress had gotten ripped, all right.

Lacey said simply, "Maybe I can help you fix it. I've done a pretty good job of repairing my own dresses from time to time."

"No… I don't think so. It's ripped beyond repair."

Her heart aching for Rosie, Lacey looked at the sign in the window and said, "It seems there are a few more dresses left at reduced prices."

Rosie turned back hopefully toward her. "How do you know that?"

"It says so right there on the sign." Lacey read, "'Only six dresses remaining at greatly reduced prices.'"

"I won't get paid for another few days. Does it say how much longer Madame will keep the prices reduced?"

Lacey looked back at the sign. The sign was clearly written in bold letters. Momentarily confused by the question, Lacey responded, "No, that's all it says."

Realization then struck her, and Lacey asked, "Don't you know how to read, Rosie?"

Rosie stiffened and took a backward step.

"Rosie?"

Rosie's lips wobbled. "No."

"Oh."

"My Ma and Pa died in an accident when I was six. My uncle didn't have any choice but to take me in." She shrugged. "That's what he said, anyway. He raised me until I was ten. I guess he figured a girl like me wouldn't have no use for book learning."

"A girl like you?"

Rosie ignored the question. "He ran off when I was ten."

"He left you alone?"

"He said I always had too much to say."

Lacey took a breath, then forced a smile. "Well, I suppose I wouldn't know how to read, either, if it wasn't for my grandpa. He took me in when my mother died, too, you know."

"I know."

Lacey's brows rose with surprise.

"Everybody at the Nugget knows that story. Your grandpa was killed, and before he died, he told you to go to town and ask for Scully, so Scully could take care of you. Then Scully sent you back east to school, so you could learn to be a lady."

A lady.

Rosie had used that word with profound admiration, and Lacey felt her own eyes moisten. She heard herself say, "Yes, Scully did all that for me, but I could already read by the time I met him. My grandpa taught me easily enough. I could teach you, too."

"No, it's too late for me."

"Oh, pooh! I never heard such nonsense!" Realizing she had startled Rosie with the sudden vehemence of her response, Lacey continued more softly, "I'd really enjoy teaching you to read, Rosie. It would be fun."

"Everybody would laugh at me. Besides, Scully wouldn't like it if you spent too much time with me."

"He wouldn't care."

"Yes, he would."

Rosie was adamant. Aware that she was losing the battle, Lacey said, "Then we don't have to tell anybody I'm teaching you to read."

"That won't work."

"Yes, it will."

A glimmer of hope shone in Rosie's eyes as she said, "You really think I could learn…it's not too late for me?"

"Of course it's not too late."

Rosie hesitated a moment longer, then said, "I could try—but only if I can pay you for teaching me."

"Pay me? Why?"

"Men get paid for the work they do. Women should, too."

The light of principle shone in Rosie's eyes—and a

fragile fragment of a pride that was almost nil. Lacey could not infringe upon what little Rosie had left.

Lacey replied, "All right, I'll teach you to read if you'll—" Lacey continued smoothly after a moment's hesitation "—if you'll make me a basket just like yours. It's beautiful."

"That's not a fair exchange."

"We'll both be getting something we want. What's fairer than that?"

Rosie hesitated.

"Well, is it a deal?"

Rosie hesitated a moment longer, then nodded.

Elated, Lacey said, "We'll start tomorrow! You can come to my room at the boarding house when I'm done with work in the restaurant and we'll—"

"I couldn't do that. Mrs. McInnes wouldn't like it."

Lacey did not bother to argue the point. After a moment's thought, she said, "In that case, I know the perfect place."

Lacey walked out onto the boardwalk and waited as Scully closed the restaurant door behind them. She smiled up at him, then took his arm as they began walking. Yes, the day that had started out so badly had made a complete turnaround. She'd had a lovely afternoon with Scully and had taken the first step toward helping someone desperately in need. She had simply turned her perplexity over into His hands, and the Lord had provided the way to help Rosie. All she had needed to do was listen to His response.

Her heart rejoiced.

Lacey's smile briefly faded at the thought that night was approaching, and with it the possibility of the nightmares, which had increased in frequency. As pleased as she was that the situation with Rosie appeared to be headed in the right direction, she was forced to admit she had been unsuccessful in combating the shifting shadows of the terrors she faced in her dreams. Lacey glanced at Scully. Her inclination at that moment was to confide in Scully, to tell him about the nighttime anxieties she could not seem to overcome, but she was determined not to take a step backward in her independence, nor to allow fear to intrude even briefly into the beauty of the day they had shared.

Forcing those thoughts aside, Lacey watched as Scully observed the street with a practiced eye. Her gaze lingered. His skin had darkened to a golden hue while they had frolicked in the water. His eyes, always his most outstanding feature, appeared a lighter, softer gray in comparison, and his smile more brilliant.

She said candidly, "You're a very handsome man, do you know that, Scully?"

Scully looked back at her with a suddenly wary expression.

"Well, you are. I can't possibly be the first woman to tell you that."

Scully's gaze narrowed. "No, you're not…but, in my experience, that compliment is usually followed by a request for something extravagant."

"Scully…" Lacey replied sincerely without hesitation, "What could I possibly want from you that you haven't already given me?"

His expression unreadable, Scully did not respond, and Lacey continued with a hint of a smile, "I have something to confess, though. I didn't really remember what you looked like when I came home that first day.

I saw that tall, gray-haired rancher who was in town when I stepped off the stage, and I thought he was you."

"Tall, gray-haired…" Scully frowned. "You mean Tom Belcher?" At Lacey's nod, he said, "He's more than fifty years old."

"I figured you had to be at least that old since you were already an adult when I first met you. I figured you'd be needing somebody to take care of you in your old age. I wanted to be that person."

"You wanted to spend your life taking care of an old man?"

"Not *any* old man. Just Jake Scully. But the joke was on me. You're young and handsome…and you're still taking care of me." Lacey sobered. "You're not only handsome, Jake Scully, but you're a good man."

Scully did not smile as he said, "Did you ever stop to think that I might not be the Good Samaritan you think I am?"

"Scully…you've read the Bible!"

"Does that surprise you? Do you really think I could've lived with your grandfather for a year without learning something?"

Lacey asked with a sober bluntness, "Is that why you left Grandpa? I know he didn't ask you to leave."

"No, that's not the reason." Scully's voice dropped a note softer. "I left because your grandpa set a criteria I needed to emulate. He was a man who had set his own goals and established his own way of life with standards he refused to compromise. As far as I was concerned, whether he ever struck it rich or not didn't really matter. I admired him. Although my own ambitions or standards weren't as clearly defined, I knew it was time for me to make my own way, too. Your grandpa understood that."

"My grandfather and grandmother were cut from the same cloth. I don't know if you knew that. Grandpa told me my grandmother could've stayed in a nice, comfortable home back in Illinois when he went west, but she chose to go with him. He said she accepted every day they had together as a blessing, no matter how difficult their circumstances, and he'd never forget that. It broke my grandpa's heart when she died in an epidemic. He raised my mother by himself, and when my mother died in an epidemic, just like my grandmother, he raised me, too."

"Your grandfather was a good man."

"You are, too."

"I'm not your grandfather, Lacey. Don't ever mistake me for him."

"I won't. I couldn't."

Appearing uncomfortable with their conversation, Scully turned his attention back to a cautious scrutiny of the street. He had behaved in the same way when the previous weekend was approaching. She supposed it was a reflex that had become instinctive over the years in a territory where civilization sometimes seemed to lapse when celebration took over, but she didn't yet feel the same way.

Twilight was a special time in Weaver. In that brief period before the darkness of night, Weaver came alive with lamplight, imparting a fairy tale quality to the primitive scene. The greatest transformation performed was on the Gold Nugget Saloon. The building glowed, boasting bright lights and gaiety that came to full blossom only after the sun had set. She knew the sometimes cruel light of dawn would dispel that metamorphosis, but she never failed to enjoy the deceiving sight.

Lacey's smile dimmed as Scully's step slowed. His gaze had halted on a couple locked in a passionate embrace in a dark alleyway beside the Gold Nugget. Scully drew Lacey determinedly forward.

Out of view of the embarrassing scene, Scully turned to her and said, "I'm sorry to have exposed you to this kind of thing, Lacey. As far as Lucy and the rest of the women who work in the Gold Nugget are concerned, the Gold Nugget is a dancehall. That's all I expect of them when they entertain my customers. I can't control what the girls do on their own time, but I don't stand for that type of behavior while they're working. I'll tell Lucy she's no longer employed at the Gold Nugget tomorrow."

Lacey turned to glance back at Lucy as the smiling dancehall girl freed herself from the cowboy's embrace and they walked arm and arm back into the saloon. She said instinctively, "Don't do that, Scully."

He turned darkly toward her.

"I know Lucy's not behaving properly, and I really don't know her, but I do know if she leaves the Gold Nugget, she'll probably end up someplace where more might be expected of her than it is here. Warn her, first. At least here she has a chance to discover the error of her ways."

"I don't have time for warnings. She knew the rules when she took the job."

"If you warn her and tell her what'll happen if there's a next time, she'll understand you meant what you said."

"I don't operate that way at the Gold Nugget."

"Please."

Still frowning, Scully said, "Why do you care what happens to Lucy?"

Lacey replied, "Why should I not?"

Silent a moment longer, Scully replied, "I guess that's as good an answer as any. All right. I'll give Lucy fair warning tonight. The rest is up to her."

"Thank you, Scully." Greatly relieved, Lacey tucked her arm more tightly under his.

Scully regarded her intently. He said, "You look tired."

"Thanks. I was feeling pretty good until now." Lacey gave him a wry smile, then admitted, "But you're right. I am tired."

"I'll walk back with you to the boarding house."

Aware that Scully's night had only begun, Lacey withdrew her arm from his and said, "You don't have to do that. I don't have far to walk, and you have a business to take care of. I'll go back by myself."

"I'm not leaving you alone on the street at this time of night."

"It's barely dark." Lacey glanced around them. "There are any number of women still on the street."

Scully motioned toward four cowboys riding briskly toward them and said, "I don't have to look around to know those fellas wouldn't look twice at any of those other women—but they would at you."

"Scully..." Lacey could not help but laugh. "I'm a big girl now."

"That's the problem."

Suddenly realizing he was deadly serious, Lacey said, "I surrender."

"It's not a case of winning or losing, Lacey. It's a matter of being safe."

And of not becoming a burden to a man overly concerned for her welfare.

Yes, she understood far better than Scully realized.

That thought in mind, Lacey responded, "All right, let's go back now. I have a feeling Mary may be waiting for me. She treats her boarders like her children, you know."

"Lacey..."

"I really am tired, Scully."

They had reached the boarding house door when Mary called from inside, "Is that you, Lacey?" In the doorway within seconds, the dear woman said, "I'm glad you brought Lacey home early, Scully. I managed to save her some of my special apple pie, but it won't last much longer if any of my other boarders see it."

Lacey walked up the boarding house steps as Mary chattered on. She looked back as Scully tipped his hat and walked back down the street.

Barret stood at his office window, watching the growing activity on the street. Friday night, and the influx of weekend revelers had just begun. Within the hour, all respectable residents would be in the safe refuge of their homes and the streets would be abandoned to pleasure seekers. Hayseeds...hicks...ignoramuses. The town was full of them, and not a single one of them had any idea of the level of enjoyment one could reach in more civilized environs. Yet he had no desire to go home yet. As deficient as his office was in the refinements to which he was accustomed, his home was worse. It was by far the largest house in Weaver's small residential area on the next street, but it was still a miserly abode when compared to the mansion that had been his family's San Francisco home.

His life in Weaver was a bore. The only thing that made it bearable was a dream now held in abeyance in the dainty hands of Lacey Stewart. He needed to shake her up somehow…force her to make a move—which would be difficult indeed with Scully dogging her every step.

Barret's eyes glazed over as he stared out onto the street. He needed to think…and plan.

Lacey looked up from the page she had been reading as a thought struck her in the silence of her room.

Strangely enough, she'd had no desire to sleep after Scully dropped her off at the boarding house door and she was safely secured in her room. Sitting alone in the advent of night, her mind again deluged with uncertainties, she had reached for her grandfather's Bible, which had given her so much comfort through the years. She was uncertain how long she'd been reading when it came to her in a flash that if Rosie could not read, she could not write—and if she could not write, she could not read. There was no way of separating the two. The lessons needed to be taught concurrently. She had everything she would need in order to teach Rosie to read. It was all contained in the one book she held in her hand. Writing, however, was another matter.

Paper and pencil—Rosie needed that much, at least, so she could practice in private between lessons. Without those simple supplies, Rosie would be at a disadvantage that might even discourage her enough to make her abandon the effort.

Lacey shook her head. She couldn't let that happen

to a young woman with such low self-esteem that she
believed no one, including God, truly loved her.

Lacey looked out her window at the darkening shadows of the street below. There was no way she'd be able
to purchase the necessary supplies in the morning or
after she finished up work in the restaurant, without
Scully's notice. She would have to get them now, before the mercantile closed for the night.

She didn't have much time.

The brisk business of the saloon constant behind
him, Scully nodded to familiar faces in passing as he
pushed his way out through the Nugget's swinging
doors onto the boardwalk. He walked a few steps into
the shadows of the overhang, then leaned back against
the false front of the building, frowning as the boisterous music and heavy smoke from the saloon filtered
out onto the street.

What in Sam Hill was wrong with him? Admittedly,
his lifestyle had been beginning to pale of late. He had
supposed he was getting older. He had thought it might
be time to broaden his horizons. He had even considered moving on, but, somehow, none of those solutions
had seemed the answer.

Then Lacey returned to Weaver, and his scrutiny
of Weaver and the lifestyle he had adopted became
sharper…clearer. It was almost as if Lacey's confidence in his "goodness" made him even more aware
of his deficiencies; as if her innocent trust made him
aware of the tawdry side of things he had previously
accepted; as if her faith in the Lord and her devotion to
His teachings made him conscious of the many ways
in which he fell short.

Yet he felt none of the resentment he would have considered an ordinary reaction to his new consciousness. And the reason was simple. Lacey had brought him to those conclusions with only honest praise for him.

Rose-colored glasses.

She was too innocent, and too beautiful. She didn't realize how a man could be intrigued by that combination, or what he could be thinking each time she smiled at him so guilelessly. He wished he could make her realize those things, but he didn't want to if it would change her. He liked her the way she was, honest—outspoken, earnest…feisty, anxious to fight the good fight. He'd never met a woman like her.

"Well, stranger."

Scully turned toward the sound of the familiar female voice. The dazzling color of Charlotte's red hair was distinctive even in the limited light, as was her teasing smile as she continued, "I haven't seen much of you lately. I reminded you of that once before. I also reminded you that you knew where to find me, but it looks like it's time for me to stir your memory." She walked an intimate step closer as she said, "So, here I am. And don't tell me you've been busy. I won't accept that excuse. I know a man always makes time for things that are important to him." She halted for effect, then said, "Which brings me to a very unflattering conclusion."

Scully could not help but smile. Charlotte…out in the open…never mincing words. He could do no less than return the favor in kind.

"You're right, Charlotte, honey. A man does make time for the things that're his top priorities."

Charlotte sobered. She responded bluntly, "You're making a big mistake, Scully."

Scully was suddenly as serious as she. "Lacey's my responsibility, Charlotte. She's out of her element here. She needs guidance, and I'm the only family she has."

"Are you sure you're the one who should be giving her guidance?"

"Yes."

"Oh...ho!" Charlotte was smiling again. "You didn't even hesitate!"

"And what does that tell you?"

"That tells me you haven't changed as much as I thought you had." Charlotte reached up to stroke Scully's cheek with her smooth hand as she whispered, "And it also tells me, if I just relax and have some fun while I'm waiting, you'll walk right back into my arms."

Charlotte stood up on tiptoe unexpectedly and pressed a fleeting kiss against Scully's lips. Contrary to the reaction she expected, Scully drew back and said, "You haven't changed a bit, either, Charlotte—but I think it's time for us both to get back to business."

Scully slid his arm casually around Charlotte's shoulders and turned her back into the saloon. Charlotte hadn't bothered to be subtle. Even if she had been, he knew all the signals. The truth was, he wasn't interested anymore. He'd been as truthful as he could be with her. Lacey was his responsibility, and that was all that counted.

Lacey stood still in the shadows of the boardwalk. The street teemed with activity around her, but she was somehow unable to move. She had watched the two figures standing intimately close under the Gold Nugget's overhang. The brightly dressed, redheaded woman was Charlotte, who had never been overly friendly to her while she resided at the Gold Nugget. The other person was Scully.

Lacey had caught her breath as Charlotte stood up on tiptoe and pressed her mouth to Scully's. She saw the whispered conversation that followed when he drew back, and she glimpsed the smile on Scully's face before he slipped his arm around Charlotte's shoulders and they walked back into the saloon.

Lacey took a shaken breath. Although the kiss had been fleeting, Scully and Charlotte were obviously more than friendly.

Hard questions tormented Lacey. Had she imposed herself upon Scully's life to the extent that he had no time for the woman he loved?

Had she been so self-absorbed and determined to regain her past since returning to Weaver that she hadn't given a thought to Scully's hopes for his future?

Uncommon distress shuddered through Lacey when the answer to those questions became painfully clear.

Lacey swallowed past the lump in her throat, then forced herself on toward the mercantile. She needed to change all that now. She needed to allow Scully time for his own life by immediately taking full charge of her own. It wasn't only fair, it was the right thing to do. And if that necessity had somehow formed an aching knot inside her, she need remember to be thankful for the blessings God had given her and not lament the loss of something she had never owned.

As for Scully, she would have to depend on the Lord to guide him.

In the meantime, the mission that had brought her out onto the street at that late hour had not changed.

Her smile fixed, Lacey walked into the well-lit mercantile.

Barret blinked. Still at his office window as he liberally imbibed in the solitude, he struggled to clear his vision, then laughed aloud as Lacey stepped out of the boardwalk shadows and walked to the mercantile store.

Lacey had seen Scully and Charlotte together. He had seen the prim Miss Lacey Stewart's shocked expression when the sultry redhead kissed Scully boldly. He knew it had not missed her notice that Scully and Charlotte had looked quite cozy when they walked back into the brightly lit saloon.

Barret snickered with true enjoyment. It appeared he had judged Lacey harshly. He now believed she had been sincere in her enjoyment of Scully's attentions. She might even have been considering taking him with her when she went to locate her grandfather's strike.

However, if Lacey had entertained that intention even for a moment, she had obviously abandoned it now. And since she now knew her hero's true worth, he might even have been provided with a way back into her good graces. All he needed was a careful word here, and an inference there. That was his forte, after all.

Yet a simple point nagged at him. Scully was a clever, experienced man. It didn't make sense that he was so completely taken in by Lacey's innocent pose.

Could it be…?

Barret went suddenly cold. Did Scully suspect Charlie had made a strike? Was it possible that the old man had hinted at it during their conversation that last day?

If so, he probably believed the strike existed because there was no other reason anyone would go after the old man.

Barret followed that trend of thought: *If* Scully believed Charlie had made a strike and *if* he had waited ten years to find out, he probably figured the payoff should be his.

Barret was suddenly deadly sober.

But *if* Scully had come to that conclusion...he would soon discover he was wrong.

Chapter Seven

"Oh, I'm sorry, Scully. I should've told you sooner that I couldn't have lunch with you." Her regret was sincere even if her excuse was deliberately misleading. Lacey continued, "I promised to be at the church after I finish work at eleven. I've been wanting to do something positive since I arrived in Weaver, and this is my chance to do it."

The early morning hum of the restaurant continued on around them as Scully questioned, "Is that smart? Doesn't Reverend Sykes think that's asking too much of you?"

"It isn't Reverend Sykes's decision."

"I know your intentions are good, Lacey, but the restaurant is so busy that you go without breakfast most of the time. Now you won't have time for lunch."

"I'll find time to eat. Don't worry."

"But I do worry about it." Seated alone at a corner table, his untouched breakfast in front of him, Scully scrutinized her intently.

Lacey squirmed mentally under his stare.

The semidarkness before dawn...the fire...her grandfather's gasping words. The fear...

It had all returned the previous night, in nightmares so vividly terrifying that they had left her shuddering. She knew she had awakened overly wan because of the sleeplessness that had followed.

As if reading her mind, Scully said, "You're pale this morning, Lacey. Are you all right?"

"I'm fine." She smiled. "I have to go back to my customers."

Scully asked abruptly, "Has somebody been giving you trouble here?"

"No."

"Is the work too heavy for you?"

"No."

Scully did not appear convinced.

Lacey responded sincerely, "I don't want you to worry about me. I wasn't able to attend services regularly while traveling back to Weaver. I sorely miss my connection to the Lord's word, and this is good for me."

"I don't think the Lord would want you working yourself into the ground because of a sense of duty."

"It's not duty. It's pleasure."

Scully considered her reply, then said, "I'll come to get you at the boarding house at suppertime."

Lacey was about to make an excuse, but Scully's scrutiny was so intense that she was certain he'd see right through her if she tried.

Deciding to put that off for another day, Lacey said, "I'll be waiting."

Lacey was about to leave Scully's table when his touch on her arm stayed her. She swallowed as Scul-

ly's sober gaze met hers and he said, "You'd tell me if
something was wrong, wouldn't you, Lacey?"

"Scully..." Lacey sighed. "Of course, I would."

Of course, I would.

Lacey had said those words so sincerely. So, why
didn't he believe her?

Scully watched as Lacey moved back and forth between the restaurant tables, smiling at the customers as
she snatched up empty plates from some and returned
with filled plates for others. She was becoming more
adept at her job with every day that passed, and he
needed no one to tell him that Sadie was pleased. Neither did he need anyone to tell him that Sadie's customers—the majority of whom were male—were pleased
as well.

Scully picked up his fork, poked at the hotcakes on
his plate, then looked back up to watch Lacey's progress across the room. Todd Fulton was there again. The
youthful cowboy couldn't take his eyes off her. Hiram
Watts, Jerry Livingston and Mitch Carter had obviously also taken to coming in as often as their sched-
ules allowed.

Could one of them be the reason Lacey was effectively distancing herself from him?

No, she wanted to make time to work at the church.

He understood.

Yes...he did.

"I'll never be able to do it." Rosie shook her head.
Tears brimming, she glanced up from the slate on the
table in front of her. "It's too confusing."

"No, it isn't."

Lacey slid her hand over Rosie's. Rosie's hand was trembling, and Lacey's heart ached. They were seated in the small anteroom that Reverend Sykes had made available when she had confided in him about Rosie's lessons the previous day. She had known he wouldn't refuse her space to conduct Rosie's lessons, and she had been equally sure he would respect her confidence. True to their agreement, he had allowed them complete privacy, and Rosie had appeared pleased. A half hour into the first lesson, however, the situation had taken a drastic change in course.

"I told you, it's too late for me." Rosie wiped away a tear with an angry hand. "What do I need to learn to read and write for, anyway? I've done all right so far without it."

"You're a good person, Rosie. I can't imagine how difficult it was for you just managing to survive, being out on your own as young as you were."

Rosie did not reply.

"But you can do even better, and doing better starts with feeling better about yourself."

"Marjorie knows how to read and write, and she's working at the Gold Nugget."

"That's Marjorie's choice. You didn't have a chance to make a choice."

"Nothing will probably change, even if I do learn to read. I'm a Gold Nugget girl, and everybody in Weaver knows it. I'll probably always be a Gold Nugget girl, either here or somewhere else."

"That could be true, of course, but even if it was, that doesn't mean you wouldn't profit from reading—even if it's only in the way you feel about yourself." When Rosie did not respond, Lacey picked up her Bible. She opened it to a familiar page and smiled. "Do you see these small drawings in the margin, Rosie? My Grandpa drew them to illustrate some of the stories when he was teaching me to read. Some of the drawings are faded and almost illegible, and I don't remember when he drew some of the others, but they all represent his love to me—a love that was an extension of God's love. Being able to read these words is a treasure beyond value that my Grandpa shared with me. One of the reasons I came back to Weaver was because I wanted to remember even more—about things that the night my grandfather was killed somehow made me forget. I expect I'll be able to clear up those memories when I finally get the courage to ride out and face the ruins of the cabin my grandfather and I shared. But since returning to Weaver and learning how others in situations similar to mine have suffered difficult lives, I've begun wondering how I could show my appreciation for being blessed with Scully's care over the years. I've found the answer, Rosie. I can show my appreciation by sharing my blessings, just like Grandpa and Scully shared theirs with me."

Her voice suddenly husky with emotion, Lacey whispered, "I know learning to read and write will be hard at the beginning, but it'll get easier. I know you can do it."

"It's too late, I'm telling you." Rosie's pale eyes were red-rimmed. "I don't know much, but I know I've done a lot of things that go against what's in the Bible. Just like my uncle said, everybody gave up on me—including God."

"Look…right here, Rosie." Lacey pointed again to the drawings on the Bible's page. "Do you see these two birds my Grandpa drew in the margin? He drew them when he read this to me.

"'Are not two sparrows sold for a farthing? And one of them shall not fall on the ground without your Father. But the very hairs of your head are all numbered. Fear ye not, therefore, ye are of more value than many sparrows.'"

Rosie remained silent as Lacey whispered, "You see? You'll always have value to the Lord. It'll never be too late for you to Him."

Rosie took a breath. "Is that what it says...truly?"

Lacey nodded. "I'll read more to you from the scriptures—every day if you want me to. But when we're done with these lessons, you'll be able to read it all for yourself."

Rosie swallowed.

"It all starts with the alphabet you're scratching on that slate, and ends up with reading a book."

Rosie's lips wobbled as she said, "If you won't give up, I won't, either."

"It's a deal." Lacey cleared the thickness from her throat, then took the chalk from Rosie's hand. "D...for dog, that's how you write it." And as Rosie struggled to form the letter, "That's good, Rosie...really good!"

"She's at church, boss. The way she went sneaking off, I figured she'd finally be leading us somewhere important, but that's where she went, all right."

Barret stared at Blackie and considered his statement. Lacey had sneaked off to church.

Sneaked.

Confused and frustrated, Barret returned, "She must've seen you following her."

"No, she didn't boss."

"Why else would she waste her time going to church in the middle of the afternoon?"

"Maybe it has something to do with that Rosie from the Gold Nugget. She went into the church a few minutes after Lacey got there."

"Rosie…" Barret shook his head. If Lacey was enlisting that girl's help for some reason, she was making a big mistake. Rosie couldn't even help herself get out from underneath her abusive boyfriend's thumb. Barret said abruptly, "That doesn't make sense."

"Well, she's been in that church with Rosie for the past hour."

"Where is she now?"

"Still there, I suppose."

"You *suppose?*"

"Don't worry, boss. Larry's watching her. She ain't going nowhere without one of us trailing behind."

"Where's Jake Scully?"

"He's at the Gold Nugget, I guess. He saw Lacey at breakfast. The two of them looked real cozy, too."

Cozy? He had seen Lacey's expression when she saw Scully and Charlotte together the previous evening. That didn't sound right, either.

"She's up to something. Keep your eye on her," Barret ordered. "She's not going to get away with anything. I've waited too long."

His agitation increasing, Barret followed Blackie's progress as his hireling exited his office and started back up toward the church. Blackie was useless when it came to the subtleties of situations, but both Larry and he had learned the value of maintaining his confidence. They were the best he could do right now.

Barret took a breath, then made a decision. He presently had only one recourse.

"I thought I saw you approaching, dear."

Lacey looked up to see Barret standing in her path as she walked back down the boardwalk from the church.

Lacey attempted to stifle the surge of annoyance his appearance elicited. She had just begun feeling things might take a turn for the better. The midafternoon sun was shining and the heat of the day was bearable. She had stopped off to see Careful on the way back, and the burro's enthusiastic, braying welcome, as well as his sympathetic silence when she shared her troubles with him as she had done as a child, had soothed her sagging spirits. Most comforting of all, however, her first session with Rosie had gone exceedingly well after its rough start.

Lacey recalled Rosie's flush at the end of the lesson when she presented Rosie with a pencil and paper tablet with which to practice her newly learned skills. It had occurred to her when she saw Rosie's reaction that it was probably the first time in her life that someone had even thought to place paper and pencil in Rosie's hand. The thought had momentarily thickened Lacey's throat, but she had forced aside her emotion, determined that this instance would not be Rosie's last.

She had read a chapter of Bible text to Rosie at her request when their lesson was completed. The realization that Rosie had never heard the first chapter of Genesis or any other Bible verse before that day had stunned her. The words had become even more precious to her knowing that Rosie was hearing them for the first time, and she had been hard-pressed to keep the tears from falling. She had been inspired by Rosie's eagerness to listen and learn, and the resulting glow within had warmed her soul.

Then she had spotted Barret Gould standing in her path.

Irritated by the fact that she had not had the presence of mind to walk on the other side of the street to avoid such an encounter, Lacey did not respond to Barret's greeting.

His smile paling as Lacey remained silent, Barret continued, "I've been thinking about my unfortunate comments during our previous conversation, Lacey. I meant well but spoke in a way that was detrimental to any friendship we might form. It occurred to me in retrospect that I accused Scully of similar behavior— meaning well, but not acting in your best interest. I realize that now, and I want to apologize. I hope you will accept my apology, because it is sincerely meant."

"I accept your need to apologize...." Her eyes never moving from Barret's remorseful expression, Lacey heard herself say, "But I strongly resent what you said about Scully. You aren't his friend, so neither can you be mine."

"I hope you're wrong there, Lacey." A revealing anger flitted across Barret's expression before he continued in an almost fatherly manner, "I'm older than you, and I'm far more experienced in dealing with life's dilemmas. I saw in you an inclination to glorify Scully because of the admirable care he provided for you, and I hoped to spare you the disappointment I saw in your future."

"You needn't worry. Scully makes no pretense about himself, so he will never disappoint me."

"Dear... I was hoping to spare you disappointment of a more intimate nature."

Lacey felt the flush that transfused her skin as she responded, "Meaning?"

"Meaning, I...we..." Barret paused briefly, as if seeking the right words. He continued, "You're a beautiful young woman. You'll make a good man an excellent wife someday, and the man who wins your hand will be fortunate, indeed. I'm sure Scully feels the same way. He'd like to see you safely married with children to care for but—"

Losing patience, Lacey interrupted, "Mary is expecting me and she worries if I'm late."

"But," Barret continued with an indulgent smile, "Scully's preference for redheaded women is well-known in Weaver. It will always be his first priority, whether you realize that now or not. And that, my dear, was the main reason for my ill-advised comments that first day."

Incensed, Lacey barely maintained her calm as she replied, "Scully's social preferences, if indeed he has any, are not my concern. Neither, Mr. Gould, are they yours."

"I hoped to spare you some grief, dear."

"I'm not your 'dear.'"

"Nor did I wish to make you angry with me again."

"You've failed in that respect, too. In fact, you've made me angrier than anyone else in Weaver has since my arrival."

"That was not my intention. I'm sorry."

"You should be."

"My intentions were good, but I see they've been misconstrued."

"No, I don't think so."

Barret did not immediately respond.

Rigid with anger, Lacey said, "I don't accept your claim that your intentions were good. Neither do I believe I've misconstrued them. You stopped me today to apologize for your previous comments about Scully, then proceeded to restate them in more positive terms. Let me save you the trouble of apologizing again by telling you you'll be wasting your time. So, if you'll excuse me—"

"Lacey—"

Lacey looked down at Barret's hand on her arm as he again attempted to stay her. She objected from between tightly clenched teeth, "Take your hand off me."

"Lacey, I—"

"And don't ever bother me with your insincere apologies again."

Waiting only until Barret's hand had dropped back to his side, Lacey walked off, head high.

She was still walking resolutely, refusing to look back, when Barret's words returned to tighten the knot that had formed deep inside her the previous night.

Scully's preference for redheaded women is well-known in Weaver.

Lacey reached up toward her platinum locks with tears suddenly brimming.

Barret walked back into his office, then turned to the window to watch as Lacey continued down the street. He mumbled an epithet, abandoning any further attempt to gain Lacey's confidence. She did not respond to his guile like the average woman—but the reason was simple. She was *not* the average woman. Her facade was carefully calculated. Her defense of Scully was somehow useful to her at the moment and it would not change.

There was one area, however, where he knew his barbs had lodged deeply. His remark about Scully's preference for redheads had struck home because Lacey had seen the evidence of it with her own eyes.

Lacey slipped out of sight, and Barret turned back to his desk with a single thought consoling him. He need not worry that Lacey would consider confiding the location of her grandfather's mine to Scully now—not with Charlotte on the scene.

Barret smiled to himself with his certainty that Lacey would turn against Scully sooner or later. That was a reality he could count on.

Because that was the way women were.

Rosie was breathless with excitement when she reached her boarding house door. A small smile on her lips and a paper tablet and pencil in hand, she walked up the staircase toward her room on the second floor. She had worked so hard during her first lesson, but she honestly believed Lacey had worked even harder. She had seen the concern in Lacey's eyes when she had been briefly overwhelmed, and she had felt Lacey's driving desire to help her learn. She was no longer puzzled why a lady like Lacey would care about someone like her, because she now knew the answer. She'd have the answer to all her other questions, too, when she was able to read the Bible for herself.

Rosie reached the top of the stairs and turned toward her door, then glanced down at the tablet she carried. Lacey had printed her name on the first page.

Rosie Burns.

She had copied the letters with Lacey's instructions, and she would practice again as soon as she could.

She would be reading soon.

Very soon.

Rosie tucked her tablet under her arm as she pushed open the door to her room. One step inside and she froze. She looked at the half-empty bottle of red-eye on the nightstand beside the bed where Riley was reclining. She was unable to move as Riley sat up and demanded, "Where were you? I've been waiting for you for an hour."

Rosie tossed her precious tablet and pencil casually onto a chair, leaving the door open behind her as she said, "I didn't expect to see you here until tonight."

"I asked you where you were."

"At the boutique. I need a new dress."

"You didn't get one, though, did you?"

"No. I didn't have enough money."

Riley stood up and started slowly toward her. He was slight, wiry, tightly muscled. Rosie remembered a time when the sight of him—his curly blond hair, warm brown eyes and little-boy looks—had started her heart pounding with anticipation.

Now her heart pounded only with fear when he halted close beside her and whispered, "I don't believe you."

"But—"

"I went past the store and looked inside for you, but you weren't there."

"Maybe I was at the mercantile."

"You weren't there, either."

"Or the apothecary. I needed something for…"

"Stop lying! Who were you with?"

Rosie took a shaken breath. Riley looked at the chair where she had dropped the tablet. She took a step toward it as he reached over and picked it up. She held her breath when he opened the tablet to the first page where her name was printed, where her own, primitive attempts at drawing the letters were clearly visible.

"Rosie Burns…your name." He laughed aloud. "Well, either a kid is learning how scribble, or somebody's trying to teach you to write your name. Which is it?"

"Riley…"

"I asked you…" Riley grasped her arm painfully tight. The smell of liquor was heavy on his breath as he said hotly, "Which is it?"

Tears squeezed out the corners of her eyes as Rosie replied, "I bought the book in the mercantile, and I asked Mrs. Wilson to print my name in it…so I could try to copy it."

"Why?"

"Because."

"You're thinking after you learn to write your name, you'll be too good for me, huh?"

"No, I didn't think any such thing. I just wanted to know how to write my name, is all."

Riley released Rosie so abruptly that she staggered back a few steps. She watched as he picked up the pencil Lacey had so carefully sharpened. He turned toward her and broke it in half, then, laughing at her gasp, tore the sheet containing her name out of the tablet and tossed it onto the floor. He was tearing the other pages out one by one when Rosie charged toward him.

"That's mine! Give it to me!"

Riley raised his hand to strike her when Jewel appeared unexpectedly in the doorway and said, "Leave her alone!"

Rosie looked up to see the derringer in Jewel's hand was pointed directly at Riley.

When Riley turned to advance toward Jewel, Jewel warned, "Don't make that mistake, Riley. I'm not afraid to shoot."

Riley slurred, "You wouldn't do that, would you, Jewel? I thought we was friends."

"We're not friends, and we never will be. You're drunk. Get out of here."

Riley took a step. "I'm not going nowhere."

"You'd better."

"If you're thinking that boyfriend of yours can protect you when that gun's not in your hand, you're wrong."

"I can protect myself."

"You think so, huh?"

Jewel aimed the pistol pointedly. "Either you get out of here now, or I'm going to fix it so neither Rosie or any other woman will ever have to worry about you bothering them again."

Riley went still. "You wouldn't do that."

"Wouldn't I?"

Riley turned back to Rosie and demanded, "Tell her, Rosie, honey. Tell her I didn't mean nothing."

Rosie stood stiffly. She did not respond.

Jewel did not blink. "Get out."

"You'll be sorry about this."

"Yeah, I know. Get out."

"You will, too, Rosie."

Rosie remained silent.

Riley took a lurching step forward as Jewel stepped

aside. He mumbled under his breath as he walked out through the doorway.

Following him at a safe distance, Jewel watched as he stumbled down the staircase and out the front entrance, slamming the door behind him.

Back in Rosie's room, Jewel closed the door behind her, then looked at Rosie where she stood against the wall with tears streaming. She said, "Come on over to the washstand and wash your face. You'll feel better."

Rosie swallowed. She moved abruptly to gather up the broken pieces of pencil and the sheets torn from the tablet. She was still clutching them close when she walked to the washstand.

Sunday morning. The sun beamed down from a cloudless sky. Weaver's main street was silent. The Gold Nugget Saloon was dark.

Lacey stepped out through the boarding house doorway and started toward the small church hidden from view around the curve of the main street. She had intended to wait for Mary, but the older woman had waved her on ahead when the last-minute details of cleaning up after breakfast had taken longer than expected.

Dressed in her Sunday best, a simple blue cotton with a matching hat and reticule, Lacey walked at a modest pace, somehow feeling more alone than she had ever felt in her life. She clutched her Bible tightly and smiled at Weaver's prominent citizens as they emerged from their doorways, but she made no attempt to join them. She searched the growing parade and saw Wilson and Janine Parker from the mercantile store walking with Doc Mayberry; Rita Johnson, the apothecary's niece, with her stiff-necked mother and father; Noelle Leach, the blacksmith's daughter and her father, Noah, just turning the corner of the street ahead. She nodded at Hiram Watts, Jerry Livingston and Mitch Carter as they lounged against a storefront on the opposite side of the street and tipped their hats in her direction.

The church bells began ringing as if on cue, and doorways opened along the street as additional church-goers emerged to join the silent parade. Lacey scanned the street, her spirits sinking lower when the person she had hoped to see did not appear.

Lacey thought back to her conversation with Barret Gould, and her anger again simmered. It was not Christian and her thoughts were not worthy of the Sabbath, but she truly disliked that man. Even more, she despised what he had said.

Scully's preference for redheaded women is well-known in Weaver.

Those words haunted her. They seemed to confirm what she had witnessed the previous night between Scully and Charlotte. They had stolen the joy from her successful first lesson with Rosie. They had left her silent and uncommunicative with Scully at supper later that night. They had made her more vulnerable than ever before to the nightmares, which had assaulted her vividly every time she had dozed during the night.

She was angry with herself because she hadn't had the courage to release Scully completely from the bondage of sharing his daily meals with her. Her excuse had been that Scully didn't appear to resent that ritual, but she vacillated, still uncertain. She had prayed for direction only to have awakened that morning still suffering indecision.

Lacey's step momentarily stilled as Barret Gould

walked onto the main street to join the stream of worshippers. Frowning, she wondered at his reason for going out of his way to take the Main Street route to church instead of the shorter route from his house on the next street.

Barret was dallying. Lacey realized abruptly that at the present rate she was walking, she would soon reach his side.

No, that would never do.

Silently imploring the Lord's forgiveness, Lacey crossed the street to avoid Barret completely. She could not be sure that his dallying was a deliberate effort to again place himself in her path, but she rationalized it was far better to avoid interaction with him than to chance her reaction if he attempted to start another conversation.

The irrational ache in the pit of her stomach remaining, Lacey cast another surreptitious glance around her, then chastised herself for entertaining the hope that Scully would appear somewhere on the street to accompany her. Without saying the words, Scully had made it clear the first day she had met Reverend Sykes that he had no intention of taking the reverend up on his invitation to attend Sunday worship. She did not choose to judge him for that decision. Scully had already gone out of his way to accommodate her—far more than she had realized until she had glimpsed him with Charlotte.

The unhappiness inside her expanded.

"Lacey...good morning."

Lacey turned at the sound of her name. Todd Fulton stepped out from the shadows and walked up to her side. She noted that the young wrangler's dark hair was neatly combed underneath his hat as he tipped it politely, that he was freshly shaven and was wearing clothes that were obviously newly purchased as he confessed, "I was waiting in the doorway for you to pass. I knew you'd be going to church this morning. I was hoping you wouldn't mind if I joined you."

"Mind? Of course not." Lacey forced her smile brighter as she looked into Todd's uncertain expression. "I'd enjoy your company."

"I was hoping you would. I was also hoping you'd have dinner with me tonight. It would pleasure me greatly."

"I...well..." Lacey took a breath. If this was a sign, she couldn't ignore it. Her decision made, she forced herself to say, "I'll be happy to have dinner with you."

Todd was conversing easily as they approached the church, but Lacey's thoughts wandered. She was no longer walking alone...yet she still felt strangely alone.

Lacey scanned the street one last time as she approached the church doorway. Resigned, she walked inside.

Scully watched from a position out of sight of the procession making its way to church. Lacey disappeared through the church doorway with Todd walking proudly beside her. Scully lingered only until the church doors closed and the singing began before walking back in the direction from which he had come.

Somehow, he couldn't put a name to the feelings inside him. Nor could he quite understand what had driven him to the street to see Lacey so early that morning after the especially active Saturday night he had had at the Gold Nugget. Was it because she had been so quiet at supper, because he had sensed a distance widening between them, or was it because, if Todd hadn't stepped up unexpectedly to accompany her, he might've been the man to walk beside her though the church doors for Sunday service?

No matter. Todd was with her now, and as long as the cowpoke behaved himself, he supposed Lacey was better off.

Yes, of course, she was.

He was sure of it.

Chapter Eight

The fire burned hotter. It singed her skin.

Her lungs were on fire.

There was no way out.

She cried out, "Help! Help me..." but her scorched lips refused to allow the sound passage.

She was outside the burning cabin—but the danger remained.

Grandpa was dead! They had killed him, and still they lingered.

They came closer...nearer.

Help! Help me!

Lacey awoke with a start, her heart pounding. She struggled against the terror remaining in the silent shadows of her boarding house room. She closed her eyes, then snapped them open again, telling herself it would soon be Monday morning, the beginning of another week. She had only had another nightmare, like the many others she had suffered through before. She would survive. Dawn would bring relief from her fears.

Lacey sat up slowly in bed. She was still trembling and a glance at the window revealed that dawn was hours away. Determined to take charge of her emotions, Lacey forced herself to lie back again. She firmly closed her eyes. She would not surrender to fear.

Grandpa's image appeared vividly in the darkness of her mind's eye, and Lacey smiled. Those sparkling eyes and that dear, bearded face... But, the image was changing. It was being replaced by a sober, handsome face and a serious, gray-eyed gaze that held hers intently. That gaze warmed her, held her safe and she abandoned herself to its comfort.

Scully.

Of course.

He would always keep her safe.

Lacey emerged from the boarding house doorway and glanced up at the lightening sky. It was Monday morning, and dawn had not fully consumed the night, but she was already dressed and on her way. Sadie would be surprised to see her at the restaurant so early and she—

Lacey gasped as a figure stepped out of the shadows.

"Lacey."

Her fear dissipated.

"Scully, what are you doing here so early?"

Scully walked to her side and Lacey felt his warmth pervade her. His handsome face, his sober gaze, the sheer size and masculine power of him—all was gentleness and understanding in his dealings with her.

She had felt that gentleness and understanding when she had explained the previous day that she would be having Sunday supper with Todd. She had seen the flicker of an unnamed emotion in his gaze before Scully had nodded and accepted her decision without comment. She had reasoned that the strange sense of abandonment she had felt when Scully left her at her door was unrealistic, that she needed to become more independent for Scully's sake, as much as for her own. She had enjoyed Todd's company that evening and had even tentatively consented to see him again, while still scanning the street for a sign of Scully in the hope of seeing *him* again before the day ended.

It had occurred to Lacey that her most recent nightmare—a dream more vivid and more terrifying than its predecessors—might have been related to that sense of abandonment, but she had forced that thought away. Scully had a life of his own. She needed to remember that.

Yet she did not question her joy at Scully's unexpected appearance in the predawn shadows as she smiled up into his uncertain expression and he said, "If I didn't know better, I'd think you're happy to see me waiting here for you this morning."

"And you'd be right, even if I'm surprised to see you, since the Gold Nugget probably only closed a few hours ago."

Scully sobered as he scrutinized her surprising lack of color and the dark shadows under her eyes. He said, "You look like you didn't sleep well, Lacey. Was it the nightmares again?"

"You always seem to open our conversations by telling me how tired I look." Lacey continued her light rejoinder with a shake of her head. "Everybody else tells me how *good* I look...."

"You do look good—better than any woman in this town—but that doesn't mean I can't see that you had a fitful night's rest."

"You see right through me, don't you, Scully?"

"No. If I could, I wouldn't be here this morning, wondering what's going on."

"What do you mean?"

"I'm glad you and Todd have struck up a friendship, Lacey. I'm glad to see you're settling in—but I have a feeling there's something else going on." Scully hesitated, then continued, "I want you to talk to me, Lacey. I have the feeling you're trying to shut me out, even though you say you're glad to see me this morning."

"I told you, I *am* glad to see you."

"So?"

"Oh, Scully…" Unable to avoid telling him the truth any longer, Lacey blinked back the sudden heat of tears and said, "I'm trying not to be selfish."

"Selfish!"

"I've been claiming all your time since I came back to Weaver—as if I have a special right to it."

"You do have a special right."

"No, I don't. You have a life of your own. It doesn't necessarily coincide with mine, and I shouldn't expect it to. I came back to Weaver for a few purposes. I explained the first—to take care of you in your old age—which was a misconception on my part. The second was to lift the shadows from the memories I have of my grandfather. The third—" Lacey shrugged, unable to express a thought not totally clear in her own mind. "Well, it looks like I haven't done so well on any of those fronts."

"So you figure to start by pushing me out of your life and pretending you're no longer my responsibility."

"I'm an adult now, Scully. I'm responsible for myself. That's something I've had to make myself face."

"Why?"

"You need to go on with your own life."

"What's all this concern about my life all of a sudden?"

"'All of a sudden...'" Lacey's spirits sagged. "I guess that says it all."

"No, it doesn't. You came back to Weaver expecting I'd help you settle the past and situate yourself in the present, and you had a right to that assumption. So...what happened? Why has everything suddenly changed?" And when Lacey averted her gaze, he asked, "Come on, Lacey, tell me."

Lacey looked back up at Scully. How could she explain? How could she make him understand?

Truth was the only answer.

Lacey responded bluntly, "I saw you with Charlotte outside the Gold Nugget the other night. I'm sorry, Scully."

"Sorry about what?" Scully's broad frame tensed noticeably. "Charlotte's a friendly acquaintance, but neither of us have made our friendship out to be more than that."

"I saw you kiss her, Scully."

"I've kissed a lot of women in my life."

"There was something special about that kiss."

"Not on my part."

"Scully..."

"Is that what this is all about—a simple kiss? Lacey, you've been sheltered all your life, but the truth is, a kiss doesn't signify commitment. That's all it is—just a kiss."

Scully flushed as a thought suddenly struck him. He asked, "Why? Did Todd try to kiss you last night?"

"Of course not!" Lacey's reply was spontaneous. She then added, "But why would it matter if 'a kiss is only a kiss'?"

"Because you seem to think it means more."

"A kiss is an expression of caring, Scully. I'm not so *naive* that I don't understand that. I've been tempted to kiss you myself a few times."

Silent a few moments, Scully replied unexpectedly, "So, why didn't you?"

"Because I thought it would be forward. I thought you might resent—"

"I wouldn't have resented it."

Lacey was uncertain of the reason for the sudden thickness in her throat as she replied, "All right, then."

Standing on tiptoe, Lacey pressed a lingering kiss against Scully's cheek. Somehow dissatisfied, she impulsively slid her arms around his neck and hugged him close. She whispered, "I do love you, Scully. I always will. You're the best friend I'll ever have...dearer than anyone I know...closer to me than if you were actually my family, but I don't want my feelings to become a burden to you. You have a life of your own that's separate and apart from me. I want to make sure you don't end up resenting me for keeping you from it."

Scully's strong arms closed around her, and the tightness in Lacey's throat thickened as she said, "Please understand... I'll always love you, Scully, no matter how many Charlottes there are in your life."

Thrust abruptly an arm's length from him, Lacey looked up into Scully's stern expression as he repeated, "Charlotte is an *acquaintance*. That's all."

"I'm just using Charlotte as an example." Lacey hastened to explain, "I know you prefer redheaded women and I—"

"Who told you that?"

Lacey went still.

"It's untrue, and I want to know who said it."

"Does it matter?"

"Yes."

"I've already set him straight about it. I told him your personal preferences are nobody's business but yours, and they certainly aren't *my* business."

"Tell me who it was."

"No."

"Was it Todd?"

"No!"

"Who—"

"Don't ask me again, Scully. It doesn't matter."

"Yes, it does."

"Scully, please! I made a mistake mentioning it. Don't make me regret it even more than I do now. It doesn't matter, really it doesn't. He won't repeat what he said to anyone else. If he was trying to warn me against you, I've made it clear I didn't feel I had any need to be warned. I also told him I'm not interested in anything else he has to say, whether it's about you or anyone else."

"Was it Reverend Sykes?"

"Scully, I told you... I won't answer you."

"All right." His chest heaving with the anger he suppressed, Scully continued, "You won't tell me, so I'll make this point clear right now. That kiss you witnessed between Charlotte and me meant nothing more than casual friendship. I've kissed a lot of women and held a lot of women in my arms."

Unexpectedly drawing her against him, Scully

brushed a kiss against her cheek and said, "Now I've kissed you, too. I'm also holding you in my arms, and you can believe me when I tell you that brief kiss I just gave you means more to me than any of those others."

When Lacey did not reply, Scully drew back and whispered, "I kissed you, Lacey, and you aren't even a redhead."

Lacey's spontaneous laugh was the signal he appeared to have been waiting for. Scully slid Lacey's arm through his and said, "Enough said. Come on. Sadie will be wondering where you are. Besides, I'm hungry, and I haven't been to bed yet. I'm going to take care of both those necessities in that order, as soon as possible."

Lacey walked beside Scully. Her cheek burned from the touch of his lips. His warmth filled her when he looked back down at her and added, "Now that all that nonsense is settled, I'll be back at noon to take you to lunch."

"Oh, no." Lacey shook her head regretfully. "I have to be at the church."

Scully's gaze narrowed. "Supper, then?"

"Yes."

They turned onto the main street's boardwalk and Lacey clutched Scully's arm unconsciously closer. The day was brighter and her heart had lightened.

How had she come to be so blessed?

"I'm going with you."

Rosie looked at Jewel as the taller saloon girl stood illuminated by a shaft of afternoon sunlight in the doorway of her room. Jewel's color was more vibrant than her own and her demeanor was more assured, but Rosie knew only too well that underneath her outward composure, Jewel was like her—still the abandoned child she had once been, still struggling to find her way. Their common backgrounds had made them instant friends after meeting at the Gold Nugget two years earlier, and the common problems they had shared since that time had brought them even closer.

Yet there were basic differences between them that made Rosie question Jewel's motivation as she replied, "You don't have to come to my lesson with me, Jewel. Riley won't be back for a few days. It always takes him that long to come to terms with the way he acted. Besides, he doesn't know anything about my lessons. He thinks I bought the tablet."

Jewel responded unexpectedly, "Did it ever occur to you that I might want to go with you because I'm as eager to learn as you are?"

"No." Rosie replied honestly, "I didn't think it mattered much to you."

"It doesn't, but it won't hurt, either."

"Then you're not coming with me because you think Riley will be waiting for me somewhere?"

"No."

"Truth, Jewel…"

"That's not my only reason."

"But you want to take your derringer with you."

Confidence returned to Jewel's expression. "I'm never without it."

"Lacey wouldn't want you to take a gun into the church."

"Don't tell her, then."

"Jewel…"

"I'm coming with you—like it or not."

"Jewel, please, leave the gun here."

"I told you, I don't go anywhere without it."

"You can go to the church without it."

Jewel did not respond.

"Jewel..."

Rosie saw the myriad of emotions that raced across Jewel's expression. She was not aware she was holding her breath until she released it when Jewel reached into her pocket, withdrew the derringer, then took a few steps into the room to shove it underneath a bed pillow and said, "Are you happy now?"

A smile her only response, Rosie picked up her torn tablet and broken pencil, and turned toward the door.

Scully awakened abruptly from his sleep. He glanced at the bright sunlight against the window shade of his bedroom, then at the clock on the wall. It was almost noon. He had slept for a few hours and had awakened automatically as if his inner clock, always so dependable in the past, was telling him he had an appointment with Lacey for their noon meal.

But he didn't.

Scully slid his arm underneath his head in a deceivingly casual pose that did not reflect the many conflicting thoughts that had plagued him since his conversation with Lacey that morning. He remembered the moment she had walked out of the boarding house door into his view. Her startling beauty had been luminous even in the limited light of morning, but the true significance of the moment had come when she heard his voice and turned toward him with true joy in her smile. That moment of reality had hit him hard. He hadn't realized how much he had been depending on her reaction to seeing him there that morning.

Scully shook his head. Lacey's attempt to distance herself from him had been more obvious to him than she'd realized, and whether he cared to admit it or not, the thought had tormented him. He'd been determined to discover why—for many reasons. He had told himself that Lacey was too beautiful, too honest and trusting for her own good. He had reminded himself of the many dangers she would face because of that potent combination of attributes—dangers she was unprepared to handle. He had purposely recalled to mind that Charlie had entrusted him with her future, and that he had a right to his intense interest in her welfare. Keeping all those thoughts in mind, he had deliberately ignored the deadening ache that had twisted tight inside him when he became certain she was avoiding him.

But that was all changed now.

Almost.

It was now clear that for some reason he could not fathom, someone was trying to turn Lacey against him. He would be able to understand it, if not condone it, if that person had been Todd. Yet Lacey's instinctive re-action had dismissed that possibility. Was it Reverend Sykes or Doc Mayberry? He'd had difficult conflicts of opinions with both those men in the past, and they didn't especially approve of him. He wondered if, pos-sibly, Janine Parker was spreading harmful gossip at the mercantile these days, or if Rita Johnson or Noelle Leach had made that untrue comment to Lacey about his preference for redheads—a remark he wouldn't have given a moment's thought to, if not for Lacey's reaction to it.

He had scrutinized Sadie's customers as he had eaten breakfast in the restaurant that morning. He had searched his memory for those who had become regulars since Lacey had begun working there. He'd thought of Hiram Watts, Jerry Livingston and Mitch Carter, all bachelors who hadn't disguised their interest in Lacey. He'd remembered Barret Gould, who had paid her special attention. He had searched his memory for the faces of Weaver residents who had expressed disapproval of him at any point in the past, and had considered the possibility of their interference. Lastly, he had then recalled the reaction of the Gold Nugget girls to Lacey. He'd known that "preference for redheads" comment had been a direct reference to Charlotte, but he'd dismissed Charlotte's possible involvement. That wasn't Charlotte's way.

No…male or female, this person was sly. Scully couldn't figure out his or her agenda, and that worried him.

His discomfort dismissing any further thought of sleep, Scully threw back the coverlet and walked to the washstand. He splashed cold water against his face in an attempt to clear his mind, rubbed his hand against the shadow of a beard on his chin, then stared at his reflection as he dried his face. He wondered what Lacey saw when she looked at him.

She'd said he was handsome. He considered himself in the mirror more closely.

His hair was thick and dark, but he'd recently seen a gray hair or two at his temple.

His features were passably regular, but he'd been told

his frown was too harsh and his smile too infrequent. He supposed there was truth in that.

In examining his broad-shouldered, tightly knit frame, he saw only hard muscle and sinew.

Lacey had said she had come back to Weaver expecting him to be an old man, that she had been surprised to find him so young. He supposed that comment had come back to roost uncomfortably with her when the person who had made the "redhead" comment made her consider everything that remark entailed.

Then Lacey had said she loved him.

Loved him.

She'd said it so easily, with an affection so obviously heartfelt that he'd been left momentarily speechless. He remembered the totally innocent touch of her lips against his cheek, the warmth of her arms around his neck, the sweet contact of her body pressed to his. It had seemed so right when he had closed his arms around her and held her close. And when he had kissed her cheek, he remembered the fleeting thought again returning, that her lips had been only a hairsbreadth away.

He had said he loved her, too.

The words had come easily, he supposed because, in a way, he had loved her from the first moment he had seen her as a sick, injured child.

But Lacey wasn't a child anymore.

That last thought the only clear reflection in his mind at that moment, Scully turned away from the washstand and reached for his clothes. He was too restless to sleep any longer, and he was hungry.

Scully glanced at the clock again. Lacey would be at the church by now. He was glad she was making a life for herself in Weaver.

Yes, he was.

Scully forced himself to retain that thought as he dressed and turned toward the door. But he had things to do.

"Oh, I see you've brought a friend."

Lacey glanced between Rosie and Jewel as the youthful saloon girl entered the silent church anteroom. She took another backward step to allow Jewel to enter as Rosie responded, "I hope you don't mind that Jewel came with me. We figured it would be just as easy to teach two of us as it was one." Rosie added, "You don't have to worry, you know. Jewel's smart. She learns fast, and I'll share my tablet with her."

"Of course, I don't mind." She looked down at the broken pencil and damaged tablet Rosie clutched and asked with concern, "What happened? Did you have an accident?"

Lacey saw the tense breath Rosie took before she responded, "I fell. I told you, I'm clumsy—but I saved all the pages that got torn out of the tablet and I'll still be able to use them."

Lacey scrutinized Rosie's flushed expression, then said, "I know there's more to it than that."

"It's nothing you have to worry about," Jewel responded in Rosie's stead, her expression void of emotion. "We can handle it."

We.

Meaning the two of them.

Saddened to be excluded, Lacey was silent for a few moments before she said, "I need to know, Rosie, does it have anything to do with your association with me?"

"Oh, no! He doesn't know about you. I mean…he…"

Rosie halted abruptly, her face flaming. With a concerned glance at her friend, Jewel repeated, "We can handle it."

Her expression unexpectedly softening, Jewel then said, "I'd like to stay if you don't mind, Lacey."

"Of course you may stay. I'm truly happy to welcome you." Lacey offered, "You can use my pencil while we practice."

"No."

"Please. I have others."

Jewel reluctantly nodded.

With those words meant to lessen Jewel's discomfort fresh on her lips, Lacey picked up her slate and chalk. She'd replace the pencil at the mercantile after the lesson was over. She hoped the Lord would forgive her stretch of the truth meant to alleviate Jewel's hesitation, then dismissed the thought from her mind.

Lacey glanced at the broken pencil Rosie clutched. She looked at the fading bruise on her cheek.

Despite Jewel's protestations, she could ignore the obvious no longer.

"Is that all you have to tell me?" Barret's narrow nostrils twitched as Larry stood a few feet across from his desk, his report completed. The odor of unwashed body permeated the distance between them as Barret said, "So you're telling me Lacey is now meeting with *two* saloon girls at the church—but you don't know why."

"How are Blackie and me supposed to know why? We ain't mind readers."

"But you do have eyes, don't you?"

"Yeah...so?"

"And ears."

"What are you getting at?"

"You couldn't get close enough to *see* what they were doing through a window, or possibly to *hear* what they were discussing?"

"You didn't say nothin' about that. You just told Blackie and me to follow Lacey and report back to you."

Barret's smile was cold. "But you aren't reporting anything."

"I told you that Jewel woman's with them other two now, didn't I?"

Barret took a secure hold on his patience. "Yes, but I don't know much more than I did before about the reason they're there. So now I'm telling you to find out what they're *doing* in that church."

Larry shrugged. "It can't be nothin' too bad. It is a church, after all."

His forbearance snapping, Barret ordered, "Find out!"

Larry responded defensively, "Me and Blackie always do the best we can."

"So far it hasn't been good enough. Get back there, and don't let Lacey out of your sight."

"Right."

"And take a bath!"

Larry scowled. He was about to respond when Barret ordered, "Go. We're done talking."

His eyes trained on the door through which Larry had disappeared, Barret paused to consider his situation coldly. He could not be truly certain how much ground he had gained in turning Lacey against Scully, and the reason for Lacey's association with the Gold Nugget women was a total mystery. If things did not change, Blackie and Larry's ineptitude would force him into a premature move that would not be totally wise. Yet impatience was tearing at his innards.

Barret took a deep breath and made the only wise decision available to him. He needed more time to assess the situation. He needed to be certain what he was walking into before he took any drastic steps.

That decision made, Barret growled a soft warning into the silence of the room.

"But don't waste too much time in making your move, Lacey, or... I'll make it for you."

"I don't want to bring trouble to the church, Reverend."

Her smooth brow knit with concern, Lacey looked at Reverend Sykes with uncertainty. She had waited patiently until Jewel and Rosie had left the church at the end of their lesson and had walked out of sight before seeking out the reverend where he was working in the small church garden.

Responding to her statement in his typically soothing manner, Reverend Sykes said, "You're not bringing trouble to the church. You're doing the Lord's work. That's what the church is here for."

Lacey hesitated, then said, "Rosie's beau beats her, Reverend. She doesn't want to admit it, but most everybody who knows her realizes it by now. Jewel came with Rosie to her lessons today. She said she needs to learn how to read and write, too, but I think there's more to it than that. She's so protective of Rosie. I have the feeling she thinks Rosie's beau will be a problem if he finds out the reason she's coming here every day."

"You're doing the Lord's work, Lacey."

"But—"

"You're taking Rosie a step in the right direction, and Jewel is following, whatever her reason. You're succeeding."

"But—"

"Don't be concerned about anything else. Things will work out. And don't worry about the church. It will continue to stand. Just remember, in the short time you've been back in Weaver, you've given more thought to the future of those two women than anyone in this town ever has."

"That can't be true."

Reverend Sykes did not reply.

"What about Rosie, Reverend? Her beau—"

"The situation is longstanding, isn't it?" At Lacey's nod, the reverend continued, "You know Rosie will most likely retreat from you, that you'll probably lose her and Jewel, too, if you attempt to speak to Rosie about her beau at this early stage. It's probably taken all the courage she could muster to make this first attempt at improving herself. A step at a time, Lacey."

"But—"

"You'll be in a better position to have her listen to what you're saying if you wait."

"But—"

"You can't expect fast progress when attempting to reverse the conduct of years." He added with a smile, *"'Let us not be weary in doing good—for at the proper time, we will reap the harvest.'"*

Lacey sighed.

Patience.

Yet somehow she had to do more.

* * *

"We'd better hurry. We're going to be late for work."

Jewel turned toward Rosie as they rounded the corner and approached their boarding house. Rosie had been scanning the street nervously since they had emerged from the church. It was obvious that she was worried Riley might be lurking somewhere nearby, but they had also stayed at their lesson longer than they should because things had been going so well. With a day's head start on her, Rosie had actually begun printing her name so that the letters were recognizable. She'd never seen her friend so excited.

Jewel gave a mental shrug. She had no doubt she'd soon be writing her own name, too, but Rosie had been correct in her assumption that the lessons didn't mean as much to her. Rosie's sense of self-esteem was somehow tied to her progress. She was happy to see Rosie's enthusiasm, but she didn't fool herself that paper and pencil could change their lives.

Rosie was breathless from hurrying, and Jewel urged, "Slow down, Rosie. The Gold Nugget won't shut down if we get there a few minutes late."

Rosie nodded, her chestnut curls bobbing.

Chestnut curls.

A familiar knot of pain clenched tight in Jewel's gut. Cynthia's hair had been that same color. Her baby sister had also been small and slender like Rosie, and had had brown eyes so similar to Rosie's that she had caught her breath the first time she met Rosie a few years earlier.

Rosie and Cynthia were similar in so many other ways, too. Both were honest and totally forthright, with a way of looking directly into a person's eyes that elicited from Jewel a strong need to protect the trusting nature that in Rosie's case had been so badly abused.

Jewel fought back a familiar distress. Cynthia, her baby sister—dead at the age of twelve. Cynthia and both their parents had been victims of the fever that had swept through their small cabin. Jewel still could not comprehend why she had been spared. Alone and devastated afterward, she had fervently wished she had been taken, too. Yet it was later that she realized fully how merciful that would've been.

She had been orphaned at fourteen.

A trace of innocence had still remained at fifteen.

By the age of sixteen, however, she'd fully absorbed some of life's most painful lessons.

Those lessons had changed her.

It had stunned Jewel—and made her sad—to realize, when she met Rosie a few years earlier, that despite all that had happened to her, Rosie was still trusting at heart. Anybody with half an eye could've recognized Riley for what he was when he cozied up to Rosie with flattery and promises that first day, but he had said all the things Rosie wanted to hear, and Rosie had told herself she was "in love."

Jewel looked at Rosie's bruised face. That's what "love" had gotten her.

Jewel was determined that she'd never let herself be that kind of a fool.

Jewel's step slowed when the boarding house came into view and she saw the slim, dark-haired man leaning against the wall beside the door. She did not smile when his face brightened at the sight of her and he started toward them.

"Buddy's been waiting for you, Jewel."

Jewel nodded. "That's what it looks like."

Buddy reached her side and tipped his hat to Rosie as she hurried past with a nod. Then, turning his attention fully toward Jewel, he said, "I'm glad you got back. The boss sent me into town for some supplies, so I figured I'd use the time to see you while old man Parker was filling the order at the mercantile. I was starting to worry you wouldn't get back before I had to leave. Where've you been, darlin'?"

"That's my business, Buddy."

Buddy's smile faltered. "Yeah, I know. I didn't mean nothing by it." He hesitated, then said, "But it could be my business, too, if you'd let it be."

"That would be a mistake."

"Not for me, it wouldn't." Suddenly solemn, Buddy looked directly into her eyes and said, "I don't mean to blow my own horn, Jewel, honey, but I need to tell you again—I'm honest, loyal and a hard worker, and I'd never look at another woman if you'd say the word. I could make a good life for us."

"Like I said before, that would be a mistake."

"Why?"

Jewel forced a hard smile. "You know that old saying, 'Too much water has passed under that bridge.' Like I told you, right now I'm just floating with the current, and that's the way I like it."

Momentarily silent, Buddy responded, "That isn't the way it seemed when we was together a few nights ago."

Jewel's smile twitched. "That was then. This is now."

"Is that right?"

"Why would I say it if I didn't mean it?"

"I don't rightly know, but I don't intend to quit until I find out."

"You're a fool, Buddy Cross."

"A fool who loves you."

Love.

Jewel responded coldly, "I'll be late for work if I waste any more time here."

"You wouldn't want that."

Jewel did not reply.

"I'll see you tonight. Save the last dance for me. I'll take you home."

Jewel turned toward the boarding house door without responding. She looked up at Buddy when he stayed her with a touch on her shoulder.

Despite herself, her throat tightened when Buddy whispered, "I love you, darlin'. I'll put that ring on your finger yet."

Jewel shrugged off his touch and walked away without looking back.

The evening was balmy, and Lacey's hand on his arm felt right as Scully and she walked toward the livery stable after their evening meal.

Scully looked down at Lacey as she maintained her silence. She had been preoccupied throughout their meal. Something was bothering her. She had mentioned she hadn't stopped off to see Careful that morning and he had suggested they visit the feisty little critter after they finished eating. She had easily agreed, but her still diverted gaze spoke volumes.

Yet Scully was unprepared when Lacey looked up at him unexpectedly and asked, "How long has Rosie Burns been working for you?"

Scully was suddenly wary. He had spent a long, tedious day indulging town gossips and making inquiries that had led him nowhere. There had been nothing but sincere greeting in Janine Parker's expression when he had entered the mercantile. Their conversation had been open and friendly, and it had taken him no more than a few minutes to decide she wasn't responsible for the talk that had reached Lacey's ears. He'd met Jerry Livingston on the street a little later and had just as quickly dismissed him and his friends from his list of possible rumormongers. He had then visited Doc Mayberry and waited a half hour for him to finish with another patient before seeing him. The doc had appeared honestly concerned about his feigned complaint. The doc had prescribed an Epsom salt bath, which Scully had no intention of taking, and he had left the doc's office certain he'd have to look further for the culprit. He had already cancelled out Reverend Sykes, knowing Lacey wouldn't have gone back to the church if the reverend had been the one who had tried to poison her mind against him. He intended to talk to his Gold Nugget girls later that evening, but he didn't really expect any one of them to be guilty of carrying tales.

That left Barret Gould. He had never liked or trusted that man. Neither did he like the two men Barret employed to do odd chores for him. He did not believe that dishonest men could be honestly employed by a man with as questionable a character as Barret Gould's. He supposed it was for those reasons that he had preferred to eliminate all the possible gossipmongers from his mind before considering him. Unfortunately, his opinion of Barret's character and choice of employees was not shared by the majority of Weaver's more respectable citizens.

He had been considering Barret's possible complicity more closely before picking up Lacey for supper, but all thought was presently struck from his mind by Lacey's question.

Scully thought back. "How long has Rosie been working for me? About two years, I guess."

Scully saw the effort Lacey expended to hold back her response before she blurted, "You know her that well, yet you didn't notice the bruises she's worked so hard to cover up since she met Riley Martin?"

Scully frowned. "I saw them, all right."

"And you didn't try to help her?"

"How would I do that?"

Lacey's astounding eyes widened with incredulity and her flawless skin flushed. Scully noted absentmindedly that she was somehow even more beautiful in the throes of her sudden anger as she replied hotly, "How? Are you asking me how you could've helped her?"

"That's right. I'm asking how I could've helped Rosie when each time she showed up with a split lip or a black eye, she told me and everybody else who asked that she had fallen, or walked into a door, or she had just made the mistake of applying too much makeup that night."

"But you knew Riley was responsible."

"Did I? Rosie denied it, and when Riley came to the Gold Nugget a few nights after she showed up with new bruises, they looked even cozier than before."

"She's afraid of him!"

"You wouldn't think so if you saw them together."

Lacey blushed.

Aware that he had embarrassed her, Scully said more kindly than before, "If I've learned nothing else while running the Gold Nugget, Lacey, I've learned to let the girls who work there handle their own problems unless it interferes with their work."

"But Rosie is being physically abused."

"She chose Riley. I didn't."

"She made a mistake."

"Maybe she did, but it's her life, and I'm not responsible for it."

Lacey's step slowed. Her face paled as she looked up at him solemnly and said, "I suppose you would've felt the same way about me, then, if you hadn't owed my grandfather a debt of gratitude."

They were beginning to draw the attention of passersby, and Scully urged Lacey forward into the livery stable. Breaking his silence when they finally emerged through the back door at the corral where Careful was confined, he responded quietly, "Don't compare yourself with Rosie, Lacey. You would never have turned out to be a Gold Nugget girl, whether your grandfather had sent you to me or not."

Scully noted the shaky breath Lacey took before she said, "I'm not so sure about that." And she added, "But you didn't answer my question."

"Your question…meaning would I have seen to your needs all these years if I hadn't owed Charlie a debt of gratitude?" Scully stared down into Lacey's expectant expression. He responded truthfully, "It took only one look when you wandered into my saloon all those years ago, and I knew I could never have turned my back on you, whether you were Charlie's granddaughter or not."

"Why, Scully?"

Why, indeed?

Scully responded, "I can't tell you why. I can only tell you the way it was."

"Scully…"

Uncomfortable, Scully said gruffly, "I don't want you getting involved with Rosie's problems, Lacey. I told you before, and although the reality of it doesn't seem to have sunk into your mind yet, this is the Wild West and all that goes along with it. That means there are men and women out here who handle their problems with a gun rather than go to any authority—whether it's personal or business problems they intend to solve."

"Because people don't help them."

"Because they don't *want* anybody to help them."

"That's not true."

"True or not, Lacey, how the girls at the Gold Nugget handle their lives is none of your business."

"Why?"

"That should be obvious."

"It isn't, to me."

Scully said flatly, "I don't want you getting involved with Rosie or any of the other girls at the Nugget."

"Too late."

"What's that supposed to mean?"

Lacey turned away without responding.

"Lacey…"

"I don't want to discuss it anymore."

"I told you—"

"I said… I don't want to talk about it anymore."

A welcoming bray turned Lacey toward the corral fence as Careful slid his head through the bars and nudged Lacey's hand. Lacey frowned as she stroked Careful's muzzle.

Silence reigned heavily between them before Lacey turned back toward Scully with a shaky smile that tore at his heart and said, "I'm sorry. It's my fault. I made a mistake bringing the whole thing up. Please, let's not argue anymore, all right?"

"All right."

It was a long moment before Scully realized that whatever Lacey wanted, whatever she said, would ultimately be all right with him.

It was a wonder to him.

A wonder *why.*

Chapter Nine

The evening shadows filled Weaver's main street as Jewel stood in the doorway of the Gold Nugget Saloon. She turned her back on the heat and din within and walked out onto the boardwalk outside as the noise began overwhelming her. She nodded with a smile at the wranglers lounging there, her composure gradually returning.

She had dressed in a scarlet gown that was her favorite that evening because of the way it complemented her brunette coloring. She had used that dress to bolster her morale many times when it was faltering—and she needed it badly this night.

Jewel joked briefly with a smiling wrangler as he pushed his way through the swinging doors. She employed a facade she had perfected over a period of years, a facade that had hidden a multitude of emotions. She glanced at Rosie where her friend stood a few feet down the boardwalk. Rosie was smiling, her expression open as she laughed and conversed with the men on either side of her. That was Rosie's gift, the ability to keep her fears at bay for short periods of time, but Jewel did not possess that skill.

Jewel slipped her hand into the pocket of her dress that allowed her access to the derringer holstered in her garter. Small and potent, the gun was a reassurance that gave her confidence. She was especially in need of that confidence tonight because she had just learned Riley was back in the area.

Jewel laughed encouragingly at a comment made by the fellow at her elbow, then looked offhandedly down the street. Billy Watts had mentioned seeing Riley outside town a few hours earlier. Billy had remarked that Riley wouldn't like seeing Rosie enjoying herself with those two friendly customers when he came back to see her.

She had hidden her reaction with an expert smile and a wink, but her heart had begun a nervous thudding. She had sworn to herself the last time Rosie had come home beaten and bruised at Riley's hands that she would not let it happen again. She had not been able to save Cynthia, but Rosie—as dear and innocent at heart as her baby sister—was not beyond her help.

Jewel took a breath and responded appropriately to the man who walked up beside her. She breathed in the fresh air, grateful for a moment to think after speaking to Billy. She had the feeling she would especially need a clear head tonight.

Three days had passed since she and Rosie had returned from their lesson and found Buddy waiting at her boarding house door.

Three days...

So much had happened since then. Rosie's and her lessons had continued, and they were both advancing rapidly under Lacey's patient tutelage. She could already print her name as well as Rosie could, and both Rosie and she were working successfully on the alphabet. Lacey concluded each session by reading a chapter from the Bible at Rosie's request, and while peering over Lacey's shoulder, she had already become familiar with a few of the words.

Trust in the Lord with all your heart... He will direct your path.

Rosie had received more comfort from those words than she had, but the passage lingered in her mind. Perhaps it was easier for Rosie to trust in the Lord than it was for her, but she didn't understand how that was possible with all that Rosie had suffered. The only thing she knew for certain was that she would not allow Rosie to leave the Nugget with Riley that night if there was fear in her eyes.

As for Buddy...

Jewel smiled more broadly to conceal a surge of emotion. Buddy had come to the Nugget that evening three days previously as he had promised. She had been unable to deny her spontaneous joy at seeing him when he walked through the doorway, or the way she had warmed to his touch when he slipped his arm around her. She had saved the last dance for him. She hadn't been able to help herself.

Jewel swallowed against the lump that choked her throat. Buddy said he loved her, but he was a fool. Only a fool could love a woman who had so little love left in her. Only a fool would believe a woman like her could change her past simply by changing her future.

Only a fool believed in redemption.

As if bidden by her thoughts, Riley rode into view

at the end of the street, and Jewel tensed. She watched as he rode gradually closer.

Slight, with curly hair, warm brown eyes and a youthful appearance, Riley looked deceivingly harmless. No one would initially believe he was capable of the cruelty hidden behind that benign exterior. Neither would anyone see through him as quickly as she had.

Experience was an unforgiving teacher.

Jewel noted the moment when Riley spotted Rosie standing between the two friendly wranglers a few feet away. She saw his mouth twitch into a hard smile as he drew his horse up to the hitching rail.

Scully briefly scanned the activity in the saloon as he walked down the stairs from his room. The clamor of merrymaking was increasing as the hours progressed, but he somehow had little patience for it all. He hadn't finished dinner that evening and he was hungry. He needed to get to the restaurant before it closed for the night.

Scully acknowledged the greetings of Joe Mullens, a graying cowman, as he made his way across the crowded floor toward the swinging doors. He joked briefly with Harve Stone as he passed. He responded with a short comment to Willie Johnson as the wiry fellow looked up with a greeting, and he reacted with a laugh to Ness Green's quip before emerging out onto the street. His expression changed when he saw Riley Martin dismounting.

One glance, and Scully knew the reason for Riley's rigid posture. Rosie was standing farther down the walk with two wranglers who were obviously enjoying her conversation. She hadn't seen him yet, and she was laughing at a comment one of them made.

Scully saw the twist of Riley's lips as he started toward her.

Scully paused to scrutinize the men standing with Rosie. They were both wranglers from the Diamond R ranch. Both of them were decent men, and Rosie knew enough not to cause trouble when she was working. She'd handle it. She always did.

Turning his back on the scene unfolding, Scully continued on down the street.

Rosie gasped as Riley turned her roughly toward him. His hand still on her shoulder, he said, "You didn't see me, huh? You wasn't expecting me, neither, or you wouldn't be out here with these two fellas."

"What's your problem, boy?" The bearded fellow on Rosie's right eyed Riley more closely, then said, "The lady and me are just having some fine conversation."

"She doesn't need your conversation, do you, Rosie?" Riley's hand tightened on her shoulder as he repeated, "Do you, Rosie?"

Fear choked Rosie's throat. She needed no one to tell her that Riley was looking for trouble. She had been warned about him causing a ruckus at the Nugget. He knew it, too. He also knew how much she needed her job, and he was counting on it.

Despising him more at that moment than ever before, Rosie smiled at the cowpoke beside her and said, "It's all right, Johnny. Riley and me are…good friends. He gets mad sometimes when I enjoy myself too much with other fellas."

"That's too bad for him, ain't it?"

Riley looked at Rosie, his gaze menacing. "Tell him, Rosie. Tell him you don't want him hanging around you anymore."

"Johnny's a nice fella. We were only talking."

"Yeah, only talking. I know you better than that."

Johnny's expression hardened as he warned, "I'd watch what I said, if I was you, fella."

Rosie saw Jewel advancing toward them out of the corner of her eye. Jewel had a strange look on her face. It frightened her, and she said in an attempt to placate Riley, "Johnny won't mind if I spend the rest of my time with you while I'm here tonight, will you, Johnny?" She looked at the frowning cowpoke almost pleadingly and said, "There's not a girl in the Nugget who won't be happy to take my place beside you once you walk back through those doors."

Rosie gasped as Riley's grip twisted painfully tight and he said, "You don't need *his* permission. You don't need anybody's permission but mine—'cause you know what'll happen to you if you don't listen to what I say."

Jewel was coming closer. Rosie felt a trembling begin somewhere in the pit of her stomach when she saw Jewel slide her hand into the pocket of her dress. So intent was she on Jewel's advance that she gasped aloud when Scully appeared unexpectedly behind them and jerked Riley around to face him.

Rosie felt the color drain from her face at Scully's tight expression. His tone was all the more compelling for its softness when he said in a voice barely audible over the din of the saloon behind them, "It's time for you to leave, Riley."

Bold in his arrogance, Riley replied, "I ain't leaving unless Rosie leaves with me."

Scully looked at Rosie, his expression cold. Rosie took a backward step at the intensity of Scully's gaze when he asked, "Do you want to go with him?"

Somehow frozen, Rosie was unable to respond. She heard Jewel answer in her stead, "Rosie doesn't want to leave with him. She doesn't want any part of him!"

Ignoring Jewel's interjection, Scully asked again, "Do you want to go with him or not, Rosie?"

Rosie shook her head.

Scully pressed, "Answer yes or no. Riley needs to hear you say it."

"No... I don't want to go with him."

"You heard her, Riley." Directing the full weight of his threatening stare at Riley, Scully said, "Either you leave now under your own power, or I'll personally escort you out of town."

"No, you won't."

"Try me."

Rosie recognized the rage burning in Riley's gaze. She saw his hand twitch the second before it moved toward the gun at his hip, then heard Riley's startled grunt of pain when Scully jammed his fist into Riley's ribs, halting him. She was breathless as Scully drew Riley's gun from his holster with a quick twist of his other hand and tossed it to the wrangler beside them, saying "Give this to Bill at the bar. He'll know what to do with it." Turning back to Riley, who was still gasping for air, Scully then said, "Let's go."

Incredibly, the activity on the boardwalk continued unaffected around them as Scully pulled Riley into the shadows of the alleyway between the buildings.

Rosie turned back to the wranglers beside her with a start when Johnny said, "I guess we don't have to worry about that fella no more with Scully taking care of things. What do you say we go back inside?"

Rosie nodded. Shaken, she started toward the swinging doors with as steady a step as she could manage.

Jewel hesitated and glanced toward the alleyway where Riley and Scully had disappeared. She looked again at Rosie, who was doing her best to appear as unaffected by the episode as the two wranglers beside her.

Never more conscious of the small gun holstered on her thigh, Jewel did not choose to consider how close she had come to using it this time. She would not have hesitated, and if not for Scully's intervention—

Jewel preferred not to take that thought any further. Scully had taken over, and he would set Riley straight for the time being. His warning wouldn't last long, but Rosie would be free of the threat Riley presented for a few more days.

And so would she.

Jewel turned toward the cowboy who had stepped up beside her. She smiled as he accompanied her back into the Nugget. Standing companionably beside Rosie a few minutes later, she squeezed Rosie's arm in a comradely gesture before joining in the easy banter around her.

Scully stood in the shadows of the alleyway with Riley still breathing raggedly beside him. Speaking in a cold tone that did not reflect the heat of his stare, he said, "Before you leave, I want to make sure you understand you're not welcome at the Nugget anymore, Riley. Don't…come…back."

Riley's response was a muttered expletive that caused Scully to respond more forcefully, "There's nothing more to say about it, so just get on your horse and git!"

"I want my gun!"

"You can pick it up at the sheriff's office tomorrow morning, after you tell him what you tried to do with it here."

"I didn't do nothin'!"

"Tell it to the sheriff."

Still mumbling as Scully escorted him forcefully to his horse, Riley mounted up. His boyish face was dark with fury when he turned back to say, "You think you won, but you made a mistake tonight, Scully. This ain't the end of it."

Scully stood fast as Riley kicked his horse into a gallop and thundered down the street. He waited until Riley disappeared from sight before turning determinedly back in the direction of the restaurant. In truth, he had lost his appetite just about the time the image of Rosie's terrified expression had forced him to retrace his steps and face Riley down.

Scully was nearing the restaurant when he finally acknowledged despite himself that his conversation with Lacey had probably influenced the action he had taken a few minutes previously, that she would probably approve of the way he had defended Rosie. Admittedly, he felt better knowing Rosie wouldn't have to fear Riley that evening; yet it troubled him to realize—where Lacey would not—that the effort had most likely been a waste of time.

Rosie and Riley would probably be back together before the week was out. That was the way of things—the way it had always been, and the way it would remain.

Scully paused at the restaurant doorway to look back at the brightly lit Nugget. He had no doubt that Rosie and Jewel were laughing and talking inside, continu-

ing on as if the scene on the boardwalk with Riley had
never happened.

Yes, that was the way of things, too.

Music and laughter from the Nugget reverberated
on the street around Scully as he then glanced up at
the starlit night sky overhead, knowing Lacey's room
was silent and peaceful, that she was probably sleeping
soundly, her beautiful face composed serenely in sleep.

The sleep of the innocent.

Scully pushed open the restaurant door and walked
inside.

"Help me! Help me!"

*The cabin was burning behind her. She had escaped
from the flames, but she still struggled to breathe.*

There was blood on Grandpa's chest. He was dying!

"Take the Bible, Lacey. Let it show you the way."

The shadows surrounding her began moving.

They started toward her, and she ran.

She heard pounding, footsteps following her.

She heard ragged breathing coming closer.

They were right behind her!

"Help me! Help me!"

"Wake up, Lacey!"

Lacey awakened with a start. She gasped at the
shadow leaning over her bed, her heart pounding.

"Are you all right, dear?"

Lacey attempted a calming breath. She recognized
the soft voice even before her gaze penetrated the flickering light. It was Mary.

"I heard you calling for help. I thought you were sick,
but you were having a nightmare."

"I know." Lacey breathed more deeply. "I'm sorry if I woke you up."

"No, that's all right. I'm here whenever you need me." Mary's tone was motherly as she probed gently, "You seem so restless at night. Are you bothered often by those frightening dreams?"

"Just sometimes, but I'll be fine, now. Please, go back to bed. I'm sorry I disturbed you."

"It isn't because you don't feel safe in this house... I mean, you do know no one can hurt you here, don't you? Scully was concerned how you'd do here, but I reassured him that you'd be fine, that I'd look out for you."

"I *am* fine. These are just dreams left over from my childhood. Scully understands that, but please don't mention it to him. I don't want him to worry."

Mary's face moved into lines of concern. "I think I know Scully better than most of the people in town because I've known him since he came here with only a few dollars in his pocket and a sack full of determination. He was living in this boarding house when my husband died. He helped me in so many ways, although he wouldn't especially like it if he knew I'd told anyone about it. He's a fine man, even if there are some in town who wouldn't agree."

"I agree."

"I know you do, dear." Mary smiled, then said, "Would you like me to get you anything before I go back to bed...some tea, perhaps?"

"I'm fine, really."

"Well, if there's nothing else I can do for you now, just call me if you should need me."

"Thank you."

Lacey closed her eyes when Mary pulled the door

shut, taking the flickering light with her. She let out a shaken breath. The nightmares were worsening, becoming more frequent and more terrifying. They were changing in ways that she couldn't quite define.

She didn't understand the reason they continued to plague her.

She didn't know how to handle the panic they stirred.

Lacey brushed away the tear that squeezed out from underneath her closed eyelids.

And she didn't know how to make them stop.

"You're looking mighty pretty this morning, Lacey."

Lacey forced a smile for Todd's benefit. He had been sitting at a corner table waiting for her to make her way across the crowded restaurant floor toward him. She had not been particularly efficient at her job after the sleepless night past, and he had been extremely patient, as had Sadie's other customers. But she was not patient with herself.

Lacey withheld the sudden rush of tears. She was a fraud. She had taken on adult responsibilities, but it was all a pretense. She couldn't even defend herself against her own childish dreams.

"Lacey…?"

Lacey snapped back to the present. "I'm sorry, Todd. What can I get for you this morning?"

"The usual."

"Bacon, eggs, some of Sadie's fine biscuits and coffee."

"Right." Todd reached for the hand Lacey rested on his table. He held it lightly for a moment, his expression earnest. "I've been missing you these past few days, Lacey. I was wondering when we would get to spend some time together again—maybe a picnic. The stage won't be running this Saturday and my boss won't need me."

"Saturday..." Lacey raised her palm to her forehead. She was perspiring. It was so warm. She shook her head. "I can't really say. I have some things to do."

"Maybe if I talk to you later on in the week."

"Yes, maybe then."

Lacey made a fast retreat to the counter where Sadie seemed to be laying out filled plates with astonishing speed. She placed Todd's order there, then glanced at the door and heaved a sigh of relief when Scully walked in and sat at his customary table. The sight of him some-how calmed her.

"Lacey..."

Lacey turned at Sadie's summons.

"Jack's steak, and Shorty's ham and eggs are ready."

Lacey delivered them to the waiting customers. End-less moments passed before she reached Scully's table, but he wasn't smiling. His expression spoke for itself.

Anticipating his comment, she said, "Good morning, but don't say what you're thinking. You don't have to."

"You don't look rested."

He had said it.

Ignoring him, she asked, "What do you want for breakfast?"

"Didn't you sleep well last night?"

"Hotcakes and eggs? Do you want ham, too?"

Scully glanced at Todd's table and frowned.

"Don't look at Todd like that. He certainly isn't the one who's exhausting me." Realizing she had made an admission she hadn't wanted to make, Lacey said, "All right, so I'm tired. Maybe I just work too hard."

"Maybe."

Scully was still searching her face with his sober, gray-eyed stare. Its touch was almost palpable as it brushed her forehead, her eyes, her cheek. She felt a sudden rush of heat as it halted briefly on her lips.

"I'll get you your breakfast."

Lacey beat a hasty retreat from Scully's table. He was going to ask questions again, questions she didn't want to answer.

But questions or not, Lacey's heart was pounds lighter when she reached the counter. Scully was there. That meant everything would be all right.

She had deliberately ignored his questions. She was telling him in so many words he didn't have the right to ask them.

She was slipping away from him.

Scully sat at the table as Lacey hurried back to the counter at Sadie's summons. He glanced at Todd. There was no mutual exchange of friendly greetings when their glances met. Todd resented his association with Lacey. He admitted to himself for the first time that the feeling was mutual.

Scully considered that spontaneous thought. Actually, he had always considered Todd Fulton a nice fellow, but it bothered him that Todd might be the reason Lacey had begun shutting him out. He also knew it was unrealistic of him to think Lacey would always remain as close to him as she had been that first week after she arrived in Weaver. While living upstairs in the room near his at the Nugget, his had been the first face she had seen upon awakening, and the last face she had seen at night. It hadn't mattered to him that the reverse hadn't been true for him. As many familiar faces, both male and female, that he had seen before his long night was over, Lacey's was always the last face he saw before closing his eyes at night.

It was a beautiful face, all the more endearing for the unspoken bond that had existed between them from virtually the first moment she had returned home.

Yet although he still saw Lacey every morning and they were again eating their evening meals together, he still sensed a subtle distance between them. Lacey was holding something back. He didn't know what it was, but he knew it weighed heavily on her mind. He felt it. It was part of the bond they shared...innate...a part of him, just like Lacey, herself.

Those thoughts remained on Scully's mind as he finished his breakfast. Without any further reason to remain, he placed his coins on the table and left with a tip of his hat to Lacey and Sadie alike.

He had been late arriving at the restaurant. He had stopped at Sheriff Connolly's office to drop off Riley Martin's gun and tell him what to expect. Riley was no stranger to the sheriff. Scully's mouth twitched wryly with the admission that he wasn't, either.

"Scully, wait a moment!"

The familiar voice turned Scully toward Mary Mc-Innes as she hurried toward him. She glanced at the restaurant, then drew him out of its view and away from the early morning sidewalk traffic as she said softly, "I wouldn't want Lacey to see me talking to you."

Scully went still at Mary's anxious expression. His heart began a sudden pounding.

"What happened?"

"Nothing happened. I didn't mean to frighten you,

Scully." Mary hesitated, then continued in a rush, "I've been debating whether I should talk to you about this for days, but last night—"

"What happened last night?"

Mary's lined face grew earnest. "I suppose you know about Lacey's nightmares."

Scully did not reply.

"They're probably nothing new to you, since Lacey's obviously been having them for a long time. The only thing is…"

Scully waited with growing impatience as Mary floundered. He prompted, "Lacey's always had the nightmares, since early childhood."

"They're getting worse. She cried out so loudly in her sleep last night that I went in to make sure she was all right. I don't think anyone heard her but me, since her room is on the first floor close to mine, but she was terrified, Scully."

"What did she say?"

"She said the nightmares weren't a problem. She was fine."

Of course.

"But she isn't fine. She's reliving that night when her grandfather was killed, and the dreams are becoming more intense. I could tell by her reaction to them. Something's bothering her, something she doesn't quite understand herself. She won't talk to me, Scully, but she trusts you implicitly. I think she'll talk to you if you try."

"I've tried, Mary."

"Then maybe there's something else you can do. She's a lovely girl, but she needs help." Mary hesitated again. "I didn't want to burden you with this. I know Lacey is close to the scriptures and she depends on them to console and guide her. I know for a fact that she's spent time talking to Reverend Sykes, but I don't think she feels as close to him as she does to you."

Scully said abruptly, "I'll take care of it, Mary."

"I hope you're not angry."

"No."

"If you choose to tell Lacey that I spoke to you, please tell her it was because I was concerned for her welfare."

"Lacey knows that. I know it, too. Thanks, Mary."

Scully watched as Mary returned to the boarding house. When he turned back toward the Nugget, his decision was made.

Blackie grasped Barret's arm, halting Barret on the street as he returned from his afternoon meal at home, and Barret struggled with soaring anger. His housekeeper had been particularly friendly upon his noontime arrival—her first offense. He had fought to conceal his contempt for her pride in the unimpressive dessert she claimed to have prepared especially for him.

The woman was as common as everyone else in Weaver, as were her culinary efforts. They would not have been considered fare fit for pack beasts at the gourmet restaurants he had frequented in San Francisco—restaurants he was *determined* he would patronize frequently again.

He had emerged back out into the afternoon sunshine and started toward his office with that resolution fresh in his mind. Blackie's unexpected appearance had not improved his disposition, and the touch of the fellow's less-than-clean hand on his arm had soured his disposition further.

Barret snapped, "Take your hand off me, Blackie. This isn't the place for us to discuss business."

Blackie's hand fell back to his side. Barret did not miss the dark look the man shot him when he said, "I went to your office, but you wasn't there. You wanted Larry and me to tell you more about what Lacey Stewart was doing at that church—"

"Be quiet, you fool!" Barret glanced around them, then continued, "Wait until we get back into the office."

Barret's lips twitched with anger at the sound of Blackie's footsteps following him on the boardwalk. He turned toward Blackie the moment the office door closed behind them and warned, "Don't ever do that again."

"Do what?"

"Accost me on the street."

"Accost…what are you talking about? I was just doing what you pay Larry and me for."

"I don't pay you to announce to the world that you're watching Lacey Stewart for me."

"Nobody heard me because nobody was listening."

Barret ground his teeth with frustration, then repeated, "Don't ever do that again, do you understand?"

"Yeah, I understand."

"So?"

"So, what?"

"What did you come to tell me?"

Blackie's bearded face darkened. "You wanted to know what Lacey was doing with those two saloon women at the church."

"So?"

"She's teaching them to read."

Barret did not immediately respond.

"And write."

Barret shook his head. "There has to be more to it than that."

"She reads the Bible to them, too."

"How do you know that?"

"Because Larry sneaked up to the window and peeked inside while I watched to make sure nobody saw him. He listened long enough to get a good idea what they was doing."

"Larry is stupid. He isn't capable of understanding the subtleties of situations. He's missing something."

"No, he ain't. He said those saloon women was working hard trying to write, even if he figured they was wasting their time."

"Wasting their time?"

"Like they need to know how to read or write with the kind of work they do. Besides, Larry and me don't know how to read or write, and we're doing fine."

Barret stared. Blackie truly was an imbecile.

Barret questioned, "When Larry was listening, did he hear Lacey ask the women any questions, or tell them she wanted them to find out anything for her?"

"No."

"How can you be so sure? Did you ask him?"

"Larry said they was learning to read and write. That was all."

Struggling to retain his patience, Barret asked, "Why didn't Larry come here himself and tell me what he heard?"

"He's watching Lacey, like you said—not letting her get out of our sight."

"You could've remained behind to watch Lacey so he could come."

"Yeah," Blackie sneered, "but Larry didn't take a bath yet, so he sent me."

Really. As if Blackie smelled any better.

Choosing to keep that thought to himself, Barret instructed, "She's up to something. She'll be ready to make her move, soon. Keep your eyes on her."

"Yeah...anything you say."

His temper exploding at Blackie's mocking tone, Barret retorted, "You and Larry are involved as deeply in this whole situation as I am, so watching Lacey Stewart should be as important to you as it is to me!"

"Sure."

Imbecile was too generous a description.

Barret strove to control his anger as he repeated, "Don't let her out of your sight."

"How many times are you going to say the same thing?"

"As many times as I have to in order to make you understand."

"Larry and me understand. We ain't dummies."

Sure.

Barret watched as Blackie walked out onto the street, slamming the office door behind him.

One thought remained in Barret's mind. He would soon have no recourse in what he must do.

Lacey glanced up at the position of the sun as it dropped past the midpoint in the clear sky. As she made her way back from the church at the conclusion of Rosie and Jewel's lesson, it occurred to her that she'd seen nothing but clear skies since she had returned to Weaver. She had somehow forgotten that detail during the long years spent at school in New York. A rainy spring and fall was more the norm in that city, with undependable weather in between. Somehow she'd forgotten how bright the Arizona sun was, how vast the sky could be, and how blue.

Careful's welcoming bray brought a smile to Lacey's lips as she turned into sight of the livery corral. The dear burro had been expecting her. It hadn't taken him long to become accustomed to her routine and to expect her visit on her way back to the boarding house each afternoon. However, Careful's uncanny comprehension of human activity had turned out to be a drawback for her in this particular case. She had known he would be waiting and had not wanted to disappoint him, even though she was exhausted after her sleepless night and wanted nothing more than to go back to her room to rest before she met Scully for supper.

Scully...so intent on her welfare, so perceptive, and so *annoyingly* outspoken in his observances. Lacey scratched Careful's muzzle and the patient animal practically smiled. The unusual attachment between them had resumed as if her ten-year absence did not exist for the burro. She could not express how much that simple continuity meant to her. It was a link to the past that she treasured and she—

"Lacey."

Lacey jumped with surprise when Scully walked out of the livery stable into her view. She gasped, "You startled me!"

"Did I?"

"You walk as silently as a cat. You'd make anybody jump."

"You're on edge because you're tired."

Lacey did not reply.

"Your nightmares are getting worse, aren't they?"

"Mary told you."

Scully did not confirm or deny.

"I frightened her, Scully. I'm sorry about that."

"There's only one way to stop those dreams. You know that as well as I do."

"I'm not ready, yet."

"You're as ready as you'll ever be."

"Besides, I don't have time. Sadie needs me at the restaurant."

"She can get Millie to replace you for a day."

"I have…things to do at the church."

"They can wait."

"No."

"Listen to me, Lacey. You won't be free of your nightmares until you face them head-on."

Lacey felt panic rising. "I won't go."

Scully's voice softened. "You don't have to be afraid. I'll be there."

"No, I can't."

"You have to face the shadows in your dreams sooner or later."

The sudden fear in Lacey's expression stopped Scully cold.

"What wrong, Lacey?"

"Nothing."

"Tell me."

"It's just… I don't know if I want to face them. The shadows scare me, Scully. I don't want to remember anything about them."

"Shadows can't hurt you."

"I know, but—"

"But what?"

Lacey's eyes filled. "You won't always be there for me, Scully. What will I do then?"

The question suddenly more than he could bear, Scully slid his arms around Lacey and drew her close. She trembled as he stroked her hair and said, "Who said I wouldn't always be there for you? That might be wishful thinking on the part of some young fellas in Weaver, but I expect to be around as long as you need me."

Lacey drew back from him. Suddenly embarrassed, she said, "Are you disgusted with me, Scully?"

"Disgusted?"

"I keep telling you I'm an adult and I'm responsible for myself, then I end up shaking like a child because of a dream."

Scully gripped her shoulders, forcing her gaze up to his when she looked away. He said, "Those nightmares aren't simple bad dreams. They're memories that have been lurking in the back of your mind for ten years, waiting to be finally put to rest. You have to remember whatever it is that's frightening you, or you'll never be free."

Lacey did not reply.

"I'll get the supplies together and tell Sadie to talk to Millie."

"I didn't say I'd go."

"We'll go tomorrow."

Silence.

"Tomorrow, Lacey."

Scully watched as Lacey turned and walked away. She did not look back.

Chapter Ten

S̲he couldn't believe she was doing this. She didn't want to believe it.

Lacey glanced at Scully as he rode beside her on the trail lit by early morning sun. Scully sat his mount easily, his weathered hat pulled down low on his forehead to shade those sober gray eyes; his broad shoulders erect; his boots fitted firmly, but naturally, into the stirrups as his long legs hugged his mount's sides with instinctive skill.

It occurred to her that no one would believe this fit, alert cowboy was the same man whose dark, custom-tailored suit, brocade vest and dark Stetson normally marked him the owner of the area's largest and most successful saloon. Nor would they believe that the strong, callused hands presently holding the reins also dealt cards with consummate skill.

The truth was, Scully was at ease in whatever setting he chose, with a competence and self-confidence he had earned the hard way while overcoming difficult years.

Self-confidence in which Lacey was presently, sadly, lacking.

The day had barely dawned before Scully was at the boarding house door with the day's supplies carefully packed on his saddle, and with Careful trailing behind. They had stopped only for breakfast before mounting up and leaving town. They had eaten breakfast in virtual silence, the same condition that had existed between them since Scully had insisted on the journey they were presently taking. They had been on the trail for hours with hardly a word spoken between them.

In thinking back, Lacey didn't remember actually agreeing to Scully's plan. He had merely announced during their supper meal the previous evening that the supplies would be ready for their journey in the morning, that Millie White would replace her at the restaurant while she was gone and they would be leaving at dawn.

She supposed her consent had come when she had slipped out of the boarding house after Scully left her there and had gone to the church to leave the day's lesson for Rosie and Jewel with Reverend Sykes.

She had returned to her room afterward and retired to her bed with true trepidation for the night to come. Yet, surprisingly enough, she had slept nightmare-free.

Lacey's mount moved relentlessly forward, appearing unaffected by the heat of the day even as perspiration beaded her forehead and upper lip. Scully looked her way unexpectedly. Their eyes met, and her throat choked tight.

That observant gaze.

Scully said, "We'll be stopping soon. There's a stream not far from here where the horses can drink and we can rest for a few minutes."

Lacey nodded, then looked away. She felt the weight

of Scully's stare, but she refused to look back. Her eyes were still averted when they stopped and Scully dismounted.

Dismounting as well, Lacey walked to the narrow rivulet sparkling in the afternoon sunlight. She leaned down and splashed her face, then looked up to see Scully crouched beside her.

She was unprepared when Scully asked softly, "Are you still mad at me, Lacey?"

Mad at him?

Was she?

"I'm not angry, Scully. I'm just…" She took a breath. "I'm just *afraid.*"

Her emotions bursting free with that admission, Lacey began sobbing in earnest. How could she make him understand that as much as she wanted to remember every detail of the time her grandfather and she had spent together, she feared remembering the night she had lost him?

But Scully's arms were around her. He was murmuring soft reassurances against her hair, and the realization belatedly dawned that she had no need for explanations, or the attempt to make Scully understand.

Because he understood instinctively—without any explanations at all.

"What's going on down there?"

Larry adjusted his spyglass and studied the shaded spot where Scully and Lacey had paused at the stream. His view was partially blocked by low-lying bushes thickly shielding the area, but that did not halt his response as he turned to his cohort and said, "What do you think's going on, Blackie? They're cooling off at the stream while we're baking out here in the hot sun."

Blackie grabbed the spyglass from his hand and focused it carefully. He heard Blackie's low curse as he studied the scene, then lowered the glass and said, "It don't seem like they're going to be stopping there very long—just to water the horses and wet down a bit. I expect they'll be moving on soon."

"To find her grandfather's strike." Larry gave a harsh laugh. "You know what I think? I think there ain't no strike at all. I think that old coot Charlie Pratt never did strike it rich like the boss thinks. I think it was all in Pratt's head, and now it's stuck in the boss's head, too!"

"You're crazy."

"No, it's the boss who's crazy." When Blackie shook his head, negating his statement, Larry continued hotly, "If there was gold out there, how come we couldn't find it?"

"Because we didn't know where to look, that's why."

"We checked every inch of ground for weeks after we killed that old man. No, we couldn't find that gold because there wasn't any to find."

"That isn't what the boss thinks."

"He's crazy, I tell you! And since Lacey Stewart came back, he's been getting crazier."

"Maybe." Blackie lifted his hat and wiped his arm across his forehead. "And maybe not. All I know is that he puts money in my pocket, and that suits me fine."

"It don't suit me too fine. I don't like it out here, sizzling my heels in the sun while he sits back in his office, all cool and fine, waiting to tell us how dumb we are for not being able to find a claim that don't exist."

Blackie responded, "Did you ever stop to think that

woman down there wouldn't be so determined to go back to a burned-out cabin in the middle of nowhere unless there was a good reason?"

"Her grandpa's buried out there."

Blackie's expression was skeptical. "Would you ride all the way out here just to look at a grave?"

Larry did not reply.

"And if you'd been living in a big city for ten years, and you grew up to look half as good as she does, would you come back to Weaver just to work in a restaurant?"

Still no reply.

"So maybe the boss ain't so crazy after all."

Larry's tight expression did not change as he replied, "All I know is that I'm getting tired of doing *hoity-toity* Gould's dirty work."

"But here you are, ain't you?"

Larry took an aggressive step. "You ain't thinking this whole thing through. What do you think the boss is going to do if he finds out there ain't no gold strike out there for him to cash in on?"

"I don't know, and I don't care. It's no skin off my nose either way."

"He ain't going to take it kindly, I'm telling you."

"Yeah…sure."

"There ain't no telling which way he'll jump when that happens."

"*If* it happens." Blackie raised the glass back to his eye, then reported, "They're leaving. Get yourself ready."

"For what?"

"We're going to sit ourselves down by that stream when they get far enough away, and we're going to cool ourselves off for a while."

"But I thought—"

"You thought, what—that I'd say we'd better keep on their tails? What for? We know where them two are heading. We can catch up with them anytime we want. They won't get away from us."

Larry considered that thought, then grabbed the spyglass from Blackie's hand and raised it back to his eye. "Yeah, there they go, all right, traveling at a snail's pace. We can be right behind them when they get to the grave with no trouble at all."

Larry turned back to Blackie, smiling for the first time as he said, "Now, that's using your head."

He must've been imagining things.

Scully scrutinized the terrain around him cautiously as the sun burned hotly on his shoulders. The first portion of Lacey's and his journey had been fraught with tension, a part of it of his own making. He'd been unable to pinpoint the source of his discomfort, but a sense of being watched had plagued him, setting him on edge. The sensation had waned inexplicably as they neared their destination.

He had begun wondering if the heat had been getting to him, and had then dismissed the thought, grateful that the former strain that had existed between Lacey and him earlier had also dissipated.

I'm afraid.

With those two words, the dam had broken, releasing Lacey's fears. The truth was, he had known it would be difficult for her to return to the site of her grandfather's grave, yet he had not realized the depth of her misgivings.

Nor had he realized how difficult it would be to release Lacey after he had held her comfortingly close again in his arms.

Emotion twisted tight inside Scully. He was disturbingly affected by Lacey's distress, so much so that he knew he would gladly have assumed her fears if he could, no matter how great their proportions, but that would've been too easy. Instead, he was forced to watch while she suffered through her terrors.

He was beginning to learn it was the hardest thing he had ever done.

Scully glanced at the mountains in the distance. They were drawing closer. They'd be arriving at the site of Charlie's cabin soon. He looked at Lacey where she rode silently beside him. She would soon be faced with memories she had avoided for years.

How would they affect her?

What would she do?

Scully knew only one thing for sure. He would take care of her—and, yes, he would protect her with his life.

Rosie's forced smile began failing as the sun fell from its apex. She had started work early at the Nugget, only a few hours after Jewel and she had gone to the church and found Reverend Sykes waiting to tell them Lacey couldn't make their lesson that day, but that she had prepared some work for them to do. They had accepted the paperwork Lacey had left and had departed immediately, uncomfortable in the pastor's presence.

They had been stopped by Bill, the bartender, on the way back to their boarding house. He had notified them that in Scully's absence, he needed them to come in to work a little early.

The realization that both Lacey and Scully were gone

had momentarily panicked her. The safety that the Nugget afforded had relieved that anxiety temporarily. However, the extended hours spent there had come back to haunt her.

The surrounding din rebounded, and Rosie's head pounded in time with the sound. She took an unsteady breath as she looked out at lengthening afternoon shadows on the street, then stood stock-still as her stomach lurched perilously close to revolting.

Rosie attempted to steady the queasy waves engulfing her. She was more upset than she realized, and her stomach was paying the price. The problem was, she had just begun believing things could change.

It had been incredible to her that she could actually write her name. She had also been touched in a way she had never been before when she realized that Lacey was almost as excited as she at her progress.

Then Scully had stood up for her, and when he had sent Riley packing, she had felt almost *worthy*.

Now they were both gone.

Rosie glanced to where Jewel was talking with a bearded, smiling wrangler. She knew Jewel felt somehow responsible for her welfare. She wasn't quite sure how that had come about, except that Jewel and she had become closer than most sisters she knew. Yet, if only for that reason, she didn't want Jewel taking the risk of getting involved in her problems.

Her stomach lurched, and Rosie hastened out through the swinging doors onto the street. She took a few unsteady steps toward the alleyway and gulped in fresh air free of the smoke and closeness of the saloon. She caught her breath when she was jerked unexpectedly backward, then dragged into the shadows between the buildings. She shuddered when a familiar voice whispered into her ear, "You ain't too smart, are you, Rosie?"

Riley.

Riley turned her around to face him as he said, "Did you think your protector would spend all his time looking out for you? No, he's got better things to do, and you ain't one of them."

Rosie struggled to free herself from his painful grip as she said, "What are you doing here, Riley? Scully's inside right now. If I call him—"

"He ain't in town, and you know it!"

Rosie's blood went cold.

"Did you think I wouldn't hear about how he's out somewhere having fun with that fancy woman he's been supporting all these years? He chose her over you, Rosie, and he left you for me."

"It's not like that—none of it! You're twisting things like you always do."

"But he's not here now, is he?"

Failing to free herself, Rosie asked abruptly, "What do you want from me, Riley? Everything you said to me about how much you love me was a lie. You know it, and I know it."

"No, it wasn't. You're just saying that now because somebody made you think you can do better than me." Riley crushed her closer. "You need to get it through your head that there ain't nobody who'll ever treat a Nugget woman any better than I treat you."

"Let me go." Rosie refused to listen. "Let me go!"

"I ain't letting you go, and there's no way you can make me." Still holding her cruelly tight, he said, "Set your mind to it. You're *my* girl, Rosie. You're going to stay *my* girl until I'm ready to let you go."

"No, she isn't."

Rosie gasped at the unexpected sound of Jewel's voice.

Her expression emotionless, Jewel entered the alleyway and advanced toward them. Her hand closed around the handle of her concealed derringer as she walked closer. She had known it would come to this sooner or later, just as she had known what she would do when it did.

"Get back into the saloon, Jewel." Rosie's voice shook revealingly. "Riley and me are just talking."

The panic in Rosie's tone was obvious as Jewel continued her approach, ordering softly, "Let Rosie go, Riley."

"Sure—like I'm going to take orders from a Nugget woman like you."

Jewel's finger curled around the trigger of her derringer. The metal had warmed to her skin. It felt strangely comfortable in her hand, as if it were a part of her.

She repeated more softly than before, "Let her go."

"I told you I ain't letting her—"

Riley's reply was cut short when Buddy slipped unexpectedly into the alleyway beside him and ripped Rosie from his arms. Thrust back against the Nugget wall, Riley stared, aghast, gasping as the lean cowpoke glared at him warningly with his gun drawn.

Jewel held her breath as Buddy directed, "You and Rosie, get back into the saloon—now. I'll take care of this."

Jewel shook her head. "I'm not going anywhere."

"Get out of this alleyway, both of you."

Jewel stared at Buddy. She had never seen him like this before, so cold, so...determined. She said abruptly, "Let's go, Rosie."

"No! I want to—"

"Let's go!"

Ignoring her protest, Jewel pushed Rosie out onto the boardwalk ahead of her. Time stood still as Rosie and she stood rigidly inside the swinging doors, waiting. Jewel released a pent-up breath just short of a sob when Buddy finally nudged his way through the swinging doors into sight.

Jewel searched Buddy's expression, inwardly trembling. She hardly breathed when he directed his first comment to Rosie, saying, "You don't have to worry about Riley anymore."

Jewel saw the relief that flickered across Rosie's face as she mumbled her thanks. Buddy then walked to the bar, tossed Riley's gun to the startled bartender and said, "Get rid of that for me, will you, Bill?"

Jewel asked shakily when he turned back toward her, "What happened?"

"Riley's gone."

"Gone?"

"I told him not to come back again…not if he expects to keep breathing."

Rosie gasped.

Jewel remained silent.

His expression pure ice in the brief silence that followed, Buddy then said, "It's over."

The desert landscape slipped into afternoon shadows as Lacey turned a shaken glance toward the remains of her grandfather's cabin a distance away. She clutched the Bible to her heart.

I can do everything through Christ, who strengthens me.

Lacey had read that passage often. She believed it sincerely, yet as the area became more familiar, trepidation had made persistent inroads into her mind. She searched out Scully's figure as he tended to the horses, then glanced away.

The landscape—barrel, cholla and prickly pear cactus; giant saguaros outlined against purple-tinted mountains; with palo verde and mesquite trees in between—all had gained gradual familiarity as they had continued their steady approach to this spot. Yet her first view of the charred debris of her grandfather's cabin earlier had sliced open old wounds that had begun bleeding profusely.

Memories had returned in a swelling rush, reviving the beauty of long days spent under Grandpa's loving care: hours passed wandering the desolate terrain as she followed her grandfather on his prospecting excursions into the brush; leisurely moments spent while Grandpa wielded his pick and shovel with relentless determination; the discovery of shaded places where she would close her eyes and rest through the heat of the day with Careful at her side.

The trickle of a narrow stream nearby had stirred recollections of wading delightedly as Careful drank, of Grandpa's voice calling her back to the cabin and the sound of Careful's hoofbeats behind her as she returned. She had remembered simple but joyful celebrations, while Grandpa played his fiddle and she sang loudly and enthusiastically, songs ranging from "Oh, Susannah" to "Amazing Grace." Then, best of all, she had recalled the quiet times as twilight changed into night, when she would sit on Grandpa's lap and he would read to her from the Bible—familiar passages, precious words on which he had based the conduct of his life.

But Grandpa was gone. His voice had stilled, and the music was silent. All that remained were shadows.

Lacey turned abruptly toward the grave marked by a simple, wooden cross. The shadow enveloping it was somehow symbolic. Her recollection of that fiery night still limited, she remembered the roaring flames, her grandfather's whispered words and a pain that was more than physical as she had watched him breathe his last breath.

Would she ever remember more?

Did she truly *want* to remember?

Unaware that she was trembling until Scully's strong arm slipped around her, Lacey melted into his strength. She could feel Scully's breath against her hair as she whispered against his chest, "Why would anyone want to kill my grandfather, Scully?"

"I don't know." Scully's husky whisper rang with frustration. "Nobody could figure that out. Your grandfather wasn't rich in much of anything except his faith and his belief in the future."

"It's funny…all the happy memories flooded back at first, but now everything's changing."

"There's nothing to worry about here, Lacey." Scully's deep voice was earnest. "You know I wouldn't let anything hurt you."

Lacey drew back with an effort at a smile. "When will we be leaving?"

"We'll leave anytime you want to—sooner or later. It's up to you."

Lacey began slowly, "I know why we came, and I appreciate all you've done." Lacey could not restrain an apprehensive glance around her. "I've remembered so much already, and I—"

Somehow unable to finish that statement, Lacey said simply, "Thank you, for helping me remember so many of the good memories, but I'd like to go back now."

"All right, just as soon as we have something to eat."

Scully slipped his arm around her as they walked back to the horses. Lacey tried to relax. She had forgotten how bright the desert sun could be, how hot it could get...and how desolate this location was.

She had forgotten so many things...just as she had forgotten the memories that still lurked in the shadows of her mind.

"Warm water and jerky." Larry turned and spat on the ground in contempt. He looked back up at Blackie and motioned toward the campfire in the distance. "But they're down at that stream refreshing themselves in the water and eating like they're out on a picnic."

"Stop complaining, will you, Larry? We can't afford to go nowheres near that stream and chance them seeing us, and you know it." Blackie tossed away his last bite of jerky and stood up in exasperation. "You ain't been the same since that day the boss told you to take a bath."

"That don't have nothing to do with it!"

"Don't it? You ain't had a good word for anything he's told us to do since."

"Are you telling me this whole trip isn't a waste of time? Scully and the woman ain't doing nothing down there but walking around, staring at that charred wood for a while, then going back to look at that grave. From the way Scully was packing up a while ago, they're not going to be staying much longer, neither."

"You should be happy about that."

"I ain't, because the boss ain't going to be happy when we tell him Lacey didn't even make an attempt to locate that strike."

"Maybe she saw more than she's letting on."

"It didn't look like it to me."

"Maybe she don't want to share that strike with Scully, no matter what he did for her."

"That don't seem likely, either."

"Likely or not, you don't know nothing more than I do!" His patience short, Blackie said, "I don't want to hear nothing more about it. The boss said to follow them, so we followed them. He said to report back to him, and we'll report back to him what we saw—which was nothing. And that's the end of it."

"He's not going to let it go, I tell you."

"I don't care if he does or not."

"He's crazy. There's no telling what he'll do."

"You're the one who's crazy."

"Yeah…sure." Larry turned his back on his cohort, then muttered into the silence that followed, "He's crazy, I'm telling you. We're going to have to watch our step."

The shadows of the endless day were lengthening and the streets of Weaver would soon be brightly lit. The Gold Nugget was already ablaze with light and merriment, but the atmosphere between the three sitting at a table in the corner was restrained after the tense confrontation with Riley earlier.

All three turned toward the smiling cowpoke who unexpectedly tapped Rosie's shoulder and said, "How about a dance, Rosie?"

Rosie nodded. She turned with a forced smile toward Jewel and Buddy as she took the cowboy's arm and said, "I'll see you later."

Jewel swallowed a strange sadness as Rosie walked away. Rosie was Rosie. She'd make the best of things, if only to alleviate their concern.

Jewel looked up at Buddy as he moved his chair closer. She felt the press of his warmth against her and her heart skipped a beat as she forced herself to say, "Thank you, Buddy."

"For what?"

"You know the answer to that question. If you hadn't showed up when you did, things might be a lot different right now."

Buddy whispered soberly, "You're thanking me for stopping you from what you intended to do to Riley out there, so I'm telling you not to thank me for it. I didn't do it for you, or for Rosie, either. I did it for myself."

"Buddy—"

"You would've shot him."

"I just—"

"Don't deny it. I know about that hidden gun you carry, remember? But I don't understand how you got it into your head that it's your job to fight Rosie's battles for her."

"Rosie made a mistake trusting Riley, and I'm not going to watch Riley make her pay over and over for it. She doesn't deserve that."

"You don't deserve a lifetime of paying for Rosie's mistakes, either. That's what would happen if you did what you intended to do out there."

"She's my friend, Buddy. I won't desert her."

"So, Rosie's your friend. What am I to you, Jewel?"

Jewel averted her gaze.

"Look at me, Jewel." Buddy's gaze grew intense. "I want to know."

"You're my…friend."

"What else?"

"What else is there?"

"Don't pretend."

"I'm not pretending. I'm accepting a truth that you won't face. There *is* nothing else—there *can't be* anything else between you and me."

"I don't believe that."

"I told you, what you want and what I want are different."

"I don't believe that, either."

Jewel took a shaky breath, then continued in a voice barely audible over the surrounding din, "I appreciate what you did, Buddy, more than you know, but it doesn't change anything. What I said may not be true for you, but it's true for me. If you can't accept that we already have all there can ever be between us, then you're wasting your time with the wrong woman."

"Are you telling me to find somebody else?"

A breathtaking pain stabbed sharply inside Jewel, so deeply that she was momentarily unable to respond. Regaining control, she whispered, "You're the only one who can answer that question."

Buddy's gaze lingered in the extended silence that followed Jewel's response. She saw his expression tighten as he drew himself slowly erect. She watched his gaze go cold. She felt a moment coming that she had always anticipated, yet now dreaded more than she had believed possible.

A voice at her elbow shattered the silence of the moment as a man interrupted to ask, "Hey, Jewel, Buddy's been monopolizing you long enough. How about a dance?"

Jewel glanced up at the grinning cowpoke. Willie Johnson was a nice fella, and dancing with the customers was her job.

Intensely aware that Buddy had remained silent, Jewel stood up, only to feel Buddy's touch restrain her as he stood up beside her. Her throat choked with emotion as Buddy responded softly in her stead, "Find yourself another girl, Willie. This one's mine."

Scully worked with the horses as they prepared to leave. Lacey scanned the landscape around her for a lingering look at the remains of the cabin that had once been her home and the lonely grave nearby. The shadows were lengthening too quickly to suit her and a strange agitation was expanding inside her at the thought of all that the darkness at this location might bring.

Lacey turned abruptly at the sound of Careful's bray and Scully's annoyed response to see the determined burro break unexpectedly away from his tether to start back toward the cabin debris.

Starting after him instinctively, Lacey reached the burro as he stopped beside the charred timbers. She reached for his broken tether only to freeze into motionlessness as familiar images began inundating her mind....

Flickering shadows and darkness...she needed to cover Grandpa. She couldn't leave him lying cold and alone.

But the shadows were moving. They were coming

closer. She yelled at them to stay back, but fear gripped
her throat and no sound emerged.

She started to run, then tripped and fell.

She got up to run again.

Grandpa, help me!

No, he was dead.

The shadows were right behind her.

They caught her by the hair!

Help me! Somebody, help me!

"Lacey, what's wrong?"

Breathless, shaking with terror, Lacey stirred from
the onslaught of the paralyzing images as Scully
grasped her shoulders.

"What happened, Lacey?"

Lacey struggled for breath. She strained to focus on
the features of the man supporting her with his grip. It
was Scully, and the threatening darkness had evapo-
rated into the brightness of day.

"Are you all right, darlin'?"

Scully's rough palm stroked her cheek. He drew her
closer as Lacey whispered, "The shadows almost caught
up to me, Scully. I could feel their hands on my hair."

"You're safe now." Regret rang in his tone as he said,
"I shouldn't have brought you here. Coming has only
made things worse."

"No, I'm all right now." Lacey tried to smile. "It was
only a flash of memory—something I have to learn to
face."

"Not *only* a memory, Lacey."

Scully brushed her mouth unexpectedly with his,
then whispered, "You don't have to be afraid anymore,

not with me beside you. Remember that, darlin'. Keep it close to you."

Slipping his arm around her as he picked up Careful's tether, Scully urged Lacey back toward the horses.

Lacey felt no need to respond as they reached their mounts and Scully swung her up into the saddle. No words were necessary. She'd be all right now. Nothing could happen to her with Scully so near.

Besides, he had kissed her.

And…he had called her "darlin'."

Lacey had stopped shaking.

As they rode, Scully looked at Lacey. She had not spoken a word since they started back toward Weaver. Nor had she taken her eyes from the trail ahead.

Scully remembered with a tight knot deep inside him the way Lacey had turned to him in her fear. She had looked up at him with the same trust in her eyes that he had seen that first day so many years ago.

And he had drawn her close instinctively.

He recalled the brush of her fair hair against his chin as he had held her against him. The memory of her sweet scent stirred him, as did recalling the warmth of her lips as he had brushed them with his own.

She was so beautiful and so innocent…and so terrified of shadows that stalked her darkness.

Scully unconsciously touched the gun on his hip. He looked at the Bible that Lacey gripped tightly as they rode.

A potent combination.

Scully admitted to himself with sudden, silent

candor that there was nothing or no one who meant more to him than Lacey did.

"They didn't do nothing, I tell you!"

Incredulous, Barret stared at his two hirelings. He attempted to read their expressions as shadows held them in dark relief in the doorway of his home, but it was to no avail.

Both frustrated and grateful that his housekeeper had left for the day, Barret ushered the two men inside. He glanced at their grimy boots as they carelessly tracked residue from the livery stable across his spotless hallway floor.

Unable to bear another step, Barret slammed the front door closed behind them and ordered, "That's far enough. Now repeat what you just said."

Blackie spoke up, his weak grin displaying an uneven row of yellow teeth as he said, "How many ways do we have to say it, boss? Scully and his girlfriend just got back to Weaver from the old man's burned-out cabin. We came back a safe distance behind them. We didn't let them out of our sight for a minute, like you said, but we ain't got nothing to tell you. Them two didn't do nothing at the cabin but stand around."

"Impossible. They didn't go there without a reason."

"Well, that's all they did. The woman and Scully went to stand beside the old man's grave for a bit, then they wandered around what was left of the cabin."

"They didn't check a map...search out the nearby terrain...trek up farther into the wilderness."

"No."

"Tell me exactly what they did from the moment they got there."

Blackie shot Larry a glance before replying, "Like I said, they looked at what was left of the cabin, then they looked at the grave."

"And? And?"

"They talked. They went to get water from the stream. They made their camp. They ate. Then they packed up and left."

"You weren't watching closely enough."

"We didn't miss nothing."

"They must've seen you watching them."

"They didn't see nothing. We was too careful."

"The woman was the one you needed to watch closely. What did she do?"

"She didn't do nothing but hold onto that Bible every minute she was there. She hardly let it out of her hand, even when she took that burro to the stream to drink… even when she walked around the grave, and all the while Scully was sticking to her like glue."

"What do you mean?"

"They was talking to each other all the time, and Scully didn't let her out of his sight."

"Even when she was reading the Bible?"

"I told you—"

"That's it!" Barret felt a surge of pure jubilation as the thought struck him. "The secret is in the Bible. The old man must've drawn a map to his claim in it, and his granddaughter was doing her best to coordinate the direction without letting Scully see what she was up to."

"No, I don't think so, she—"

"I'm not paying either of you to think." Barret's glance was scathing. "I'm the one who does the thinking, and I'm telling you the secret to that old man's claim is in that Bible."

Barret paused. His heart was racing. Ten long years of staring at that gold nugget in his drawer was about to come to fruition.

He declared, "I want that Bible."

Speaking up for the first time, Larry said, "And we're supposed to get it for you? How're we supposed to do that? She always has it with her."

"Always? She doesn't take it with her when she goes to work at the restaurant in the morning, does she?"

"No, but—"

"Get it then."

"That won't be so easy. She—"

"I didn't say it would be easy. I just told you to get it."

Barret noted the glances the two men exchanged, and his temper flared. "Is that so hard to understand? Go to the boarding house when she leaves, find the Bible, and bring it to me!"

"What about Old Lady McInnes?"

"That's your problem. I want that Bible in my hands tomorrow."

"But—"

"Tomorrow."

Barely in control of his agitation, Barret watched as Blackie and Larry walked out. His patrician face flushed, he told himself he need be patient only a little longer. His hirelings were dolts, but they were more than capable of the task he had set for them. They were also necessary for the manual labor that would be needed to verify the strike before he could register it in his name. He'd dispense with them when they weren't needed any longer.

And good riddance.

Barret smiled at the thought. Yes, a very good riddance.

* * *

It was night when Scully faced Lacey beside her boarding house door. They had returned to Weaver and had gone to the restaurant for a warm meal, which Lacey had picked at sparingly. It was now time to say good-night.

But Lacey was frowning when she looked up at him. Her gaze lingered on his face and Scully felt the knot inside him tighten. The distance they had covered and Lacey's confrontation with the past had been emotionally exhausting, but, strangely, he had treasured every moment. He didn't want to leave her to go alone to her room where the demons of her dreams might haunt her again. He wanted to keep her close to him, to know that she'd always be near.

The direction of his thoughts brought a frown to Scully's brow as well. He said gruffly, "You should go right to bed. You're tired and you're going to have to be up early in the morning."

"I suppose." Lacey hesitated. She glanced in the direction of the Gold Nugget. Music and laughter spilled out through its portals, echoing on the night breeze as she said with a forced smile, "I guess you'll be busy for a while though."

Scully shrugged. "Maybe."

Lacey said unexpectedly, "I'm sorry for all the problems I caused you out there today."

"You'll never be a problem to me."

Scully noted the uncertainty in Lacey's expression when she nodded and looked away. He said, "About your nightmares, Lacey—"

Lacey's gaze snapped back up to his.

"If you'd feel better sleeping at the Gold Nugget until

they fade, I could ask Helen to come back to stay for a while."

"No." Lacey shook her head emphatically. "I'm responsible for handling my nightmares."

He asked softly, "Is it because you couldn't be comfortable at the Nugget anymore?"

"I didn't say that!" Lacey gasped. "I'd *never* say that."

"But...?"

"It would be taking a step backward when I'm supposed to be an adult."

"Don't make the mistake of thinking your behavior is immature, Lacey. Your nightmares are a small price to pay for survival."

"I should have them under control by now." Lacey paused. "I *will* get them under control."

"The nightmares are growing clearer because you're getting closer to remembering everything your mind couldn't face when you were a child. They'll end when your memory of that night fully returns."

Lacey replied, "Even if I'm not sure I want to remember it all?"

"I don't think you have a choice." Scully paused, then said, "I wish I could help you, darlin'. The only thing I can say is that I'll always be close by if you need me."

"I know."

Scully stroked a pale wisp of hair back from Lacey's cheek. He ached to hold her again in his arms, to feel her close against him. He lowered his head to brush her mouth lightly with his.

The brief, sweet taste of her...

Scully jerked back, then said gruffly, "Go to bed,

Lacey." And when she hesitated, he added, "Go ahead. I don't want to leave until you're safely inside."

His heart was pounding when Lacey closed the boarding house door behind her, and Scully struggled to regain stability. What had he been thinking? It could never work...a man like him who had strayed so far from The Word during his lifetime, and a young woman who believed in every syllable that was written, and who lived her life accordingly.

Scully turned back toward the Gold Nugget with long, determined strides. No, it would never work.

"I told you he's crazy."

Blackie rubbed his stubbled jaw at Larry's comment and glanced back briefly in the direction of Barret's house as the two men turned onto Weaver's main street. He shrugged as he responded, "Maybe you're right, after all. The boss sure is acting crazy enough with all that talk about Lacey Stewart's Bible—"

"As if he's going to find a map to the old man's strike in it, even if we do get it for him."

"What do you mean, 'if'?"

Larry gave an amused snort. "So you're telling me you want to follow through on his orders?"

"Is there any reason we shouldn't?"

"Because he's crazy!"

"So?"

"What's going to happen when he gets that Bible and doesn't find what he wants in it?"

"That's his problem, not ours."

"I'm telling you, he's like a powder keg waiting to go off."

"I don't think so."

"I do."

"What's that supposed to mean?" Blackie halted abruptly on the walk. He turned to glare at the cowpokes behind them who had walked up their heels, then looked back at Larry and lowered his voice as the cowpokes walked past. "Are you telling me you don't want any part of getting that Bible for him?"

"I don't know."

"Well, I do. I'm going to get it for the boss *because* he's been the boss for the last ten years, his money's good and even when things didn't go as planned, he handled it. Yeah, he might be slipping toward the edge with the way he's talking, but it'll be simple enough to walk away without nobody even giving us a thought if it all turns out to be a problem. In the meantime, I'm going to ride this gravy train as long as I can. If that means getting him that Bible, that's all right with me."

Larry shrugged.

"What're you saying now?"

"I guess you're right. Getting that Bible ain't the hardest thing he ever asked us to do."

"As a matter of fact, it'll be easy—especially since we know Lacey's room is nice and handy on the first floor of the boarding house."

"With Old Lady McInnes standing watch."

"I can take care of that."

"You can?"

"Just watch me."

Yea, though I walk through the valley of the shadow of death, I shall fear no evil: for thou art with me; thy rod and thy staff, they comfort me.

Lacey raised her head from her Bible and glanced

out into the darkness through the window of her room. The day of Scully's and her trek into the wilderness was coming to an end as she read the 23rd Psalm. She had read it countless times before, but the words had never struck as close to her heart as they did that night.

Music from the Gold Nugget wafted in on the night breeze, and her mind wandered.

Thy rod and thy staff, they comfort me.

Scully's and her visit to the devastating terror of her childhood had resulted in the return of memories, both good and bad. Although shadows still remained, the experience had also proved to her beyond doubt that the Lord had chosen Scully to be the unlikely *rod and staff* to guide and comfort her. She was grateful—but she was keenly aware that her feelings for Scully were rapidly surpassing ordinary gratitude.

Lacey raised trembling fingers to her lips. The touch of Scully's kiss was still vividly real, raising a desire within her that was just as vivid and real. She had wanted to slide her arms around Scully's neck and draw him closer, to feel his mouth press more tightly to hers. Yet Scully had drawn back from their kiss so abruptly.

When she had previously declared her platonic love for him, he had responded in kind, and she had known he spoke truthfully. That bond remained firm and unbreakable—but this was more.

Uncertain, Lacey clutched her Bible more tightly. As always, when she did, it was as if she could feel Grandpa's presence, as if his gnarled hand again held hers. She treasured that link to the dear man she had lost in the violence of that fiery night.

She missed his counsel.

She missed his solace.

She missed…him.

Scully's image returned at that moment, so intensely bright in her mind's eye that Lacey caught her breath. Yes, she had lost Grandpa, but Scully now stood stalwart at her side. He would never desert her.

That thought a somehow aching consolation, Lacey stood up and walked to her bed. She placed her Bible on the nightstand. She then lowered the lamp, lay down, and drew the coverlet up across her shoulders as music from the Gold Nugget echoed through her room.

"He loves you, Jewel."

Jewel paused in the doorway of her room. She had come in late after spending some private time with Buddy after her work at the Nugget was done—private hours that she told herself meant nothing more to her than those she had spent with other men before him. But it had been harder than usual to part from Buddy after his tenderness, after his loving words—words she had heard before and would not allow herself to make the mistake of believing.

Rosie had been waiting for her in her room. Rosie had greeted her with the words she had just spoken so solemnly.

Jewel pushed her bedroom door closed behind her and said, "Buddy loves me, huh? Didn't you learn anything with Riley? How many times did he say he loved you? How many times did he say he needed you?"

"That's different. Riley's a liar. He doesn't love anybody but himself. I didn't know it then, but I know it now. Besides, Riley never said he wanted to marry me."

Jewel went still. "How'd you know Buddy wants to marry me?"

"So he *did* ask you."

"So you were guessing."

"Yeah, but it wasn't hard to figure out. It's easy to see the kind of fella Buddy is, and nobody can miss the way he looks at you." Rosie paused. "He risked his life when he faced Riley down, Jewel. He did it for you—not for me."

Jewel did not respond, allowing Rosie to say, "Buddy saw the look on your face, and he heard the threat in Riley's voice. He stepped in before you could get hurt. I'm telling you, if I had a man like that wanting to marry me—"

"What Buddy and I do is none of your business, Rosie."

"Just like what Riley and I do is none of *your* business, you mean?"

When Jewel did not answer, Rosie stood up and said, "I don't mean to seem ungrateful, Jewel. You got in the middle of things for me, and if you didn't and Buddy hadn't interfered, I don't know what would've happened."

"Riley's not a fool. Scully backed him off the first time, and Buddy took care of the rest. Riley won't be back because he knows what'll be waiting for him if he does."

"That's right, Buddy took care of the rest—and he'd take care of you, too, if you'd let him."

"I don't need anybody to take care of me."

"Why are you so stubborn, Jewel? Buddy loves you!"

"I don't believe in love."

Silent for a moment, Rosie said, "I don't think I could live with believing that."

"So you're telling me *you* believe in love after you've

been lied to and tossed aside by every man who ever said those words to you?"

"Those words do mean something to some people."

"Oh, I forgot. You're the expert."

Rosie glanced away and Jewel took a conciliatory step toward her. "I'm sorry. I shouldn't have said that. It's just that no man I've ever trusted has proved worth his salt, so I've learned to depend only on myself."

"Buddy's not like that."

"No, I don't really think he is." Startling Rosie with those words, Jewel blinked back the moisture that had sprung into her eyes and said, "But if he isn't, he deserves better than getting stuck with a Gold Nugget woman for the rest of his life." Jewel forced an expression of emotionless acceptance as she continued, "Buddy will get tired of waiting when he figures out I'm not what he thinks I am. Then he'll find himself a woman who's everything that I'm not. Until then, whether it's right or wrong, I'll enjoy things as they are. Can you understand that, Rosie?"

Her eyes moist, Rosie rasped, "I can understand it, but I don't think—"

"Don't think, Rosie. Just let me be. Will you do that for me?"

"Jewel..."

Jewel waited for Rosie to continue. She stood still as a tear slipped down Rosie's cheek. She remained silent as Rosie hugged her tightly, then slipped out of the room without another word.

Chapter Eleven

Mary McInnes looked at the disreputable-looking fellow standing on her doorstep, then at the sun that had barely risen in the morning sky. It was early...too early to open the door to an unwashed undesirable like Blackie Oaks, and *far* too early to be subjected to his overwhelmingly unpleasant body odor.

Mary's lips tightened. She could never understand the tolerance the good people of Weaver had for this man and his partner. Nor, for that matter, could she understand the respect most townsfolk had for Barret Gould, the man who "so generously" employed Blackie and his partner at odd jobs. As far as she was concerned, the town of Weaver would be better off without the three of them. For that reason, she had never been overly friendly with any of them—and for that reason she had been surprised to find Blackie standing at her door so early in the morning. She had been even more stunned at his question.

Somehow incredulous, Mary shook her head. "You're asking me if I have a room to let to you in my boarding house, Mr. Oaks?"

"My name is Blackie, ma'am." Blackie's mouth widened in an unappealing smile as he continued, "I heard in town that you had a room available, and I rushed right over here to see if I could get it."

"There must be some mistake. I don't have any empty rooms. Almost all my boarders are of long standing."

"You're sure... I mean, maybe somebody told you they might be moving, or maybe—"

"Nobody's moving out of my boarding house at this time. You were misinformed." Mary took a backward step in an attempt to avoid the man's aroma. Unable to escape it, she brought the conversation to a quick halt by saying, "I'm sorry you wasted your time. Good day."

"Wait a minute, ma'am!" Blackie jammed his foot onto the doorway, preventing Mary from closing the door. He smiled at her annoyance as he said, "I've been hearing about the great meals you serve your boarders. Even if you don't have a room to let, I was wondering if you'd have room at your table for me and my partner on a regular basis. We ain't been getting too many decent meals lately, and we'd be willing to pay any reasonable price you'd set."

"That's out of the question."

"Why? I mean, couldn't I talk you in to it?"

"No, definitely not. Sadie serves very good meals at her restaurant, and she serves everyone. You should have no complaints if you go there. Now, if you wouldn't mind taking your foot out of my door..."

"Oh, sorry, ma'am." Blackie smiled again. Mary cringed at the sight as he continued, "I just want to say that I hope you'll keep Larry and me in mind if things should change here."

"Yes...of course."

Mary closed the door with a firm click, and Blackie's smile sagged into a sneer as he turned away. He wondered what the old lady would say if she knew that he wouldn't take a room in her old rattletrap of a house even if *she* paid *him.*

Still mumbling under his breath, Blackie turned the corner of the street and waited impatiently for the sound of a familiar footstep. As Larry came into view, he whispered, "Did you get it?"

"Yeah, I got it." Larry tapped the sack he held in his hand. "But I barely got in and out of the boarding house before the old lady came back into the hallway. It's a good thing that Bible was in clear view or by the time I found it, she might've seen me climbing back out through that window. Then I would've had to fix her good, and the boss wouldn't have liked that too much."

"The boss is going to be happy about this."

Larry gave him a look. "I wouldn't count on it. He ain't going to be too happy if he doesn't find the old man's map in there."

"And if he does find what he's looking for?"

Larry did not bother to reply.

Barret paced his office floor, then glanced out the window at the sunlit morning street beyond. He was perspiring profusely. He glanced at the small wall mirror in passing, and noted that sweat was leeching through the underarms of his custom-fitted jacket in the most common way.

With a grunt of disgust, he pulled off his jacket and tossed it onto the chair, then pushed back a straying strand of dark hair and mopped his handkerchief across his brow. Work was piling up on his desk...mundane

work, boring work, in a town that was just as mun-
dane and boring, and which he had barely tolerated for
the past ten, endless years. He had come to his office
without stopping to eat the breakfast his housekeeper
had prepared, and had been forced to suffer her disapproving glances as he left. He had been waiting for
what seemed an eternity for his hirelings to bring him
the small volume that would eliminate his present torment forever.

They still had not arrived.

Barret looked again out his office window, then
stopped dead in his tracks. He did not move until the
door opened and two unkempt figures pushed their
way into the room. He glanced down at the small sack
Blackie carried, then asked, "Did you get it?"

"Of course." Blackie's smile was cocky. "Did you
think we wouldn't?"

Barret snatched the sack from Blackie's hand with
a sound that clearly bespoke the response he had not
needed to utter. He looked into the sack and took a relieved breath. It was there. He had it in his hands. The
waiting would soon be over.

"Get out."

Blackie and Larry both frowned at Barret's tone,
but they did not move. He repeated, "You heard me."

Blackie blustered, "We thought you'd be—"

"I don't know what you both thought, and neither
do I care. I intend to examine this prize you've brought
me *privately,* without interruption. That means, I will
do it behind closed doors with the drapes drawn. Do
you understand?"

"Yeah, but—"

"Privately means without either of you present."

"But—"

"I'll call you when I need you. Get out."

Blackie stumbled backward at Barret's admonition. Tripping over Larry behind him, Blackie hardly waited for his cohort to clear the doorway before pulling the door shut behind him.

Barret shook his head with disgust. Their behavior was so typical of their limited mentality that it was not even amusing.

Barret took the few steps to the door in an expect-ant rush. He turned the key in the lock and pulled the heavy drapes closed over the windows before return-ing to his desk.

His heart pounding, Barret withdrew the Bible from the sack with an extravagantly ceremonious gesture.

His moment had come.

"It's gone, just like I told you. It's just...gone!"

Lacey took a breath and swallowed against en-croaching tears as she faced Scully solemnly in the silence of her room. She had come back to the board-ing house after finishing work at the restaurant. Her intention had been to pick up her Bible and the next lesson she had prepared for Rosie and Jewel. The pa-pers had been where she'd left them, but the Bible was not. She had searched the entire room, but it was nowhere to be found.

Panicking when she realized further effort would be wasted, she had left her room and asked Mary if she had seen her Bible, only to remember belatedly that Rosie and Jewel were waiting for her at the church. She had then returned swiftly to her room, snatched up the written lesson and dropped off the papers for the two women with a brief explanation before rushing back to search her room again.

Lacey attempted to swallow the lump in her throat. She wasn't certain when Mary had sent for Scully, but he had arrived at the door of her room a few minutes previously. Relaxing her rules as she had once before, Mary had again allowed him inside to help with the search, leaving the door open at her silent exit.

They had not found her Bible.

Lacey fought to control her trembling. "Where could it be, Scully? I left it on my nightstand. I always leave it there."

Scully did not reply.

"Do you think somebody took it?" Immediately she countered, "But that doesn't make sense. Why would anybody steal an old Bible? It isn't worth much to anybody but me."

"Somebody obviously took a fancy to it."

"Who would want a Bible enough to steal it, especially since Reverend Sykes would gladly provide one for anybody who asked? And how would somebody get into my room? Mary has been home all morning."

"Was your window locked?"

"It was when I left."

"Your door?"

"I don't have a key, just a latch on the inside, but Mary said her boarders are totally dependable. She's never had a problem with anything being missing."

Scully walked out into the hallway, then returned to the room, his expression dark. "The hallway window is open."

"Mary always leaves it open. She says it's cooler that way."

Scully did not comment. He asked, "Has anybody shown an interest in your Bible lately?"

"No, nobody except—" Lacey halted abruptly. Rosie had remarked several times how fortunate she was to have something so precious, but Rosie was too sweet and sincere to be at fault.

Scully pinned her with his gaze. "What were you going to say?"

"Nothing…except some people at the church have remarked about the care I take with it."

Scully remained silent and Lacey took a shuddering breath. With an attempt to face reality head-on, she said, "It's gone, Scully. I'll never get it back."

That thought suddenly more than she could bear, Lacey collapsed against Scully. She pressed herself instinctively tight against him as she whispered, "I know it's only an old Bible, but it's important to me. It's taken me through so many difficult times, and it's all I had… all that's left of my grandfather…of my past."

Scully clutched her close. Tilting her chin up toward him, the sincerity in his gaze clearly visible, he whispered huskily, "That's where you're wrong. You have me, Lacey. You'll always have me."

She had known that, just as she suddenly knew, as Scully lowered his mouth toward hers, that he was going to kiss her again.

But Scully's kiss was different this time. He kissed her slowly, gently, with a tenderness that continued when he finally drew his mouth from hers and pressed his lips to her eyelids, her cheek, the curve of her jaw. Held breathless by the soaring emotion he evoked inside her, Lacey encircled Scully's neck with her arms to draw him closer. She was lost in the glory of the moment when Scully pulled back from her with startling abruptness. She was unprepared when he said, "I'm sorry. That was…a mistake."

Lacey shook her head, uncomprehending. How could it be a mistake when being in Scully's arms felt so right? Surely he—

"Don't look at me like that, Lacey. You're upset. I shouldn't have taken advantage of you."

"You didn't. I—"

Scully took a backward step. "You're feeling lost and vulnerable right now. You aren't thinking rationally, or you'd be telling me to get out of your room."

"Why? I don't want you to leave."

"You don't know what you're saying, Lacey."

"I'm saying that something bad has happened. Someone came into my room. Someone stole my Bible. I don't know who would do such a thing, or why, but the only person I really trust is you."

"Maybe you shouldn't trust me too much right now."

Lacey took a forward step. She whispered, "Why, because you kissed me? I'm glad you kissed me, Scully."

"This is wrong, Lacey, more wrong than you realize. Your grandfather wouldn't have wanted…he didn't expect…" Scully shook his head. "It's time for me to leave."

"No."

"I'll get your Bible back for you. That's a promise."

"But—"

"Keep your window locked. I'll tell Mary to lock the hallway window, too." He paused. "I'm sorry."

"Don't go yet, Scully!"

Lacey watched as Scully walked out the doorway and disappeared from sight.

Stunned, she stood motionless. She had never felt more alone.

I don't want you to leave.

Lacey's simple statement rang over again in Scully's mind as he exited the boarding house. Out on the street at last, he took a deep breath. He had come so close to losing control when Lacey was in his arms.

Scully forced himself to face a truth he had so diligently avoided. He loved her. Not in the way he had always loved Lacey, as he loved a dear, young girl left in his care; or in a way he might've thought he had loved any woman before her—but as a man truly loves a woman.

I'm glad you kissed me, Scully.

She shouldn't have been.

Don't go.

He hadn't wanted to, but the truth had never been more evident than when he had drawn back from kissing Lacey, barely in control of the emotion building inside him, and had seen the innocence in her eyes.

He wasn't the man for Lacey. Too many years had passed in between, with too many nights for him to ever hope to erase. He had slipped into a lifestyle that was in too great a conflict with hers. Lacey didn't realize that now because her thoughts were in a turmoil, but when her life was back on an even keel, she'd begin looking at him differently. She'd see him for the man he was—a saloonkeeper, a gambler, a man who took his pleasures at will, while giving little thought to the

Book she cherished or its message. No, he was not the man she imagined him to be.

Lacey needed him right now, but when a decent young fellow like Todd Fulton decided to make his move—

Scully forced that painful thought from his mind. He filled the aching void with details that he needed to examine more closely.

He had no doubt that Lacey's Bible had been stolen. She would never have misplaced it. Accepting that conclusion then shed a different light on the sensation he had had of being watched as Lacey and he had traveled to the remains of Charlie's cabin.

Were the two incidents related?

If so, who was behind it all, and why?

Possibilities sprang to mind, but Scully was certain of only one thing.

Someone would pay.

"It's not here!" Barret glared at Blackie, then flashed a similarly heated glance at Larry before continuing, "There's no map in this Bible. What did you do with it?"

Momentarily speechless as he faced Barret across the still darkened office to which he and his cohort had been summoned, Blackie replied, "We didn't do nothing with it, boss."

Barret shuddered with wrath. He had spent the greater part of the morning going through the pages of Lacey Stewart's Bible—and he had found *nothing*. In frustration, he had shaken out the aged volume, checked the binding and gone so far as to rip some of the binding loose with the thought that the map might be concealed inside. As a last resort, he had tried to discover a pattern in the crude, faded illustrations Charlie had drawn in the margins of some pages, obviously for Lacey's benefit when she was a child, but he'd been unable to make sense of the birds, angels and trumpets randomly sketched.

He had almost begun believing that his dream had ended. He had then withdrawn the small sack from his drawer and removed the gold nugget Charlie had left with him, and his dream had been restored anew.

The nugget was real, and so was the strike.

Barret insisted with growing vehemence, "The map was in the Bible. It had to have been."

"If it was, somebody took it out before we got there, boss." Larry continued defensively, "Blackie and me never saw it. We ain't dumb enough to try to cross you. Even if we did, we'd be long gone by now."

His chest heaving, Barret considered Larry's response. Neither of the two were smart enough to get away with stealing that map from him, and they knew it. They'd have to kill him first. Of course, they had killed before, but he prided himself on the fact that they had become too subservient to him to give even a moment's thought to the possibility of slaying him.

Barret gradually drew his breathing under control. So, if the map hadn't been in the Bible, it had to be somewhere else. Old Charlie had to have left some kind of signs leading to the location of the strike. The old man wasn't a novice. He knew even the most experienced prospector could become confused in the wilderness without leaving some kind of markings behind him.

Lacey was the only person who could possibly know what those signs were. Since she hadn't made a move toward the strike, she'd obviously gone out with Scully only with the intention of refamiliarizing herself with the territory. Now that she had gotten her bearings, she would make a move on her own soon.

Barret muttered a soft curse. Stealing the Bible had been a mistake. Lacey was now alerted to the fact that someone might be on to her plans. It might cause her to be more careful...to take her time.

Barret took a firm hold on his frustration. All right, he'd waited ten years. He could wait a little longer.

Barret looked again at his henchmen, then said, "I believe you. You didn't take the map, but if the map wasn't in the Bible, it's in Lacey Stewart's head."

Barret almost laughed at the startled expressions his statement evoked. He saw the wary glances Blackie and Larry exchanged when he said, "Lacey Stewart has waited as long as I have to claim this strike. Her deviousness proves she's as determined as I am to get it. Unfortunately for her, she's not as smart as I am. I'll win out in the end."

Barret added more intently, "She's nervous, but she'll make her move sooner or later, so don't let her out of your sight."

"What about Jake Scully?" Blackie grumbled. "I ain't too anxious to come up against him."

"You don't have to worry about Scully. It should be obvious to you that if Lacey was going to cut him in on the claim, she would've done it already. No, she's going after it by herself."

Barret was momentarily, perversely amused as he added, "Under different circumstances, I might even be tempted to say Lacey Stewart's a woman after my own heart."

Sobering abruptly, he continued, "But right now I'm telling you both that whatever happens, one thing is certain. That claim is mine."

Chapter Twelve

"The Lord is my shepherd: I shall not want. He maketh me to lie down in green pastures. He leadeth me beside the still waters."

Lacey halted at that point in her reading. She glanced at Rosie and Jewel as they waited for her to continue, but she was suddenly unable to speak past the thickness in her throat.

The lessons had been going well. She had been stunned at both women's quick grasp of every advance in learning she had attempted. The full depth of their desire to learn was never more evident, however, than when they requested that she read to them from the Bible Reverend Sykes had given her. Their questions were quick and instinctive as they peered over her shoulders, following her finger as she pointed at every word.

Lacey swallowed again. Rosie had requested that she read this particular psalm. Rosie had remembered abstract portions of it from her childhood, portions that had remained with her through the years. Lacey had recognized the lines immediately when Rosie had quoted them, but it was more difficult for her to read the psalm than she had ever imagined it would be.

Because of Scully.

Because he was slipping away from her.

Lacey breathed deeply to stabilize her emotions. Two weeks had passed since her Bible was stolen...since Scully had kissed her and stirred her so deeply. She had wanted to talk to Scully about the moment. She had regretted telling him that she was glad he had kissed her, because she had realized belatedly that Scully was not.

She had recalled, just as belatedly, beautiful, red-haired Charlotte's easy manner with Scully as they had walked back into the Gold Nugget that night. There had been no tension between them. Charlotte obviously asked for no promises from Scully, and Scully appeared to prefer things that way. She had told herself in retrospect that she needed to accept Scully's apology for those brief moments she had spent in his arms. She had told herself that if he wanted it that way, she would accept his apology—but Scully didn't seem willing to give her the chance. He had forced a painful distance between them since that morning, which he began by skipping breakfast at the restaurant while she was working there, by not appearing until evening, when he spoke to her briefly, often with an excuse why they couldn't have supper together.

Her Bible was lost to her.

Her nightmares continued.

And she had lost her best friend.

"Lacey, are you all right?"

Lacey looked up into Rosie's querulous expression, then back down at the Bible in her hand. She replied past the lump in her throat, "I'm sorry. My mind must've drifted."

Aware that they were waiting, she continued softly and sincerely, *"He restoreth my soul."*

Scully walked solemnly up the street, his expression forbidding. It had been a long two weeks since he had last held Lacey in his arms, and he ached inside. He wasn't sure when it had happened, when his feelings had slipped past protectiveness and friendship. Yet he knew the distance he had put between them was not only necessary. It was urgent.

Urgent, because he did not want to make the mistake of telling Lacey he loved her.

Scully lengthened his stride as the storefront he sought came into view. He needed no one to tell him that more had to have been at stake than an old Bible in order for someone to secretly follow Lacey and him on their long, tedious journey into the wilderness. During the week past, he had discreetly talked to everyone who could've been on the street the day Lacey's Bible was stolen, but no one had noticed anything unusual. Then he had gone back to talk to Mary.

Scully remembered Mary's annoyance at her off-handed recollection of Blackie Oaks's visit to her front door. She had said, "His inquiry was a complete waste of time, and what irritated me most was the half smile on his face that made me think he was aware of it. All that talk about rushing right over to talk to me when he heard a room might be available in my house—then all that hogwash about how he and that other ruffian friend of his wanted to pay to eat at my table every night because they hadn't been eating well lately…as if I'd ever allow it!" She had shuddered. "That Blackie fella actually had the nerve to stick his foot in my doorway so I couldn't close it on him!"

With those comments under his belt, Scully had then talked to Harry Rice, who usually ate breakfast at the restaurant at that time of day. Harry had nodded and said, "I did see Blackie and Larry on the street when I left Sadie's that morning. I remember thinking they must've fallen out of bed to be up and out on the street so early, but then when they went into Barret Gould's office, I figured he must've sent for them."

Blackie Oaks *and* Larry Hayes...

Yes, there had to be more to the theft of the Bible than was obviously apparent.

Scully had strained to remember that last day when Charlie and he had talked. Strangely, what he remembered most was the way Charlie had smiled when they had reminisced about the time they had spent working together years earlier. In retrospect, however, it seemed they had passed the greatest portion of the time discussing how Scully had come into the unexpected ownership of the Gold Nugget. He remembered his surprise when Charlie mentioned his granddaughter, saying she was a gift in his old age, and that he treasured her more than he could ever treasure the gold strike he had prospected for all his life. He had said he'd left her behind at the cabin to take care of Careful, who had seemed to be ailing, but he'd bring her in to meet Scully the next time he was in town—which would probably be soon.

Scully wondered why he hadn't asked what would be bringing Charlie into town again so soon, especially when he knew Charlie spent as many hours as he could squeeze into the day prospecting for the gold that he always expected he'd find in the next shovelful of dirt to be turned over.

He now wished he had.

Scully halted outside Barret Gould's office, his expression grim. He pushed open the door and walked inside.

Scully fixed his gaze on Barret's neatly shaven face as Barret stood up behind his great mahogany desk. He noted the fellow's forced smile as Barret said, "Well, well…if it isn't Jake Scully. How may I help you?"

Silent, Scully remembered the day that impressive mahogany desk arrived in town. The outlandish scene Barret had made as he had directed the unloading of that prestigious piece of furniture from the delivery wagon had amused some onlookers, but it hadn't amused him. The true nature of the man had been revealed that day, and he hadn't liked when he had seen.

He still didn't.

Scully responded, "I can't rightly say if you can help me, but maybe you can answer a few questions that have been bothering me of late."

"Questions?" Barret's smile froze.

Scully pressed, "You know Lacey Stewart, of course."

Barret shrugged. "Yes, I do. She's a lovely young woman."

"You also know she's Charlie Pratt's granddaughter."

"I assume that's general knowledge in Weaver."

"Nobody ever did find out who killed Charlie."

"So?"

"Or why."

"What does that have to do with me?"

"I was wondering if you had any business with Charlie Pratt years back."

"Charlie? No, not that I recall. Why do you ask?"

"Charlie never did say why he came into town that last day."

"I should think you'd know better than anyone else in this town the answer to that question. Like all the other prospectors who frequent your establishment, Charlie was most likely hot, thirsty and in need of a break from prospecting. A visit to your saloon was a natural choice."

"Charlie wasn't like 'all the other prospectors.'"

"I didn't know the man well enough, so I can't comment on that."

In order to see the lawyer's reaction, Scully prevaricated, "There are some folks in Weaver who seem to remember Charlie paying a visit to your office when he was in town."

"They'd be mistaken."

Noting Barret's instinctively defensive posture, Scully added, "There's been more than a usual interest in Lacey's comings and goings lately."

"That's understandable, don't you think? She's quite a beauty."

"She's also had something very important stolen from her recently—something old Charlie gave her."

"So?"

"Aren't you curious about what was stolen?"

Barret shrugged again. "Not really. I can't imagine that old man would have left his granddaughter anything that could possibly be of interest to me."

"Really?"

Barret's posture grew rigid. "Are you accusing me of theft?"

Scully did not reply.

"You're insane. I don't have the slightest interest in Lacey Stewart's meager possessions."

Scully pinned him with his gaze. "Maybe. Maybe not."

"It's time for you to leave."

Scully paused, then added, "Charlie put Lacey in my care. I want you to know that I take that charge very seriously. Anybody who tries to harm her in any way will answer to me."

"You're wasting your time and mine. Please leave."

"I'll leave in my own time, Barret, but first I want to make something very clear. If you have any intentions toward Lacey Stewart, back off. Otherwise, you'll end up a sorry man."

"Is that a threat?"

"If the shoe fits…"

"Get out."

Scully allowed his gaze to linger for a few tense moments before he turned slowly toward the exit. He did not bother to look back as he pulled the door closed behind him and started back down the street.

He had seen what he had wanted to see.

Barret Gould had the look of a guilty man.

The office door closed behind Scully, and Barret felt a flush of pure fury.

The gall of the man, to approach a respectable citizen in his own quarters and accuse him of petty thievery when Scully, himself, was nothing more than a barkeep!

Barret took a shuddering breath and walked to the

window to watch Scully as he strode down the street. The man was a fool for warning him, but now that he had, it appeared Scully would have to be taken care of when everything came to a close. That's where Blackie and Larry would again earn their keep. A bullet in the man's back wouldn't cause either one of them much stress.

Or him, either.

Scully turned the corner of the street and Barret whispered into the silence, "You came here to give me warning, Scully, but you succeeded in doing only one thing. Fool. You've signed your own death warrant."

"You look like a man on a mission."

Scully turned at the sound of the familiar, throaty voice. He paused, his hand on the Gold Nugget's swinging door, and looked down into Charlotte's smile.

"Can't manage a smile for an old friend, Scully?" Charlotte chided him softly as she ran a dainty hand against the upward sweep of her blazing red hair. "I must be losing my touch."

Scully swept her with a glance. Charlotte was wearing a small straw hat and a simple green gown that emphasized her natural assets clearly. Scully smiled. Even in her street clothes, Charlotte dressed to be noticed, a fact that she never denied. He had always admired her candor.

Scully had the feeling he would be subjected to her candor in another way when Charlotte began, "I've been missing you more than ever, Scully. I was expecting I'd start seeing more of you when things started cooling down between you and Lacey."

"I'm Lacey's guardian, Charlotte. That's all I've ever been to her."

"Right, and like my mama told me, the moon is made of green cheese." Charlotte slanted him a half smile. "You used to be one of my biggest admirers, Scully."

Scully reluctantly returned her smile. "I still admire you, Charlotte."

"So, what's going on?"

"I've been busy."

Charlotte's smile faded. "Have you and Lacey had a falling-out?"

"No, I told you—"

"I know what you told me, and I know what I see." Charlotte moved a step closer. "You're a man in a million, Scully. I don't expect to give up on you easily."

"Give up on me?"

"Let me clarify…turn you over to another woman."

"Like I said, there's no 'other woman' involved. I've been busy."

"And like I said, I know what I see. Scully…" Charlotte's voice dropped a note softer as she said, "I've always been a woman who said what she thinks. As you know, I have no shortage of admirers, but I've been missing you—because you make me smile inside. It's a good thing to smile inside. I miss that, too."

"Charlotte…"

"Give what I'm saying a little thought…and remember that I'll be there for you."

"Charlotte…"

"I said, think about it." Charlotte suddenly laughed. "And don't look so serious."

Standing on tiptoe, Charlotte brushed Scully's mouth with hers and whispered with a wink, "There's more where that came from, darlin'." She walked off down the street with a practiced sway. Scully stared after her for an extended moment, then turned back to push his way through the swinging doors. He did not stop until he reached his office at the rear, then closed the door behind him.

Charlotte dismissed from his mind, Scully stood still in the silence, recalling the look on Barret's face when he left. Yes, Barret had the look of a guilty man...an *impatient*, guilty man.

If he was right, Barret would make things start happening soon.

Lacey stood, shaken, in the shadows of the mercantile doorway. Her new Bible in hand, Rosie and Jewel's paperwork under her arm, she had been making her way back to the boarding house when she had seen *them*.

Her breathing uneven, her throat tight, Lacey struggled against tears. She had seen the kiss Charlotte and Scully had exchanged. She had also seen the expression on Charlotte's face when she had turned to walk back down the street, and the way Scully's gaze had followed her. Their short conversation and that kiss had been laced with a history between the two of them that could not be denied.

Lacey could avoid the truth no longer. Scully was a man of the world. The kiss he had given her had been merely an expression of affection and an appreciation of her distress. By reading more into it, she had made him uncomfortable, and the former ease that had been between them had disappeared in an instant, never to be reclaimed.

Lacey forced up her chin and started toward the

boarding house. She was such a fool. In his mind, Scully was still her guardian and nothing more.

Lacey brushed away the tear that slipped down her cheek, then raised her chin higher. Another truth that she could deny no longer was that she loved Scully in a way that surpassed friendship. She could think of no greater joy than that of spending the rest of her life in his arms as his wife and the mother of his children. But he regarded *her* as a child.

That thought doused Lacey with sudden, cold reality. Scully thought of her as a child because she had been behaving like a child—dependent, needy, uncertain. Her dependency was a disservice to Scully, to the man who had cared for her for the greater portion of her life. He deserved to be set free of the responsibility that had been fostered upon him by her well-meaning grandfather. He needed to be freed to take steps toward settling his own future—a future held in abeyance because of her; a future that included a woman who would love him the way he was meant to be loved, and who would bring him back to a more stable way of life.

Sadly, that woman would not be she.

Still struggling for control of her emotions as she reached her boarding house door, Lacey was about to push it open when a slim, dark-haired cowpoke stepped unexpectedly into view.

Lacey gasped with a start, and the fellow said politely, "I'm sorry if I frightened you, ma'am, but we have a mutual friend, and I'd like to talk to you a moment if I can."

Lacey struggled to regain her composure as she responded, "A mutual friend?"

"Jewel Nichols. My name's Buddy Cross."

"Oh, yes, I remember." He had appeared with Jewel at the boarding house door that early morning after Riley struck Rosie. Lacey managed an uncertain smile. "You wanted to talk to me?"

"Yes, ma'am." Buddy continued soberly, "I wanted to make sure you knew how much the lessons you're giving Jewel and Rosie mean to them."

Lacey was momentarily startled. "You know about the lessons?"

Smiling for the first time, Buddy said shyly, "Yes, ma'am. Jewel doesn't keep too much a secret from me." His smile faded as he continued earnestly, "But Jewel does hide her feelings from most folks. She's not like Rosie, who wears the way she feels out in the open, so I figured it was important to let you know, in case she didn't, how much the lessons mean to Jewel, too."

"I—I'm glad to hear that, Buddy."

"I wanted to make sure you knew that Rosie and Jewel both consider you a friend."

"I *am* their friend."

"Ma'am…" Buddy hesitated as he searched for the right words. He continued, "I needed to tell you that being Jewel's friend makes you my friend, and you can call on me if there's anything I can ever do for you."

"Thank you, Buddy."

"No, I'm the one who's thanking you, ma'am. You're the only person besides me who's ever given a thought to making Jewel's life better, and I appreciate that… a lot."

Lacey was momentarily unable to reply.

His face flushing, the slender cowhand continued, "You see, I'm Jewel's friend, but I also hope to make her my missus someday."

His words causing a lump to tighten in her throat, Lacey extended her hand and said, with true warmth, "Buddy Cross, I'm so pleased to meet you."

Buddy's heartfelt declaration lingered in Lacey's mind as Buddy tipped his hat with a polite goodbye and walked back to the horse he had tethered nearby.

Pushing open the door to her room with a determined hand moments later, Lacey felt the weight of her former decision returning. It was time to take adult steps to correct the situation between Scully and her…to relieve him of the responsibility that was weighing him down.

Her decision steadfast, she knew she could do that in only one way.

"Lacey's upset." Rosie shook her head as she and Jewel walked down Main Street. They had finished their lesson a short time earlier, had waited the required minutes after Lacey left the church before leaving behind her so no one would suspect that they had been working together. Silent since Lacey closed the church door behind her, Rosie had then stated the obvious as a way of breaking the silence. She continued with a glance at her friend, "She's trying to hide it, but Lacey's miserable."

"You don't need to be a mind reader to see that."

"We need to help her, Jewel."

Jewel's quick glance was sharp. "It's none of our business, Rosie."

"Like it was none of Lacey's business that we couldn't read or write, you mean?"

"Don't start that again. It's not the same thing."

"Isn't it?"

"Rosie…" Jewel stopped dead in her tracks and

turned to face her friend, "You can't fix everybody's life, especially when you can't even fix your own."

Sobering, Rosie replied, "You're right. I couldn't fix my own life, but Riley's been out of it for more than two weeks now. He won't be coming back this time, all because a couple of friends helped me out. I'm also learning to read and write because another friend is taking the time to teach me, so I figure I owe something in return."

"Rosie..."

"I know having her Bible stolen was hard for Lacey. I still can't imagine why anyone would take it, but I don't think that's all that's bothering her. Maybe I should tell Scully and he can—"

"No!"

Rosie's pale eyes narrowed. "Why?"

Jewel shook her head.

She repeated, "Why?"

"Haven't you noticed that Scully and Lacey haven't been seen around together very much lately...that Scully's been spending more time at the Nugget than before...that Charlotte's been sashaying around him again?"

"Yes, but—"

Jewel looked at her pointedly.

"Oh, no, that can't be it!"

"Maybe not, but it's obvious that Lacey and Scully have had some kind of a falling-out. The only thing I don't know is what Lacey's thinking."

Her eyes filling with sudden tears, Rosie whispered, "She must feel so alone. What can we do to help her?"

No response.

"Jewel?"

Jewel sighed. "We can't change Scully's preference for redheads, if that's the problem. I suppose we can only watch and wait, and be there if Lacey needs us."

Rosie nodded. She supposed Jewel was right. What other strategy could two women employ to help a friend when their own lives were too far from perfect to enable them to give advice?

Yes, they'd just have to watch and wait.

Yes, she could relieve Scully of the responsibility he felt for her in only one way.

The dawn sky was still streaked with night as Lacey, dressed in riding clothes, made her way toward the livery stable with that thought foremost in mind.

Lacey reviewed her decision as she neared the dimly lit stable. As painful as it was, the message from Scully the previous day, saying he'd again be unable to meet her for supper, had been a clear confirmation of the conclusion she had forced herself to face. She had taken a job at the restaurant and attempted to face her fears when she went to the site of her grandfather's cabin to see his grave, but she had continued to lean on Scully by refusing to face those fears. She needed to eliminate her nightmares forever by forcing herself to remember the lost details of the night her grandfather was killed.

She needed to do that for herself; but mostly, she needed to do that for Scully—to set him free.

It was the least she could do.

Because she loved him.

Resolved, she had taken immediate steps toward that goal. She had made arrangements with Sadie to have Millie replace her at the restaurant until she returned. She had prepared Rosie and Jewel's lessons for a few days and had delivered them to their door. She had bought the necessary supplies at the mercantile store and had arranged to have them packed on the mount that would be ready for her when she reached the livery stable that morning. She would be on her way within minutes—a step she hadn't had the courage to take until now.

Her heart pounding as she entered the stable, Lacey met Barney Pettit's concerned glance. She returned it with a forced smile at the livery stable proprietor as he said, "You're sure you want to do this, ma'am? Riding out alone in this country is dangerous for a young woman like you."

"I won't be alone...not really." She patted the new Bible Reverend Sykes had given her before slipping it into her saddle bag. Touched by the old man's concern, she continued, "Besides, it's no more dangerous now than it was for an eight-year-old girl who made it to Weaver alone ten years ago. I did it then without supplies, and by walking a good part of the way. Surely I can do it now, as prepared as I am, and with a good, strong horse under me."

"I don't know..."

"Don't worry, Barney. I traveled this country with my grandfather when he was prospecting, remember? I know it quite well." Aware that her statement was a stretch of the truth, Lacey patted Barney's arm reassuringly. "I'll be fine."

A sudden braying from the corral in the rear turned Lacey in its direction. "And you don't have to worry about my getting lost, since I'm taking Careful with me. He knows these trails better than most people in these parts do. He'll get me back."

"Well, he's as ready to go as he'll ever be."

Like her.

Mounted within minutes, Lacey turned her horse out onto the street with Careful trotting behind.

"Lacey Stewart isn't working in the restaurant this morning, and do you know why?" Barret glared at his sleep-drugged hirelings as he harangued, "Because she left town at dawn...while you both were sleeping!"

Barret was apoplectic as he faced the two men in the cabin they shared at the edge of town. He had arrived at their quarters moments earlier as the morning sun began rising, and had found both Larry and Blackie asleep in unclean bunks unfit for man or beast. Infuriated almost as much by being subjected to the rank odor of the cabin as he was by their ineptitude, he said, "I told you she'd make her move soon. I told you to watch her...not to let her out of your sight!"

"You didn't say nothing about watching her all night long."

"Do I have to spell everything out for you? Anyone with half a brain—anyone who was doing his job and watching her closely enough—would've realized what she was planning and would have been prepared."

Barret continued, "You know as well as I do where Lacey's headed. I want you to catch up with her and follow her covertly. That shouldn't be hard for you to do. She'll lead you right to the strike."

"What if she don't?"

Turning on Larry with sudden venom, Barret said, "Then do what you must to *make* her tell you where the strike is located. I'm tired of waiting."

"That's easy for you to say, but if Scully—"

"She rode out *alone,* you fool, just as I said she would! You'll never have a better chance."

"Alone…" Blackie exchanged a glance with his partner. "Where's Scully?"

"Who cares? Scully obviously doesn't even know she left. He hasn't been meeting her for breakfast lately, and if the rumors around town are correct, he won't miss her until suppertime tonight. That should give you enough time to accomplish what you need to do."

"But when Scully finds out—"

"He's going to have to be taken care of eventually anyway." Barret's expression hardened. "You might even be able to kill two birds with one stone if you're smart enough."

"Two birds with one stone." Blackie grinned unexpectedly. "That sounds fine to me."

But Barret did not smile in return. Instead, he warned, "I'm telling you now—I expect results. I don't expect to have waited ten years in vain."

"We'll find that strike for you, boss."

"Yeah, we'll make her talk. You can bet on it."

Barret paused for a last, lingering stare at the two men before he turned toward the door.

That sounded right to him. He *would* bet on it, too. What they did not know was, at stake would be their lives.

"When did she leave, Barney?"

Tension twisted tight inside Scully as he stood in the livery stable awaiting Barney Pettit's response. He still couldn't believe it. He had gone to the restaurant at midmorning expecting to get a glimpse of Lacey while she worked. He had wanted to make sure she was all right, as he had done countless times during the past two weeks without her knowledge. Startled this time to find Millie replacing her, he had spoken to Sadie and had then gone directly to the boarding house, hoping to find Lacey there.

Trepidation had expanded inside him as he tried to convince himself that Lacey wouldn't be foolish enough to venture out into the rough, dangerous country surrounding Weaver alone, that she was too smart for that. One look at Mary when she opened the boarding house door, however, and he knew he had only been fooling himself.

"She left at dawn." Replying to his question, Barney eyed Scully's stiff expression with a frown. "I figured it was kinda strange that Lacey would be going out to visit her grandfather's grave alone, being's you was looking after her and all, but she said she'd be fine because she knew her way around these parts."

Scully glanced toward the rear of the stable. Anticipating his question, Barney said, "Yeah, she took Careful with her. She said she didn't have to worry about getting lost as long as that old burro was along."

Dreading Barney's response, Scully questioned tightly, "Did you see anybody else leave town after she did…anybody you didn't expect to see?"

"Funny you should ask." Barney shook his head. "I was tending to one of the mounts a fella left for me at the hitching post out front when Larry Hayes went running into the blacksmith's shop next door a little while after Lacey left. Noah told me Larry was in such a rush that he didn't even wait for Noah to reshoe his horse before riding off like a bat out of you-know-where, heading for parts unknown."

Scully went cold. He had no doubt where that degenerate had been heading. He instructed tensely, "Get my horse ready for the trail, Barney. I'll be right back to pick him up."

Cold fear expanded inside Scully as he pushed open the door to his room minutes later and changed into his riding clothes.

You'll never be free of those nightmares until you face them down, Lacey, and there's only one way to do it.

Scully shuddered as his words returned to taunt him. Lacey had gone back to old Charlie's cabin because of him. Because of his feelings for her and emotions he was unable to control, he had abandoned her to her fears and left her with no recourse but to meet them alone.

He should've known. He should've realized what he was forcing her to do.

His hands shaking as myriad images flashed across his mind, Scully drew open his dresser drawer. He hadn't warned Lacey of his suspicions about Barret because he hadn't wanted to frighten her. She had no idea of the possible danger she faced. She was vulnerable and alone, and hours ahead of him on the trail.

Scully reached for the gun belt in his drawer, fear for the woman he loved shaking him to the core. Lacey was at the mercy of men who had no mercy at all, yet he could not help her unless he could reach her in time.

His need profound, Scully felt the desperate stirring of a part of him that he had thought long dismissed. He sank slowly to his knees and raised his eyes toward the God so familiar to him in his youth, the supreme power with whom he had become estranged. His throat tight, he reminded himself that Lacey was unlike him, that this same God was the source of her strength, that she was devoted to His Son's teachings and had charted the course of her life accordingly. He began earnestly, "I've strayed from you, dear Jesus. I've done my share of sinning. I've done little to deserve your love or intercession, but I'm not asking for your help for myself. I'm asking for you to help Lacey. She's familiar to you, I know, and far more worthy of your protection than I ever was. I'm asking you…pleading for you to find a way to keep her safe from whatever bad intentions are stalking her until I can reach her. I'm asking you to keep watch over her and hold all evil at bay until I stand at her side. I'll take it from there, Lord. I'll fulfill the promise I made to Lacey's grandfather at any price that's asked of me. That's my promise to you, Lord Jesus, and it's a promise I will not break."

Pausing for a stabilizing breath, his eyes brimming with the power of his plea, Scully added hoarsely, "I beg you to answer this prayer, my dear Lord Jesus, not for my sake, but for Lacey, who is so worthy of your love."

Shaken by his heartfelt appeal, Scully stood up and strapped his gun belt around his hips. He would honor his promise to Charlie, and he would fulfill the sacred promise he had just made. He would do it, at any price.

The day had turned hot and bright. Lacey glanced at the position of the sun in the cloudless sky as she followed the dusty trail at a steady pace. Her expression sober, she ignored the perspiration trailing down her cheek from underneath the damp band of her hat. She scrutinized her mount, then looked back at Careful as he trotted behind. Like her, both animals were thirsty and tired, but they'd reach her grandfather's gravesite soon.

Lacey paused at that thought as her mount continued dutifully forward. Strangely, the same terrain that had seemed so foreign to her previously had now become familiar. She took each turn in the trail instinctively, with certainty in her direction. She was able to calculate the time it would take for her to reach her grandfather's cabin easily when she had been formerly at a loss. She sensed this change in her had no relationship to her previous journey with Scully. Instead, it was as if a part of her was gradually returning to life—a part that had been asleep, or had been paralyzed by the terror of a fateful night.

More certain than ever before of the necessity of the journey she had undertaken, Lacey glanced at the emptiness surrounding her as her thirsty mount increased his pace. The emptiness stirred memories... painful memories of a long, exhausting walk while her head had throbbed incessantly and her weakened legs had seemed ready to fail her. She recalled her fading consciousness and the echo of her grandfather's gruff, beloved voice that had urged her on. She remembered the name of the man he had sent her to seek with his dying breath.

The name rebounded again inside her.

Jake Scully.

It seemed ironic that years earlier she had walked this same trail hoping to find Scully, while she was now making this journey hoping to find the courage to leave him.

That thought raised the mist of tears to Lacey's eyes as the remains of the cabin came into view. Somehow unwilling to immediately face the blackened timbers and the small mounded spot a short distance from it, she headed to the stream to water her animals. Dismounting, she released Careful so he might drink more easily. She then kneeled at the stream's edge to cup the water in her palms and splash it against her face.

Refreshed and resolute, she stood up and looked back at the cabin debris. She had come to confront her past and to face her future. She would not leave until she met them both.

Chapter Thirteen

The sun dipped slowly toward the horizon with colors expanding brilliantly against the darkening sky. Immune to the glorious display, Lacey struggled to subdue the trembling that had begun inside her with the advent of twilight shadows.

Feeling an overwhelming sense of dread, she looked at the charred remains of her childhood and gathered her strength as she determinedly kneeled to set up her bedroll. She glanced back at the mound marked with a simple wooden cross. The lonesome sight revealed none of the goodness of the old man who had lived and worked nearby. It reflected nothing of the generous nature and loving qualities that compounded the tragedy of his death, and Lacey was suddenly alone—more alone than she wished to be.

Her skin was burning hot, and choking smoke filled her lungs.

She was afraid, but Grandpa held her hand tightly as he dragged her from the flames.

Disoriented, she looked up at Grandpa. Her head

hurt. She wasn't sure what had happened, why the cabin was burning, why Grandpa was looking at her so strangely.

She gasped as Grandpa fell to the ground clutching his chest, and she saw the bloody wound there.

Grandpa!

She was trembling so hard that she could hardly talk when Grandpa clutched her hand and started to speak. She—

A playful tug on her hair snapped Lacey back to the present with a gasp. Her heart pounding, she looked up into Careful's expectant expression, then raised a shaky hand to stroke his graying muzzle. With supreme strength of will, she shook off the images that had made determined inroads into her consciousness and stood up. She was an adult now, not a child. She could not afford to surrender to her fears.

Lacey surveyed her camp, then turned her attention back to the patient burro, still feeling truly alone.

"The boss ain't going to like this."

Blackie's mumbled words ended the silence that had prevailed between Larry and him as he watched Lacey's camp through his spyglass. It hadn't taken them long to find Lacey on the trail, but that's where the problems had begun.

Blackie adjusted his spyglass and studied the scene more carefully. Something was wrong. Lacey Stewart had made her way directly to her grandfather's old cabin site as expected, but that's where the expected had ended. In the time since, she had done nothing but water her animals and walk around the camp she had set up. She had shown no interest in the surrounding terrain, had made no attempt to forage out into the wilderness for old trails or possible signs her grandfather might have left indicating the direction of his strike. In fact, she had shown no interest at all in anything but the old man's mounded grave. What was she up to?

"What do you mean the boss ain't going to like this? Give me that glass!"

"Hey!" Protesting when Larry snatched the spyglass out of his hand to survey the scene for himself, Blackie added, "You ain't going to see nothing more than I did, no matter how hard you try, 'cause there ain't nothing to see."

A low growl his only comment, Larry watched the camp a few moments longer, before lowering the spyglass and replying, "I'm not going through this again, you know—watching and waiting who knows how long for that woman to make a move. I'm tired of the boss making out like I'm dumb, and I'm tired of taking his guff. I *ain't* dumb, and I ain't letting no woman lead me around in circles. I'm telling you now, Lacey Stewart's going to point out where that strike is located, and I ain't going to take no for an answer."

"I know what you mean." Blackie studied his cohort's flushed expression. "But you know what'll happen then. Scully will be on us faster than chain lightning."

"You heard what the boss said about him."

"Yeah, but I'm thinking taking care of Scully will be easier said than done."

"The boss don't care about what you think! All he wants is for us to come back with a map of that strike, and that's what's going to happen."

"But—"

"He wants what he wants, and I'm going to make sure he gets it."

Blackie did not immediately respond to Larry's unexpected turnabout in attitude. He supposed Larry was thinking differently now because the boss had been so mad that they'd let Lacey get a head start on them, and because, like Larry said, the boss was crazy when he was mad. The truth was, like Larry, he didn't fancy the thought of the boss getting any madder at them than he already was.

Blackie said belatedly, "We told the boss we'd get him what he wanted, one way or another."

Larry stared at Blackie malevolently, then demanded, "Say it again, Blackie…like you mean it, or I'll take care of both of them by myself, if I have to."

"Don't worry about that." Embarrassed to be reprimanded by his cohort, Blackie repeated with conviction, "We'll get the boss what he wants together." He hesitated, then questioned, "How do you think we should do it?"

"It ain't going to be as easy as the boss said it would be, that's for sure. I don't fancy waiting for that Stewart gal to make her move. If she don't show me something soon, I'm going to move first."

"What are you saying?"

"You'll see."

"Larry…"

"I told you, you'll see!"

Blackie took a backward step, then turned toward his horse. As far as he was concerned, Larry was beginning to act as crazy as the boss he was always complaining about.

And he wasn't sure he liked it.

* * *

Lacey forced herself to finish her meager supper as the wilderness shadows darkened into night. Her hands trembling, she dropped her canteen, then stood abruptly still in an effort to bring her emotions under control. She despised her realization that her courage had seemed to dissipate along with the waning light. She had striven to keep foremost in her mind the reasons she had made her expedition into the wilderness and the memories she hoped to revive. In that effort, she had stood at her grandfather's graveside and had talked to the dear old man buried there, but while tears had welled, the blank spots in her memory had prevailed. She had missed the solace of holding her old, worn Bible and knowing her grandfather's gnarled hands had turned those same pages so many years ago. But most of all, she had longed for Scully's presence beside her, and the loving warmth of looking up into sober gray eyes that seemed able to read her heart.

Lacey blinked back the persistent tears, knowing the worst was yet to come. She would not wait for sleep knowing that Scully was nearby. She would not close her eyes knowing he cared. She would not hear the echo of his whispered reassurances or feel his comforting touch. She had lost those moments forever.

Lacey glanced back toward her horse at the sound of his nervous whinny to see that Careful had disappeared into the shadows. She heard him bray abruptly, and she frowned. She had not bothered to tether the faithful burro, but neither had she expected that he would wander from her sight in a darkness that held possible danger for him.

Myriad thoughts filled her mind when Careful

brayed again. Lacey started spontaneously toward the sound. Her mount was moving restlessly at his tether when she paused at the edge of the campfire's light and called out, "Careful...come here, old fella. Come on."

Silence.

Lacey swallowed against a gradually expanding fear. She remembered the ancient six-shooter her grandpa had kept handy for varmints that foraged in the night. She had not thought to carry a similar reassurance, and she repeated tentatively, "Careful...?"

When no response was forthcoming, she walked tentatively into the shadows, only to stumble and fall to her knees over an unexpected obstacle on the path. She reached out and gasped when she touched a male figure lying on the ground. The sound choked in her throat when a shaft of moonlight illuminated the face of a man whose forehead was streaked with blood.

It was Buddy Cross!

The sound of footsteps in the darkness behind her brought Lacey to her feet with a jolt of terror. Somehow mesmerized, she watched as dark shadows materialized into hulking, male forms moving rapidly toward her....

Grandpa lay motionless on the ground as their cabin collapsed into a flaming heap behind them.

He wasn't talking. He wasn't breathing.

She stood up, staring transfixed with horror as the flickering shadows came to life in the silhouettes of two men.

She fled blindly as the men started toward her at a run. Slipping and falling, she got up to run again as the heavy footsteps drew closer.

They were directly behind her when a rough hand grabbed her by the hair and jerked her backward. She glimpsed the faces of the men then—terrifying, vicious faces—the second before a brief, shattering burst of pain brought darkness closing down around her....

Lacey returned to the present with a start as the advancing shadows neared. Terror shot up her spine when the faces of the men became visible at last.

It was they, the same men, with the same, deadly intent in their eyes!

Somehow unwilling to move, Lacey demanded, "Who are you? What do you want?"

"You know what we want!" The men halted a few feet away. The smaller of the two glared as he said, "We want the same thing we wanted all them years ago, and you're the only one who knows where it is."

"I don't know what you're talking about!" Lacey's heart pounded as she said, "All I know is that you killed my grandfather and tried to kill me. And now you killed Buddy."

"We spotted him out there watching your camp. We couldn't take any chances with what he was doing there, so you can thank him for what's happening now, not us." The taller fellow continued hotly, "Just like your grandpa pulled a switch on us when we tried to find out where his strike was all them years ago. He sneaked up on us with a gun when we was watching the cabin. He made us shoot him."

"No!"

"We didn't have no choice. We threw his body into the cabin and set it on fire so's it would look like an accident. We didn't know there was anybody else in there, and we figured we'd find his strike sooner or later without him."

"What strike?"

"Don't act like you don't know what we're talking about."

"You're crazy...both of you! My grandfather never struck it rich. You killed him for nothing."

"No, you're the crazy one if you think we're going to believe you came all the way back here from that fancy school in New York just to see your grandfather's grave."

The smaller of the two men advanced menacingly closer as he said, "All the trouble can stop here if you want it to, you know. Just tell us where your grandpa made his strike, and we'll let you live."

Lacey glanced down at Buddy's still body, then replied with shaken conviction, "No, you won't, but you won't get rich by killing me, either, because my grandpa never made a strike."

"Yes, he did."

"He didn't."

"Liar!" The smaller of the two men raised his fist threateningly. "I'll teach you to—"

"Don't try it!" Scully's deep, familiar voice sounded from the shadows, stunning the scene into motionlessness as he stepped forward into view with his gun drawn.

Incredulous at the sight of him, Lacey watched as Scully ordered, "Drop your guns, both of you."

"No." The smaller of the two men almost grinned. "You ain't got the guts to shoot us head-on, Scully. You're just a cardsharp...a gambler. There ain't nothing in your veins but—"

A sudden blaze of gunfire shattered the silence of the clearing as the taller of the two men snapped his gun from his holster and fired—as Scully and the second man fired simultaneously, and the campsite was suddenly filled with gunshots that left only Lacey standing.

Stunned, Lacey was momentarily unable to react. She gasped with horror as the gun smoke cleared and she saw Scully lying on the ground, a bloody wound on his chest.

She rushed to his side, a voice inside her mind screaming, no, not again!

She could not lose Scully for the same, senseless reason that she had lost her grandfather.

Determined that she would not, Lacey untied her neckerchief and pressed it tight to his wound with trembling hands, hoping to stanch the flow of blood. She pleaded, "Talk to me, Scully. Please talk to me."

Panic made inroads into Lacey's mind when Scully's eyes remained closed. His chest moved shallowly underneath her palm and she leaned closer to rasp, "Don't leave me, Scully. I need to know you'll be all right. Please tell me you'll be all right."

Buddy staggered into the circle of the fire's light behind her. He brushed away the blood still streaming from his head wound as he checked the two lifeless men briefly, then came to crouch at her side.

Hardly aware of Buddy's presence, Lacey whispered again, "Please, Scully…open your eyes."

Scully heard her voice. He felt her touch. A teardrop fell on his cheek, and he realized Lacey was crying.

He struggled against the heavy weight of his eyelids. It hurt to move—to breathe—but Lacey was calling him.

His eyes opening into narrow slits, Scully saw her. She was beautiful, even in tears. He wanted to tell her that. He wanted to say he had never known any woman more beautiful than she, but he needed to tell her something more important, to warn her."

"Talk to me, Scully."

Scully struggled to speak. He needed to tell her it wasn't all over yet. She was still in danger.

"You're a part of me, Scully. If you die, a part of me will die, too."

No, he didn't want that! He wanted to protect her... keep her safe.

Buddy's face appeared in Scully's line of vision, and the panic inside Scully lessened. Buddy was a good man. He'd do his best to protect Lacey for the present, but Buddy didn't know Barret was the man behind her grandfather's death, either.

"Scully, please..."

Lacey was pleading with him to talk to her, but his stiff lips were unable to form a response. He tried harder, but his strength was fading. He wouldn't last much longer.

He managed to say, "Lacey..."

Scully heard Lacey's intake of breath as he spoke her name. He felt the responsive tightening of her hand on his as she whispered, "We'll get you back to Weaver, Scully. You're going to be all right, you'll see."

He had to tell her about Barret first. She wouldn't be safe there unless she knew.

But consciousness was fading; Lacey's tears were still falling; the words were going unspoken.

And as the silent darkness closed in around him, Scully realized he had not even said he loved her.

Chapter Fourteen

The undertaker's wagon rolled almost ceremoniously slowly down Weaver's main street as it returned from the site of Charlie Pratt's burned-out cabin. The sky had turned suddenly as gray as the town's mood—as dark as Barret's disposition.

He glanced down the street at the many townsfolk who stood watching in their doorways. The unexpectedly violent turn of events at Charlie's cabin had elevated Lacey's story to the point of folklore in Weaver. He supposed it was to be expected in a town with so little to amuse it. After all, a child of eight had survived an attack from unknowns that had left her grandfather dead and their cabin burned. She had trekked through the wilderness to arrive in town wounded and dragging a limping burro behind her. She had gone to the saloon where her grandfather had sent her to be raised by a local barkeep, had been sent away to finishing school and had returned ten years later beautiful and cultured, only to be attacked again by the same men who had killed her grandfather.

And in the face of all odds, she had survived a second time.

Incredible.

And infuriating!

The wagon drew to a halt in front of the undertaker's parlor as Barret watched coldly. An unmarked hole in the ground was more well-deserved than the spot on Boot Hill that had already been marked for the burial. He had displayed the proper amount of shock at what had happened in order to satisfy the town, but he was yet incapable of feigning any other emotion.

The truth was, the way things now stood, he would be glad when the last shovelful of dirt covered the graves. As far as he was concerned—despite what anyone in Weaver might expect considering his former association with the deceased—the matter was cut and dried.

Goodbye, Blackie.

Goodbye, Larry.

And most definitely—good riddance.

It was time for him to take over.

He was hot, and the pain was deadening. Spiraling images filled Scully's mind. He saw Blackie's hand flash to his gun. He felt the bullets strike him as he returned fire.

Lacey's face materialized before him and he caught his breath. He had to tell her Barret was behind it all. She didn't know.

He called out, shouting Barret's name, but the words emerged cruelly distorted.

"Lacey..."

He said her name, but the sound was indiscernible to his own ears.

He could not protect her.

Consciousness again began fading and Scully mumbled the name of the only One to whom he could turn.

He whispered, "Jesus…"

"I don't know if he'll make it."

Lacey stood rigidly still outside Scully's bedroom doorway as sunset trailed into twilight on the street beyond. A burst of laughter resounded from the saloon below, the levity in sharp contrast with the dire circumstances in Scully's upstairs room.

Lacey stared at the elderly doctor's sober countenance. She told herself she hadn't heard him correctly. Scully had been gravely wounded in the gunfight that had brought about final justice for her grandfather's death. She remembered the moment when Buddy walked unsteadily into the circle of the fire's light. His head was still bleeding as he checked the two lifeless men lying a few feet away, then came to crouch at her side and whisper, "I'm sorry I let those two sneak up on me, ma'am. Jewel figured out where you were heading after you left the lessons for her and Rosie. She asked me to follow you and watch out for you, but I didn't see those two others until it was too late."

Buddy, sent by Jewel to watch over her. She knew if it hadn't been for him and the travois he had fashioned from two blackened cabin beams and the blankets from her bedroll, Scully would not have survived the long, grueling journey back to Weaver.

Her fears had heightened as Scully's fever rose, but she had truly believed the worst of it was over when he was carried through his bedroom doorway at last and Doc Mayberry walked into the room.

Yet Doc Mayberry's expression was now grave as he said, "I'm sorry, Lacey. It just doesn't look good. Scully lost a lot of blood, he's having trouble breathing and his temperature is soaring."

Hysteria nudged at Lacey's mind as she replied, "Are you telling me he's going to die?"

"My dear..." Doc Mayberry took her hands gently in his. "I know how much this man means to you. He's the rock that has sustained you through difficult years, and he was willing to risk his life for you."

Lacey replied, "I just need to know how I can help him now that he needs me."

"You're doing all you can, Lacey."

"But it's not enough! You said it's not enough."

"We've both done all we can for him. I'll continue to care for him, of course, but the rest is out of my hands. All you can do for him is to make sure he gets the medicine I left for him every hour. Otherwise..." He shook his head, "I'm very sorry, dear."

Silent as Doc Mayberry walked down the staircase toward the saloon floor, Lacey turned abruptly and walked back into Scully's room.

Out of his hands.

The phrase Doc Mayberry had spoken reverberated in Lacey's mind as she looked down into Scully's tormented expression. His eyes were closed, but despite his weakness, he hadn't been still for a moment. He continued to writhe in the throes of an inner tribulation she did not understand. He called out sharply in his delirium, his voice sometimes raised to a shout, but his words were unclear. She had strained to understand him in the hope of offering him reassurance that would allay his torment, but she had failed.

Lacey brushed away the tears that slipped down her cheeks, despising their weakness. She had no time for tears. Doc Mayberry had said it clearly. He had done all he could for Scully. The rest was out of his hands.

Lacey briefly closed her eyes. She knew in whose hands Scully's life now rested. She had always known, and she had prayed. Now looking down at Scully's pale, fevered countenance, Doc Mayberry's dire words rang again in her mind.

Her heart full, Lacey kneeled beside Scully's bed. She closed her eyes and clasped her hands tightly together as she whispered, "Dear Heavenly Father, I beg You to shed Your healing power down on Scully now. You are his only hope. You know him well. He made his own way in a difficult world, and in doing so, he strayed from Your word at times, but his heart is good and his spirit generous. He risked his safety for me, and he now teeters between life and death. I can't understand why he would so easily trade off his own safety for mine, except that he can't accept that his word, once given, should ever be rescinded.

"My dear Father, since returning to Weaver, I have come to comprehend the true significance of Samuel's words when he said, *'For the Lord seeth not as man seeth—for man looketh on the outward appearance, but the Lord looketh on the heart.'* Those words have offered me understanding and consolation, and I pray that You will see in Scully not the man he has occasionally been, but the man of great potential that he is. My eyes and my heart see that man clearly. My faith is full and strong that his life will one day come to reflect Your Son's teachings in a way that will be apparent to all. I believe that in Your goodness, You watch over us all, and that Scully was 'the rod and staff that comforted me,' because You deigned it to be so.

"Heavenly Father, I now kneel at Scully's bedside in the hope of returning just a portion of all You have given me through Scully with Your blessings. I beg that You hear my prayer when I beseech Your aid for Scully, and ask that in Your benevolence You will look with favor on my plea and make Scully well and strong again. I ask this fervently, in the name of Your Son, the Lord Jesus Christ. Amen."

Lacey wiped the dampness from her cheeks as she drew herself slowly to her feet. Scully's restless contortions continued, and the ache inside her deepened.

Barret paused as he picked up his suitcoat from the chair. He looked out his bedroom window, anxious anticipation fluttering inside him as twilight began fading into night. He slipped on his suitcoat and turned to his dresser. He picked up the derringer lying there and slipped it into his breast pocket with a hard smile. He had waited ten years for the moment fast approaching.

Barret adjusted his collar and stepped back to scrutinize his appearance. His performance when he visited Mary McInnes at her boarding house that afternoon had been touched with genius. He had been so clearly affected when he admitted regretting that he hadn't been particularly friendly with Scully in the past. Properly contrite, he had then said he admired Scully for the sacrifice he had made for Lacey's safety, that he was pained at the thought of his former attitude toward him, but even more distressed that the men he had innocently employed for so many years had murdered Charlie Pratt.

He had said he wanted to make amends by offering both Scully and Lacey his support.

It amused him to recall how taken the old woman had been with his sincerity. She had actually asked him into her parlor for tea. During the course of the following half hour, he had learned all he needed to know about the events that had taken place at the campsite. Mary had told him that Lacey was grateful it was finally over and the men who had killed her grandfather had paid for their crime at last. She claimed that Scully had ridden out after Lacey simply because he had feared for her safety in the wilderness—an act that had proved prophetic in the eyes of the town.

Regarding Scully's care, she said that Lacey hadn't left Scully's bedside since they had returned to town, but however conscientious her care, Scully was failing. She said she had delivered Lacey a tray each mealtime, only to take the previous tray back untouched; that she had begged Lacey to rest, but Lacey had ignored her pleas. She said she feared for Lacey's health and had made the decision that she would go to the sickroom that evening when her work was done at the boarding house, and would insist that Lacey return to her room for a little while, if only to refresh herself. She had said she would not allow Lacey to refuse this time.

When looking at the old woman's determined expression, he had been certain she would not...and the plan he now intended to carry through had been born.

Dear Lacey, sweet Lacey, so concerned about her guardian's welfare—*and so determined to keep the secret of her grandfather's strike to herself.*

He had waited too long. He would get the information he wanted from her tonight, without delay.

* * *

The sound of Scully's labored breathing filled the otherwise silent bedroom. Sitting on an upholstered chair beside the bed, Lacey watched the rise and fall of his chest, her gaze lingering on the bloodstained bandage wrapped across it. The stain was dry. The wound had stopped bleeding. She supposed that was a good sign, but she wanted so much more. She wanted to feel the fever leave his body and see his constant tossing become a restful sleep. She wanted to see him well and strong again. She prayed the Lord would answer her prayers and she—

Lacey stood up at the sound of a knock on the door. She managed a smile for Mary when she entered the room. Mary looked at Scully, then looked back at Lacey with a sad shake of her head.

Without spoken comment on Scully's condition, Mary addressed Lacey, saying in a motherly tone, "You look exhausted, dear." She added, "You'll notice I didn't bring you a tray this evening."

"That's fine, Mary. I'm really not hungry."

"I know you aren't, but that isn't the reason I've come empty-handed. You haven't left Scully's side since he was put into that bed. You've refused everyone's help, including Helen's and mine, but I won't let you refuse me any longer, dear. I know Scully. He wouldn't want you to wear yourself out the way you have been."

"I can't leave him, Mary."

"He'll be angry when his fever breaks and he sees you looking totally spent."

Lacey did not reply.

"I want you to go back to the boarding house—"

"No."

"Just for a little while, dear. I've left a tray for you on the kitchen table, and I want you to make yourself eat, if only to keep up your strength."

"No, Mary, I—"

"Listen to me, please, dear. Scully will be angry with me if I failed to look out for you while he was ill. I have great affection for the fellow, you know, and I certainly wouldn't want that to happen."

"I'm sorry. I'll explain it all to him when he recovers."

"You don't look well," Mary continued with determined bluntness. "You're pale, and your appearance is disheveled. You don't want Scully to see you that way when he wakes up."

"He won't care."

"But he will—for your sake! Please, dear, go back to the boarding house. Take an hour for yourself so you may return refreshed and renewed. That's what Scully would want."

"No, I—"

"You owe it to him, Lacey, to be your best when he opens his eyes."

Lacey looked into Mary's sweet countenance. The dear woman was so obviously sincere.

Lacey paused in reply, uncertain. Maybe Mary was right. She hadn't eaten or slept more than an hour or two in the last few days. Nor had she looked in the mirror. She couldn't go on this way, and she knew it. She needed to look strong and fresh in order to set Scully at ease while he recovered.

Those thoughts in mind, Lacey forced herself to say, "You're right, of course, Mary. I owe it to Scully to be the person he expects to see when he's lucid again." She swallowed against the tightening lump in her throat and continued, "I'll go back to my room and refresh myself, but I'll return in time to give Scully his medicine in an hour." She paused, then added, "You will send someone for me if...in case Scully..."

"Dear, please go. It's only an hour, after all."

With a lingering look at Scully, Lacey left the room. She avoided the saloon floor and turned toward the newly repaired rear staircase where she might exit into the alley and elude comment about her red-rimmed eyes.

Lacey emerged from the alleyway and kept to the shadowed building overhangs on the street in order to evade concerned questions for which she had no answers. Within minutes she had slipped through the boarding house door and was headed for her room.

Cursing low in his throat, Barret watched as Lacey turned the corner toward the boarding house and disappeared from view. He had been just a few minutes too late and had missed her. The old woman had obviously finished her work at the boarding house and had come to relieve Lacey earlier than he had expected.

Just his luck!

Barret tensed as music wafted out onto the night air through the Gold Nugget's swinging doors.

More waiting. More wasted time.

No. He would not wait another day. He would not return to his home without the information he sought, even if he had to wait all night for Lacey to return.

Determined, Barret glanced around him, then faded back into the shadows of the Gold Nugget's alleyway.

The thought that he was above skulking like a thief in the night flashed briefly across his mind, but he forced back its taunting. He would be a rich thief—a *very* rich thief—before this night ended. And he would see to it that no one, including Lacey Stewart, got in his way.

A knock on the bedroom door turned Mary toward it with a frown. She looked back at Scully, uncertain. His fevered contortions had ceased abruptly a few minutes earlier. Frightened, she had rushed to his bedside to discover that his forehead was cool and his breathing even. Elation had brought momentary tears to her eyes.

The knock sounded again and Mary walked quickly toward the door. She drew it open to Rosie's surprised expression at seeing her there.

Fearing that the necessary explanations would disturb Scully's restful sleep, Mary slipped out into the hallway and drew the door closed behind her. Smiling, she drew Rosie a few steps away and started to speak.

Jewel looked up at the exposed portion of the Nugget's second floor where Rosie and Mary stood by the railing. Her stomach tense, she watched their faces as they talked, hardly conscious of the cowpoke who stood beside her.

A chill worked down Jewel's spine. The reported violence at Charlie's campsite days previously had left her shaken. She remembered Lacey and Buddy's entrance into town, dragging the travois on which Scully lay. She recalled the instant when she saw the gash on Buddy's forehead, then realized that except for a twist of fate, Buddy might have been the man at death's door on that travois—or worse, that he might be lying back at the campsite just as dead as the two men who had tried to kill him.

The realization that she had sent Buddy into harm's way to watch over Lacey, and that he had gone simply because he loved her, had twisted the knife of pain in her stomach even tighter.

Yes, she loved Buddy. That reality had never been clearer in her mind than at that moment, but neither had it ever been clearer to her that Buddy might have given his life to please her.

To please *her*—when she wasn't worth the sacrifice.

Her heart aching, she had known what she must do, and she had done it. She had sent Buddy away. She had told him it was over between them, as she should have done so many months earlier.

She supposed she would never forget the look on Buddy's face when she told him. She knew she would never forget the pain of the moment when he left.

The anguish was with her still.

But with Lacey, it was different. Lacey was good and kind. Lacey was worth any sacrifice Scully could make for her. She hoped Scully would recover, for his sake as well as for Lacey's. She knew how important it was to Lacey that he did get well. She knew Lacey would never forgive herself if he didn't.

As for herself, she only wished—

Suddenly unable to finish that thought...unable to bear the weight of her distress a moment longer, Jewel rushed toward the swinging doors. She needed air, and some time by herself. She needed to put her sadness behind her...if only she were able.

* * *

Familiar voices outside his bedroom door awoke Scully to the silence of his room. He raised a heavy hand to his chest and felt the bandage there, then closed his eyes.

He remembered gunfire at the cabin campsite... Larry's startled expression before he fell...the hard ground underneath his own back and the pain in his chest that stole his breath. Most vivid of all was his memory of Lacey's stricken expression as she looked down at him.

Blackie and Larry were dead. They couldn't hurt Lacey any longer.

Total recall flushed Scully's mind with sudden panic. But Lacey had not even an inkling of Barret's part in her grandfather's death, or the fact that she was still in danger!

The conversation outside his bedroom door caught Scully's ear as he heard Mary say, "Lacey isn't here right now. She hasn't left Scully's bedside for a minute since their return to Weaver, so I sent her back to the boarding house to take an hour for herself. She's exhausted."

"I know." It was Rosie. "That's why I came. I wanted to know if I could do anything to help. I figured nobody would miss me downstairs if I stayed here for a while so Lacey could rest."

"You are a dear, Rosie." Mary's voice deepened with sincerity. "So many people have offered their help... Sadie, Helen, Janine Parker, Millie White, Jewel and you. Even Barret Gould came to my door today to offer his services."

Scully tensed. Barret Gould.

"He feels so guilty that he had at times employed the men who killed Charlie and shot Scully."

Scully's heart pounded.

"I told Barret we appreciated his offer, but Lacey was taking care of Scully. I also told him that when I finished work at the boarding house, I would come here and *insist* that Lacey go back to her room to take some time for herself. He seemed happy to hear it."

Scully's mind raced. Barret had been asking about Lacey. He wanted something from her...something he was willing to kill to get.

"Lacey should be back any minute. To tell the truth, I expected her back before this, but I guess she took my advice and decided to rest up a bit."

Scully glanced at the bedroom window. It was dark, and Lacey was alone on the street. He needed to find her before Barret did.

A loud crash from the saloon floor rebounded in the room, startling Scully from his thoughts.

"What happened?" Mary's voice rose a frightened notch outside his door.

"It's a fight downstairs." Rosie gasped, "Old Pokey fell. He's going to get trampled down there!"

The sound of footsteps running away from the door signaled Mary and Rosie's departure down the staircase.

His mind racing, Scully threw back the coverlet and slung his legs over the side of the bed. One purpose in mind, he forced himself upright.

Pain slashed at his chest and his senses reeled. A new gush of blood heated the bandages there as he pulled his trousers from the chair and slipped them on. Staggering, he fell against the dresser drawer and pulled it open. He grasped the handgun inside and turned toward the door.

Hardly aware of the commotion continuing in the saloon below, Scully staggered toward the rear staircase. His strength was rapidly failing. He reached for the doorknob, but it eluded him. His focus blurred. His knees weakened. He railed silently against his infirmity as consciousness dimmed and he sank slowly to his knees.

Lacey walked back toward the Gold Nugget, inwardly trembling. More than an hour had passed since she had left Scully's bedside. She hadn't intended to stay away from him so long; but she had been clumsy in her haste and everything had seemed to go wrong. She had finally managed to freshen up and was forcing herself to eat some of the food Mary had left for her when a full glass of milk slipped from her shaky fingers and spilled onto her skirt. Rushing to change for the second time, she had then snapped the bodice button off her only other cotton frock, and had been obliged to take the time to repair it.

The thought of Scully's fevered countenance driving her, Lacey turned into the Gold Nugget's alleyway and started toward the rear staircase at a run. Mary was taking good care of him, she was sure, but she needed to see Scully, to hear the sound of his breathing. She needed that visual proof, that assurance that he would survive.

She was also late in giving Scully his medicine. Doc Mayberry had not looked particularly encouraging when he had handed her the bottle, but she had—

"Lacey."

Lacey jumped with a start at the sound of her name. She squinted into the shadows of the dark alleyway and frowned as Barret emerged into view. She questioned, "Barret, what are you doing here?"

"I came to see you, Lacey."

Barret walked closer, and Lacey caught her breath when she glimpsed the gun in his hand.

"What do you want? I have to get back to Scully. He needs his medicine."

"No, he doesn't."

"Yes, he does. Doc Mayberry said—"

"Stop pretending, Lacey!" Barret interrupted her, his expression suddenly vicious. "You've fooled everyone else, but you can't fool me. I know why you came back to Weaver."

"Why I came back?" Momentarily at a loss, Lacey said, "What are you talking about?"

"You came back to claim your grandfather's strike."

"My grandfather's strike?" Incredulous, Lacey said, "That's crazy! I told those other two and I'm telling you, too—my grandfather never struck it rich."

"I know better."

"Then you know better than I do." Impatient, Lacey said, "I don't have time for this. Scully needs me, and I'm going to him."

"Try it, and you won't make it past your first step."

Barret spoke with icy control. The realization that he meant every word registered sharply inside Lacey as she said slowly, "Someone misled you, Barret. My grandfather never struck it rich out here. He died just as poor as he lived every day of his life."

"Did he? Maybe you need proof before you'll understand that you can't bluff me anymore." Barret pulled a small leather sack from his pocket and threw it toward Lacey with a sneer. Lacey caught it in her palm as he ordered, "Open it!"

Complying, Lacey shook a large gold nugget out into her hand. She looked back up at Barret.

"Beautiful, isn't it? Your grandfather gave it to me in payment of the legal work he wanted me to do for him. He wanted to make sure *his strike* would be legally registered in both your name and his. He left the nugget with me without disclosing the claim's location. He said he'd be back, expecting that I needed time to draw up the papers."

Barret continued harshly, "You thought it was a secret. You thought no one knew about your grandfather's strike. You thought you'd be able to pull the wool over everybody's eyes with that act about coming back to Weaver to see your grandfather's grave, when you really came back for the gold. Well, you almost succeeded. Your grandfather didn't tell anyone about his strike— only me. But as it turned out, telling me was enough."

Barret sobered. "I never intended to kill him—not if he cooperated. He could've been alive today if he hadn't turned the tables on Blackie and Larry when I sent them out to follow him. Then those two fools foiled my plans by killing him before he could tell them the location of the strike."

Incredulous, Lacey said, "You sent Blackie and Larry out after my grandfather, and you sent them out after me."

"I did."

"And you waited all these years to find out where my grandfather's claim is?"

"Not really. I had written the entire episode off as a

failure until you came back to Weaver and gave your-self away."

"I don't know what you mean."

"You should've been more careful. I heard you talking to Wilson Parker at the store shortly after you arrived. You said you had plans that didn't include Scully or waiting for the 'right fella' to turn up. You didn't think anyone would suspect what you really meant by that—but then, you didn't think anyone knew about your grandfather's strike, either."

"My grandfather never made a strike. This nugget…" She looked down to consider it again. "I don't know where it came from."

"Liar!"

"I'm not a liar. My grandfather would've told me if he had finally made a strike."

"You know where that strike is. You went back to the cabin to get your bearings. I want to know where it is—now. I've waited ten years to leave this miserable town in style, and I'm not going to wait any longer."

"I told you, you're mistaken. There is no strike."

"I'm warning you—"

"You can warn me all you want. My grandfather never struck it rich."

"That strike won't do you any good if you don't live to enjoy it."

"Can't you hear me? There is no gold. My grandfather never made a strike."

"Are you trying to make me believe—"

"How many times do I have to say it? There…is…no…strike!"

Suddenly shaken, Barret snapped, "Shut up!"

He stared at her for long, silent moments before saying, "Congratulations! You've convinced me that you're telling the truth and you don't know the location of your grandfather's strike—but that was a mistake. Do you want to know why? Because in doing so, you've just sealed your own fate."

"What are you saying?"

"Walk back farther into the alleyway, Lacey."

"Why?"

"Do it!"

"No."

"I'll shoot you right here, if that's what you want."

"If you shoot me here, somebody will hear the shot. You'll never get away with it."

"You're wrong. No one will challenge me." Barret suddenly smiled. "You see, I'm Barret Gould—educated, respected, the town's only attorney. I'm above reproach and above suspicion. Whatever story I make up will be accepted by the cretins that inhabit this town, simply because they don't know any better."

Barret's expression sent a chill down Lacey's spine as he then added in a lifeless tone, "No one will *dare* to challenge me. Goodbye, Lacey."

Shots rang out in quick succession, and Lacey took a staggering step backward. She gasped for air. She was somehow unable to move as Barret slumped slowly to the ground with round circles of blood rapidly widening on his chest.

Lacey looked up at the Nugget's rear staircase where Scully stood halfway down, swaying weakly, a smoking gun in his hand. Beside him in a moment, she had slid her arms around him supportively. Only then did she see Jewel standing in the alleyway, the gun in her hand also smoking.

Clutching Scully close as he sagged down onto the step, she saw Jewel turn and walk back out onto the street—directly into Buddy's arms.

Struck with the determination to fight for the man she loved, Lacey separated herself far enough from Scully to whisper, "I love you, Scully. You're a part of me. You always have been. I want to be with you always. I know that now, just as I know we were meant to be together. Speak to me, Scully, tell me—"

Lacey looked up toward sounds on the staircase above them the moment before helpful hands lifted Scully to his feet and turned him back toward his room. Hardly aware of the scurrying footsteps and the mumbling of deep voices in the alleyway below as onlookers gathered around Barret's body, she remained close beside Scully, refusing to surrender his hand.

Lacey stood anxiously beside Scully's bed when Doc Mayberry appeared in the doorway minutes later. She heard him mumble as he approached, "That fella down in the alleyway won't be needing my help, so let's see what I can do here."

Lacey said shakily, "Scully's going to be fine, doctor." She bent down toward Scully to conclude in a whisper, "Because we were meant for each other."

Startled when Scully's eyelids lifted and his sober gray eyes met hers, when he curled his palm unexpectedly around her head to press her mouth down to his, Lacey leaned into his brief kiss.

She was breathless at the love reflected clearly in his gaze when Scully released her and he said weakly, but with conviction that came clearly from the heart, "That's right, darlin', we were meant for each other... and I'll never let you go."

Chapter Fifteen

❧

The ranch house bedroom was large and airy, with flowered wallpaper in pale shades of blue. The early morning sun shone on the large bed that dominated the center of the room—the bed where Lacey and Scully lingered with their infant son lying beside them.

Lacey looked down at her sleeping child, at the spiky lashes lying against his smooth cheeks, knowing that underneath his closed eyelids, Jacob Scully, Junior's eyes were a clear and sober gray like his father's.

Her heart was full.

At Scully's touch, Lacey looked up to find his gaze searching her face. He whispered, "Is something wrong, Lacey?"

Wrong?

The thickness in Lacey's throat briefly precluded speech. How could anything be wrong? She was lying beside her husband, the man she loved, the man who had recuperated fully from his grievous wounds more than a year earlier. He was the same man who had re-linquished his former life at the Gold Nugget to become a rancher—not because she had demanded it of him, but because he had accepted a need to follow the Lord's word more closely…and because he loved her. In the time since, she had borne him a son, and the love between them had expanded in ways she had never even dreamed.

Yet there was more.

Lacey recalled the beautiful moment almost a year earlier when Jewel and Buddy came to Sunday church services; when afterward, they asked Reverend Sykes to marry them. It had never been determined whether it was Scully's or Jewel's bullet that ended Barret's life. She supposed it was better that way because both Scully and Jewel had made a difficult, split-second decision for which she would be forever grateful.

Jewel had confided that she hadn't expected to see Buddy on the street when she emerged from the dark alleyway that fateful night. Yet when he was there with his arms open and waiting, she had walked into them instinctively, suddenly sure his love was true and his fidelity would never fail her.

Jewel had also confided that in that moment, she had resolved she would become worthy of Buddy's love, and of God's love as well. In truth, that was all she had ever wanted.

Lacey remembered the day shortly after Jewel and Buddy's wedding when Rosie came to tell her she was quitting her job at the Gold Nugget, that she had saved up enough money to leave town for a job farther west where she would start over using her new skills at reading and writing to good advantage. Lacey knew Rosie would succeed because the dear girl's heart was pure and open to the Lord's word.

Lacey glanced at the night table where her grandfather's Bible lay. Scully had recovered it from Barret's office, further proof of Barret's guilt, although, in reality, no proof had been needed. She had been overjoyed to be able to touch it again with the feeling that Grandpa was always near. Scully had accomplished that for her, and in doing so, had ended her nightmares and rounded out her circle of love.

She was so blessed.

"Lacey?"

Lacey responded belatedly, "No, nothing is wrong, Scully. I was just thinking."

Anticipating her need to hold the precious volume in her hands, Scully took her Bible from the night table and handed it to her. She fingered it lightly, then turned to the page where her grandfather's simple drawing noted a familiar passage: *Thou will show me the path of life; in thy presence is fullness of joy; at thy right hand there are pleasures for evermore.*

She remembered the moment when it all came together in her mind. Her grandfather had read that passage to her often, but he had read it to her with particular significance while drawing a small critter resembling Careful beside it before he left for Weaver the day he was killed. The truth of that passage had guided him throughout his life, and she suddenly realized that he had meant for it to guide her in other ways as well.

Lacey stroked the miniature drawing with her finger. She and Scully had followed that thought to fruition so simply. They had returned to her grandfather's gravesite, had loaded prospector's tools on Careful's back as her grandfather had done countless times before. The loyal burro had then turned instinctively to follow a trail through the wilderness that he had walked with her grandfather. He had stopped automatically at the last location her grandfather had worked—*the site of his lost strike.*

Lacey remembered the moment when the first nugget was uncovered. She had met that moment and her grandfather's legacy with tears of bittersweet joy.

So many good things had come from that legacy—improvements on the ranch where Scully and she would spend the rest of their lives, Weaver's newly repaired church, the clinic that Doc Mayberry had always wanted to found.

Scully drew Lacey from her meandering thoughts as he nudged, "You were just thinking—about what, Lacey?"

"Weaver already has a school, but I was thinking how fine it would be if Weaver had another kind of school." She looked up at him, her clear eyes suddenly intent. "For people like Rosie and Jewel who aren't able to read and write because they never had the chance to learn."

Scully responded, "That sounds like a fine idea to me. I could talk to Reverend Sykes about it if you want."

Lacey's eyes filled. "And maybe…possibly… Rosie could come back to teach others to read."

"Maybe she could."

Suddenly solemn, Scully took a silky lock of Lacey's pale, unbound hair in his hand as he whispered, "But I want you to know, darlin', that when all is said and done, this gold is my true treasure. You mean more to me than any other legacy Charlie could possibly have intended."

His voice growing hoarse with emotion, Scully continued more softly still, "Charlie meant you for me…

I know that now. That was that old man's purpose in sending you to find me that last day. He meant to keep you safe, which you will always be in my arms. He also meant to turn my life back onto the right path with love—which he did." Pausing briefly, Scully said, "Because I love you, Lacey."

Lacey saw the truth of Scully's words reflected in the planes of his handsome face. She felt it in the touch of his lips as they lingered on hers, then glimpsed it in his eyes as he looked down at their son when he stirred.

Lacey comforted their son softly. She then leaned back to luxuriate in Scully's embrace as she held close a truth that was etched into her heart. In sending her to Scully, her grandfather had left her the most precious legacy of all—a legacy of love more precious than gold. A legacy that would last a lifetime.

* * * * *

Allie Pleiter, an award-winning author and RITA® Award finalist, writes both fiction and nonfiction. Her passion for knitting shows up in many of her books and all over her life. Entirely too fond of French macarons and lemon meringue pie, Allie spends her days writing books and avoiding housework. Allie grew up in Connecticut, holds a BS in speech from Northwestern University and lives near Chicago, Illinois.

Visit the Author Profile page
at Harlequin.com for more titles.

MASKED BY MOONLIGHT

Allie Pleiter

For now we see in a mirror, darkly;
but then face to face: now I know in part; but then
shall I know fully even as also I was fully known.
But now abideth faith, hope, love, these three;
and the greatest of these is love.
—*1 Corinthians* 13:12–13

For Georgia

Dream big dreams, little one

Chapter One

San Francisco 1890

Set up, turn, release.

The whip sliced cleanly through the night. Without the expected crack.

Matthew Covington pulled the whip behind him again, blowing out an exasperated breath. *That's twice you've missed.* The moonlight and shadows should have eased his overwrought spirit. He checked the last few inches of the whip, making sure they were intact. He knew they would be. His own frayed concentration was at fault here, not his whip. *Come now, man. Gather your wits.* He rolled his shoulders and flexed his fingers around the hilt. *Why still so tense?* He'd doffed his collar and waistcoat. Fled that dark, fussy office where his duty to be the respectable guardian of the Covington family honor accosted him at every tight turn. Surely out here, in shirtsleeves, in the noisy darkness of unfamiliar San Francisco, Matthew could find the space he craved.

After a moment's consideration, he put the whip

down and flipped open the latch on a long wooden box at his feet. Moonlight caught the sword's edge as he lifted it from the dark blue velvet. *Whhhish.* Matthew listened for the blade's soothing whisper. Although a formidable opponent with any of his weapons, he cared little for combat. He was drawn to the marriage of tool and muscle, the form and stretch of putting the weapon through its courses. The exertion. The application of skill. *Whoosh.* Matthew's whole body seemed to exhale as he sent the sword curving through the cool darkness.

He wasn't satisfied. Fencing often eased his knotted shoulders, but he'd just had a long, excruciating day, and it simply wasn't enough. Tonight, his tension needed the whip's power more than the sword's grace, and Matthew's hand returned to the whip's hilt seemingly on its own.

"I told you!" A sudden voice broke the quiet. Two figures burst into the end of the alley. Matthew froze, glad he'd replaced his white lawn shirt with a darker one as a last-minute precaution.

"It ain't worth nothin', I reckon," one said.

"Lemme open it." The larger man bumped his companion aside and reached into a small bag.

"I git half, remember."

"You get a third. Aw, will you look at this?" The big one held up a handful of coins, obviously disappointed.

"You pick a runt to rob and expect to get gold? We ain't gonna get anywhere if you keep—" A stack of boxes fell over as someone new ran into the alley.

Someone small.

"Gimme that back!" the thin voice panted. It was a boy—no more than ten years old, from the looks of him.

Matthew's chest constricted. His fingers tightened

around the whip. *Covington, stay out of this.* He backed up against the wall.

But not before taking a half-dozen silent steps toward the action.

"Aw, looky here, what followed us." The pair flanked the boy, each man pushing up his sleeves.

Nothing needs saving, Covington. Certainly not by you.

"It's mine. I want my money back!" The boy put up a pair of tiny, heroic fists.

Don't don't don't don't don't...

The large man dangled the bag out of the boy's reach, taunting him. "Life ain't fair, runt. Better learn it now. Unlessen you're in a hurry to meet your maker."

"Give it to me!" The lad lunged at the smaller of the men, who caught him easily. Matthew glimpsed the glint of a blade against the boy's throat.

How could he not?

Matthew took four huge strides, readying the whip as he went. Silently, staying in the building's shadow, he lifted his arm. *Set up. Turn.* He sent the long arc of leather hissing through the air, to crack angrily half a foot to the right of the boy's captor. The knife was too close to the lad's throat to chance it, but the crack had the effect needed. As the burly man yelped and flinched, Matthew sent his whip out again, this time around the small bag.

He gave a precise yank, sending the purse sailing into the air to land a few feet in front of him.

"What the...?" The other man spun in Matthew's direction, his own blade raised. At least the lad knew enough to bolt out of his captor's grasp the second he flinched.

Matthew drew a breath to hiss something threatening when his brain cautioned him to stay silent. His British accent would give him away in a heartbeat. Or at least make him easier to identify. Instead, he sank as far into the shadow as he could and pulled the whip back a third time. This time it wrapped around the legs of the second man and pulled him down on top of his companion.

Why didn't the boy run to safety? Matthew remembered the bag. He considered throwing it to the lad, but that would force him to step into the light again, and the men were already scrambling to their feet. When Matthew noticed the pair lacked guns or holsters—a rare but fortunate circumstance—he calmly drew the revolver from his side. The unmistakable click of the hammer stopped them cold. He let the silver tip of the gun catch the moonlight, and the pair promptly fled, disappearing around the corner.

Exhaling, Matthew holstered the gun and picked up the bag. The boy stood gaping at him with wide eyes. Matthew tossed the bag to the lad, who was too busy straining to see into the shadows to catch it.

There was a long pause. Matthew held his tongue, but finally nudged the purse with his foot.

"Oh. Uh-huh." Still staring, the boy crouched down and groped for it.

Matthew forced himself to focus on coiling his whip. When he looked up, the child was gone.

Then, just as he turned back toward his box, Matthew heard it—the long wail of a running boy calling, *"Thanks,* mister!"

If Georgia Waterhouse was going to save the world one child at a time, someone had beaten her to it.

At least as far as the scrappy newsboy before her was concerned. Snapped from the very jaws of death, to hear him tell it. And tell it he had. He was on his fourth rendition of the morning, the pertinent details growing with every repetition as they sat in the Grace House Mission hallway.

"I thought you said he had one whip last time, Quinn. Now he's wielding two." Georgia smiled and put down the package of clothes she was wrapping. She knelt in front of the boy, tight as they were for space as they moved packages from the hallway into the mission linen closet.

She handed the boy a shirt to hold. "You know, Quinn, this is a pretty tall tale. Men don't just appear out of the shadows with whips and guns in the middle of the night to save boys." She knit her brows together as she reached behind her for another garment. "And what was it you were doing out so late, in any case? Did anyone know where you were?"

He shot her a look that said she didn't know anything. *"Everyone* knew," he said, with the whine of someone who felt he was stating the obvious. "I *always* run back to Uncle Hugh with the coins from the newsstand."

"At three in the morning?" Georgia pivoted around to pack up the shirts she held with the ones she took back from Quinn. The mission was running out of storage space. Again.

"No, most times it's closer to two."

She sighed. The fact that ten-year-old newsboys were ferrying money through back alleys at three in the morning was exactly why God had asked her to save the world—or at least San Francisco's corner of it—here through Grace House Mission.

"You know, Quinn, it'd be easy to make up a tale that some man saved you and your money from those robbers, especially if you thought people might admire you if you did. God—and I—would rather you tell the truth."

"I *am* telling the truth. *God* knows that, anyhow!"

Georgia pointed to another pile of clothes and switched tactics. "Hand me those, will you, please? I'm simply saying that it's all right to make up stories. I do it all the time. But passing them off as real is another thing altogether."

Quinn's eyes took on a nasty edge. "I *knew* no one'd believe me." He threw the pile onto the hallway floor. "Prob'ly not even God, and *He* should know better." Disgusted, he tore off around the corner, leaving the clothes scattered on the floor behind him.

Georgia heard Reverend Bauers call out down the hall as he dodged out of Quinn's angry path. The clergyman appeared at Georgia's side a second later, looking down the hall after Quinn's exit.

"Told you the tale of his midnight hero, has he?"

Georgia gathered up the clothing. "Four times. It got more heroic with every telling."

Bauers chuckled. "How many whips in your version?" He was a jovial soul of solid German stock, and Georgia was very fond of him and the work he'd done here at Grace House. The struggling "South of the Slot" neighborhood—named for its position south of the cable car line—was far better off for his efforts.

"I stopped him at two."

"It got to the point where I thought our hero would resort to cannon fire in my set of renditions," he grunted as he bent his considerable frame to gather the last of the shirts. "Oh well, I can't say as I blame the boy."

Georgia eyed him. "Telling lies?"

"More like exaggerating, I'd say. I believe *someone* got Quinn out of a scrape last night. Whether or not he wielded a trunkful of weaponry, I am not so sure. But boys need heroes, and San Francisco is in painfully short supply."

Chapter Two

❧

"Georgia, you always get these kinds of ideas after you've been to Grace House."

Georgia stared at her brother. They sat talking over breakfast in the family dining room. The sun had overpowered the morning fog, to produce a victorious wash of bright light. Unlike the estate's massive formal dining hall, this was a warm and comfortable room. Georgia had seen to its welcoming palette of honey-colored wood, gold and tan wallpaper, with a few hints of green and burgundy in various accents. She loved that the petit point chair cushions were their late mother's needlework. That the impressive gold candlesticks and clock on the fireplace mantel had been a favorite of their late father's. Even though they were long gone, this dining room was one of the places she most felt her parents' presence. Perhaps that's why she had chosen to launch her extraordinary plan over breakfast here.

"That place has cost me thousands of dollars in your brand of philanthropy. They've got you hoodwinked," her brother was saying.

Georgia gathered strength from the room around her

and silently held her ground. Or, as she liked to think of it, she held ground for God.

Stuart finally looked up from his paper. "You're not serious."

"I am." With one hand she instinctively gripped the cushioned arm of her chair, as if her mother's needlework would support her cause.

"Peach, I can't just run something like that in the *Herald*," said her brother, who often called her Peach, especially when being difficult. "You know that."

"You run whatever you please in that paper, Stuart. Facts or no facts." Georgia knew she had him there. Stuart Waterhouse ran a highly successful but highly disreputable paper.

"Peach," he moaned at her display of determination, "be reasonable. We've already had a Black Bandit Bart. People aren't going to believe that some man with the same name as that stagecoach robber has suddenly sprung up to play the noble hero. They aren't going to believe it *at all*. It's *fiction*."

Fiction. How funny of him to use such a term. She wondered what he called half of his paper's contents, since Georgia knew the term "fact" hardly applied. Quite clearly, Stuart viewed fiction as something beyond his dealings, even though Georgia imagined half of San Francisco might think otherwise.

"I know very well what it is. And believe me, Stuart, if I had a set of good deeds for your reporters, I'd tell you. But, as you so often point out, this city seems steeped in bad news. And you gave Black Bandit Bart a lot of coverage, so why not a new Black Bandit?"

Stuart rolled his eyes. "Oh come now, Georgia, times aren't as bad as all that."

"Aren't they? Have you visited Grace House? Seen what kind of people come there asking for help? Things are going from bad to worse lately. You know it. I worry that you thrive on it, for goodness' sake." She reached for the morning's edition of the *Herald,* which lay on the table between them. The cool black-and-white newsprint stood out against the honey-toned wood that surrounded them.

Georgia unfolded the paper and held it up to her brother. "I don't see a piece of good news in here, Stuart. Can you show me even one story?"

He evaded her challenge, as she knew he would. "I'm not going tit for tat with you on this." He rose and walked to the window, slipping his hands inside the pockets of his crisp gray trousers. He was a fastidious dresser, her brother. He always looked sharp and strong, his meticulously tailored coat rarely unbuttoned. "Write all the stories you like, tell tales to your heart's content," he said, gazing out the window. "Just don't ask me to run them in the *Herald.*"

The servants brought in breakfast, interrupting the exchange. The siblings ate in silence, he thinking he'd ended the conversation, she regrouping for another attempt.

When he'd finished the last of his eggs, Georgia slid the paper over to his side of the table once more. She would not back down. Not again. "We don't have any good news, Stuart. We're going to have to make our own. Fiction reminds people of what *could* be. Stories touch their hearts. This city isn't suffering from a lack of facts. Folks already have more than enough facts to fill their heads. It's suffering from a lack of heart. A lack of faith. Stories reach that part of us."

Stuart's expression told her she was speaking about things he neither understood nor valued. He ran his empire, and cared little for lingering over breakfast to discuss San Francisco's moral failings.

He didn't concern himself with the citizens' hearts or souls.

Their wallets, however, commanded his full attention.

Georgia looked at the candlesticks, massive and ornate. Her father had brought them back from a trip because he'd felt they caught one's eye. They were, in fact, the first thing anyone noticed when entering the room. She needed to catch her brother's eye, then, and put this in terms he could appreciate. She altered the tone of her voice.

"If there's one thing you know, Stuart, it's how to give your readers what they want." She handed him a small stack of handwritten pages. "Read this. Just read it once, that's all I'm asking." She sent up a prayer that he would do so. "See what those famous instincts of yours tell you about what people might think of this."

Stuart reached for a piece of toast and glared at her.

She did her best to glare back. *Lord, please let him read it. Only You can do this.*

Slowly, Stuart's hand moved toward the pages. She straightened her spine, trying to look as if she'd never leave the breakfast table until he granted her request. If the sun could conquer the fog this morning, she could stand up to Stuart.

He took hold of the pages while biting into his toast.

Georgia waited. *Show him, Lord. Let him see it. See what I see.*

She studied her brother's face as he began to read.

After a paragraph or two, Stuart stopped chewing. He let out a little humming sound as he turned the page.

"It's fine work, but I..."

"You ought to have thought of this yourself, Stuart. You ought to have *written* it yourself. It would do you a world of good to pen something that might actually be categorized as...uplifting."

Stuart dismissed the idea with a snort. "I haven't any talent for *this* sort of thing." He put down the toast, half-eaten, and emptied his coffee cup instead. "'Uplifting' doesn't sell."

Georgia tried out her newfound glare once more. "But you know this will sell. And don't try to deny it—I see it on your face. Everyone needs a hero. And if they need one bad enough, he doesn't even have to be real. That little boy at Grace House made up his own personal hero so he'd believe he had someone looking out for him. So he could believe that good might just conquer evil, after all. Hold up a little piece of good for once, Stuart. It won't hurt you. And won't cost you a dime."

Her brother was right in one respect: he *couldn't* have written it. There was nothing ideological about Stuart. He'd built a fortune on his keen grasp of the public's insatiable hunger for news. *His* brand of news. Sharp, eye-catching, unabashedly partisan news. In all honesty, her brother's outlandish character sold as many papers as his headlines. Stuart Waterhouse wasn't exactly known for his respect of facts, but his opinions were the stuff of legend.

Well, she could be a legendary Waterhouse, too. And Georgia knew, just as God did, that the public's appetite for something good was just as strong as its craving for slander.

"Run it, Stuart. One installment. As a favor to me."

"Georgia, I'm not—"

"Please, Stuart. For me."

A wry smile crept across his face, and she knew she had him. "Oh, very well, then, I'll run it."

Thank you, Father!

"On two conditions."

Well, if she hadn't known that was coming, it was her own fault. She should have guessed there'd be *conditions*.

Stuart held up one finger. "Pen name."

"But…"

"*Male* pen name," he asserted.

So the victory goes to a George, not a Georgia, hmm? She rolled the idea over in her mind and decided that the prospect might be acceptable. As unconventional as Stuart could be, even *he* knew that writing as a man was a safer idea. Still, would it be deceitful? Georgia looked at the *Herald,* lying crisp and bright on the table between them. Tomorrow's paper would contain her story. *Her story.* Even "George" couldn't dampen the thrill in that. She waited for some sense of a heavenly warning, but none came. Just the joy of seeing the story come to light. That was confirmation enough for now.

She nodded.

"And second, speaking of favors, I'm having someone over to dinner tomorrow night…."

That one Georgia had seen coming a mile off.

Chapter Three

"And in that instant, the Black Bandit flung himself onto his gleaming mount and rode off into the night. In his wake, he left his injured enemy slumped at the sheriff's feet. And behind them, the huddled group of children, astounded and grateful. Justice had prevailed in the bravery of a soft-spoken man whom no one could name."

"Well, hang me, Peach, you really can turn a phrase. Astounding." Stuart had actually interrupted his breakfast to read her the Bandit's debut installment. "How does it feel, *Mr. George Towers,* to have your dashing hero introduced to the world?"

Georgia couldn't deny her joy. Nor could she deny the blatant admiration in Stuart's voice as he read the piece. It was identical to the handwritten words he'd read yesterday, but the man's love affair with ink and newsprint was overwhelming. It struck Georgia that her Bandit was her brother's exact opposite: larger than life, just like him, but a man of impeccable heroic morals, where Stuart was a man of… Perhaps it was more polite to say his morals were rather in question.

Her Bandit was a shamelessly inspirational hero. A dark and brooding champion. Georgia had taken the seed of an idea planted by Quinn and his fantastic tale, woven in a touch of Robin Hood, and then spiced it with the distinct grandiosity of the American West. She envisioned him like King David in his glory: distant and handsome, strong, compelled by an unshakable code of justice. Like all good heroes, he had the knack of sweeping in just when all hope seemed lost.

"Here's the way I see it, Peach. Do you notice where it's placed? On the back page here? I've posted your story right where someone else can see it while a man reads the paper." Stuart held up the issue in a classic pose, then peeked above it at Georgia. "You can read about your hero while I read the other pages. I see wives across San Francisco catching a glimpse of our Bandit while their husbands scan the business column. Brilliant, don't you think? Our man George ought to be a hit by week's end."

Georgia eyed her brother. Why did it surprise her that he was managing to capitalize on this? Only Stuart could take something so noble and turn it into a way to sell more papers. Not to mention his sudden partnership in the idea. *Our* Bandit? *Our* man George?

"It's how Dickens got his start, you know," offered Stuart in response to her look. "Serialized in the dailies."

Georgia was not Dickens. She wasn't even sure how she felt about being George Towers. She'd prayed over it for hours after her agreement, waiting for God to put His foot down and end the charade. Instead, she continued to feel as though God had opened this window and wasn't in any hurry to shut it. It was an idea born of good intentions, given directly to her by the Almighty— or so it felt. But it was still a deception of sorts. One couldn't ignore Stuart's manipulation of her, nor their partnered manipulation of the public's imagination.

But oh, there it was. Sprung to life in the *Herald*'s wonderfully immortal ink. Sparking some hope in the troublesome world that was San Francisco these days. She thought of the spark in Quinn's eyes.

"Peach? You've got that far-off look again. I always worry when you look like that. I'm not always fond of what shows up afterward."

Georgia set her teacup down with a resolute clink and stared straight into Stuart's inquiring eyes. "Stuart, thank you."

"My pleasure. For what?"

"For being important."

He merely returned her stare, and she could watch him resign himself to the oddities of his sister. And that's precisely how Stuart viewed Georgia's faith: as one of her oddities. "Speaking of my vast importance— not to mention that favor you owe me—Matthew Covington's coming to dinner tonight."

"Covington? The dry goods company?" Georgia surveyed the flowers brought in for tonight's dinner table. They were almost right. Not enough bright colors. The gardener was forever forcing pastels on her.

"He's that English fellow I was telling you about," replied Stuart, plucking a blossom from the center of the cuttings for his own lapel. "The flesh-and-blood heir to that dry goods company. He's here doing the family duty, showing up to play at keeping his eye on things."

"And, of course, you asked him to dinner."

Stuart launched into a chorus from Gilbert and Sullivan.

"Because he is an Englishman!
And he himself has said it, and it's greatly to his credit,
For he is an Englishman.
He i-i-i-i-s an E-e-e-ennn-glish-man!"

Just before he ducked around the corner, Stuart looked back at her. "He's vastly important and very wealthy. I want him to have a grand time while he's here. That's where you come in. Fire up your charms, Peach, I want the man dazzled."

Oh yes, with Stuart there was always a deal.

Matthew eyed his valet as the old man held up the remains of a newspaper. Pages had been sliced to ribbons. "You do know, sir," said Thompson wearily, "that a large portion of Englishmen *sleep* at night?"

"Yes, Thompson," he replied, finishing up his collar, "I'm well aware of that. But no one has yet expired from a bout of sleeplessness, so I gather I'm safe to live another day." He shrugged into the coat Thompson held out, offering the most challenging look he could muster. The old man merely opened the door and handed Matthew a thick file, looking as if he might nap the minute Matthew left the room.

"Remember your dinner engagement at Stuart Waterhouse's home this evening. Shall I order up a double set of tonight's papers, sir, so you can read them *and* duel them?"

Try as he might, Matthew couldn't think of a clever enough response. His valet was always getting the last word. Probably what kept him alive all these years.

As Matthew boarded the carriage bound for the Covington Enterprises offices, Matthew's family duty spread before him like a dull column of orderly figures. He merely had to inspect what was presented and tally up the sum. There seemed so little art to it. Like the predictable shot of a rifle. None of the arc or parry he found in the foil or the whip. Pull. Aim. Shoot. Obey.

"How are you finding San Francisco, Mr. Covington?"

"Lovely, thank you."

"I'm glad to hear you're enjoying your stay." Miss Waterhouse gave him a charming smile. "San Francisco is not…everyone's taste," she continued. "I'm afraid we've not quite grown into our big-city shoes."

"What my sister means is that we're still a bit rough around the edges, Covington," interjected Stuart.

"Not at all, Waterhouse." Matthew forced his gaze away from the man's sister. "I find it refreshing to be someplace where everything isn't hundreds of years old. Tell me, Miss Waterhouse, aside from the very formidable task of keeping an eye on your brother, how do you spend your days?"

She caught the jest, and smiled at him. Her eyes turned up just enough at the corners to give the impression that she was keeping a secret.

"Attending to Stuart's conscience is only one of many interests, Mr. Covington. I play the harp, and I work a great deal with Grace House, our local mission.

It serves the city's many needy families. But you are correct—Stuart is my most pressing cause."

"I spend hours trying to outwit my sister, Covington." Stuart gave her a look that held both boundless annoyance and deep affection.

"All of San Francisco thanks you for your efforts, Georgia," replied another of the evening's dozen guests, Covington Enterprises' local manager, Dexter Oakman.

"And what would you say to this new fascination of ours, Covington?" asked Stuart. "Have you got any such heroes in Britain?"

"Pardon?"

"Robin Hood!" Oakman chimed in behind a mouthful of potatoes. "He's an English hero, isn't he?"

"Yes, he was," Matthew answered carefully. "The legend overshadows the real man, but often the best heroes are embellished, wouldn't you say?"

"Oh, no, Mr. Covington," Miss Waterhouse replied. "I quite disagree. The very finest heroes are the ones that aren't fictionalized."

"Fine, perhaps, but exceedingly rare," Matthew stated.

His hostess held an indefinable look in her eye as she murmured, "I would not argue with you there."

Stuart lifted his glass. "To heroes, then."

"Will we drink to all of them, or just this new fellow in your paper, Stuart?" inquired Oakman.

He rolled his eyes. "Drink to the Bandit if you must, but I'd much rather you drink to me."

"One must first do something heroic, Stuart," teased his sister.

He sighed dramatically. "To be so misunderstood."

"Is the fate of most great men," Matthew finished for him.

"Ah, Covington, I knew you'd come through for me. To our Bandit, then, and great—or should I say greatly misunderstood—heroes everywhere."

"And what do you think of our Bandit?" asked Mrs. Oakman, a round, rather witless-looking woman who had been engrossed in the minute dissection of her pork for most of the meal.

"Bandit, Mrs. Oakman?"

Stuart made a gesture as though he'd been stabbed through the heart. "I'm wounded, Mr. Covington. You don't read my paper?"

Well, that had been foolish. Thompson had truly seen to it that two copies came up to the room, but Matthew had fallen asleep over them, too exhausted to read the issue. And now Waterhouse knew. This trip was supposed to be Matthew's declaration that he could carry the family name with respect and reserve. He didn't need Georgia Waterhouse's fascinating eyes spurring him on to what his father called "his fantastic talent for making a spectacle of himself." Oh, the evening had taken a bad turn.

"Forgive me, Mr. Waterhouse. I pledge my loyal readership for the rest of my visit." It wasn't a very good recovery, but it would have to do.

Evidently not one to miss an opportunity, Stuart handed him a copy of the *Herald* the minute dinner had ended. Folded over to a back page, where some sort of serialized story had been printed.

Matthew read the first four paragraphs.

What?!

He quickly read them again, squelching the urge to gasp aloud.

Chapter Four

No.

Impossible.

Matthew sat down, hoping he showed no sign of the storm going off in his gut. He read the rest of the story, willing himself to look casual. Evidently the other night had been a spectacularly bad idea.

Don't jump to conclusions, he admonished himself. He knew who had witnessed the conflict in the alley that night, and none of them were reasonably able to document it. Several details were different.

Smile and leave it, Covington. Leave it alone. Leave it... "Who is this George Towers?"

"Fine storyteller, isn't he? He's one of my, shall we say, hidden assets. The tale's been the talk of the town today. I hadn't been eager to run fiction in my paper until now, but I must admit I'm insanely pleased."

Talk of the town. Marvelous. Father would be so very...*intent on killing him.*

"I'd imagine you are." *Waterhouse had said fiction, hadn't he?*

"We haven't got a bumper crop of real heroes in San

Francisco these days, so this author came to me with the idea of making one up. Seems to have hit a nerve. We may give your man Dickens a run for the money, eh?"

"Indeed…" That was all Matthew could spit out.

"I'll run one of these every week if the attention keeps up," Stuart announced.

"If I know you, Stuart," chimed in Dexter Oakman, "you'll run *two.*"

Matthew made a mental note to never step out of his bedroom door after dinner *ever again.*

Which was ridiculous, wasn't it? Yes, the Bandit used a whip, and he wore dark clothes. And he had saved a child—granted, it was a small girl in this story, but in other details the story was alarmingly similar to what had happened.

Stop it. This was pure coincidence. It had nothing to do with Matthew. He had nothing whatsoever to do with bandits, black or otherwise.

He had just gotten his doubts under control when Georgia Waterhouse walked into the room.

"There's someone at the door to see you, Stuart. He's being rather insistent. Something about the presses."

She was slim and graceful. Her skin was the palest he'd ever seen, but it lacked the blue tint that lurked in so many of London's pale complexions. No, hers was infused with rose and gold.

Oh, Covington, his brain cautioned, *now's hardly the time.*

Stuart left the room barking instructions for Georgia to stay and seek Mr. Covington's opinion of his paper. The Englishman had the newspaper in quite a grip and for some reason she noticed his thumb was lying across the "George" of her byline.

"It seems my brother's not won the instant subscriber he was expecting, Mr. Covington."

"Pardon?" their guest swallowed.

"I gather you're not fond of the *Herald?*"

"Why would you say that?" he replied quickly.

"You're holding it as if it were a goose you planned to behead for supper."

It proved an effective metaphor. Covington made such a show of loosening his grasp on the paper that he nearly dropped it. Dexter Oakman laughed.

"Perhaps I should say I found it rather *gripping reading,*" Covington said wryly.

She smiled. "Stuart would like that."

The Englishman raised the paper again with a far gentler touch. "What is your opinion of your brother's venture into fiction, Miss Waterhouse?"

In all the hubbub about the story, Mr. Covington had been the first person to ask *her* opinion. And, perhaps most pleasing of all, he looked at though he really desired to know, and wasn't just making polite conversation. Perhaps it would not be such a difficult favor to keep him entertained, as Stuart had asked.

"It is one of the rare things Stuart and I agree on."

"I've no doubt," he murmured, in such a way as to make Georgia wonder if he'd intended to say it aloud. There was something, a sort of puzzlement, coloring his words. He stared at her for the briefest of moments before shifting his attention to the fire. He had extraordinary eyes, Georgia thought. Dark blue, beyond indigo. As if God, forgetting that most dark-haired men had brown eyes, had given him blue eyes at birth, and then darkened the blue to cover the oversight. The inky blue-black of stormy waters. They strayed back to her for a moment, and she quickly looked away.

"Who is this George Towers? A local writer?"

"I know many things about the way my brother does business, Mr. Covington."

"But…"

"But I wouldn't be privy to half of them if I didn't know the value of a secret." Georgia allowed herself to hold his eyes for a moment. "Especially one that is becoming rather sought after." People wanted to know who George Towers was. The office had received numerous inquiries over the course of the day. Georgia was almost heady with pleasure at readers' response to her story. Having it be a secret only intensified the effect. She imagined she had looked like the cat that swallowed the canary all day.

Stuart burst back into the room. "All is well—or at least until the next disaster. Thank you, Peach." He gave her an affectionate peck on the cheek.

"You're welcome," she said, preparing to return to the ladies in the salon.

"Stay just a moment." Stuart took her hand. "I want you to hear what our guest thinks of the Black Bandit."

"I've yet to finish the story, Waterhouse," Covington protested. "You can't very well ask me to comment when I've read only a handful of paragraphs." He didn't much care for the article. Georgia could tell. And she knew in a heartbeat what Stuart was going to do next. Covington didn't stand a chance.

"Well, then, read the thing." Her brother smoothed out the crumpled paper and motioned to one of the high-backed chairs near the fire. "Better yet, read it aloud to all of us."

"Stuart…" Georgia began, thinking he was going a shade too far.

"No, really, Peach. The test of any good story is how it sounds aloud. Covington, you've a fine voice—that accent and all. Why don't you read it to us?"

"I…"

Stuart was having fun with her, Georgia knew. Giving her a chance to secretly enjoy her talent. It was a dreadful thing to do to a guest, especially one who clearly didn't relish the prospect, but she could help herself no more than Stuart could. The opportunity to sit and watch people listen to her words was far too enticing. She wanted to hear him read it. Very much.

"Please, Mr. Covington," she found herself saying. "Indulge us."

"Men who refuse Stuart Waterhouse live to regret it," teased Oakman, "generally in the next day's headlines!"

Covington knew he was cornered. Gathering his dignity, he sat down, took a deep breath and began to read the inaugural installment of the Black Bandit's adventures.

His voice flowed on, deep and musical. But there was an odd note in it, whether of shock or of fascination, she couldn't tell. And his whole body seemed to be reacting to the story, albeit subtly. His hands clenched the margins, and he shifted his weight two or three times. He stumbled on the paragraph that described the Black Bandit as tall and lithe, dark and powerful.

He put the issue down quickly as he finished, and Georgia thought, *Well, here's one reader not won over by the Black Bandit.*

Chapter Five

Desperate for the sleep that continued to evade him, and determined not to set foot outside and risk any association whatsoever with any bandits, real or imagined, Matthew settled for swinging his fencing foil around the hotel room as quietly as possible that night. He tried to block and parry as softly as he could, since he'd already roused Thompson once by knocking over a water pitcher. Even so, Matthew's final thrust skewered an item from the fruit basket on the sideboard.

He hoisted the fruit high, its weight making the foil wobble slightly as a sticky stream of juice began sliding down the blade.

Pathetic.

His San Francisco visit was not going well. And if he didn't sleep soon, he wasn't going to have a lick of business sense by the time he visited the shipping docks tomorrow. Matthew thought it a cruel irony that while he was forced to spend his day listening to the sleep-inducing rhetoric of Dexter Oakman, the combination of a silly newspaper story and a stunning woman made nocturnal sleep impossible.

He stared at the pair of *Herald* issues that lay on the table, taunting him. They were staring back, ganging up on him, their dark headlines glaring unblinkingly. *No,* he thought, nearly declaring it out loud, *I will not read it again.*

It wasn't as if he needed to. He'd reread the piece enough times that he could practically recite it. Checking over and over for hints and similarities, for any sign that George Towers had been hiding in some dark corner of that alley. No, it was impossible.

Wasn't it?

Matthew took his handkerchief and wiped down the foil, licking sweet juice off one finger.

Georgia Waterhouse. What was it about her that intrigued him so? Some of it was obvious. Her relationship with her brother fascinated Matthew. He'd known sibling teasing from his younger brother, David, but there was far more competition than companionship between them. David was highly critical of Matthew, the principal heir. Entirely too eager, he suspected, to have the position for himself. David and his father seemed to agree on so much in life. Matthew had long felt that Covington Senior had never quite forgiven his wife for having their sons in the wrong order.

No, affection was a longtime stranger to the Covington household. In recent years the fighting had cooled to an impassionate, rigid tolerance.

Stuart and Georgia, on the other hand, had something unique, an obvious but indefinable bond. As if they knew a secret the rest of the world would never share. Matthew had seen such a look flash between his twin cousins. Something beyond language or gesture.

Then again, knowing Stuart Waterhouse's social and

professional prowess, chances were those two *did* know a few secrets the world might clamor for. Hadn't she said she'd been "privy" to a few of Waterhouse's "hidden assets"?

A beautiful woman with big secrets. *Perfect.*

The downstairs clock chimed three. Georgia adjusted her pillow for the thousandth time. Sleep rarely eluded her, and she found this fit of wakefulness annoying. Try as she might, even with the help of her favorite psalms, her mind refused to quiet itself for the night.

Granted, it had been a splendid day. Spending hours watching people carry the *Herald* to and fro, listening to visitors at the newspaper office gossip and wonder about George Towers and his captivating Bandit.

"*My* captivating bandit," she declared to the curtain fringe, which offered soft, frilly nods in the breeze. She cast a sheepish glance heavenward. "Well, *ours*. Thank you, Father," she sighed, "for using Stuart and me in such a…satisfying way. Even if Stuart doesn't see it as such."

Georgia rolled over and elected to take stock of the evening. Entertaining wasn't really her gift, so perhaps analyzing the dinner and its guests might sufficiently bore her that she could sleep. She was a competent enough hostess—goodness knows Stuart invited people over constantly—but not the kind whose soirees made the papers. At least not without her brother's direct intervention. He usually whipped up a dramatic paragraph or two when the mood struck him, more for the titillation of his dinner guests than any further need to see his name in print. Georgia knew full well it was Stuart's power, and not her social prowess, that lured guests to the table. In truth, that suited her fine.

The Oakmans were dull but useful, present tonight because of their association with Covington Enterprises, Georgia guessed. No, it was clear Stuart had focused his attention on Matthew Covington. Aside from her brother's passion for all things English, Georgia guessed he'd sought out Covington—and asked that she do the same—for far more than his accent. The name Covington was familiar to businessmen in San Francisco. Their import holdings were considerable; Stuart told her that Covington Dry Goods kept half the finer stores in San Francisco stocked with European products. Stuart deemed them important enough that he made sure any Covington representative who came to town appeared at the Waterhouse table. The elder Covington had even been to dinner once, although a long time ago. Georgia didn't remember *him* looking like the man who'd come to dinner tonight.

What she'd noticed most about Matthew Covington was the extraordinary command he had of his body, which was athletic and graceful. Stuart galloped around a room, Oakman toddled, but Matthew Covington *strode*. It seemed an odd thing to notice—not like hair or eyes or a smile or such—but it struck her in a way she couldn't put a name to.

Georgia wondered how high those British eyebrows would go if he knew a *woman* had come up with the story of the Black Bandit. *And* penned it.

The clock chimed half past. No reasonable woman would be up at three-thirty in the morning considering her publishing strategies.

Well, then, she thought as she reached for her wrap, *if*

*Georgia Waterhouse oughtn't to be up, perhaps George
Towers can be awake.*

She smiled as the opening sentence came to her.
Why not?

Dipping her pen, she began:

"The Black Bandit finished cleaning his sword
as the sun dawned over the mountains. Sleep had
eluded him that night...."

"I had one hundred seventy-three reasons to decline
your brother's invitation," Matthew said when he escorted Miss Waterhouse to an event a few days later.

Why he chose this to be the first thing out of his
mouth when she entered the parlor, he couldn't say. He'd
meant it as a compliment, but as the words escaped his
lips he realized how insulting they could be.

*Fine opener, Covington. Did you leave your man-
ners in England?*

Thankfully, she seemed to guess his intent—and his
instant regret—for a small grin played across her face.
Her response pleased him.

"Yet, at the moment," he continued in complete honesty, "I can't recall a single one of them."

"A clever save, Mr. Covington. Perhaps you might
fare better if you told me why you said yes," she countered, adjusting the ribbon on her hat.

"First off, it's been made quite clear to me that one
takes one's life into one's own hands when declining
Stuart Waterhouse."

"True."

"And secondly, you make infinitely better company
than sums and inventories."

She scowled. "I'm afraid I don't find that much of a compliment. In my opinion, *most of the world* makes better company than sums and inventories."

"It depends on the sums," replied Matthew, holding the door open for her as they stepped out into the afternoon light, "and very little of *most of the world* could convince me to endure a musicale."

"Endure? But it's Gilbert and Sullivan. At Tivoli Gardens, no less. Stuart's favorite—and very British."

Matthew grimaced and offered her his elbow. "My point exactly. I don't like tea, either, you know."

She laughed. A lovely, bright laugh. "Well, there will be some of that, but I expect Stuart might be able to find you a cider. He'll be joining us a little while after the concert starts. Some paper emergency." She sighed. "There's *always* some paper emergency."

It was a grand spring day. Matthew felt the crisp bay breeze—and the delightful company—lift his spirits. Admit it or not, he'd been wondering how he could see her again. He'd have said yes if Stuart had asked him to escort Georgia to a quilting bee. "I expect your brother thrives on crises, doesn't he?"

"He seems to. Anything less would bore him."

"Stuart Waterhouse bored. It wouldn't be a pretty sight." Matthew gave a chuckle, thinking of how the man had sped around the room at the dinner party. How he seemed to everywhere at once, and hardly ever sat down.

Georgia suddenly stopped walking. She turned and looked up at Matthew with intensity, the sun playing across her hair and cheeks. "I spend a tremendous amount of time talking about Stuart, Mr. Covington." She lowered her eyes, as if her own comment caught her by surprise. "I... I should like it if that were not the case with you."

Matthew gazed at her, a sudden sympathy filling him. "I would like that very much." *Yes, very much.*

She broke the spell, picking up the pace again, a bit flustered. "I'm sorry. I don't know what made me say that."

"I do." It was Matthew who stopped this time. "You're much different than he. But people lump you together just the same. I've been lumped together with my father for ages, and we couldn't be more different. Yet everyone assumes I'm just like him. I have to admit I don't always enjoy the comparison."

"So you understand," she murmured quietly, but said no more.

Chapter Six

It seemed ages before the portly soprano and her equally portly tenor husband ended their first act. Matthew wondered how the usually fidgety Stuart could sit transfixed by such music, but he was clearly enjoying himself.

"Today's edition, Peach," he announced as he pulled a paper from under his arm at the intermission. "I'll go fetch us drinks."

Georgia folded the pages directly to the back cover. "Ah, here it is," she said. She began to read.

Before he could stop himself, Matthew leaned over her shoulder to peer at the headline: Returning by Demand: Another Episode of the Black Bandit's Adventures. He read on, drawn in despite himself.

"The Black Bandit finished cleaning his sword as the sun dawned over the mountains. Sleep had eluded him that night, as it had many nights of late. The exertion of his battles, the welcome partnership of arm and whip, the song of the sword as it sliced the night air—these things eased his spirits. But lately, even they had failed to give him rest."

Matthew blinked and stared.

Blinked again. Read and reread, his throat tightening.

It was all there. Again. As if George Towers had somehow crept inside his life. How could someone he'd never met put words to his thoughts with such wrenching eloquence? Towers seemed to understand the solace sought in exertion—but the two of them had never met. Sleep surely eluded many men, but how many understood the art of weaponry such as swords and whips? Who *was* this man?

Matthew turned away. *No,* the connections weren't there. The tension and the sleeplessness must have drawn his nerves too tight.

As he turned back, he saw that Georgia was still entranced by the story. He stared at her, sensing how completely opposite their reactions had been. Matthew wanted to put as much distance as he could between himself and that confounding piece of newsprint. She, on the other hand, looked as if she would crawl into the story if she could.

She must have sensed his stare, for she glanced up. Her eyes had a soft quality, as if she'd been someplace faraway and wonderful. Matthew tried to soften his own expression, but it was too late. She had seen his reaction—the fact registered on her face.

"You're not fond of the Bandit stories, are you, Mr. Covington?" Matthew swore there was disappointment in her voice.

"No, it's not that." He gulped almost instinctively,

then groped for some reasonable explanation to give her, wanting to banish the gulf that had just stretched between them. "They're a bit...overwrought...for my taste."

"I see." Her words were cool and clipped.

"I'm sure there are many people who enjoy such tales," he stated, trying to salvage the conversation. But the damage had been done. Why did she seem to care so much about what he thought? Why did it bother him so to disappoint her? Matthew opened his mouth to say more, then shut it with a sigh, convinced that anything he added would only worsen the situation. *Well, Covington, you've botched that one thoroughly. Where's Stuart with those drinks?*

Georgia's hand tightened around the newsprint. She'd wanted him to like it. Which was nonsense, really. He hadn't enjoyed the first episode, so why should he suddenly relish the second? It was even more effusive than the first.

But she wanted him to like it. Her disappointment was as sharp as it was surprising. She drank her tea in silence while the men found something acutely businesslike to discuss.

She had been sorry when her brother sat between her and Matthew Covington before, but now was grateful to have Stuart between them for the second act. Yet, sure enough, Stuart pleaded yet another crisis once the applause ended, and asked Matthew to see her home. In his usual obliviousness to other people's feelings, her brother focused solely on his goal: ensuring that Georgia and Matthew saw a good deal of each other. She'd have to put a stop to that soon, favor or no favor.

They spent most of the walk home engaged in forced bursts of small talk, grasping for the close atmosphere they'd enjoyed earlier. It seemed just beyond their reach. By the time they turned the final corner to her house, the gaps of silence grew uncomfortable.

Ten steps farther he stopped. He fiddled with his pockets some more, then looked up at her and said, "Would you...would you like me to read you the episode? You said you enjoyed it so much the other night at dinner. There's been so much rain, it seems a shame to go inside when the park looks so inviting." She watched him fumble, trying to cover his all-too-obvious desire to set things right between them. "I suppose we don't even need to discuss anything at all, just take in the view and..."

"Yes," she agreed eagerly. "I'd like that very much."

He smiled, a wonderful, warm smile. And when he pulled her hand into the crook of his elbow to cross the street, she felt the earlier glow come back.

He saw her seated on a wrought-iron bench under the shade of an enormous budding tree. He sat opposite her and made an amusing fuss of folding the paper to just the right spot. She sensed he was doing it purely to please her. What an appealing thing that was.

Clearing his throat so dramatically that it made her laugh, he began to read. Oh, gracious, his voice was wonderful when he read like that. Deep and refined, as if the words were both surprising and familiar at the same time. *How can he dislike the story and yet read it like that?*

"The night crept by, allowing him time to think of all he had done, and all he had lost. Justice seemed little comfort, and yet it was comfort enough. He could no more stand by and let evil run its course than he could quench his heartbeat."

Covington stopped reading and glanced up at her with an almost baffled expression. He seemed as if he didn't want to like her tale, but couldn't help himself. The words—*her* words—were affecting him; she knew it. He began to read again, and his voice seemed to wrap around her in the crisp air.

Matthew Covington was an exceedingly handsome man.

Mighty nice.

Stuart congratulated himself again for having the foresight to build the *Herald*'s offices so near his home. He hadn't realized until today what an advantageous view of the park the windows offered.

There was no mistaking the pair on the bench across from his front steps. Covington was reading the paper—his paper—to Georgia. And she was looking as if she enjoyed it immensely. Stuart smiled.

"Dex?"

"Yes, Stuart?" Dexter Oakman came up behind him, to stare out the windows.

"Will you look at that?"

"Seems your sister is playing hostess quite well. How'd you convince her to do it?"

Stuart turned. "My secret, Dex."

Oakman smirked. "You and your secrets."

"How far did Covington get in his audit this morning?"

"Halfway into last year's first quarter."

Stuart smiled with satisfaction. "I doubt it will be too difficult to see that he doesn't get much further than that."

"Sure looks like it."

Stuart brandished his file like a banner as he sang,

"I am the very model of a modern Major-General,
  I've information vegetable, animal and mineral…"

Georgia set the paper down on the Grace House kitchen table and looked at Quinn. "Well, what do you think?"

The boy tore another large chunk of bread off the loaf she'd set in front of him before she began reading the original *Herald* installment aloud. He narrowed one eye as he pointed at her with the bread. "I *knew* somebody was watching." He grabbed his mug of juice with the other hand. "But a girl? Who's dumb enough to let a girl run the money home?" He took a gulp of milk large enough to make Georgia wonder if he was eating at all outside the meals she gave him at Grace House.

"That Bandit man'll be busy if things like this keep happening," Quinn said, raising his voice to be heard over the banging of pots and dishes in the mission's kitchen. He thunked his mug down on the rough wooden table where Georgia had set a place for him after he'd missed lunch by turning up late for the second day this week. Georgia winced a bit at the lavishness of her own home compared to the squalor she saw South of the Slot. The more she got to know Quinn, the more desperate his situation seemed. And there were so many more like him.

"Really," she said, still unable to find a way to convince him the *Herald* wasn't reporting actual Bandit sightings. Quinn seemed to take such hope from the tale, she couldn't find it in herself to try any harder to take it away from him. Not that she hadn't attempted to. Quinn, it seemed, just wasn't interested in being convinced. She gave in to his insistent belief, half because she couldn't fight it, and half because she found she no longer wanted to.

"I hope Bandit Man gets to sleep during the day. If he's out all night, he needs to keep his strength up." The boy swiped his hunk of bread around the tin plate, picking up every last bit of food before he stuffed the bread in his mouth. "More egg?" he asked, his cheeks puffed out as he chewed.

Georgia rested her chin on her palm and raised an eyebrow at the grimy lad. He stared right back at her, until it apparently dawned on him what she was expecting.

"Fine." He grumbled, swallowed, then sat up straight. "May I please have another egg?" A more reluctant show of manners could not have been conceived. He made a face, as if the words left a bad taste in his mouth. The fact that he acquiesced to "please," "thank you" and napkins at all was further proof of how truly hungry he must have been.

Georgia smiled. "Most certainly. As a matter of fact, why don't we wrap up half a dozen so you can take them home." She leaned toward the boy as the house cook slid another egg—Quinn's third—onto his plate. "Does everyone have enough food at your house, Quinn?" While the answer seemed obvious, she wanted to hear his assessment of his own situation.

The lad looked at her as if she'd asked if the sky

had recently fallen. "'Course not. Who does? I mean, 'cept for here." Somewhere in the background, Reverend Bauers's off-key baritone resounded as he worked. Georgia often felt God had never created a man more enthusiastic but less gifted in song. Still, San Francisco was a good place for him. The city's faults and vices could easily overtake a more sensitive soul.

"Da was yelling about being hungry just last night. Something about still not getting paid, but I think it was mostly his leg again. I sure hope he goes back to the docks soon. He's sour about having to sit around all the time."

A fight two weeks ago had injured Quinn's father's leg. The wharves seemed less safe with each passing week. Reverend Bauers had been patching up too many victims of dock fights recently. Georgia had to ask half her women friends to donate old shifts to be cut up into bandages. She'd even seen the reverend resort to whiskey to tend to wounds, because the medicinal alcohol was running low. Reverend Bauers had no musical talents, but he excelled at making do with what he had.

"I'm sorry to hear that, Quinn. I hope things will get better for you soon," she told him. "I'll see if Reverend Bauers can stop by and take another look at that leg." No matter how one viewed it, things seemed to be going from bad to worse in San Francisco lately. How long would Grace House be able to keep up with the load? What would happen when its small team buckled under the strain? *Heavenly Father,* she sighed, *stretch out Your mighty hand over this city. Things feel so desperate. What can be done?*

Georgia couldn't shake the sensation that God was answering when Quinn poked at the paper she was still holding. "Miss Waterhouse, would you read it to me again? I like the part with the swords and all. I haven't seen his swords yet."

Again she felt the necessity of telling Quinn the stories were just made up by a man at Stuart's paper. And again, pity stopped her. If the Bandit kept one boy coming to Grace House, then the hero really *was* saving lives.

And Georgia Waterhouse could live with that paradox—at least for a little while.

Chapter Seven

"**Y**ou can't be serious!" Matthew bellowed, trying not to let his splintered nerves get the best of him. One more sleepless night and he was going to become a threat to himself and others.

"I'm afraid I am, sir. I'm woefully sorry, but there it is."

"How? Exactly *how* did my whip go missing? It's not as if I leave the thing lying around, Thompson."

The valet, ever calm, seemed only mildly repentant—but then, the man's face was so professionally inexpressive that he could have been miserably guilty over the mishap and Matthew might never know. "It is hardly the type of thing to be left out in the open," Thompson said.

Matthew began overturning chair cushions. "Which is why I keep it locked up."

"Indeed, sir, you normally do."

He froze, cushion held midair, and glared at the old man. "'Normally'?"

"I must admit I was quite astounded to see it lying about. Not having the combination to your arms case, I thought it best to at least put it out of sight. Under your linens, to be precise."

Matthew dropped the cushion back in place, heading for the bedroom, until logic stopped him. "But it's not there, is it?"

"I cannot see why the hotel staff would have thought to replace the linens twice in one day, sir. The bed had already been made. A mistake, I suppose. Change in chambermaids."

Matthew stood in the doorway between his bedroom and the sitting room, raking his fingers through his hair as he desperately analyzed the facts at hand. "So you put the whip in the sheets, and they took away the sheets, whip and all. Have I got it?"

Thompson folded his hands together, with just the mere hint of a wince. "I believe you do, sir."

What to do now? One couldn't go traipsing around a foreign city asking for a wayward whip. Matthew had visions of himself, crimson necked, trying to explain his odd choice of exercise to the hotel laundress. Then again, this was San Francisco. It might not prove to be the oddest thing she'd seen. He'd pay a discreet visit to the laundry, then, rather than have to deal with the hotel clerk or someone more likely to raise eyebrows.

Matthew pulled out his cuff links and offered them to Thompson. "I'll just have to go hunt it down, then, won't I?"

The valet looked at him askance. "Sir?"

Matthew dropped the links into the man's outstretched hand and started undoing his necktie. "I can't very well waltz into the hotel manager's office and demand my missing whip, can I? It's undoubtedly found its way to the laundry, and I'll just go fetch it back."

"Now?" As if to emphasize the lateness of the hour, Thompson produced his pocket watch and checked it.

"Better tonight than at breakfast tomorrow, don't you think? I can slip down to the laundries and slip back unseen if I'm careful."

In a rare show of disapproval, Thompson looked as if he found that a very bad idea.

Well, no, it wasn't a stellar plan, but Matthew had to get that whip back, and he wasn't swimming in good alternatives at the moment. "Have you a better solution, man?"

Thompson returned to a stone-faced silence.

"Very well, then. Don't wait up." Matthew rolled up his shirtsleeves in an attempt to look more common and less gossip worthy, should the laundry staff prove to have loose tongues. "And for goodness' sake, don't go hiding my belongings again, whatever you think may be the consequences."

Are you laughing, Father? Snickering in your velvet smoking jacket at the vision of your son, the indubitable Covington heir, sneaking toward the hotel laundry like some kind of cornered culprit?

Matthew's father had hated the whip from the moment his brother, Matthew's uncle, had given him the unusual weapon. "Ridiculous and overdramatic," Reginald Covington had declared with a frown when Matthew had showed him the first trick he had mastered. Here it was, the first accomplishment that was not just a mere shadow of his father's strengths, and it was dismissed with scorn. The whip was, and had continued to be, something entirely Matthew's own, which brought him a joy he couldn't ever quite put into words. Maturity had not yet changed that fact.

What a lark you'd have with my current pickle, Matthew thought, the familiar slant of his father's scowl coming to mind. *'Tis a good thing the Atlantic is as wide as it is.*

Why couldn't Thompson have misplaced the sword? It would prove so much less a problem, attract much less attention.

As he descended the third flight of stairs and caught the distinct scent of soapy water, Matthew thought of his valet's amazing ability to disappear. Somehow, Thompson could stand in the back of a room and evaporate into the wallpaper. One hardly even remembered he was there, until he would materialize—with a startling sense of timing—just when he was needed. The man anticipated needs with such uncanny skill that the rest of the household staff often declared he could read minds.

When Matthew was a young boy, the mere threat of Thompson's presence could stop him in his tracks. No matter how well Matthew hid his mischief, the man would always know.

Hesitating on the landing now, Matthew was struck by the irony that here he was, decades later, hiding mischievous deeds again. And Thompson still knew.

As he turned the last corner, the noise and scent told Matthew he'd found the laundry at last. He listened to the lilt of a woman's voice as she gossiped with someone over her work.

If he was careful, he could imitate their speech enough to hide his accent and, hopefully, his status. That had been a favorite trick of his youth—mimicking others' voices. It drove his father to distraction—

which was, of course, its highest value. By the age of twelve Matthew could imitate relatives enough to fool even his sire momentarily. More than once Covington had threatened to ship his son off to the most vile form of punishment imaginable—the theater. Matthew knew, though, that the threats were hollow; the Covingtons would have endured anything before allowing an *actor* to taint the family name. Trouble was, young Matthew had more than once thought the stage might be a better life than one under his father's constant glare.

"Ain't it amazing what shows up in the laundry?" asked a gravelly old voice from the steamy room to his left. "Fine entertainment it is." A fowl stench hit Matthew as he inched closer to the open door. "Most of the time. Nicky, my boy, what is you boiling up back there? Smells like six-day-old fish!"

A man snickered. "You ain't so far off. Some old salt in one of the rooms done died, and nobody found him for two days. The manager got so mad he sent the entire staff back to change every bedsheet in the hotel all over again."

"I told you that man ain't got no more sense than I got eyesight," the old woman snarled.

"I ain't never fought you on that one, Neda. And him telling us to do somethin' so useless. Like it's our fault some girl missed a room, so's now we got to do double loads of wash to keep up."

The old woman grunted. Numerous piles of linens along the hallway confirmed that the laundry staff would be working through the night to catch up. Matthew poked his toe at one or two of the piles, hoping to detect the hilt of his whip among the soft folds. He wasn't so fortunate—the bedding billowed gently.

"If we're washing clean sheets all over again, then what's that awful smell?"

"The dead man's linens, Neda. Can you believe it? I said we should throw them out, but the manager says if we bleach 'em enough times they'll be good as new. Not me—you'd never catch me sleeping in sheets some old coot died in."

Matthew flattened himself against the wall and wrinkled his nose against the dreadful smell. Good thing no one had to come out into the hallway to do away with the questionable bundle.

"Well, whatever you think, take it outside, why don't you? I'm too old to be smellin' dead people's things, you sniggering fool."

"I *was* just hauling it outside, Neda. If you could see through those eyes of yours, you'd know that. Now stay where you are so you're out of my way whiles I go past."

So the laundress had bad eyesight. Matthew would never get another chance like this. He could be in and out with the whip—if she had it—by the time Nicky came back inside. Matthew let his head fall back against the wall. *I must be daft.* Reaching up, he mussed his hair and rolled his shirtsleeves higher.

"Hey," he said brightly, raising his voice in pitch and adopting the rusty Southern drawl he'd heard from the woman. "You all found a big black whip, by any chance? I'd heard it was down here."

"I told Nicky somebody'd come lookin' fer it." Neda was an enormous woman with dark, shiny skin and eyes that were a milky, unfocused gray. She sat precariously balanced on a small stool, surrounded by baskets of linens. A stack of perfectly folded facecloths rested in her lap. She swiveled her round head, with its knot of thick, braided hair, toward a shelf to Matthew's left. "That it?"

"Sure is," he said, wincing at his own comical effort to alter his voice.

"Well, fetch it on back to your master then, boy, 'fore Nicky decides to sell it, like he was plannin' to." She squinted at him, blinking repeatedly. "Big one, ain't you?"

Matthew grabbed the whip, keeping his eye on the door through which Nicky might return at any second. He hid his relief as his hand wrapped around the familiar hilt. "Huge, Mama says. Thanks!" he called as he ducked out the doorway, feeling as though he'd just gotten away with far more than he deserved.

He heard Neda chuckle loudly as he crept back down the hallway. "Hey Nicky, guess what? The Black Bandit just came and got his whip back. And you missed him. What do you think of that, Nicky boy?"

Chapter Eight

"That's servants' gossip." Georgia scowled. "Haven't you better sources than that?"

Stuart broke a flower off the hall arrangement—from the center again, as he always seemed to do, no matter how many times the house staff had asked him not to—and slipped it into his lapel. "Better sources than servants? They're the best sources there are, Peach. Now that our Bandit's a public mystery, everyone wants in on the fun. Of course, the promise of a few coins for Bandit stories doesn't hurt, either."

Georgia planted her hands on her hips. "You've wasted your money. Really, a whip loose in the hotel laundry? That's nonsense." She took a step closer to him. "Honestly, Stuart, isn't the Bandit selling enough of your papers? Now you pay people to invent collaborations?"

Stuart pouted. "You think so lowly of your own brother? Your own flesh and blood?"

"You are perfectly capable of such a thing."

He snatched his hat from the hands of the waiting butler. "Loath as I am to disappoint your high moral standards, this tale just happens to be genuine. A black whip showed up in the laundry at the Palace Hotel last night, and some tall young lad snatched it back before anyone could get a good look at it or at him. Absolutely Bandit-worthy, in my humble opinion, and straight from the mouth of a highly respected source."

Georgia frowned. "I've never known your opinion to be humble. Highly respected sources? In a hotel laundry?"

"On Mama's grave, Peach," Stuart said, leaning in and lowering his voice, "the whip's for real." He put on his gloves. "I wouldn't be surprised if it's the talk of dinner tonight at the Hawkinses. Mrs. Hawkins has become one of the Bandit's most ardent fans. Imagine that."

Georgia winced. Stuart knew his strategy. Bedillia Hawkins was by far the most excitable woman Georgia had ever met. If by some remote chance the newspaper account of a Black Bandit whip sighting didn't stir the public's imagination, Bedillia Hawkins would surely finish the job. It would be the town's juiciest gossip by sunrise. Stuart had probably made sure they would be dining at the Hawkinses tonight for just that reason.

"Don't you think, Georgia, dear?" Bedillia inquired of her obviously distracted dinner guest.

"Mrs. Hawkins?" Miss Waterhouse blinked, pulling herself back to the topic at hand. Matthew couldn't say he blamed her for her wandering thoughts. The conversation had been frightfully dull until the subject of the Bandit came up.

"I was saying, Georgia dear, how so much gossip seems to be coming out of the Palace Hotel these days," repeated Mrs. Hawkins. "I was asking Mr. Covington if he finds it tiresome to be staying there, with so much going on. Bodies, thefts and whips—dear me, what will we see next?"

Matthew tried not to wince. He supposed he should be grateful they'd made it through the soup course before someone raised the dreaded subject.

The whip. Thompson's expression had been unbearable when he'd held out the *Herald*'s account of the wayward whip. There, next to the latest installment of the Black Bandit's adventures, was a tantalizing article about how a mysterious whip had surfaced in the laundry of the Palace Hotel. How a suspicious individual had stolen into the laundry and taken it back. Could the stealthy young man have been the Black Bandit himself? The text hinted at a variety of things that could set tongues and imaginations into motion all over the city. Based on Mrs. Hawkins's fascination with the subject, it had been successful.

"Do you think he's real, Miss Waterhouse? This bandit of your brother's invention?" Mrs. Hawkins winked at Stuart while she asked the question. It made Matthew wonder just how often people used Georgia to get to her brother. Judging from her expression, it happened frequently, and she found it highly irritating.

"The bandit or the author?" Miss Waterhouse nearly succeeded in hiding the edge in her voice.

"Why, the Bandit, of course. Everyone knows who the author is, even if they aren't saying." Mr. Hawkins raised his glass in Stuart's direction and let out a hearty laugh.

"Hawkins, you flatter me," Stuart said, lifting his glass in turn. Matthew noted he neither denied nor confirmed the insinuation.

Miss Waterhouse had to work to raise her voice above the resulting hubbub. "I find myself wishing he were real," she said, more sharply than he guessed she meant to. "I certainly would welcome him. San Francisco seems to be in dreadfully short supply of men with noble character—present company excepted, of course."

Matthew wondered, by the way she said it, if she'd added the last remark out of sheer obligation rather than any genuine respect for the men in the room.

"Georgia doubts my sources, Mrs. Hawkins. She feels I manufactured the whip's appearance to sell papers. That I'm printing shameless gossip rather than verifiable facts. As if I'd ever print anything but the honest truth."

"Stuart Waterhouse," laughed the rather besotted man next to him, "when have you ever printed the honest truth?"

"Miss Waterhouse, it seems to me that you endure much on your brother's behalf," Matthew offered, because it seemed that no one else in the room gave a thought to her obvious discomfort. "How do you find the strength?"

She smiled—just a bit, and only for a second, but it was a smile nonetheless. "Hours and hours of prayer, Mr. Covington. I have been known to take my frustrations out on the upper strings of my harp—I am forever breaking them—but mostly it requires endless prayer." She kept her tone light and conversational, but he noted an edge of weariness in her glance.

Matthew looked around the table and thought Miss Waterhouse must have a penchant for lost causes. "That's far too large a load for such delicate shoulders. Perhaps one ought to leave such a Herculean task to the likes of the Black Bandit." The last remark jumped out of his mouth seemingly of its own accord, before he had one second to think better of it.

"Speaking of Herculean tasks, Mr. Covington," declared Stuart, "I think it's high time you visited Georgia's precious Grace House. They're always working to save the world over there. What do you say to a tour tomorrow?"

"Appealing as it sounds, I am expecting some documents to arrive from Sacramento in the morning. Perhaps another time?"

Dexter Oakman nearly jumped out of his seat, opposite Stuart. "Oh, gracious, I'd completely forgotten, Covington. Meant to tell you before dinner." He put down his glass. "Those documents won't be in until Tuesday, perhaps Wednesday. The wire came in this afternoon."

"Well," said Stuart, smiling broadly, "events are conspiring in your favor, aren't they? Tour Grace House, then. Reverend Bauers and his high-minded companions will make excellent chaperones. I've even heard nuns work there."

"I hardly think Reverend Bauers has time to conduct social outings," said Georgia.

"Nonsense," her brother replied. "You might even convince Covington to send over a spot of money to help the needy." He turned to Matthew. "Mind your pockets, Covington. My sister can be most compelling when it comes to philanthropy."

Of that, Matthew had little doubt.

Chapter Nine

The clock chimed quarter past the hour as Stuart refilled his glass and Oakman's. "Did you have any trouble?"

Dexter winced. "Some. It took a bit more grease across the palm to get them diverted, but we'll see those ledgers from Sacramento before Covington does. We'll have to be careful."

Stuart picked up the poker and stirred the fire. The gold-orange flames flickered, reflecting in amber liquid in his glass. "I'm always careful. Georgia's just making my job that much easier. We practically waltzed into that tour of the mission this evening. I hadn't yet worked out how I was going to get Covington out of the office for a few hours in order to switch things. Honestly, I couldn't have planned it better myself."

"I did follow your line of thinking, Stuart." Oakman groaned, rubbing his leg. "Was it really necessary to bash my shin under the table? You've left a mark."

"Sorry about that, Dex." Stuart replaced the poker and walked over to the chair where he sat. "I hadn't time to be subtle. And speaking of marks..." He lowered his voice even though they were completely alone. "You're sure of this fellow? They'll be no trace of the alterations?"

Oakman drained his glass. "He's the top man, they tell me."

Stuart frowned. "Remind our friend that it won't go at all well for him if anyone can notice his...handiwork."

"Oh, I believe he knows." Oakman smiled.

"Make sure," Georgia's brother said, sipping from his own glass. "Show him your shin if you think that will help. I want no slips on this. Not one."

The man nodded, forcing a weak laugh. "Without a hitch, Stuart. It'll come off without a hitch."

Waterhouse began loosening the knot in his cravat. "Tell your wife there'll be a lovely piece about her dress tonight in the social column this week. She looked stunning at dinner, and we haven't run something about her yet this month. She deserves it."

"She'll be very pleased to hear that, Stuart. You're always so good to her. And Caroline does love to see her name in the columns, you know."

Everybody does, thought Stuart. *Everybody always does.*

"It's not a grand cathedral, but I rather fancy God enjoys it here." Georgia ran her hand across the adobe arch of the mission's side doorway, and a piece of the facade crumbled under her touch. "She's put up a grand fight over the years, and she's still standing. Reverend Bauers excels at what he calls 'making do at making do.'"

"That really means finding new sources for bandages, making food go three times as far, and squeezing yet one more use out of most any object," explained the reverend as he led Georgia and Mr. Covington out into the gardens.

They'd not gone three steps when a noisy commotion started somewhere off to their left, by the kitchens. Within seconds a pair of youths burst through the door, bundles in their hands. It was clear they hadn't expected to find anyone in the garden.

"Thief!" a voice cried from inside. "Stop them!"

Georgia gasped as she realized what the boys were carrying. Poking out of one of the bundles was a gold cross from the mission's tiny chapel. After glancing quickly at each other, they split up, running around the garden fountain toward the gate. Without any discussion whatsoever, Mr. Covington and Reverend Bauers set upon them, Covington taking the larger of the pair.

Georgia backed up to the fountain rim as a brawl broke out around her. "Help! In the garden!" she called as arms and legs thrashed.

As large as they'd seemed coming through the door, the boys were still rather young, and it was only a minute—albeit a dreadfully long one—before each was subdued. Grunting, they struggled against the grip of Reverend Bauers and Mr. Covington.

"How dare you!" the reverend huffed at his captive, as angry as Georgia had ever seen him.

In that second, the larger boy managed to pull out of Covington's grasp and slide something metal from his boot. It was a knife, which he quickly waved at Matthew.

No one moved. The mission cook burst through the door, only to freeze on the threshold as she saw the weapon in play. Mr. Covington, however, somehow used that momentary distraction to grab a long stick from a

pile behind him. He planted his legs in a defiant stance.
How could he hope to defend himself with just a stick?
Oh, Lord, help him!

Both combatants brandished their weapons, and it
was instantly obvious that Mr. Covington knew exactly
how to wield his, whereas the boy had evidently just
grabbed a kitchen knife. Slowly, the man angled his
body sideways, his rear arm high while he swung the
stick through the air, coolly meeting each of the lad's
angry thrusts.

The cook disappeared back through the door—going
for help, Georgia hoped. She clutched the fountain rim,
not caring if she soaked her sleeves, trying desperately
to think of something she could do.

The smaller boy suddenly stomped on Reverend Bauers's foot, sending the two of them doubling over. Immediately, the larger boy lunged at Covington, who
tossed aside his stick, trying to wrestle the knife from
his opponent's hands. The lad only fought harder, slash-
ing wildly at Covington's chest.

Lord Jesus, save him! Georgia nearly fell into the
fountain, and a scream left her throat. The smaller boy
took off through the gate with no thought for his con-
spirator. Reverend Bauers yelled for help as Covington
struggled with the larger lad and his knife.

Georgia stood frozen and shocked. In all her time
here, in all she had seen, no one had ever had the audacity to steal from Grace House.

Three men finally came rushing out the kitchen door,
just as the blade sank into Covington's forearm. Georgia flinched at the sound of it ripping through the fabric of Mr. Covington's jacket. The Englishman gave a
roar of pain, at which the wiry lad squirmed out of his

grasp and leaped through the gate his companion had left swinging.

"We draw no blood in Grace House!" Bauers bellowed after him, rushing to Covington's aid.

Georgia was still clutching the fountain, unable to move as she watched scarlet ribbons creep out from between Mr. Covington's clenched fingers. He'd been stabbed. She'd seen Cook cut herself with a kitchen knife, but had never witnessed anyone being *purposely stabbed.* Her brain seemed unable to accept the concept.

"Georgia!" the reverend called. "Come here."

Covington's eyes locked onto hers. She tried to breathe, but it was as if her corset had tightened into a vise. Dimly, she saw him force a smile.

"Shall we go find me a bandage and dry you off?" he asked.

A thick, red drop of blood fell from his clenched hand and splattered on the flagstone, snapping her out of her stupor. She let go of the fountain, and the breath she'd been trying to take rushed suddenly into her lungs.

Reverend Bauers took off his coat and wrapped it around Georgia's shoulders. She really wasn't that wet, but she shivered as the clergyman slipped Mr. Covington's waistcoat off his good arm and bundled it around the injured one. "Since we've ruined your coat already, it might as well serve as a bandage until we get you inside. We might have to stitch you up, Covington. There are medical supplies in the next building—can you walk?"

Chapter Ten

A sharp scent made Georgia gasp. She felt the warmth of a hand on her shoulder.

"Miss Waterhouse?" a genteel voice was saying. It sounded foreign and yet somehow familiar. "Miss Waterhouse, can you hear me?"

"Hmm?" She rolled her head in that direction, waiting for the smoke all around her to clear. The sharp scent came to her again, making her cough.

"Georgia, my child," said a second voice, "wake up. You've been far too brave today. Open your eyes, child." A cold, wet cloth touched her brow, and she recognized the voice as Reverend Bauers's.

The sharp scent returned a third time, making her lurch forward and rasp in a breath. She grabbed the reverend's hand as the room spun around her.

"You fainted, Georgia," he said, with an affectionate laugh, "I told you to go home, and that there was no reason to sit through my stitching Covington up. You are more stubborn than that brother of yours at times."

With a white-hot flash that made her eyes open wide, Georgia recalled her circumstances. How foolish she had been to insist on staying through the gruesome task. "Dear me. I'm so dreadfully sorry to have caused such a fuss."

"It's I who should be offering the apology," said Mr. Covington, looking much better than the last time she remembered seeing his face. "This was no place for a lady. Even a very brave lady." He held up a bandaged arm. "You'll see I've made a fine recovery, and I should never forgive myself if you do anything less than the same." He leaned in, his dark brows furrowing in concern. "Are you quite all right, Miss Waterhouse?"

Georgia blinked and took a deep breath, then dabbed at her face with the cool cloth the reverend offered. "Yes. Yes, I think so. Although I'd find a glass of water very welcome."

"Stay off your feet, Covington," said the reverend, pushing himself up from the floor, where he knelt in front of Georgia. "I'll go fetch our brave Miss Waterhouse a glass of water, and perhaps a bit of apple for the both of you. It's been a trying morning, wouldn't you say?"

"Most trying, indeed," she said, fussing with the reverend's coat, which was still wrapped around her. She really wasn't as soaked as everyone seemed to believe. "I'm afraid I've proved a miserable guide, Mr. Covington."

"Not at all," he replied. "I can't remember the last time I've had such a lovely lady swoon on my account." A wide, warm smile flashed across his face. "It's done marvels for my spirits." He nodded toward his bandage when Georgia blushed. "And the arm should heal quickly." He returned his gaze to her face and let it linger for a moment.

Georgia felt the room begin to spin again. "Gracious, I don't believe I've ever seen a larger needle." She fanned herself with the cloth and sat up a bit straighter.

Covington cast a glance toward the table, still cluttered with the bloody tools of his treatment. "I must admit, I have seen smaller, and I'll confess to an unkind thought or two toward the beastly thing in the last hour." He turned to face her again, and she noticed that his hair was in disarray, spilling wildly over his forehead. He had such dark, glossy hair for one with eyes of blue.

"But I *am fine,* Miss Waterhouse, and I have no doubts whatsoever about my full recovery." He fumbled with his shirt collar, struggling to raise his injured arm high enough to fasten the button. "I'll be summing up ledgers by the day's end, I'm afraid."

Georgia reached out to help him, then stopped herself. Red-faced, they both retreated, suddenly aware of their inappropriate proximity. Even under the unusual circumstances, they were sitting entirely too close. Mr. Covington cleared his throat and used his good arm to draw his chair toward the table.

It seemed an eternity before the reverend returned. He offered a small cup to Georgia. "Here's water for you now, but I think it's best we have something to eat in the dining room and let them clean up here. Take my arm, Miss Waterhouse, and mind you walk slowly."

When they were seated in the mission's meager dining room, Reverend Bauers produced a small packet, which he placed on the table. "I regret your visit wasn't a pleasant one, Covington. So I'd like to give you this. It comes with a bit of a story that I think you'll appreciate, given the circumstances."

"There's no need," the Englishman argued.

Reverend Bauers huffed and pushed the packet toward Georgia. "Open it for him, will you, child? I'd just as soon that wounded arm stayed resting on the table, Covington."

Georgia opened the wrinkled brown paper—on its sixth or seventh use, she mused—to reveal a small Bible. It was old and well used, and had a chunk missing from the middle, as if someone had carved a bite out of it, like a steak. The pages had been cut clean through to somewhere in the Psalms.

"Seen a bit of wear, this Bible has," said the reverend.

Georgia handed the small, leather-bound book across the table to Mr. Covington, who held it up and squinted at the cover. "Looks as though someone took a knife to this," he remarked.

Reverend Bauers chuckled. "As a matter of fact, that's exactly what happened. I wore that Bible in my breast pocket throughout my travels in the islands. I served our Lord setting up no fewer than four churches in Hawaii. We did not always get the warmest of greetings." He pointed to the gap. "A spear thrown at my heart took out that bit. Saved my life, it did."

He motioned for Georgia to search the coat she was wearing, and sure enough, in the breast pocket she found a small Bible nearly identical to the one Mr. Covington was holding. Only this one had a black leather binding and was still intact.

"I've taken to always wearing one over my heart. And I've been looking to pass this on to the right man ever since." The reverend paused and gazed at his guest. "I think it ought to be you, Covington."

"I can't accept this. It saved your life."

"You saved Grace House from theft, my son. And

came out much worse for your effort. No, no, I'll not be refused. You must have this, I insist."

Covington looked at Georgia. "I implore you, Miss Waterhouse, reason with him. It's far too dear a gift. I simply can't accept it." He slid the Bible across the table toward her.

She put out her hand to stopped him. "I would think it's become all too clear to you by now that Reverend Bauers cannot be refused. Accept the gift with gratitude, Mr. Covington. After all, as the reverend is all too fond of saying, God is on his side." As she spoke, Georgia felt something very close to a wink—the sort of playful glance she would give Stuart over the head of a dull dinner guest—spark in her eyes. It lasted a fraction of a second—a heartbeat, really—but seemed to stretch on in time. Their hands lingered on either end of the Holy Book, and she had the sensation of something important transpiring. It was nothing she could name or even really recognize; rather, the sort of flash one would put down to an overactive imagination or insufficient sleep. A "hunch," Stuart would have called it.

But he would have been wrong. It was something else entirely.

Reverend Bauers might have called it "the wind of the Spirit," but that would not be entirely correct, either.

Georgia spent the entire carriage ride home, and the ensuing afternoon sequestered in her rooms, trying to put a name to it.

Some part of her already knew.

Chapter Eleven

Stuart, how could you?

Georgia roamed through the house, fuming. For a moment she stopped in the dining room, but she had no taste for breakfast. Clutching the offending newspaper, she headed toward the parlor.

I cannot believe you've done this!

She pushed through the enormous double doors and stood in the center of the opulent room. It seemed stifling. Even though she'd chosen many of the furnishings, because Stuart had no patience for such things, she could see none of her own touches. Stuart's character was all over the house. He was everywhere, and Georgia seemed invisible. Frowning, she spun on her heels, heading toward his study.

He'd done the unthinkable. Betrayed their agreement in the worst way. She simply stood in the doorway, betrayal choking down all the words she wanted to say.

"Oh," he said after what seemed like hours, finally noticing her presence. How could he look up from his papers like that, as if she'd just breezed into the room to ask about the weather? "So you've seen it?" His voice was casual, almost dismissive. It incensed her.

She dropped the paper onto his desk, astounded that he—her own brother—couldn't see the pain he'd caused her. "How could you?" she finally asked, sounding so weak she wanted to kick herself.

He sighed, more in frustration than sympathy. "I own the paper, Peach. And I edit *all* my writers. Why should you be any different?"

It stung beyond her ability to describe. He would never see the enormity of what he had done. Why had she expected to be exempt from Stuart's legendary meddling?

"Because I *am* different," she retorted, wishing she had a more clever argument. "You added to my story. Something silly that shouldn't ever have been in there."

"*Embellished.* I embellished. It needed something to lighten up all that drama. Really. Carrying a Bible over his heart? With a knife mark in it? It was too much. You should be glad I didn't cut that part out altogether. I had to give the readers something a little more real. And you hadn't given him a calling card yet."

"A what?"

"A calling card. A sign that the Black Bandit had been there. It's in every good story, like a signature. Terribly dramatic. People will love it."

"A white ribbon nailed to a tree?" In Stuart's version, the Bandit had left a white ribbon nailed to the tree above the villain's head. Georgia found it ridiculous. As if her mysterious hero was wandering the streets of San Francisco with ribbon and tacks in his pocket like a hatmaker.

"Well, black seemed too morbid. It's a delicious

irony, the Black Bandit leaving a white ribbon. I thought you'd appreciate that."

She appreciated nothing of the sort. "You could have asked." Georgia had taken this astounding risk, reached for this impossible dream, and he'd run over her. Like he ran over everyone. *Lord, how could You let this happen? I was so certain this came from You. And now...*

"Trust me. It'll run like wildfire." His condescending tone sliced at her—not because he was being deliberately cruel, but because he truly had no idea how much he'd hurt her. "You'll see," he said, returning his eyes to his work. "I'm very good at what I do."

Yes, Stuart, you're very good at what you do. She stood planted in the doorway, paralyzed with frustration at not being able to tell him how she really felt.

But would that change anything? Stuart would not suddenly soften his tactics because she had been the target this time. The paper was out. The calling card had been added. Her hero had been tainted by her brother's never-ending exploitation of everything he touched. Why had she expected better of him?

"You could have asked me to add a calling card of my own design," she said after a long pause, disgusted with the weakness of her voice.

"I don't ask," Stuart declared, obviously finding her suggestion ridiculous. "Not anyone. Not even you."

Matthew stared at the six columns before him, absentmindedly feeling for the bandage knotted under his shirtsleeve. He kept seeing the face of Georgia Waterhouse, her pale lashes resting against alabaster cheeks, her head tilted against the sturdy back of the chair, her creamy fist still clenched around the handkerchief. It was absurd that he found her so stunning in a dead faint. One does not, after all, look one's best when keeling over. She had "fainted in his best interest," as he'd put it when he recounted the entire morning's events to an astounded Thompson—yes, visibly astounded, and that was worth something! The whole incident endeared Miss Waterhouse to him.

Matthew did omit one detail to Thompson. He found he did not want to speak of the small, battle-sliced Bible that the reverend had handed him with such unsettling reverence. At first, Matthew thought his reluctance to accept the token was born of the clergyman's great affection for it—he'd not merited so dear a gift from someone he'd just met. As he carried it home, he realized that the reluctance came from the feeling that he was standing on a very slippery slope. Had things not come to such dire ends with the whip, Matthew confessed he more than once thought to hide the Bible under his blankets.

When he opened the morning paper, he wished he had.

Chapter Twelve

There it was in the newest episode of the hero's adventures: the Black Bandit and his own battle-scarred Bible. It could only mean Stuart Waterhouse was writing the Bandit stories himself. Given what Matthew knew of him, it was easy to believe Waterhouse penned his paper's greatest sensation. Georgia must have told him the story of the Bible, and he'd used it in the Bandit's adventures. A foolish act, as it gave away his identity.

Or did it? Perhaps Stuart wasn't as foolhardy as he seemed. Only three people in the world knew the source of the tale, and none of them had any interest in angering Stuart Waterhouse.

"Mr. Covington, sir?" A bright-faced clerk rapped on his office door. Matthew set down his pen and looked up from the ledgers. "There's a Reverend Bauers here to see you."

So someone else has been surprised by the morning paper, Matthew thought as he stood up and pulled off the black sleeves that protected his shirt from the ledger ink. He harbored a moment's ingratitude toward the reverend as the sleeve bumped painfully over his wound.

Crude as the stitches were, he found he couldn't bring himself to have the wound redone by another surgeon. Not only would it be embarrassing to have to recount how one small street urchin had bested him in a fight and skewered his arm, but Matthew was certain the reverend would be coming to check on his "patient," and would feel disappointed that he had chosen to seek care elsewhere. Matthew's father was always boasting about the ghastly war scar on his left shoulder, and now Matthew had a ghastly scar of his own to boast about. As to its source, well, perhaps he'd omit some of the less heroic details when he told his father.

"Covington," Bauers called as he bustled into the room. He carried, not surprisingly, a copy of the *Herald,* as well as a small bag Matthew was sure presaged further medical atrocities yet to be endured. "How are you, my son?" The reverend pointed to his arm. "Healing well?"

"I had all but put the incident behind me," Matthew lied. "That is, until I read the morning paper. Seems we share a bit of the Black Bandit legend now, don't we? Do sit down." He came around his desk and motioned for the reverend to take one of the high-backed chairs that faced his desk.

"I suspected Mr. Waterhouse all along," Reverend Bauers said in a hushed voice as he eased his considerable frame into the chair. "Now we can be certain, can't we?" By his expression, Bauers enjoyed his newfound secret celebrity. "I must say I never thought I'd see the day when Stuart Waterhouse wrote about the Bible. God is full of splendid surprises." He chuckled, patting the folded paper on his lap.

"Will you reveal him?" Matthew asked, welcoming

any topic that kept Reverend Bauers from opening that bag. Diversionary, yes, but he was curious to know what the reverend planned to do regarding Stuart. Several of the "men of God" Matthew had encountered back in England wouldn't hesitate to parlay such a secret into several sizable contributions if they found themselves in the clergyman's position. Everyone knew George Towers didn't really exist, but part of the Black Bandit story's attraction was its mysterious author. Stuart knew the mystery helped line his pockets, and he probably would consent to a few "acts of charity" to preserve it. Still, Matthew doubted the reverend would be the kind of man to pursue extortion, even for the sake of his ragged little flock.

"Oh, I suppose there's some that would try to use it for their own gain," Bauers replied, echoing Matthew's thoughts. "I'm sure if I went to see Mr. Waterhouse, I would come away with several tidy gifts. I confess I thought of it, for an instant, last night when yet another chair broke in the dining room. I find myself having great fun with the secret of it all, however. And if it means Stuart Waterhouse will actually have to pen the word *Bible* a few more times, then I am all for letting him run with our tale." The clergyman leaned close. "Ah, but Mr. Covington, could you not expose him as easily as I? After all, you've got the Bible now. I do wonder what the good Lord has in the offing with this one."

Matthew had not yet considered the idea of God somehow placing this particular Bible in his particular hands. It was an odd, squeamish thought to entertain. "What do you make of the Waterhouse family, Reverend? Did you know Georgia and Stuart's parents at all?"

Bauers either took the bait or chose not to recognize

the diversion. "Alex and Audrey Waterhouse? No, but one hears things. I know Alex was the one to move the family business away from shipping into a variety of other interests, not the least of which is the newspaper Stuart now runs. Mrs. Waterhouse, from what I've been told, was a very great woman. Much like Georgia, I think. Very strong faith and a good, strong spirit. I'm not at all sure what she'd think of Stuart these days."

Matthew eased back in his chair and leaned his weight on his good hand. "And what do people think of Stuart Waterhouse these days?"

Reverend Bauers paused, stroking his chin. "He can be a very great friend. Or a greater enemy. Still," said the reverend, opening his bag, to Matthew's growing distress, "I wonder if Stuart has even an inkling of all the good he's doing."

"Whatever do you mean?" inquired Matthew, half out of curiosity and half to keep the man's hands out of that blasted bag.

"Oh, I know Stuart Waterhouse only thinks he's landed on a new way to sell papers, but God is no stranger to using bad intentions for good. Take the book of Genesis, for example. Joseph's brothers hardly had good intentions when they sold their little brother into slavery. God took their evil plot and used it to save thousands of lives." Reverend Bauers held the paper up. "If Stuart could see what I see, how people believe the tales to be true because they *need* the Bandit to be real, it would frighten him to bits. Georgia is proud of her brother, despite his motives, because he gave San Francisco what it needed most—a hero. I'd like to think you wouldn't be sporting that—" he pointed to Matthew's wound—"if our young friend had had a better start in life and more men of character to show him how to behave."

"Did you catch the thieving little urchin?"

"We did. And he was punished. Not to defend him, but you might steal as well if your father had poured all his wages into the bottom of a glass and your family hadn't eaten in three days."

Matthew fingered the knot on his bandage again. "Hard times are no excuse for criminal behavior."

"Oh, he's a bad seed, I'll grant you that. But all these boys know is cheating. Dockworkers are cheated out of fair pay as often as you and I breathe. If there's no justice around, you quickly learn to take all you can just to live. Steal to eat. Lads learn by example." The clergyman heaved a sigh and set about opening the bag again.

"Surely men of the cloth such as yourself can show them a better course," Matthew said, attempting to keep the conversation open and the bag shut.

"Come now, Mr. Covington!" The reverend spread his pudgy arms wide. "Do I look like the focus of a young man's aspirations? I've no curves to capture their hearts and no gallantry to capture their minds. Oh, no, Covington. Surely you can see why Miss Waterhouse thinks the Bandit is such a fine idea. A swashbuckling man of mystery is just the thing to turn these young imaginations around. The Black Bandit may be the best thing Stuart Waterhouse has ever done for us." Bauers chuckled as he pulled at the drawstring of the small brown bag. "Unless, of course, our Mr. Waterhouse can make his Bandit come to life. Now that'd be nothing short of a wonder."

He produced some wicked-looking scissors and a

bottle of something Matthew was sure would result in considerable pain. "Now, Covington, let's see to that arm."

His arm had been stinging for hours. That was his excuse. Surely the pain had driven him to such foolishness.

The pain and the harrowing tales he had heard that afternoon.

After Bauers had left, Matthew's arm stung so badly he decided further ciphers would be out of the question. He shifted his attention to the shipping interests of Covington Enterprises. A couple of inquiries had led him to a contact, a clerk within the offices who dealt repeatedly with dockworkers and marine merchants.

Matthew didn't like what he found.

An hour or two with the clerk not only confirmed Reverend Bauers's dire assessments, it exceeded them. Commerce on the docks, if one could even stretch to call it such, was nothing short of piracy. London's worst corners held more justice than San Francisco's docks. So far Covington Enterprises appeared innocent of such behavior, but given such a culture, Matthew couldn't be certain. It was standard practice to promise immigrant workers one wage and then pay another after a long day's labor. One company's shipments moved swiftly through the docks while another's rotted in plain sight.

Matthew had heard enough to sour his stomach.

And that's why he'd done it.

Well, that and the fact that he couldn't sleep. A man's mind plays tricks with his good sense at three in the morning. He hadn't set out to head South of the Slot at that hour—no man in his right mind would consider such a thing. He hadn't set out to do anything. It just overtook him, like a wave sweeping out to sea.

And somehow, with no forethought, as if someone else had moved within his own body and the way had been cleared for him, the deed was done.

He came back near dawn, exhausted, and astonished at his own actions. Thompson asked where he had been, but he didn't answer. Thompson stared at his exposed wound and asked if he wanted a new bandage, but Matthew still said nothing.

Mostly because he had absolutely no idea what to say.

Chapter Thirteen

"Quinn? How on earth did you find your way here?"

"You have to come, now. Reverend says so." The boy looked pressed for time, but not upset. What could bring him here this early in the morning?

"Is everything all right? Is the reverend ill?"

"No, ma'am. He's jumping around like it's Christmas." Quinn stared past her to the breakfast table visible through the dining room doors. "He sent me to get you right away. You have to come now, Miss Georgia." The boy looked past her skirts again, licking his lips. "I think he'll explode if you don't."

Georgia watched the lad's sense of urgency war with the scent of bacon wafting out from behind her. "Quinn, has no one offered you a bit of breakfast for your efforts?" she inquired, trying hard to keep the laughter from her voice.

"No, ma'am!" His eyes widened in hungry hope.

"Well, I'm all for rushing to Reverend Bauers's aid, but I have a few things to attend to that will only take a moment. Why don't you busy yourself with a plate in the kitchen while you wait. I won't be but a..."

Before she had even finished, Quinn was bounding down the hallway.

A small crowd circled Grace House, when Georgia and Quinn arrived in her coach. Several families stood in the courtyard with Reverend Bauers, chattering excitedly. Some great news had obviously reached the mission. If he already knew, Quinn's mouth was sealed; he claimed he'd been told to be silent.

It took a few moments to find it. After all, one would have expected something far larger, given the commotion. Eventually, after a question or two, she was directed to something small on the Grace House doorpost.

At which point Georgia nearly stumbled.

Money.

A good deal of money, from the looks of it.

Nailed to the doorpost with a white ribbon.

The world grew still for a moment, as if startled into silence by the sight. Her gaze swayed to Reverend Bauers, who met her eyes with an expression of astonishment that surely matched her own.

Nailed to the door with a white ribbon.

Then, suddenly, she caught sight of more white ribbons. Dozens of people clutched a white ribbon and an actual dollar bill. It may have been the first time any of them saw or held, much less possessed, paper money. A dollar was no small amount, but a *paper* dollar—that was a double surprise. God, in His infinite wisdom and humor, had taken Stuart's ugly twist and turned it into something splendid.

"See?" spouted Quinn. "The Bandit!" Georgia marveled that the child had been able to keep quiet at all, given the sparkle in his eyes as he pulled her forward.

"Can you believe it?" Reverend Bauers was beet-red from the excitement. "Have you ever in all your years…" He couldn't finish the sentence.

Georgia could only shake her head. She was afraid to speak, sure she would give herself away if she uttered even one syllable.

The money had been nailed to the top of the archway, about nine feet off the ground. The white ribbon fluttered in the breeze, and hands from the crowd reached up to touch it, as though it would bless them on contact. When she'd read Stuart's passage, Georgia had envisioned a frilly white ribbon—something off a hat or dress. This was a simple strip of white cloth—not fussy, but noble and absolutely perfect.

"Come, lad," Reverend Bauers called, pointing to Quinn. "What do you say we get this down and put it to good use?"

The boy sprinted toward the reverend, who hoisted him up to reach the nail. It did not come free easily, and in the end three men had to hold Quinn up while he wiggled it loose. When he finally succeeded, and was lowered into the crowd clutching the money and the ribbon, a cheer rose up. Georgia absorbed every detail so that she could tell Stuart. Even he couldn't remain unaffected by the scene unfolding before her.

Hope had come South of the Slot.

God had brought it. Invited by the persona of her Black Bandit.

Her satisfaction was so deep, so complete, that if the world never knew of her role, it would be more than fine.

Thank You, Lord, Georgia prayed as she watched Reverend Bauers lock the money up in the mission safe a few minutes later. Fifty dollars would go a very long way in his resourceful hands. *Thank You so very much for giving me such a laughable idea and turning it into this. I'm blessed beyond words.*

The reverend dusted off his hands and turned to her, grinning from ear to ear. "I never thought I'd have occasion to say this, child, but God bless Stuart Waterhouse."

"Stuart?"

"Come now," said the clergyman, pulling her a bit closer while he lowered his voice. "Do you think I don't know? It's obvious the Bandit is Stuart's doing, so don't try to hide it." He narrowed one eye playfully. "Although I'd mind what you say around him from now on. After this hits his presses, he's liable to pounce on any story you tell him. It's a good thing Mr. Covington seems sporting about the whole matter, I'll tell you that."

So they all thought Stuart wrote the Bandit stories.

Well, of course they did—it would be the natural conclusion of anyone who really sat down to think about it. And surely now the reverend and Mr. Covington had every reason to think Stuart was George Towers. They'd naturally assume she'd told Stuart the story of the Bible, and he'd used it. Such behavior was expected of him.

But Stuart hadn't done it, had he? No, she had. She had done something so "Stuartlike" that everyone immediately attributed it to him. Not a compliment to her character.

Still, look what God had accomplished with it. Did that mean she had done the right thing? Or that God

had made good come from her poor choice? The fact
that there was no clear answer was disturbing indeed.

"Why yes, of course, that's quite right," she said,
trying to hide her tangle of emotions. The few minutes
she'd had were simply not enough to digest today's wild
turn of events. Georgia felt as if her head and heart were
turning somersaults in twelve directions.

"It's a fine, fine day." Reverend Bauers beamed. "Just
last night I was beseeching our Lord to send help for
the back staircase. I was hoping we'd get another year
out of the floorboards, but…" He shook his head, the
tops of his ears turning pink as he chuckled yet again.
"Fifty dollars. Glory be to God! Fifty dollars."

"It is an amazing thing," Georgia said, meaning
every word.

"And long overdue in coming, my child." Reverend
Bauers fiddled with the white ribbon someone had
tucked into his coat pocket. He looked up, a thoughtful expression on his chubby features. "You must tell
Mr. Covington at once. He will be delighted, I think,
after having seen the worst of our little flock."

Georgia smiled, thinking how grand it would be to
watch news of this fly through the city. "Stuart has invited him to dinner tomorrow, so I shall make sure he
hears of our little wonder. It is a good day, Reverend,"
she said. "Go and enjoy it."

Chapter Fourteen

Georgia found Stuart standing over the printing presses. There on the stairway above the rows of black, greasy machines, he was king of all he surveyed. The day's edition had been rerun with a detailed account of what Stuart called "The Generosity at Grace House."

"Look at them, Peach." He spread his hands, gesturing to the roaring machines. "Whirring away. It's just ink and paper, but it's so much *more* than ink and paper." He burst into a chorus from *The Gondoliers*. "Did I not say it would be spectacular? I've even ordered white ribbons for the floral arrangements at dinner tonight." He stopped swaggering and crossed his arms in thought for a moment. "I may even have them string up the trees on the front walkway. Ribbons everywhere. What do you think of that?"

That was Stuart—excessive in every detail. "I think it rather much," she replied. Then again, "rather much" was what people expected of her brother. "There will be no white ribbons in my hair tonight, so don't even think of asking."

The look on his face told her she'd accurately predicted the limits—or lack of limits—of his excess. He was, obviously, planning to ask her just that. She shook her head, but couldn't help smiling at his rampant happiness. His pleasure meant something to her, because he was the only person who knew the Bandit's true source. Even if he had twisted it beyond her liking, the partnership had been fruitful beyond her bravest dreams.

At that moment, despite his faults—and the faults he seemed to drive her to—she loved her brother.

Matthew made the coachman go around the block again when he pulled up to the Waterhouse mansion. The sight ruffled him so much he needed several minutes to summon his composure.

Not that the Waterhouse mansion wasn't an impressive sight on its own, having the unmistakable appearance of an owner who didn't know when enough was enough. But tonight, it looked like a frosted cake. The ornate house and grounds were literally covered with white ribbons.

I suppose I deserve this, Matthew chided himself as they rounded the corner to see the ribbon-bedecked house for the second time. His stomach seemed to sink to the soles of his boots as they started up the inclined drive. *It always ends up in something like this, and you never learn. Never.* Matthew slumped down in his seat, wishing he could somehow render himself invisible.

But wait, you are. No one knows you were the one. Surely, if people knew, they'd have been on you like bees on honey by now. You're safe. He pulled in a breath and straightened his collar.

Just don't ruin it.

Had the invitation come from anyone but the Waterhouses, Matthew would have made his excuses and kept to his room. Even if it meant an entire evening of ignoring Thompson's suspicious glare. And the valet did suspect something. After a lifetime of Matthew's antics, the man had frighteningly good instincts about what Matthew did or didn't do out of his sight. But even Thompson, for all he might suspect, would never reveal anything.

It was worth any discomfort, Matthew decided, to see Miss Waterhouse's reaction to his little stunt. The whole time he'd been darting in and out of shadows, shredding his bandage and inventing ways to hammer silently, his mind had played with the image of her face. How she would react. How those porcelain cheeks would flush with joy at the sight of those ribbons fluttering in the breeze.

He'd done it for her. He told himself over and over that he hadn't, but the truth refused to subside. Her high expectations for mankind had tugged something out of him. So he'd done it. He'd gone out and made that fictional hero display some of the philanthropy she so valued.

It felt marvelous, reckless, and he'd never slept better.

Good thing, too, Matthew thought as he pulled himself out of the coach and cringed at the cascade of white ribbons dripping all over the house. *You'll need every wit you have about you tonight.*

Stuart Waterhouse looked as though he'd been crowned king of California. Within ten seconds of saying hello, Matthew was dead certain Stuart was the pen behind the Black Bandit. He was strutting like a peacock, cleverly dodging the constant questions about the Bandit's white-ribboned generosity. For a man who loved intrigue and sensation, today must have felt like a thousand Christmases wrapped into one.

Even with all the other secrets abounding that night, Matthew was keenly aware of the one secret he shared with Georgia Waterhouse: that he owned the Bible of Black Bandit fame. Bauers knew, and probably Stuart knew, as well, but that didn't alter Matthew's feelings.

She knew. It played across her face whenever her gaze flickered his way, driving him daft for most of the evening until sometime after coffees were poured, when Matthew managed a word with her in a corner of the library.

"My dear Miss Waterhouse," he said, astounded at his sudden craving to say her first name despite the social outrage it would have caused. "What an astounding pair of days."

Her smile ignited something in his chest. "So you've heard about our little wonder? The reverend said that you had seen the worst of our community, and now he was pleased that you were able to see us at our best."

"It is a fine thing."

"I'm so delighted for Grace House," she said.

Matthew let caution slip through his fingers. "I have a certain now-famous volume with me." He spoke the words quietly, his hand casually resting on his coat breast pocket. He knew exactly what he was doing, and it had the intended effect.

For a moment she seemed to hold her breath, and he felt it in the skip of his heartbeat. "Is that wise?" she nearly whispered.

"I have the feeling it's best kept on my person for

the time being. Imagine the spectacle should someone discover it."

Her eyes asked the question: *Will you reveal it?* What a strange thing it was to find himself in one of San Francisco's most enviable positions: knowing one of Stuart Waterhouse's secrets.

Chapter Fifteen

Surely, the Bible all but proved Stuart Waterhouse wrote the Bandit.

Ah, but Stuart still didn't know that Matthew was the one to bring the Bandit to life. Even if he never stooped to use them, holding such trump cards over Waterhouse was a rare moment indeed.

He'd rather have spent this moment in more private company with Georgia, but polite society had other plans. Instead, he found himself reduced to engaging Miss Waterhouse in a series of bland pleasantries as the other guests persisted in drifting in and out of their conversation. Stuart soared in for a moment, waving a white ribbon and pecking his sister on the cheek before a pair of his business associates whisked him away to meet someone "most important." After three more such distractions, Matthew finally secured a moment of privacy with her, and dived into the subjects he had wondered about for days.

"Why has Stuart never married?"

Miss Waterhouse put down the punch cup she was holding. "A bold question, Mr. Covington."

He tucked his hands in his pockets, rocking back on his heels. "Stuart is a bold man, Miss Waterhouse. And one of substantial wealth. Even with his...distinct character, he could have his choice of San Francisco's eligible young ladies."

Georgia turned her attention to an overlarge portrait of Stuart that hung beside the fireplace mantel. Posed in a thronelike chair beside a roaring fire, her brother looked so regal that the painting could have been hung on an ancient castle wall in Britain. The artist had also, however, captured the rebellious glint of Stuart's eyes. The sly turn of his mouth that let one know the man held a thousand secrets and wouldn't hesitate to use them.

"Stuart was almost married once," she said, her voice faraway as she touched the bottom corner of the frame. Matthew found the gesture surprisingly tender.

He liked that about her. Despite her brother's appetite for scandal, despite the fact that the floor beneath her feet and the clothes on her back and perhaps even the pearls at her neck had been very likely purchased with scandal, she wouldn't stoop to it.

Matthew held her eyes for a long moment, wanting to say so much more than was possible in the circumstances. "Still," he finally offered, "I believe marriage to be a fine and worthy institution."

"I agree." She gave a small smile and clasped her hands together. "I have seen the characters of many men highly improved by a fine marriage. I persist in my hope for Stuart."

He simply could not resist. Dropping his voice, he inquired, "And of your own hope? If I were a less honorable man, I would not resist the temptation to ask you why it is that you haven't married."

Her smile became warm and broad. She laid her hands across her throat in a mock swoon. "Oh, then it is a good thing you are an honorable man, Mr. Covington. Your resistance is most appreciated."

It was the flash in her eyes that banished the last of his restraint. "Why is it you never married, Miss Covington?"

"What of your resistance?"

"It seems to have wandered off. I shall fetch it back… eventually."

"As well you should."

He waited for her to reply.

She didn't. She simply looked at him with a sly smile. Again he saw a hint of the very complex woman lurking under all that propriety. "Then I shall answer you… eventually," she murmured.

"But not now."

"No, Mr. Covington. Not now."

Somehow, her refusal to comply was even better than any answer she could have offered. Which was a daft thought. Georgia Waterhouse drove him to sheer lunacy. His previous night's work was proof of that.

Georgia fell back on her pillows, exhausted yet wide awake. *Such a day this has been, Lord.*

One of the two dogs that lived in the Waterhouse mansion home laid its head across the foot of the bed. More than a dozen years ago a San Francisco man had been crazed enough to declare himself emperor of the United States. He'd had two dogs, one named Lazarus, the other named Bummer. When the "Emperor" died in 1880, Stuart had gone out and purchased two dogs and given them the same names. Georgia pitied the beasts, which were caught up in her brother's endless plays for power, just as she was. "Lazarus, can you imagine such a thing? Money, nailed to trees with white ribbons? How do you suppose it was done?" She flipped herself around on the bed to face the dog, scratching the thin-faced hound between the ears. "How is it that no one saw it?"

Lazarus only moaned, then turned in circles to settle himself on the thick rug. Georgia flopped back, her arms spread across the plush covers. How had it been done? The scene unfolded in her imagination, materializing out of a gray fog in tiny details. He must be tall—of course he would be tall—and athletic. Nimble but very strong. He must have dressed in dark clothes to have moved about unnoticed, she imagined. Black? Brown? No, gray. A misty gray.

Where had the money come from? Locals always used gold coin—only Easterners had paper money. What did that mean? When had he decided to adopt Stuart's white strips?

She saw him in her mind's eye—a faceless, noble silhouette sliding in and out of the shadows. Broad-shouldered, dark-eyed. A brooding personality, perhaps. A man who had known some of life's pain, she decided, although she couldn't exactly say why. A man who knew the burden of command and the power of mercy.

A man too noble, too perfect to be real. Oh, what she would give to meet such a man. He must be out there, somewhere.

"Bless him, Father. Whoever he is, wherever he is, he is my hero. And, perhaps, Yours."

Hero. The Bandit lived. Georgia fell asleep imagining the mysterious details of the man who had stepped into the Bandit's boots and changed her world.

Chapter Sixteen

"Thank you. I should have been loath to miss this." Georgia smiled at Matthew Covington as they wandered about the art exhibit.

"You live too much at the mercy of Stuart's schedule," Mr. Covington offered. "Surely you could have your choice of escorts or husbands to free you from such a fate."

She wished he would move his focus from such a tender topic. "Mr. Covington," she replied, lightening her tone intentionally, "are you trying to tell me you've rediscovered your restraint? For I must confess, I see no evidence of it yet."

He grinned, caught in the act. He seemed to enjoy trying to get her to address the one question she had clearly told him she would not answer. Not anytime soon, at least. "I've seen no evidence of your response, either."

"And you shall not." She twirled the handle of her parasol. "As such, we are at an impasse. Shall we find a more pleasant topic?"

He paused, as if searching for one, but Georgia was

quite convinced he had a list of conversational gambits lined up in his head, each one designed to land up at the reason for her unmarried status.

He took a more direct tack than she would have expected. "Your brother seems quite intent on fostering our friendship." He chose his words carefully. They both knew it might have been more accurate to say, "Your brother throws us together at every opportunity, and I suspect invents his own."

Georgia opted for a sliver of truth. "Stuart believes you to be important."

"Stuart's fascination with the English is no secret. Perhaps all he admires is my pedigree."

She stared at him with narrowed eyes. "Would he be mistaken, Mr. Covington? Am I to discover that you are in fact a dishonorable Spanish spy? A notorious German, perhaps, gifted in deceptive accents?"

Matthew bowed. "A son of British soil, Miss Waterhouse, loyal to crown and country. Although I was thought to be good with voices as a child. Used to play endless tricks on the house staff and my brother." He tucked his hands in his pockets as they turned the corner. "But I'm afraid there's not much use for such antics in the running of a proper British enterprise. Stuart is right in one respect, I suppose—I am important." He did not say the word as if it were a compliment. Quite the opposite. "I've responsibilities bearing down upon me at every turn. Reputations to maintain. Honor to uphold. Profits to tend." He gave a small sigh. "I am continually aware that should Covington Enterprises pull up stakes, many would lose their livelihood." He stopped and gazed at her, as if it was something he hadn't intended to reveal. "I believe we were in search of a pleasant subject. This hardly qualifies."

"You feel your obligations keenly, don't you, Mr. Covington?"

"Yes, Miss Waterhouse, I suppose I do."

"A very good thing. I believe God wisely places men of high conscience in charge of such sizable burdens."

They stepped out onto a small terrace warmed by the sun. "You still think God wise, Miss Waterhouse? With all that you see of man's evil toward his fellow man?"

"Of course I think God wise," Georgia said, turning to gaze at a tall row of trees. The aging newspaper minion Stuart had sent along as a chaperone had disappeared into another exhibit hallway nearly a quarter of an hour before. "Man's evils are not God's doing, but only born of the wisdom of His gift of free will." She allowed herself to turn and look at Matthew, straight into his eyes. "No, Mr. Covington, I do not think God is at all pleased with San Francisco these days."

"You hold the scriptures in high regard, don't you?" He motioned for her to sit on a bench off to one side of the terrace.

"Indeed I do." She settled onto it, taking care to ensure space between them.

Mr. Covington glanced back at the terrace gate, as if confirming the predictable absence of their "guardian." "Very well, then. Last time, you asked me to read to you. I should like you to return the favor." He removed the tattered volume from his coat pocket and handed it to her. "Surely you have favorite passages."

"I know you must have one, if not several," Matthew continued when she hesitated.

Her eyes darted back and forth, as if this was something too private to do on a terrace bench. Did the words in that book really mean that much to her?

"I'm afraid it is on a subject most men find dull," she stated, sounding as if she knew it was a useless defense.

"I care not," he said quietly, refusing to let his gaze drop from the inviting puzzle of hers.

Finally, she let her eyes fall as she feathered through the pages. She cleared her throat and adjusted herself on the bench. "'If I speak with the tongues of men and of angels, but have not love,'" she began, and then read through a poetic passage about what real love was and why it mattered above all else.

He watched how her fingers held the page with affection. She did love these words.

"'Believeth all things, hopeth all things, endureth all things...'" She paused just a moment before she finished, "'Love never faileth.'" She shut the book with a tender gesture, running her finger along the slice as if to soothe it.

Georgia Waterhouse was an extraordinary woman. She was beautiful, but it was her inner strength, her fierce devotion and hope, that pulled at him. *Can I tell you how I admire you, or would it frighten you away?*

She held the book out to him and he took it, clasping her hands in his and holding them as long as he dared. She seemed small and fragile in that moment, and he wanted to draw a long silver sword and demand the world pay attention to her, to honor her for the wonder she was. "Thank you," he said, meaning so much more.

Late that night—so late, in fact, that it was actually the next morning—Matthew sat at his hotel bay window. Sleepless, he stared at the full, creamy moon and the shadows it cast over the city. He thought of her. He fingered the jagged hole in the Bible just as she had done, feeling for evidence of her touch. Her hands had felt so small in his.

He was taken with her.

He'd been taken with women before. Struck by some stunning beauty or a clever wit. But those were quick flashes of fireworks compared to the slow burn he now felt in his chest.

"Oh, you fancy her," his brother would often say of the latest object of Matthew's affections. He would not use that word now—*fancy* seemed nowhere near what he was feeling.

Of course, nothing could be less sensible. Even if Georgia—and he enjoyed thinking of her as "Georgia," not "Miss Waterhouse," even though he'd never take such liberties out loud—was the perfect woman for him, it could never be. He was an Englishman who must someday, sooner or later, return home. And even if Stuart Waterhouse might view it as the coup of the century, Matthew couldn't see himself taking Georgia away from either her brother or her beloved San Francisco. He wouldn't uproot her like that. Even if he managed to persuade her to move with him to England—which he suspected he could—eventually she would feel uprooted and displaced.

But he *was* taken with her. So much that he could scarcely picture himself leaving California under his own free will.

And that's what duty was about, wasn't it? Handling responsibilities even when doing so clashed with one's own free will.

Matthew stared about the room, looking at the trappings of his lifetime of obligation. Files upon files. Dignified coats and hats, letters of introduction, documents piling up beside books and ledgers. Only the whip and sword felt like his own possessions.

The whip and the sword.

Put that thought away right this moment, Matthew scolded himself. *You've no right to deceive her like that.* Still, he had already done so, hadn't he? He'd made the Bandit step into the real world. And it had nearly made her glow when she talked about it.

He bolted upright, the truth of it shocking him. Matthew Covington could never woo Georgia Waterhouse.

But he knew someone who could.

Chapter Seventeen

Dexter Oakman tucked his fingers in his vest pockets and smirked. "Genius."

"The last three issues alone have sent our second-quarter figures well above projections." Stuart laced his own fingers behind his head and leaned back in his chair. "A profit is a thing of beauty, Dex."

"You'll have more profits than you know what to do with after this new venture takes off, Mr. Waterhouse."

Stuart narrowed his eyes at Oakman. "Are we on track?"

"A few snags, but you'll have the cooperation you need by the end of the year."

That was good. Stuart needed the cooperation of certain well-placed individuals. Lots of well-placed individuals, if his final plan was to be realized. Labor and commerce were simply a means to an end, tools to exert or release pressure. A port's true value was in how it could be manipulated. And if Oakman could be believed, Stuart would be able to manipulate certain valuable markets to his whim by the year's end.

Oakman picked up a copy of the *Herald.* "So what

of your real-life Bandit? Tossing money to the poor and making you look as if you called it down on the city's behalf. You want him to show up again?" Oakman turned and glanced at Stuart. "Or was it you who made him appear in the first place?"

It was, of course, the question everyone was asking. Had the *Herald* awakened a new hero, or simply installed one? Half the city—the optimists—believed the episodes had either driven a virtuous man to impersonate the Bandit, or had reported the Bandit's noble adventures under the guise of fiction to protect his secret identity. The other half of the city—the skeptics and cynics—believed the whole thing to be a clever stunt designed to sell papers.

Everyone had an opinion. It was the topic of endless discussions. Stuart, for the first time in a long time, waffled on which theory to encourage. Should he take credit for this new sensation, bolstering his reputation for sales genius? Or was the wiser move to play the noble card, humbly accepting his role in bringing out the city's inherent goodness?

It mattered not that he was, in truth, neither. Stuart had long discarded truth whenever there was profit to be made. And if profit came in the guise of a dashing swordsman invented by his sister, then who was he to turn it away?

Matthew heard the thick wooden doors shut behind him, blocking out the light as they closed. What sun still entered Grace House's tiny chapel was washed in a warm amber by the room's few small stained glass windows. The ornate churches in this city or in London never affected him. They were large and gracious and easy to dismiss as feats of architecture. This humble little chapel, however, seemed determined to seep into his bones. He'd walked through this chamber a dozen times during his visits to Grace House, but hadn't realized until this morning that he avoided lingering inside. It wasn't that he'd never had cause to be in here alone, but more that he unconsciously avoided it.

He had thought he was here to gain Reverend Bauers's partnership in a most unusual endeavor. That was why he'd come. But the sanctuary seemed to have an agenda all its own, as if it had been silently waiting for him to show up and walk into its grasp. Matthew felt ambushed by the extraordinary quiet. The room felt full and empty at the same time. He had the unsettling sensation of someone taking his insides and shaking them gently.

He breathed in the cool, distinct scent, a mix of candle wax, wood, and the smells of ritual he remembered from his infrequent visits to the cathedral in London. He'd shared his father's dislike of churches since he was young, being loath to suffer anything requiring quiet and stillness. Once, as a young lad, he'd slithered four pews away before his mother noticed his absence. Only Lady Hawthorne's shriek of surprise when young Master Covington's dusty, smiling face had peered up at her from below had given him away. His father had paddled him soundly—not for being disrespectful in church, but for sullying the family name.

Matthew figured out that day that the virtue extolled most in the Covington household was not piety, but propriety. In truth, his father cared little about the integrity of his conduct as long as its public appearance brought the family honor. If Matthew found a respectable way to enslave small children, he doubted his father would have raised an eyebrow. It all seemed so hollow.

Until Reverend Bauers and Georgia. Until here.

Matthew pulled the small Bible from his pocket. Such a tiny book with so much history and so much consequence. He'd grown uncomfortable with the thing. Like the chapel, it refused to remain a simple object. Instead, it seemed to become a force of nature. He found himself fingering the missing chunk, as Georgia had. He was constantly aware of the Bible's presence—the weight of it in his pocket, the texture of it in his hands, the space it occupied on his desk.

You're daft, Matthew told himself as he stared at the simple gold cross he had saved from theft. It disturbed him to have so personal a connection to so holy an object.

Something was here. Something he imagined others felt while gazing at the vaulted ceilings of cathedrals or the gilded intricacy of altars. It was something he heard in Georgia's voice. Something familiar, yet just beyond his recognition.

Something that was seeking him as fast as he was running from it.

He took another deep breath and closed his eyes, then found himself wishing Reverend Bauers had given him something else—*anything* else. Something that would remain a simple token. Which made no sense, for it was a tiny old book and he was a powerful British businessman.

Matthew groaned and leaned his forearms on the pew in front of him.

"So you *do* feel it," said a warm voice over his right

shoulder. Matthew nearly leaped off the pew. Clergymen should not be able to sneak up on a man like that.

"I thought so," Reverend Bauers continued. He must have seen the alarm in Matthew's eyes, for he placed a hand on his shoulder and said, "Don't be alarmed. God's pursuit is nothing to be afraid of. Startling, perhaps, but not frightening."

Matthew didn't know what to say. He found he couldn't even be sure what Reverend Bauers was talking about. At least, that's what he told himself.

"Have you opened it, or have you just stared at it?"

"At what?" Matthew retorted, almost defensively.

Bauers smiled. "Come now, my son, what kind of man do you take me for? Do you think I give such gifts lightly?"

He knew. Somehow that made it far worse. Matthew made no reply.

Bauers sat down next to him and stared up at the cross. "What do you see up there?"

"I know what that is, but I tell you, Bauers, I'm no man of God."

The reverend laughed softly. "All men are of God, Covington. Some just refuse to recognize it. Some are born knowing it, others come to see it slowly and late in life. And then," he said, turning to look straight at him in a way that made Matthew's chest constrict, "there are the few whom God goes after with both barrels blazing."

He was certain there was no safe response to that.

"If you came to return the Bible because it disturbs you, I'll not take it back. Have you opened it at all?"

He could say yes. But truly, only Georgia had opened it. He'd held it, touched it, kept it near, but somehow had no desire to open it again, even to find the passage she had read. He felt as if he didn't know what would happen if he did.

"It won't bite you. Not, at least, in the way you think. I'd begin with Exodus, if I were you. I think you'll find Moses a man to your liking in many ways. And"— Bauers pointed to the missing chunk—"I think most of it's still there." The reverend's thick hand clasped Matthew's shoulder again and squeezed. "If you still find the need to rid yourself of it after that, we'll talk. But not a moment before. You're welcome at Grace House any day, at any time. Remember that."

He started to leave, but Matthew put a hand on his arm, stopping him. "Actually, I came for another reason. One you might scarcely believe."

Bauers raised an inquisitive eyebrow. "Well then, come into my study and let's have a talk."

Chapter Eighteen

Stuart ate his dinner with an air of deliberate calculation. This, Georgia recognized, was a sure sign of impending doom. He normally either relished his food or ignored it. Food was something he enjoyed when he felt good, or simply another task to accomplish when he felt overworked. It had become one of the easiest ways for Georgia to gauge her brother's volatile disposition. On the days when he ate carefully, she knew it could only mean he was plotting.

"Peach," he began as he pushed back his chair after the main course, injecting what Georgia imagined he thought was a casual tone into his voice. Did he have any idea how transparent he was? He tinkered with the heavy silver napkin ring at his left. "Are you happy?"

The question surprised her. It was an unusual opening for one of Stuart's controlling conversations. She had best tread very carefully with her answer.

"I'm delighted you ponder the issue," she said, avoiding the question. Years of debate with this king of secrets had built her skills in that department.

One hand went to his heart. "Of course I care about your happiness. We're all we have in the world."

If there ever was a classic Stuartism, "we're all we have in the world" would be it. It was his favorite saying when he wanted something from Georgia. Usually something large and questionable. "You, me, enormous material resources, a few dozen servants, and a host of admirers?" she countered. "We're hardly in seclusion, my dear brother."

He waved his hand and took a large swig from a crystal goblet. "I don't mean that. All this—" he gestured around the dining room "—is lovely, and you keep yourself enormously busy, but are you *happy?*"

She considered several options before deciding on a straightforward answer. "Yes, Stuart, I am. My world is not ideal, I grant you, but all things considered, I am very fond of my life."

He put the goblet back down on the table and ran his fingers over its silver trim. "You don't wish for more?" Stuart did have a gift for loaded questions.

Georgia thought about the humble mission, the families like Quinn's, and the abundance surrounding her here at the estate. More? She didn't need half of what she had. But that was Stuart at his core: always trying for more. More power, more influence, more money, more satisfaction, more *more*. She mused that if the Waterhouses ever commissioned a family crest, the motto need only be *More*.

"I should like to see more of my brother, but I fear I will have to wait in line behind his many minions." She hadn't entirely objected when he'd sent word about missing the exhibit at the conservatory. It had been a most extraordinary afternoon with Matthew Covington. Still, enough of those "coincidences" and there'd be talk. Stuart craved talk, but she did not.

He caught the hidden meaning in her reply. She was forcing him to be direct, and he knew it. He folded his napkin and laid it on the table. *Ah,* thought Georgia as she leaned her elbow on the arm of her chair, *now we get to the heart of the matter.*

"What do you think of our Mr. Covington?"

Georgia smiled.

"So you *do* like him!" Stuart pounced.

She held up her hand. "My smile, brother, comes from my amusement at having guessed your real question ten minutes ago. Honestly, do you find directness so appalling that you cannot even manage to be forthright with your own sister?"

Stuart planted his elbows on the table. "Where'd be the fun in that?"

"We'll never know until you try."

"We'll never know what you think of Covington until you answer my question," he insisted.

"He seems a good and decent man. And so very important. Not to mention so very British." Georgia gave him his answer, but threw Stuart's own agenda back at him in doing so.

"I could pursue Covington on your behalf, you know. I want you to be happy."

There it was. The tender, brotherly side the rest of the world never saw. People always asked her what it was that enabled her to endure all of Stuart's larger-than-life tendencies. That quiet tone of his voice let her know that despite his questionable methods, he often had shreds of good intentions. She believed he truly did want to see her happy, though his vision of what it took to achieve that was sadly distorted. After all, despite several past chances to wed her off to someone highly advantageous, he'd never done so against her wishes. Nor would he. He might try mightily to persuade her, but would never override her decision.

"I've no wish to haul off to England and play lady of the castle, Stuart. My home is here. Should I be swept off my feet anytime in the near future, however, I'll be sure you are among the first to know."

"Among?" he cried in mock alarm. "*Among* the first?"

"A lady does need a few secrets in this world," she teased, glad to have that rough patch over with. "Especially a Waterhouse."

He rose from his chair and went to pull out hers. As he did, he leaned over and pecked her on the cheek. "Speaking of secrets," he said into her ear, "I've a request to make of George."

Stuart shut the library doors a moment later. "We're getting near the end of the quarter and I need a firecracker of a Bandit episode."

Georgia gazed up at him. He looked so much older when he slicked his hair back, close to his head like that. It made him look sleek and severe. Stuart's personality almost demanded a headful of unruly curls, not the razor-straight white-blond hair they'd both received from their mother. Their father had had dark, wavy hair. Stuart had his eyes, but mostly her efforts to see her father reflected in Stuart went unrewarded. He neither looked like him nor acted like him. Still, Stuart was her brother, and no matter how much he liked to exploit the phrase, he was indeed "all she had in the world."

"I think you overstate my... *George's* influence," she

replied. "It wasn't the words that created the sensation. It was whoever duplicated them in real life."

"Never underestimate the power of the word, Peach. It's all in the words." He tapped a succession of books on the shelf behind him.

"Meaning?"

"Meaning give our mysterious imitator something to work with," Stuart replied. "Write an episode that just begs to be imitated."

Georgia sat down. Write an episode designed to be acted out? The idea felt absurd. Why not simply hand out white ribbons with each issue of the *Herald* tomorrow? Goodness, she'd best not suggest that—Stuart might actually seize the idea. She stopped and stared at him. "You're serious. You actually want to encourage such a thing?"

"You've been encouraging people to do noble deeds your entire life. Why stop now?"

There was some odd logic to his notion, but it still felt horribly wrong. Unscrupulous and manipulative. "Stuart, I couldn't."

He pointed at her. "You could. And that's what scares you. You've hidden behind your lack of influence for too long, Peach. Now you've got it. Use it."

She didn't know how to respond. "*George* has it," she replied, mostly because she couldn't craft another answer.

"What's in a name? 'That which we call a rose by any other name would smell as sweet.' Shakespeare said that. And that man knew the power of words. Come on, Peach. Stir up a crop of heroes. Who knows what will happen if you do?"

Who knows indeed, Georgia thought.

Chapter Nineteen

Sitting at her bedroom desk, Georgia stared at her pen. Could she stir up a crop of heroes? It didn't even need to be a crop, did it? Look at what just one man did at Grace House. Then again, did she know it was one man? Who knew anything about how the white ribbons and money had appeared? She thought about Reverend Bauers's glowing face as he'd tucked the money into the mission safe. About the children playing with the white ribbons. She hadn't done any of it, but she'd inspired it. Could she inspire more?

Lord, Georgia prayed, clutching her pen inside her folded hands, *I'm toying with fire. Guide my words. I know You have the power to transform men and to work wonders, but I've no wish to play God. Shut this door if this is not Your will, and end this charade before anyone is hurt.* She waited for a sense of danger, an urge to halt, to overtake her. Instead, stories began to weave themselves together in her head. *If You have something astounding in mind, Lord, then grant me courage. I'll go where You want, but stay beside me.*

She stared at the blank sheet of paper. What would be

easy to bring to life? Something common. Something everyday that could be swiftly transformed into something wondrous. What was commonplace to people in need? An image began to form in her mind's eye. Georgia took a deep breath and wrote.

"The fog swirled thick and gray around him. The Bandit shrugged off the evening's chill as he watched the men unload the ship. They chatted casually, unaware of the priceless nature of the boxes they hauled."

Matthew woke from a delightfully sound sleep. He dressed quickly in an unassuming coat and trousers—a step or two down from his usual impressive attire—and snatched a trio of apples from the bowl on the sitting room table.

Thompson looked up from polishing Matthew's boots. He raised a salt-and-pepper eyebrow at the plain dress of his master. Matthew raised an eyebrow back, then juggled the three apples for a moment before sending one sailing in Thompson's direction.

The old man calmly caught the fruit, as if he'd been expecting it for hours. "Feeling fit this morning, sir?"

Matthew bit into the one of the remaining apples in his hands. "Indeed I am."

"May I ask why so casual?"

"No," said Matthew simply, suddenly wondering why in his seven-and-twenty years it hadn't occurred to him to say such a thing before. "You may not." It sounded rather petulant, but directness was surprisingly effective against an adversary as wily as Thompson.

Matthew started to say something such as, "I'll be

inspecting some holdings until well into the afternoon," but stopped himself. He wasn't required to explain himself at all, was he? Surely civility and decorum required such a thing, but under the circumstances...

"I'm off," he said, taking another bite, as if the two words were all the explanation required.

He strode down the hallway, imagining Thompson's jaw hanging slack behind him. It probably wasn't—there was a good chance Thompson wasn't even surprised by Matthew's unusual behavior—but it was much more amusing to think otherwise.

It had been so easy to arrange. Reverend Bauers had proved an adept accomplice, with a dozen ideas on how to give the Bandit a life of his own South of the Slot. Anonymity and money rendered such things highly doable. Matthew had the easier role: secure the needed funds without attention—which generally meant putting a sizable dent in his own personal travel allowance—and then pass them on to the reverend. The funds changed hands two or three times—each with a small cost for the transaction, unsurprisingly—in order to ensure the proper amount of confusion, and the intended target received money from a variety of untraceable sources.

Fortunately, Matthew thought with a smile as he stood several blocks away from the mercantile that was their first target, *the reverend seems as skilled a prankster as I.* For a man of the cloth, he got a very pirateworthy gleam in his eye when he smiled.

The neighborhood grocery market inhabited a wide, solid building whose front opened out onto an enormous porchlike space. Its owner was a stoic Italian named

Vincenzo Trivolatti, who had come to San Francisco to seek his fortune, and found love in the process, marrying a local Irish girl. Where Vincenzo was all business, his wife, Irene, was all heart, or so Reverend Bauers said. Aiding the cause of the Bandit, provided it proved sufficiently profitable, would appeal to both their sensibilities. It seemed an ideal match.

Despite the earliness of the hour, a crowd had already begun to form amid the neat stacks of produce and goods under the market's front awning. It was Friday, market day, and the neighborhood grocery would be bustling even under normal circumstances. Matthew doubted Trivolatti would ever know the likes of this day again. He'd seen to that.

It had taken only three hours to arrange the details. One hour before opening, a young boy was sent with a letter to the Trivolatti home, disclosing two impending arrivals at the market. The first would be a supply of white cloth strips. Reverend Bauers had prayed that God would prevent all medical emergencies as he and Matthew shredded Grace House's existing bandage supply to produce the needed tokens. Matthew had thought to himself amusingly that at the rate he was going, several of the hotel bedsheets might have to go missing in order for him to restock Grace House's medical stores. Bauers predicted that the ribbon delivery alone should catch Irene's undivided attention. No one South of the Slot had escaped hearing about the Bandit's first adventure.

The second delivery, intended to secure Mr. Trivolatti's cooperation, was a supply of funds delivered by secured guard as a deposit for the day's tally. Matthew's inspection of the Covington Enterprises shipping logs had given him enough of a working knowledge of the cost of daily goods in San Francisco. With a few simple calculations, he could guarantee that the amount delivered would be more than enough to ensure Trivolatti a healthy day's profit. The letter instructed the grocer to take no payment for any order placed today, and that if the funds provided did not cover the orders placed—which Matthew predicted would be highly unlikely, but given the speed of dock gossip, not impossible—to write down the remaining balance and it would be paid the following morning by similar messenger. Instead of demanding payment, Vincenzo was to simply hand a white ribbon to his customers and inform them that the Bandit had bought their groceries.

Irene, a generous and highly religious woman, would no doubt keep her eye on the entire proceedings. She was just the sort of principled individual who would rather die than see such a noble act abused. Times, however, were tough, and she was only one woman, so just in case greed should rear its ugly head, a banking clerk had been anonymously hired to keep tabs on the day's event. Matthew didn't much care for the idea of Irene having to single-handedly ward off a mob of opportunists. Matthew would have loved to have had the Bandit standing guard, sword gleaming in the sunshine from atop a nearby building, but such a thing was neither practical nor advisable. It was not only beyond outlandish, but Matthew's arm had not yet gained back its full strength, and should the Bandit need to swoop down and defend the poor Trivolattis, Matthew—or any mere mortal, for that matter—would hardly be up to the task.

Matthew and Reverend Bauers had opted for the power of words instead. "You will be watched," the note had concluded, "for the Bandit rewards his partners, but hunts his adversaries without mercy." True, it had been rather dramatic, but wasn't drama the point of it all?

Legends could hardly afford to be subtle. Stuart Waterhouse had taught him that.

Chapter Twenty

$\mathbf{M}$atthew leaned against a building a block away, non-descript in his workman's clothes, and observed. An old woman called out grateful exclamations as she left the mercantile, clutching the white ribbon to her breast. She spoke in Italian, but no translation was needed. Waving to a small boy across the street, she told him something in rushed words and shooed him away, presumably to spread the news. Other families came trotting up the street, nearly running in their hurry to take advantage of the windfall. Another woman took Mr. Trivolatti's face in her hands and kissed him on both cheeks when he handed her the ribbon. Mrs. Trivolatti protested at great length, only to laugh, hug her husband and enjoy their role in the spectacle.

This went on for over an hour as Matthew watched, the reactions of surprised and grateful families making him feel like a king. He had done it for Georgia, but felt such a deep personal satisfaction that he wondered which of them would enjoy it more.

When Reverend Bauers came walking down the street midmorning, exactly as planned, the ruckus erupted all over again. Men and women huddled around him to tell him the news, and he feigned surprise comparable to the best London actors. Matthew laughed to himself, thinking he had chosen a highly capable co-conspirator in the lively round man.

The hush that suddenly fell over the crowd caught Matthew by surprise. It was a few seconds before he realized the market had fallen into prayer. In the quiet, he found he could hear the reverend's words clearly.

"Most Holy Father, we are overwhelmed in thanks to You this day. We bless You for how You have provided for Your faithful. In Your wisdom and mercy, You have sent us a champion. A soldier of justice we have not seen. Bless Your servant, this Bandit, and strengthen him with the thanksgiving of those he has helped. Reward him for honoring Your calling. Protect him for future deeds of justice and mercy. May we remain grateful and hopeful, and may we continue to trust in You, because of the things You have done today." As the reverend raised his hand to pronounce "Amen," a cheer went up through the small crowd.

Matthew stood there, locked in place by the words. Bauers knew he would be within earshot. The reverend must have chosen his prayer as much for Matthew's sake as for the crowd's.

He'd called him a servant. As though what he was doing was some sort of holy mission, not just one man's ill-advised attempts at heroism.

As though it hadn't been Matthew's idea.

The concept shook him to the core. This was little more than a prank, not some crusade. He wasn't even sure it fell under the category of "good deeds." He was, when one got right down to it, showing off for a girl.

One could hardly call that divine intervention. More to the point, one could hardly take marching orders from a God one wasn't even certain existed in the first place.

Matthew shook his head, checked his watch and headed back to the hotel by a side street. California was proving to be a most unsettling place. The sooner he got back to precise, well-behaved ledgers and numbers, the better.

"Are your inspections proving satisfactory?" Thompson droned as he brushed off Matthew's coat and adjusted the lapel later that week.

"Yes, quite."

"And you've fully recovered from your injuries?" Again, the dry tone of a man compiling facts. Which was always reason to suspect Thompson. He collected facts the way a boy with a slingshot collected small stones—as tiny weapons capable of great impact.

"Nearly," Matthew said carefully, flexing his arm and twisting his wrist this way and that. He suffered an occasional sting if he hit the wrong angle, but within the week he should be up to speed. The scar was quite evident. He was grateful life rarely afforded him a reason to roll up his sleeves. The thing looked like it belonged on a war hero, not a well-bred gentleman.

Thompson had tried valiantly to repair the slashed coat, but it had been beyond helping. No matter, the finding, measuring and ordering of a new jacket had given Thompson something to do other than gather facts on Matthew.

"Your father will be expecting a report next week," Thompson said, as dryly as ever. He was a master at dropping verbal bombs without flinching.

A report. There was much to report, but not much that Matthew could be certain about yet. His review of the books had proved them clean. Exceedingly clean. Unnaturally clean, which had given rise to Matthew's suspicion that things were not what they seemed. In a town where corruption was the local currency, Covington Enterprises should not have such pristine books. A certain amount of "greasing the wheel"—he'd heard the term recently—would have to go on in any commercial enterprise as large as Covington. Yet everything lined up in the records. There was not even a simple addition error in sight.

It was, in Matthew's opinion, too perfect to be believed. He could not shake the nagging suspicion that things had been cleaned up for his viewing. Some of that was to be expected, of course, for no one hauled himself across the Atlantic by surprise. The staff had had several months' notice of Matthew's arrival. Surely they'd tidied up a bit. But this was altogether something else. Something he couldn't quite yet name.

How to report as much to his father? Should he communicate his hunch? No, Matthew preferred to delay his report until he had a better sense of Covington Enterprises' true workings. And that would take time. It would take making friends, asking around and observing carefully. One could hide shady dealings for a handful of weeks, while the master was in town, but sooner or later "business as usual" would emerge. Not that Matthew minded extending his visit. The brisk air of San Francisco suited him far better than London's cold, damp atmosphere. As did lots of other city amenities. And citizens.

As if to underscore the city's attractions, Thompson held out a sheet of paper Matthew recognized to be Stuart's personal stationery. "You've received an invitation to dine at the Waterhouse estate tomorrow evening. Shall I send your acceptance?" A wry taunt underlay Thompson's words.

Matthew had thought through his response earlier, for he was sure he'd receive another invitation from the Waterhouses. Stuart was doing a masterful job of controlling their social interaction, but it was time Matthew took the upper hand.

"No, Thompson, I'm afraid I'll need to decline. I've a business engagement to attend to that evening." He didn't, but one could be easily arranged. "Would you send an invitation for both Mr. and Miss Waterhouse to join me at the hotel for tea on Monday afternoon? It's high time I return their gracious hospitality, and I've found the Palace's tea service quite up to snuff."

Thompson raised an eyebrow. *Ha!* thought Matthew to himself, *surprised you, didn't I?* It gave him no small pleasure to foil Thompson's assumptions every once in a while. The man was simply incorrigible when he was right all the time. And he was, most of the time.

But the invitation had other advantages as well. Matthew had just read today's newspaper. The *Herald* had reported the incident at Trivolatti's grocery in glowing terms. And this week's Bandit episode continued in the same vein—as a matter of fact, it simply *begged* to be brought to life. It would be so easy to arrange, it was nearly an invitation to do so. A dare, even. As such, Matthew and the reverend had a little work to do, and Sunday night was going to be a busy one. What better way to reward a hard night's heroism than to discuss it with Stuart and Georgia the next day? To ensure a view to her reaction since he'd not seen her after the grocer's event? It was too enticing to resist.

Chapter Twenty-One

Sister Charlotte was exactly the kind of person Georgia wished to seek out for her odd confidence. The tall, energetic nun had a personality—and a past—worthy of newspaper headlines. She'd enjoyed a very successful career on the stage until she had captured the heart of a theater patron, who'd married her and given her a social life nearly as grand and public as her stage career. For a few years, Charlotte had been the darling—and perhaps the target—of San Francisco society. Then her husband had taken ill suddenly and died, ending yet another distinctive chapter of her life. Jaws of people all across the city had dropped when she joined the Sisters of Notre Dame and became a nun.

Her dramatic life made Sister Charlotte a unique woman. Highly independent for one having taken the vows. A sort of morally upright Stuart, Georgia thought, in that she had little concern for what others thought of her. She took care of people others would overlook or shun. Even before she'd joined the order, she'd engaged in what Stuart had called "taking in strays," for Charlotte often had a surprising spectrum of characters come to live on her palatial estate. The list of entertainers, scoundrels, hard cases and celebrities who'd enjoyed her hospitality would fill a year's worth of Stuart's gossip columns.

Charlotte cared about people, period. She had always been quite vocal about caring for God, too, which was why Georgia found it odd that people were suspicious of her "conversion." Sister Charlotte hadn't converted at all, merely formalized a strong faith into a holy office. Even in a stark black habit, she simply was what she was—a big-hearted woman who felt God gave her lots of things so she could share them with the world.

As she walked down the street from Grace House toward the convent a few blocks away, Georgia decided some of the Bandit's outlandish drama must have come from her image of Sister Charlotte. Were she male, Charlotte would have been a logical candidate for the Bandit, Georgia was certain. She wasn't sure some of San Francisco society didn't suspect Charlotte, anyway—she was just the kind of woman to dress as a man and run around saving the world.

Hardly the kind of wise old sage one turned to for advice.

Then again, it was hardly the normal kind of advice Georgia was seeking. To be truthful, she wasn't at all sure of what she was doing, or why she was doing it. She only knew she had to talk to someone, and this was not a subject for Reverend Bauers's ears. Or any other pastor's, even though several churches supported Grace House, and she was a member of one of them. This was a female matter. Or more precisely, a matter of female faith, which, as Georgia saw it, made it suited to Sister Charlotte's "unique" perspective.

The nun offered Georgia tea in a corner of the convent gardens. Even now, without her legendary luxury, she was a delightful hostess. Despite a habit of repeating herself, she tended brilliantly to all the little details of a warm welcome.

The tea was lovely, the setting peaceful, but never bringing up Stuart Waterhouse's name was the most refreshing thing, as far as Georgia was concerned. Charlotte seemed to see her for the woman she was, not just as the sister of the city's most prominent publisher. Charlotte was one of only a handful of people who did so, which made it a wonderful thing indeed.

"It seems to me," she said, leaning conspiratorially toward Georgia as she poured more tea, "that you're not here to discuss the bandage supply or parish funding for Grace House. Oh, no. You've got more on your mind, if I daresay so, and I do always dare to say what I think, all the time." She laid her hand gracefully on Georgia's arm. "What can I do for you, Georgia?"

"I... I have a problem of a most delicate nature."

Charlotte's smile was as quick as it was warm. "I thought so. Tell me, is it a matter of the heart, or a matter of the soul? Those are the only things that really count, you know."

"I believe it to be a matter of the heart, Sister, but I must confess that I am not at all sure."

"Sure?" she said, picking up a small biscuit. "Who is certain about any such thing?" She took a bit of the biscuit, then folded her long slim fingers together across her lap. "So now, what is this matter which you suspect to be of the heart?"

"I find myself enormously taken with a particular

man." She said it quietly, as if the trees might repeat the news if she spoke too loudly.

"Goodness, that is a matter indeed." The nun looked at her with serious eyes. "Are you in love?"

"I don't believe I can be," Georgia said.

"Nonsense," countered Charlotte, sitting back in the bent-willow garden chair. "All of God's creatures are capable of love."

"I cannot love this man," Georgia explained, feeling her cheeks grow hot with embarrassment, "because he does not exist."

That stopped Sister Charlotte dead in her tracks. "Not exist? Is this like something from one of those novels—all swashbuckling romance without a hint of how to get along in the real world?"

Georgia gulped. The Bandit was a swashbuckling novel in Stuart's eyes. She hadn't counted on such an attitude from a veteran of the theater. She'd expected Sister Charlotte, despite her current austerity, to understand the power of imagination. "It is a fascination of a…literary sort… I suppose."

Sister Charlotte took a drink of tea. "Robin Hood!" she declared, as if it solved everything.

"Robin Hood?"

"I was smitten with him when I was younger. Read everything I could get my hands on about him. Dreamed up a picture in my head, his voice, the way he walked. Suddenly, no man on earth could compare. There were men who looked like my Robin Hood. Men who walked like him, but no one who came close to being who I'd created in my mind." She tapped the crisp white rim of her veil. "You've got a Robin Hood in your head, don't you?"

Georgia was quite sure her mouth was open. "In a manner of speaking, I suppose you are right."

"Of course I'm right. I could see it in your eyes the moment I said it. And you think you're the only woman to do something so outlandish? Women with fine imaginations have found themselves in your slippers more times than I can count. And we all think we're insane for doing it. You were smart to come to me, you know." She leaned in closer and lowered her voice. "Not everyone understands these things. Especially here."

Now there was an understatement. Georgia was quite sure she didn't understand a shred of her current emotional predicament. "But you understand?" she said, not caring how relieved she must sound.

"Completely. But I doubt it's Robin Hood who has your attention, my dear. I suspect he's a little antiquated for your taste. What tale has captured you?"

"Well…"

Charlotte's eyes widened. "Wait! Say not another word! How could I not see it? How could I not have guessed? The Bandit. It's the Bandit, isn't it?"

Georgia could only nod.

"Yes," the nun said, a knowing smile creeping into her violet eyes, "I read it. We are allowed newspapers, you know. And I might have smuggled it in if we didn't." She chuckled. "All the world wants to know where your brother got him, but I suspect even you wouldn't divulge that now, even to me?"

"No." Georgia found it hard to choke out the single syllable. Charlotte seemed to find her strange delusion so ordinary, so completely understandable, that Georgia felt as if her ability to breathe had just this moment returned.

"You have taste, I'll grant you that much." Charlotte sighed. "He'd be a rare find, our Bandit, if he walked into the real world."

"Yes..." Georgia kept waiting for more words to form, but she was stuck with single syllables for the moment.

"Of course, he *has* now, hasn't he? Shown up in a few dramatic encounters of late. That does complicate things. I can see where you'd be in a bit of a state. It's not every day that the man of your daydreams appears in reality." She tsked, pouring more tea. "Presents quite a challenge." She stopped, as if a thought had suddenly occurred to her. "Have you *seen* him? Our Bandit? Has he come to you? I couldn't think of anything more romantic, really."

"No. He hasn't."

The sister draped herself across the table, leaning on one elbow. She assessed Georgia with narrowed eyes—dramatic, violet eyes that Georgia imagined had sent more than one man's heart into spasms. "That's not the issue, really, is it? There's more to this than our mysterious hero."

Again, Georgia felt herself blush. "An ordinary man," she began, but then corrected herself. "Actually, he's far from ordinary, but he's not—"

"Say no more," interjected Charlotte, throwing her hands up in a melodramatic gesture. "Now I see your pickle. And why you came to me. How did I fall for Robert Brownstone when I had all of the stage's handsome heroes fawning at my feet? How does one make a life in the real world when the fantasy is so very enticing?" She pointed a finger at Georgia. "You're a sharp one, Miss Waterhouse. You know where to go for good advice, and that's half the battle, I always say. Our real-world hero—is he sensible? Does he suit you?"

"Not at all. In that I mean I see little hope for any future between us. I'm not even sure I want one." Suddenly, Georgia found her tongue. "He has many wonderful qualities, and I do believe he is fond of me, but there are so many obstacles."

"Ha!" Charlotte exclaimed. "What would love be without obstacles? No fun at all, to hear my dear late Robert tell it. God is at His best overcoming obstacles. We'd know nothing of our Lord without the teaching of our own mistakes." She settled herself in her chair. "Now let's be practical for a moment. Have you kissed him?"

Georgia nearly dropped her teaspoon.

"Well, it's a perfectly sensible question, given the circumstances. Have you?"

She shook her head.

"Good. Don't kiss him—or let him kiss you—unless you're absolutely sure. Take it from a woman of the stage, young lady, a man's kiss can be a distraction. It can hide far too much. You'll always know a true kiss when you feel it, but a proper young lady such as yourself doesn't always know a false kiss when it comes her way." The woman drew up her chin with an authoritative air. "Only the stage can teach you that."

Georgia came away from her meeting with the sure impression that she had made a good choice in confiding in Sister Charlotte. And that the Sisters of Notre Dame didn't know half of what they had in her. Odd as she was, Sister Charlotte was the perfect blessing. Perhaps the only sort of woman to understand the circumstance in which Georgia found herself.

She was also quite sure that whatever advice she'd received on the perils of insincere kisses, she was in no danger—immediate or otherwise—of having such a challenge thrust upon her. Tea at the Palace Hotel, even if Stuart should pull another of his disappearing acts, was hardly the place where men ravished women. True, the hotel had a reputation for hosting all sorts of characters, but the more unsavory of the lot rarely showed up for tea.

Chapter Twenty-Two

"Come now, you insufferable rascals, get on with it." Matthew could hardly believe his present circumstances. The Covington heir was, at the moment, dangling a jar of camphor through a hole he'd recently cut in the top of a chicken crate.

A crate of chickens. Does a proper English gentleman allow himself to be found standing among crates of chickens at two in the morning, engaged in the questionable act of drugging poultry?

Well, thought Matthew, *not if he can help it. I'd have a time explaining myself if I got caught, now wouldn't I?*

Of course, Reverend Bauers's pacing at the back of the stockyards wasn't helping to maintain calm. Even in the dim moonlight, Matthew could see the sweat beading on the clergyman's bald head. Not that he wasn't sweating himself. He swung the rope holding the jar again, splashing a little of the liquid on the crate floor. How had he made it this many years without realizing how dreadful chickens smelled? "You all smell so lovely when roasted," he crooned to the birds, "but I can't say the same for your present state. Breathe deeply, ladies, I can't stand here all night. Take lovely little deep chicken sighs, if you will. That's it..."

As one wobbly white hen sat down and settled her head, another brown-speckled hen followed suit. A third slumped in a corner. "There we go."

"You're sure this will work?" Reverend Bauers's agitated whisper came from somewhere behind him. "No one became suspicious when you bought so many chickens?"

Of course he wasn't sure it would work. Using the liquid on a handkerchief to drug the family cat so it could be locked in his father's armoire was one thing. Buying six different crates of chickens at three different places, and arranging for them all to be delivered to a fourth location, was one thing. Drugging said crate-fuls of chickens to quiet them for a stealthy journey to the center of town was proving quite another.

He should have stuck with eggs.

The eggs were easy. Supplying a neighborhood with eggs for their Easter breakfast simply meant arranging for baskets of them to be tied with white ribbons and delivered before Easter. He could have recreated the Bandit's latest exploit without breaking a sweat—in fact, Matthew half worried someone else might try to play Bandit and beat him to it.

Chickens to go along with the eggs, now *that* presented a challenge.

More challenge than Matthew liked, to be honest. He'd thought the idea of drugging the chickens so that they could be quietly transported was brilliant. The chickens, however, weren't feeling that cooperative. It was taking twice the time he'd calculated for the feathered little beasts to fall asleep. If he used stronger solu-

tion, the Bandit's gift to the community might be crates
of chicken carcasses. Which was why Matthew Covington found himself dashing among crates of chickens at
two in the morning, waiting for them to fall asleep. His
father would be in convulsions if he knew.

To think this was the easiest part of the plan.

Reverend Bauers was just beginning to beseech the
Lord for sleeping chickens when the last of the plump
little darlings slumped into a heap and Matthew reeled
in the jar. "Got it!" For the next half hour, he and the
reverend worked feverishly to tie white ribbons to one
leg of each sleeping bird. It proved a ridiculously complicated task. Finally, they were ready. The Reverend
then took off in the direction of a large cart happily
lent by the Trivolatti store. They'd sent a note the night
before, asking to have the cart waiting empty on a particular street corner. The Trivolattis had been told to
leave the cart unmanned, but no one suspected that
would be the case; a Bandit sighting presented far too
great a temptation.

Which was why Matthew's new disguise proved such
a blessing. As he leaped out of the shadows dressed
in a gray shirt, dark trousers, black hat with a single
white feather, and black mask—the Bandit's known
costume—Matthew simply nodded at the awestruck
young man who handed over the reins.

Yes, the Bandit wore his signature costume now.
And no one could have predicted how that came to be.

Thompson, in an act that would shock Matthew until
his dying day, had appeared with the garb two evenings
before. How the valet had figured out his role, Matthew
didn't know. Nor would he ever, for when he found his
tongue again and asked Thompson how he'd guessed,

the man had only produced the widest smile Matthew had ever seen and said absolutely nothing.

Thompson—*Thompson,* of all people—knew.

Thompson approved.

Wilder still, he conspired! If Matthew was looking for signs that playing the Bandit was his destiny, then one could find no greater endorsement than Thompson's cooperation.

"It is my duty to see you properly dressed," his valet had said, after laying out the dark trousers, charcoal-gray shirt, wide-brimmed black hat and outlandish white feather—cleverly removable for discreet missions. The design of the Bandit's wardrobe had not been Thompson's; the outfit had been detailed in a recent episode in the *Herald.* Its execution, however, was extraordinary. Matthew could only imagine what it had taken for Thompson to see to its secret assembly.

True to the old man's impeccable sense of detail, Matthew noted a few smart embellishments. The pants had dozens of useful pockets and specially sewn loops to hold a unique belt. Rather like a holster, but much more elegant, the latter held both Matthew's sword and his whip. The mask, perhaps the most difficult thing of all, was outstanding. A thin leather caplike contraption, with a panel that folded down over the eyes, close to the head and neatly under the hat. The outfit was half pirate, half Musketeer and wholly perfect.

"I—I've no words," Matthew had stammered as he took the clothes from the grinning old man.

"Then none are needed," Thompson had said simply, as if the exchange were as common as a daily bath.

Something indescribable had stirred in Matthew when he put the clothing on. As if a new man—a bold, invincible spirit—had slid from the shell of the duty-bound accountant. It was as if, before, Matthew had been imitating the Bandit. But once wearing the disguise, he *became* him.

And the Bandit could do anything, including wrangle chickens.

One hoped.

By four-thirty in the morning, the crates of quieted chickens had been loaded onto the cart. Matthew sat in the driver's seat, convincing himself that the Bandit could drive a buckboard wagon at considerable speed just as easily as Matthew had raced his father's best carriage around the stable yards.

He edged the cart forward and heard a few clucks of protest from waking chickens. Now was the time.

He was just about to spur the team of horses forward when he felt Reverend Bauers's hand clasp his right foot. The clergyman bent his head and rested both hands on Matthew's shiny black boot.

"Bless this man and his bravery, Father. See that this food finds its way into homes to honor you, just as this man honors Your call to service. These creatures are given to those who dearly need food. And dearly need hope. Let us never forget Your hope and the sacrifice You paid for our sins. Protect this man with the might of Your hand as he serves Your people. Amen."

Matthew once again found his tongue tangled by the reverence this man seemed to place upon his ridiculous deeds. He was play-acting for his own vaunted reasons, not "saving" anyone. Still, something tugged at him, that same sense of being caught up in something larger than himself or his faulty motives. Tonight, he felt as if he were a shred of the hero Reverend Bauers seemed to make him.

Was it selfish to hope that Georgia Waterhouse would hold the deed in the same regard? If he was truly going about God's business, then he had no right to twist such service to catch the eye of a woman. Still, if God was as all-seeing as Bauers claimed him to be, then surely He was already aware of Matthew's baser motive. *And is most likely angered by it,* he thought. *It's a wonder I'm not struck down by lightning this very second.*

Wouldn't that roast the chickens? He laughed, thinking how they might at least smell better. As Reverend Bauers called "Godspeed!" Matthew pulled the cart into the street and spurred the horses into a quick trot.

After so much planning, the execution seemed to fly by in a matter of heartbeats. Dressed as the Bandit, he drove squarely into the middle of a predetermined intersection. They'd chosen one in the center of the neighborhood, where it would soon be noticed. He suspected he'd already been, even at that hour.

He quickly leaped from the cart and sprinted to the back, where the crates of sleeping chickens stood beside several boxes of eggs.

Now for the finishing touch. The last dollop of drama to take this episode from anecdote to legend. And the first test of Matthew's healed arm. With a deep breath, he pulled his whip from the loop on his trousers and clasped the handle. Shifting it back and forth a time or two, he let his arm recall its weight and rhythm. Then, with enormous satisfaction, he swung it back and cracked it several times just above the chicken crates, sending the sound ringing through the deserted intersection in a way that was sure to call attention.

Matthew waited only one second before dashing off into the darkness, where a hidden set of clothes waited to usher him back into obscurity.

Chapter Twenty-Three

"It sounds calamitous," Matthew said as he poured a second cup of tea. "I do wish I'd been around to see it. Chickens? Really?" It felt ridiculous to pretend ignorance.

"Hordes of them," Georgia said, a laugh stealing into her voice. Matthew could see the amusement in her face as she described the wild scene. "They were still running everywhere, even hours later, trailing white ribbons, feathers flying. I don't think I've ever seen anything like it."

"How on earth does one get that many chickens beribboned and into the center of town undetected?" he asked, doing his best to sound astonished. He forced himself, for discretion's sake, to interject a shred of disapproval into his voice. In truth, it was more than just an effort to maintain his disguise; some part of him wanted to see what Georgia would do if pressed to defend the Bandit.

"It seems to me," she replied, as she set down her teacup, "that we are dealing with a most extraordinary fellow. Quite resourceful. Very noble, but I suppose a bit reckless by some standards."

Very noble, resourceful and a bit reckless. It was funny to hear such words. If God himself had asked Matthew how he would like to be remembered, those were very nearly the attributes he would cite. And here Georgia was mentioning that about the Bandit—who was, and was not, Matthew Covington. It was an odd and yet powerful sensation.

Made more so by what Matthew could see lingering in Georgia's eyes—an admiration for the recklessness. An admiration that came close to affection for the dashing hero her brother had dreamed up. What a heady concept that was.

Which made Matthew wonder…had Stuart dreamed up the Bandit just for her? A prank to please his sister? Matthew scorned the idea of playing upon her sensibilities like that…until he realized that what he was doing was not much different.

It stung.

The Bandit was reckless. Matthew Covington could not be. Dashing midnight bravery was a luxury for imaginary men, not Covingtons.

Still, as he looked at her there, glowing in a butter-colored gown that set off her glistening gold hair, he knew he would do it again. To watch her talk of it with that look on her face, to know that she held a part of him—even an invented part—in such esteem, was enough.

It would have to be, wouldn't it? There could be no future between them. The cold gray halls of England would stifle her, and he was duty-bound to return home soon, no doubt to marry an appropriate woman of his mother's choosing.

"The eggs will help make a festive Easter for the children. I've always loved Easter eggs. I think childhood traditions are the ones we most remember," Georgia said, smiling as she evidently recalled another detail from the scene. "What are the Easter traditions at the Covington household? Do you remember any from your youth?"

Matthew toyed with his spoon. "There was always an enormous fair. There was an egg tradition there, too. Blindfolded men and women would dance across the street and try to avoid the eggs placed in their path. Many a good pair of shoes came to ruin on those days. My father took me to Spain several times to the bullfights that happen there at Easter. Ghastly business, really. I much preferred the fair at home. One could have far more fun with far less mortal injury."

"I'd love to see a bullfight," said Stuart. "So far all I've seen is that business where they walk down the street in New York. I hear in Greece they throw huge pottery jars from the windows to make noise."

"And what are the Waterhouse Easter traditions?" Matthew asked, expecting the pair of siblings to spout all manner of memories. Given how playful they were with each other, he had no doubt they'd given their parents a challenge as youngsters. Especially Stuart.

"Oh, our mother loved Easter," Georgia sighed. "We colored eggs, of course, and there would be a big cake and enormous meal waiting when we came home from church. She would fill the house with lilies and tell the Easter story with great dramatic flair." She nudged her brother. "Stuart gets his theatrics from Mother's side of the family."

"Peach had the luck to be born on an Easter Sunday, so some years it was a double celebration," offered Stuart, who had spent most of teatime surveying the room over Matthew's shoulder. Sizing up the social value of everyone present, Matthew surmised. It had become clear that to Stuart, life was a series of potential deals. He paid little attention to the moment because his gaze was forever fixed on the next big opportunity. Matthew was surprised he could contribute to the conversation at all, given how little notice he seemed to be paying to it.

"So you've a birthday coming up?" Matthew asked with a grin. Peach, hmm? It suited her, silly as it was.

Georgia blushed, and he could easily see where the nickname came from. She did have a peachy glow about her.

"Tomorrow!" announced Stuart. "Georgia's birthday is tomorrow."

"Stuart, hush." She swatted at him. "You shouldn't… oh dear." Her face fell as a waiter arrived to stand over Stuart's shoulder.

"Message for you, Mr. Waterhouse. At the front desk."

Georgia seemed to know how events would proceed from here. Once again, her brother was going to pull his infamous disappearing act.

"Back in a jiffy." Stuart pushed his chair away from the table. "Entertain our birthday girl for a moment, won't you, Covington?"

There was an uncomfortable silence as he buzzed off, responding to yet another important interruption. And then again, not so uncomfortable. Matthew enjoyed

Georgia's company tremendously. He just wished things didn't always have the feeling of being orchestrated. He would have preferred to know she sought his company by choice, not manipulation.

Matthew stifled a sigh. It must be tiring to be so continually maneuvered by someone you love. He leaned in a bit and whispered, "I give him eight minutes before he returns to tell us he's 'dreadfully sorry but he must be going.'"

Matthew's talent at impersonations paid off, for his imitation of Stuart's voice was spot on.

Chapter Twenty-Four

Georgia gave a start, shocked at Matthew Covington's mimicry and his directness. It was one thing to know what was going on, quite another to declare it openly. For a moment it stunned her, but then she discovered it felt surprisingly refreshing. As if he respected her enough not to pretend they both didn't see what was going on in Stuart's constant disappearances.

"Mr. Covington, what a thing to say." She played for a moment at being insulted, then let a hint of her amusement show. "Personally, I'd give Stuart no more than five minutes, under the circumstances."

Mr. Covington's face creased in a gleaming smile and he pulled out his pocket watch. "Shall we see who wins?"

Georgia feigned astonishment. "Am I to understand you are suggesting a wager? Here, during tea at the Palace Hotel? The very thought."

"I'd never suggest such a thing," he replied, looking all too much as if he'd be delighted to do that very thing. "Think of it as hypothesis and observation. A scientific study."

She shot him a doubtful glance. "A scientific study. Of Stuart's diversionary tactics?"

Her label evidently delighted him. "'Diversionary tactics.' Why, I do think that's a most appropriate term." He made a show of checking his watch. "Two minutes fifteen seconds."

"This is outrageous." She fanned herself, playing along. "I should be most insulted." But it wasn't insulting at all. As a matter of fact, it was satisfying to call Stuart at his own game.

"But you're not," Matthew retorted, "because you're far too smart for that."

"A backhanded compliment, Mr. Covington." She *was* too smart for this. Suddenly, she found herself wondering why she had ever put up with it.

He stared at her for a moment, almost indecisively. Then, after looking over her shoulder toward the hotel desk, as if to judge how much privacy they had before Stuart's return, he leaned in. "Then I shall pay you a true compliment, Miss Waterhouse. I find you a most delightful woman, honorable and admirable in every detail. And..." he softened his voice until it seemed to tingle down the back of her neck "...in possession of the most astounding eyes I believe I have ever seen."

He stared at her again, for how long she could not say. His expression confounded any attempt at words. He found her delightful. Honorable and admirable. Not just the sibling shadow of her outlandish brother, but *her.* And to think that he found her eyes astounding, when she could hardly think of words to describe *his.* Their impossibly deep indigo seemed to pin her to her chair.

His directness flustered her. He spoke as though her

opinion meant something to him. And that was a rare thing indeed for the sister of Stuart Waterhouse.

After a pause that seemed endless and yet far too short, Georgia saw his gaze shift over her shoulder. "Four minutes fifty seconds," he said in a conspiratorial whisper. "You win."

On cue, Stuart appeared at her right side, a stack of papers in his hand and a waiter just behind him. "Crisis at the office. I've got to run, Covington, it can't be helped. But…" He stepped out of the way to reveal the waiter holding two slices of lemon cake, a specialty of the house, and one of Georgia's favorites. "I thought this might keep you both from missing me. Consider it an early birthday cake, Peach, from me to you. You'll see her home, of course, Covington?"

The waiter set the slices down in front of them. "Of course," replied Covington, managing to look surprised despite his earlier prediction.

"My favorite. Thank you, Stuart. I almost forgive you." The words were hollow. Stuart was trying to be nice, in his own selfish, manipulative way, but somehow a line had just been crossed. True forgiveness felt just out of her grasp at the moment.

Stuart winked. "That'll have to do." And he was gone.

Covington gave her a sympathetic look before attempting to make the best of things. "*Is* this a favorite of yours?"

"My very favorite, as a matter of fact." She straightened in her chair. "And don't worry," she added in a firm voice, "I have every intention of making Stuart bring me back here tomorrow for more. He can buy my forgiveness today, but it won't excuse his obligation tomorrow, I assure you."

"Well then, I suppose I should have to reluctantly thank Stuart for the opportunity to see you again tomorrow. Perhaps we should consider tying your brother to his chair so as to insure you an uninterrupted birthday luncheon."

Georgia imagined Stuart lashed to his chair with the red velvet stanchions from the hotel lobby. "That would be something to see," she laughed. "Then one of us would have to feed him his cake."

"I do believe I'll leave that duty to you," Mr. Covington said before taking a bite of his cake. He nodded in approval of the fluffy, lemony confection, and some part of her was pleased to know he liked it as well. "Happy birthday, Miss Waterhouse." His eyes held hers for a moment, the smile in them fading to something far more unsettling.

Her hand clutched her napkin under the table. His voice had the most extraordinary smoothness when he spoke softly. It seemed to ripple over her. "Thank you, Mr. Covington." She felt as if she gulped out the words.

"Please," he said, his voice gaining even more warmth, "call me Matthew. Even if just for today."

Matthew. She'd known since they were introduced that his name was Matthew. She'd heard the name dozens of times. Yet to hear him speak it, to hear him ask her to use it, was another thing altogether. Matthew. It suddenly sounded as smooth and lovely as his accented voice.

She took a breath, dared to look in him in the eye, and said, "Thank you, Matthew."

She didn't ask him to call her Georgia. He didn't expect her to. He was almost surprised she'd granted his request and called him Matthew. Not that he hadn't surprised himself by asking her.

That woman did things to him. Unsafe things he couldn't help and wouldn't deny. It was worth any impropriety to give her that moment of feeling special, when she'd been so repeatedly brushed off by her brother.

No, he didn't mind that she hadn't asked him to call her Georgia. He liked the secrecy of calling her that in his thoughts. *Georgia.* To him, now, she was Georgia, even when he said goodbye to her as "Miss Waterhouse."

And when he went back to his hotel room after seeing her home—and after daring to plant a light kiss on her hand when he helped her out of the carriage—he knew sleep would evade him tonight.

It did. He wandered about his room, restlessly turning a thousand thoughts over in his mind until the wee hours of the morning. There, in the sleepless darkness, Matthew pulled out his sword for the first time in weeks. It did not surprise him when he thought it whispered "Georgia" as it sliced through the air.

His father was fond of saying that Matthew frequently lost his composure. Matthew was beginning to think the heir of Covington was in very real danger of losing his heart.

Chapter Twenty-Five

I've no right, Father. I owe so much to Stuart. Without him, I could have been forced into a marriage by now simply to survive. Why has he begun to grate on me so? I've withstood his tricks for years without chafing, but now it's become so much harder. What is happening?

Georgia sat in her window seat, her arms hugging her knees, her toes tucked under the hem of her shift. She pulled her wrap tighter around her shoulders as a gust of wind rattled the bay window. Droplets of rain raced each other down the panes, joining and pooling, then splitting again in a glistening web across the glass. She traced one drop's path down the window with her finger. Spring in San Francisco was always an unpredictable affair—warm and welcoming one day, damp and dreary the next.

It seemed a fitting time for a birthday, as her life seemed to be changing pace. An agitation had stolen over her in recent weeks. She'd put it down to the excitement of the Bandit, but she was coming to realize it was far more than that. It had been coming on for months, long before the dark brooding hero of her imagination had appeared. Six months ago she'd have told anyone who asked that life was perfect just as it was. That things could go on in their present state indefinitely, and she'd consider herself supremely blessed.

She could no longer answer so firmly. Things could not go on in their present state, even if she had no idea what the alternative might be.

Where are you pulling me, Lord? Are You pulling me at all? Or am I simply straying, straining against You? I've never felt lonely before. Even when people could not understand how I was content, You've given me great contentment. Why remove it now?

Perhaps it was just the passing of another year that made her so pensive. She was, after all, turning twenty-five, and that seemed like an important year. One that invited retrospection. Perhaps in a week she'd look back on all this tumult as just an emotional response to the passing of time. After all, Stuart had been sour-faced a whole month earlier this year when he turned thirty.

An hour later, the thought still held no comfort. It was almost two in the morning, and if she didn't find a way to sleep, she would spend her birthday in a sorry state indeed. She read a psalm—the one about God knitting her together in her mother's womb—for it seemed appropriate to the day. She found herself wondering if this section was one of the ones cut from Matthew's Bible.

Matthew. How easily the name slipped into her mind now. She allowed herself to imagine him, sitting up late into the night, exploring the Bible Reverend Bauers had given him. She was sure she'd sensed some reaction in him when she'd read him the passage from Corinthians. Yet he did not seem a man of faith at all. Seeking, perhaps, but no faith had taken hold, as far as she could see. It seemed unwise to nurture any fondness for a man so ill at ease with himself. Still, that was how Reverend Bauers always said God shook a man to attention. With an unrelenting ill-ease. Was God shaking Matthew Covington? What an extraordinary thing that would be.

He would be a wonderful man of faith, she surmised, without really knowing why. It was just an instinct.

I'm quite fond of him, Father. You know that. And You know how unwise a thing that is.

Despite her self-lecture, the memory of his impulsive kiss on her hand this afternoon wedged its way into her thoughts. *He is fond of me, I think, but for such unusual, rewarding reasons. He sees me. I know You see me Father, and that You know me. But to be seen, be recognized by him in such a way, was so pleasing. Thank You for that blessing. A birthday present from You, it almost felt like.*

Matthew Covington, for all his attributes, was a most unwise prospect. She could recognize this, even if she kept rubbing the top of her palm where he'd touched her. No, she'd be wise to direct her energies into something else.

Perhaps in a week or two the contentment would return. She did, after all, have another man to consider. One who depended heavily upon her affections. Who existed by virtue of the fine imagination God had given her.

She had the Bandit, and he was a most excellent place to channel all those energies.

When would the Bandit have his birthday? Would he be the kind of man to celebrate the passing of his years, or ignore them? Yes, this was a much better place to focus her thoughts. Georgia let her head fall against the glass as she wondered. Her hero needed a birthday of his own. How to give him one? The scene came to her in an instant, as if it had dropped from heaven in complete form. It was perfect; dark and brooding, just like her hero. Tragic and yet deeply poignant. She heaved a sigh of thanks toward heaven and nearly ran to the desk, flipping open the top of her inkwell with such vigor that it sent a small shower of droplets over the page.

"Black gloves laid a single white lily across the roughly hewn gravestone. Rain fell softly, darkening the granite with streaks that seemed to weep down its engraved face. She lay here, never to know the joy of flowers or spring—or her son—again. Each year the Bandit made his pilgrimage to the lonely site of his mother's grave, the woman who'd given her life in the granting of his."

"Easter is over this weekend, isn't it?" Stuart asked with annoyance. The eggs had been fine—charming even—but when the real-life Bandit had upped the ante to all those chickens, things got a little more complicated than Stuart would have wished. He didn't like someone trying to outdo him. Stuart wanted to have his hands on the reins. He wanted to know he could orchestrate events to his liking. He didn't much care for a loose cannon like this Bandit impersonator roaming his city unsupervised. He'd need to find him somehow, so he could keep him under control.

"Yes, sir," Oakman replied.

Stuart looked at him. "Who is this man impersonating my Bandit, anyway? Do we have any idea? Not that I want to stop him, mind you, but I want to know where to put the pressure if he goes too far."

Oakman leaned back, resting his hands across his belly. "There are loads of theories. But no one knows anything definite, that I can find."

"Keep looking."

"Oh, you can count on that, sir. I'm looking."

Stuart leaned against his desk and lowered his voice. "We're a month away. Are we ready?"

That brought Oakman to attention. "Near as I can tell. There are a few loose ends to tie up. One contact on the docks I'm not quite sure about, yet. I need to take a few steps to ensure his loyalty, but I don't think there'll be any problem."

A few steps. Stuart was relatively certain what kind of persuasion bought loyalty on the docks. It was a jungle down there, a predatory landscape if ever there was one. Which was just fine by him. He preferred the open food chain of the docks to the gilded treachery of Nob Hill any day.

"What about our friend Mr. Covington? Has he found anything?"

Oakman paused for a second, running his hands down his face. "He asked for a second set of ledgers yesterday. That worried me a bit. But I'm not sure it's a problem."

Stuart blew out an exasperated breath. Covington was presenting more of a challenge than he'd anticipated. Why couldn't the Brit just give in to his obvious infatuation with Georgia and stop being so studious? A healthy young man shouldn't be so hard to distract. Stuart checked his watch. "Well, I've got to meet Georgia for lunch. It's her birthday."

Oakman looked up. "Didn't you take her to lunch for her birthday yesterday?"

"No." Stuart shook his head, not hiding his exasperation. "Covington had us over to the Palace for tea. I gave her an early piece of birthday cake when you sent over the message to call me back."

"But you *told* me to send over the message to call you back, sir."

"I'm aware of that, Dex. She just didn't take it very well, that's all. Something's put a bee in her bonnet lately. She's all up in arms over little things. Told me in no uncertain terms last night at dinner that I was to take her back to the Palace today for her birthday, and that if I was to leave for any reason at all, heads would roll."

"Georgia? Said that?"

Stuart glared at his colleague. "She did. Emphatically. I don't know what's gotten her all riled up."

"What?" said Oakman, with the most ridiculous look on his face, "or whom?"

"But I've just *come* from cake." Georgia tried to resist as Quinn pulled her down the Grace House hallway toward the dining room.

The boy spun on his heels. "Don't you tell anyone that. This cake is *your* cake." He tugged on her sleeve. "Act happy to have it."

"But I am happy to have cake," Georgia replied, her heart warming at the boy's concern. "Just not so *much* of it."

"We *made* you this cake," he said, as if that should be argument enough. "Is icing supposed to be green?"

Georgia tried not to consider the possibilities. "Some is. Icing comes in lots of colors."

"We only got green. So pretend you like it." He seemed to consider it his job to manage her participation. *Just what I need,* she thought for a moment, *another male telling me what to do.* When she noticed a large splotch of something greenish on Quinn's elbow, she decided perhaps it was not as bad as all that.

Quinn halted in front of the closed dining room door. "Come in here for a moment, Miss Georgia," he shouted in a rehearsed tone, evidently providing the "cue" needed by those within. "We've got something to show you," he bellowed.

Quinn pushed open the door to a room filled with smiling faces. A pack of recently scrubbed, smeary-aproned "bakers" yelled "happy birthday" around a lop-sided green cake. It wasn't a happy green, more brackish than lime-colored, with a frightening collection of black bits, but the cheery expressions couldn't help but make Georgia chuckle. Reverend Bauers had a "we did the best we could" expression that only deepened her laugh.

The exquisite lemon cake at the Palace Hotel might have delighted her palate, but this questionable confection delighted her heart. She clasped her hands theatrically. "My goodness," she exclaimed, "I'm absolutely surprised."

"We made it!" a small child to her left boasted, pointing with pudgy green-tinted fingers as one corner of the top layer slid slightly off its base. "Can you tell?"

"Not at all," Georgia said. "It looks like you just brought this from the finest bakery in the city."

Reverend Bauers extracted himself from the sticky crowd and came around to pull out a chair at the head of the table. "Miss Waterhouse, will you share your cake with us and celebrate your birthday?"

"I'd be delighted."

As he pushed in the chair, the children scattered to their own seats, eager for a piece of their creation.

"There's room for one more, I trust?" Matthew Covington's voice came from behind her. "I missed the earlier birthday cake." Obviously, he'd not seen the cake in front of her, or she doubted he'd ask.

Georgia whirled to face him, giving him an exaggerated wink. "Oh, but Mr. Covington, I've had *no* cake yet today."

Chapter Twenty-Six

M atthew seemed confused. "Have you not just come from—"

Georgia raised both eyebrows, hoping to cue him to follow her lead. "No," she said, overenunciating and nodding almost imperceptibly to the crowd behind her, "I've been *hoping* for cake all day and had *none.*"

Matthew glanced at her, cast his gaze to the baked atrocity on the table, then looked back at her. She gave him her most blatant "play along" expression.

"Of course," he finally said, only barely hiding a laugh. "And here you were saying to me just yesterday how much you liked…" he chose his description carefully "…green cake. How very fortunate for you."

"Fortunate for *you,* you've come in time to join us," she said, nearly laughing at the situation. She was certain he was no more enamored with the idea of eating such a cake than she. She was also certain he'd play along in heroic proportions rather than disappoint such an endearing audience.

"Indeed," he said, his eyes darkening to mean any of a thousand things. "And how very…green…a cake

it is. I *must* have a piece before Reverend Bauers and I
attend to urgent business."

Did he have urgent business with Reverend Bauers?
Or was that merely a strategic improvisation? He was
holding something behind his back. Either way, she en-
vied his alibi, for she had nothing more urgent than a
role of uncut bandages to save her from so green a cake.

"But no business more urgent than this," he declared,
producing a lovely bouquet of lilies. Delicate yellow
lilies the color of lemon cake. "Since I missed our earlier…appointment. Happy birthday, Miss Waterhouse."

She took the flowers from him. Two of the older
girls cooed and poked gentle fingers at the blooms.
"They are delightful, Mr. Covington. Thank you so
very much." As she said his full name, his request to
call him otherwise echoed like a vibration through her
chest. "Do sit down."

"From the look on your face—" Reverend Bauers put
the book he was holding back on the shelf "—you're up
to something. And I daresay it's more than providing
Miss Waterhouse with a birthday bouquet."

Matthew pretended surprise. "Me? However could
you say something like that?"

The clergyman leaned forward and whispered, "Oh,
a recent event involving agitated chickens."

He stepped back with an elaborate bow. "Well, my
good Reverend, you have me there. But poultry aside,
we have a bit of work to do if a certain hero is to give
another Easter gift to his fair city."

Bauers's expression grew serious. "I've given thought
to that, Covington. I don't think it would be proper to
do anything else near Easter. It is a holy season, and

given to contemplation and sacrifice, not theatrics. I'd much rather see you at our Good Friday service than out conducting heroics. *Very* much rather."

Matthew should have known it would come to this. Sooner or later, the good reverend would try and drag him into a church service, especially at Easter. After all the man had done to aid him, did Matthew really have grounds to refuse? "I'm not at all sure," he said, stuffing his hands in his pockets, mostly because he couldn't think of a stronger retort.

"No one needs you to be sure. We just need you to be here." The clergyman raised an eyebrow. "Unless you have other plans?"

Other plans. He had no holiday plans. While he had somehow expected the Waterhouses to extend an Easter invitation, he really had no basis to expect such a thing. At the moment, it looked as if he would be spending his Easter with Thompson in his room. Or eating alone in the Palace dining room.

"Come now, Matthew," the reverend said, using his Christian name for the first time—intentionally, Matthew guessed. "Unless Stuart Waterhouse is planning to spirit you elsewhere, everyone you could call friend will be at the service here—including Miss Waterhouse. And me. And, if you must know, a couple of young men who skewered you not too long ago and have since repented."

Reverend Bauers was pulling out all stops and brooking no refusal. What had Matthew's father once said to him? *It does you no good to start a fight you can't win.* Matthew sighed. "Very well then, what time should I be here?"

Reverend Bauers clasped both of Matthew's shoulders. "I knew you'd come round."

"And how did you know that?"

With a wink, the reverend nodded toward the heavens.

Egad, thought Matthew, *that's the first time I've been in a room with one other person and been outnumbered.*

Matthew was delighted to discover Georgia was still at Grace House when he finished—if one ever truly finished—with Reverend Bauers. He'd planned to give her the flowers in relative privacy, not amidst the giggling pack of children. Still, it had been pleasant enough to catch her eye here and there in the chaotic conversation, to sneak a glimpse of her admiring the flowers as she showed them to the girls around the table. He had pleased her, and he liked that.

Which was, of course, not helpful. He must return home to England when his business was completed, and he knew in his bones that England would never suit her. Still, Matthew seemed unable to squelch the impulse to make her happy. To, when he was honest with himself, "rescue" her from the apathy of her surroundings. And that had always been Matthew's vice: rescuing even when no rescue was needed.

Even if it meant ingesting the strangest concoction to ever be called "cake." As he recalled the green-gray dessert they'd shared, he wondered if Georgia's stomach had turned over as many times in the last hour as his had. She did look a little peaked when he found her putting away the last of the bandages in the storeroom. It did not escape his notice that the lilies lay on the table beside her.

"Have you fully recovered from your party?" he asked as he leaned in the storeroom doorway.

She gave a lopsided grin and put her hand to her stomach. "I'm not quite sure. They did a most...enthusiastic...job, didn't they? I'm worried that our poor cook may never recover from the experience."

Endearing. That was the word he'd give to her expression. She looked so full of affection for this place and these people that she'd gladly have swallowed frogs. For the first time he admitted to himself how envious he was of that affection. "I'm worried myself," he said, trying not to wonder if she would put her tender hand to his forehead if he pleaded ill. "I hope you won't be offended if I admit to preferring the cake at the Palace."

"No," she said with a laugh. "Not at all."

Matthew came into the room and nodded at the bandages. "Still working? Haven't you celebrations to attend to? Ones involving *actual food?*" He regretted the question the moment it left his lips. What if she had no celebrations planned? What if lunch with Stuart was the most she received on her birthday? It stung him that he'd asked so pointed a question without thinking.

"I'll have a lovely dinner with my brother. Cook always makes my favorites. And I have many plans for Easter to pull together, so I'll be quite busy."

Matthew wondered if being born on Easter wasn't really the blessing Stuart made it out to be. The feast moved every year, sliding in and out of the path of Georgia's birthday, it was true. But to Matthew it seemed Easter was yet another force determined to overshadow this extraordinary woman. His own mother spent days elaborately celebrating her birthday—and demanding others do the same. Did everyone brush aside Georgia's birthday because it fell too near to Easter? Did she do anything other than pause for a few slices of cake before resuming rolling bandages and seeing to her household? She deserved better.

He decided on a birthday present of another kind. "Bauers's convinced me to come back Friday. I thought you'd like to know."

She blinked at him for a moment before she registered his meaning. When she did, she put down the bandages and turned to face him fully. "For Good Friday services? Oh, yes, Matthew, I am delighted to know."

She had called him Matthew without thinking about it. Her immediate blush told him so. Which meant that she had been using that name in her thoughts. Which meant she had been thinking about him. A jolt went through him.

"The service is beautiful here," she said too quickly, as if to cover up the admission, "and quite different from what I imagine you're used to. I always find it a very moving experience." Her gaze dropped back to the bandages. "I've always wanted Stuart to come, but have never been able to convince him. I'm so glad Reverend Bauers has had more success with you."

She was oblivious of her own strength. She saw Stuart's refusal as a reflection on her, instead of his own stubborn nature. Was she unaware that the prospect of seeing her again was half the reason Matthew had consented to Reverend Bauers's persuasion? Was she so blind to her qualities that these people at Grace House celebrated? Instead, focusing on the many who dismissed her? How was it she held such calm inner strength without even realizing it? How did she persevere in the face of a world that seemed to pay her so little attention?

He realized he was staring at her.

He realized he did not want to stop, nor to hide what he was certain showed in his eyes. It was doomed, what he felt for her at that moment, what he'd been feeling for days, if not from the first. It could come to no good end for either of them. And yet he could no more hold it back than he could halt the tide that would carry him back to England.

"Stuart is a fool to decline," he said quietly. He wanted to hit himself immediately. Had she not asked from the first that they not spend time discussing her brother? Was Matthew such a coward that he could only couch his hints at affection in Stuart's actions? "I'm too glad to come and see what you hold so dear," he said with more strength. "I would consider it an honor to escort you to the service."

She knew. He saw it in her eyes. No, she wasn't unaware of her effect on him. She feared it, just as he did—perhaps far more than he did. But she knew. Even if he couldn't be certain she'd known it before now, even if she'd only suspected it when he'd kissed her hand yesterday, here, now, she *knew*. It seemed as if a cannon went off in his chest. "Please... Georgia... allow me the honor."

It was a daring assumption, to use her first name without her permission, but he seemed unable to stop himself. She startled just a little bit at his boldness, but there was much more than surprise in her eyes. There was a tiny, fragile joy, a careful pleasure, that fastened itself around his heart.

"We'll...we'll see," she stammered quietly.

It was enough for now.

Chapter Twenty-Seven

Georgia was finishing up some sewing that evening when she heard Stuart's tenor ringing through the halls.

> "Oh, men of dark and dismal fate,
> Forgo your cruel employ,
> Have pity of my lonely state,
> I am an orphan boy."

She put down her work and sighed. Of course. Well, it was her own fault. She'd thought she'd penned a poignant episode of the Bandit's adventures for the Good Friday edition. She hadn't for a moment considered that she'd now employed one of the most famous running jokes of *The Pirates of Penzance* when she'd made the Bandit an orphan. She'd given the story to Stuart when they met for her birthday lunch. An episode in which readers discover the Bandit's parents are dead, which, by definition, made him an orphan. Stuart's beloved Gilbert and Sullivan pirates never harm any orphan, and are hilariously astounded when all their victims instantly "claim" to be orphans. "An orphan boy"—how had she not seen it? She was astounded he'd waited this long to come home and tease her.

It would be a long evening, even with a fine birthday meal. From now until the episode's appearance on Friday—and perhaps for weeks thereafter—the chorus would be endlessly sung to her, Georgia had no doubt.

She heard her brother's steps coming into the parlor, accompanied by a rousing chorus, *"'For he is an orphan boy, hurrah for the orphan boy!'"* Stuart's blond head popped into the room from around the corner. *"And it sometimes is a useful thing to be an orphan boy!'"*

Georgia looked up from the mound of cloth in her lap. "Most amusing, Stuart."

"And how are you, my dear orphan sister?"

It had not struck her that she and Stuart were orphans, as well. Not that she didn't know it—especially today, her birthday. But she always thought of it in terms of Stuart's phrase "we're all we have in the world." The term "orphan" seemed so much colder, despite the fun Gilbert and Sullivan had with it.

"Did you have a nice afternoon at the Grace House after our lunch?"

"As a matter of fact, I did." She smiled at the memory of the ominously green cake. Reverend Bauers had said the most beautiful prayer over it. It had tasted more like medicine than confection, but she'd made a spectacle of herself complimenting the children for their efforts. She was only outdone by Matthew Covington, whose outlandish string of superlatives reduced everyone to laughter by the end. It was truly a delightful, if not delicious, celebration.

Her brother looked puzzled. "I still say it's an odd way to celebrate your birthday. Ripping bandages."

How wrong he could be about some things, for so smart a man! Her work at Grace House was so much more than ripping bandages. These people were as much her family as Stuart. She could think of no finer way to celebrate her life than to do the things that gave her joy. And Grace House always gave her joy. The fact that Matthew had been there had given her great joy, as well—even though it felt dangerous to admit it.

She had tried not to be disappointed when he did not appear at the Palace as she and Stuart had lunch—and more lemon cake. Instead, she had attempted to reassure herself that it was just as well not to nurture that friendship. To remind herself how foolish her growing affection was.

He felt something for her. She knew it, could feel it in how he'd looked at her when he said he was coming to Grace House on Friday.

He was coming to the church service.

He wanted to come with her. *With her.* Did he realize what that meant to her?

The lilies he had given her, now standing in a crystal vase on the parlor table, had not left her side all afternoon.

She shared none of this with Stuart.

"I enjoyed my afternoon immensely, Stuart. And so did you, from the look on your face."

Stuart swept the needlework off of her lap and pulled her to her feet. "My look has nothing to do with me. It has to do with you. With your birthday present. I've come up with the most marvelous gift for you, Peach."

Georgia often felt a mild sense of alarm when Stuart got that expression on his face. "And what is that?"

"I'm going to throw you a ball."

"A ball? For my birthday?" Georgia felt the room shift a little under her feet. It was not a pleasant sensation.

"Well, not exactly a birthday ball. It's a little late to pull something like that off on a grand enough scale."

A grand enough scale? She furrowed her brow.

"A great big ball. Isn't it a fine idea?" He didn't wait for her answer before adding, "But it's not just any ball, Peach."

"What do you mean?"

He dropped her hands and crossed his arms across his chest like a conquering major general. "I'm going to throw a Bandit Ball. I'm going to throw you a ball in a few weeks and we're going to invite the Black Bandit to show his face. You're going to meet the man who's been bringing your fantasy to life, Peach. He'll never know it's you, but you'll get to know it's him. You'll meet your Bandit. Are you pleased?"

Georgia gulped in a breath. "I don't know what I am. I don't know what to say."

Stuart pulled her into a waltz. "Say the only thing you ought to say—yes!"

"I cannot imagine where he got this wild idea to throw a Bandit Ball." Georgia pushed a cart full of reading primers as she and Sister Charlotte walked through the convent school a few days later. The convent was donating some educational materials to Grace House, and Georgia was only too glad to have another opportunity to visit Sister Charlotte. "It's a dreadful idea, don't you think?"

Charlotte selected another book from the shelf behind her and added it to the cart. "Why, not at all. I think it's a grand idea. For any number of reasons."

Georgia's spirits deflated. Was she the only person who thought this a poor idea? Did anyone care what *she* thought of a ball proposed as *her* birthday present? "And those grand reasons are?"

Charlotte pushed open a supply closet door. "First of all, you'll get to meet your Bandit under the most advantageous conditions. He has no idea of your affections for him, but because of your status as Stuart's sister he'll be bound to pay attention to you."

Charlotte still had no idea that Georgia penned the Bandit's adventures. No one knew the truth, and it was going to stay that way. If Charlotte—or anyone—merely thought her interest in the Bandit was because of Stuart, or if they persisted in their belief that Stuart was really George Towers, then that was fine with Georgia. It made things infinitely easier. "True."

"You'll get to see the man up close," she continued, selecting three more books from a narrow wooden shelf, then adding some small slates and a ceramic container of stubby pencils, "not hiding behind the costume and the legend. You have no idea how illuminating it can be to see a legendary man up close. Some of them grow more compelling the nearer they get. Others, well—" she erupted into a chuckle "—let us just say they pale under scrutiny."

Georgia took the supplies and stacked them on the cart with a dubiously raised eyebrow.

"Oh, I know of what I speak. You may find the fastest antidote to your infatuation might be spending ten minutes in close proximity to the man." Charlotte handed over the last of the books and dusted off the front of her habit. "The stories I could tell! The heroes I could bring down."

As outlandish as it sounded, it made Georgia wonder about Charlotte's late husband, Robert Brownstone. What kind of man had finally won Charlotte's heart? What had he done? How had he risen victorious over so many heroic characters?

Georgia was drawn out of her thoughts by the waving of a pencil in front of her face. "Really, dear, you must stop drifting off like that. It hides your intellect." The nun waved to a young priest coming down the hallway. "Father David, would you please see to it that these supplies are delivered to Grace House?"

"Yes, Sister." Off went priest and cart.

"Now," continued Charlotte, "back to the business at hand. You're going to invite your other man—the real-life man—to the ball, are you not?"

"Goodness. I hadn't thought about that. I don't even know if he'll still be in San Francisco." Distant shouts heralded the letting out of girls from class elsewhere in the building.

"This will give him reason to extend his visit," said Charlotte. "Have you seen him since our last conversation? Have you revised your opinion of him in any way?"

Georgia felt a blush rise in her cheeks. "As a matter of fact, I have." Carefully, without mentioning any names, places or other identifying details, she told Charlotte the story of the tea and cake and her birthday flowers.

"Matthew Covington? The man is *Matthew Covington?*"

Chapter Twenty-Eight

Georgia nearly gasped. She'd taken the greatest of care not to reveal his identity. "How did you...?" She could not even finish the sentence.

"My dear girl, this is a convent, not a deserted island. We still do get asked to events and we still do meet people. Especially visiting dignitaries. And I must say Reverend Bauers has been rather vocal about Covington's dramatic scrape over at Grace House. And then there is Stuart. He likes to make sure everyone knows he knows everyone important." One hand flew to her chest. "Really. I do wonder how you put up with that brother of yours."

It wasn't as if Georgia hadn't heard that sentiment expressed many times before. She heard that remark, or something like it, frequently. But she usually fended it off with a comment about how Stuart had a big heart, or how he loved her dearly even if he did have an odd way of showing it, or how it took a big spirit to run a big paper. Today, though, she found such responses hollow and false. "I suppose I wonder myself," she said, surprised at her own open admission.

"You're not him, you know. You're not alike at all. You're the furthest thing from each other that could be."

It was as if Charlotte had given voice to a fear Georgia had never allowed herself to recognize. A thought she'd never articulated, never even dared to name. She was afraid that people thought her like Stuart. That people mistook her tolerance for approval. That people never saw her behind the glare of Stuart's high-energy personality. Seemingly out of nowhere, Georgia felt a lump rise in her throat. She swallowed hard, thinking it a very foolish thing indeed to grow teary in a school hallway.

Charlotte, however, was far too keen a soul not to notice the effect her words had on her companion. She grasped Georgia's arm and squeezed it affectionately. "That's part of it, isn't it, dear? To spend your life alongside someone like Stuart. You fear yourself invisible."

Invisible. It was as if Charlotte had chosen the very word Georgia couldn't bring herself to use. Is this what nuns did? Bring people to the point where words evaded them, and they could only nod?

"My dear Georgia, none of us is invisible to God. He sees all that we do. All that we bear. All we yearn for. Surely you know that in your heart?"

"I do," Georgia replied, her voice a bit shaky. "But..."

"But knowing something and feeling it are two different things, aren't they?"

Georgia nodded.

"Mr. Covington. Does he make you feel invisible?"

"Oh, no, not at all," Georgia replied, with more enthusiasm that was perhaps wise. "Quite the contrary."

"There is much to be said for that." Together they walked through a sea of girls toward the convent garden.

"There is also much to be said for the huge distance between London and San Francisco," Georgia murmured. "And for a heart of faith and a heart without faith."

Charlotte patted her hand. "Ah, now, that's a real issue. Oceans can be crossed. Households can be moved. A man's faith is not so easy a challenge. I daresay you are right to hesitate." She opened the garden gate. "Does he know of your faith?"

"I'm sure he does. We've spoken of it directly."

"Well, that's certainly promising. What did you discuss?"

Georgia's heart gave an unsettling flip as she remembered the scene in the park. "He asked me to read him my favorite scripture. I'm quite sure it affected him to hear it. I mean, I suppose I'm sure. You can never be sure about something like that, can you?"

"Nonsense," countered Charlotte. "I believe you can be."

"Still, admiration of faith, and faith of one's own, are very different." Georgia fingered a broad green leaf on a plant to her left.

"An excellent point. How would you describe Mr. Covington's faith?"

Georgia thought about it for a moment. Matthew had tried not to be affected by the scripture she had read, but she knew it had had an impact upon him. It was in his eyes even if he hadn't said so. And somehow, without their even discussing it, she knew he was struggling with whether to delve into the Bible Reverend Bauers had given him. Was God, in fact, "on his heels," as the reverend was so fond of saying? Was that why God had brought Matthew into her life? The thought seemed far-fetched, yet appealing. She felt a grin sneak across her face. "Ready to pounce?"

Charlotte sat down. "God has certainly been pouncing on unlikely men since the time of Moses." She spread her hands wide. "Why not your Mr. Covington?"

Matthew looked up from cleaning his sword when the clock chimed eleven. After a dreary dinner at the Oakmans', during which the couple seemed intent on securing themselves in his good graces by way of endless compliments, he'd retired to his room. As the son of a powerful businessman, he'd been the recipient of such attention enough times to recognize it. Still, he never could stomach it the way his father and brother could. They saw it as the necessary lubrication of the gears of commerce. To him it rang insincere.

It made him think of Georgia. How opposite they were. Here he was, under the glare of so much unwanted attention. Eyed by dozens of people who were watching to make sure he did his duty. She, on the other hand, went about duties far beyond and in many ways beneath her station without the slightest bit of recognition or notice. How could she endure the disparity, when it chafed at him so?

Matthew's gaze fell on the small Bible sitting at his desk. Did her faith gave her that steadiness he admired?

He was almost embarrassed to be considering the question, although he didn't know why. *Because you have no faith,* he told himself. *And you won't pretend you do. At least you respect God enough not to employ Him as lubricant to the gears of life.* One had to have faith to benefit from it.

He'd heard of people "coming to faith." There'd been

a cousin several years back, an idealistic young man who'd left a promising post with a fine firm to go off and teach natives somewhere. So obviously, one could acquire faith, for the cousin in question had been quite the rake before God got ahold of him.

But how did one acquire it? Did you hunt it down? Or did it come upon you unbidden, like an illness?

Or love.

Was he in love with Georgia Waterhouse? Matthew mused. What a mess that would be. He was taken with her. Extremely. Dangerously. But he was not ready to use a powerful word like love. He'd try not to be, if one had a choice about such things.

Georgia's faith was an inseparable part of her. One could not admire the woman without admiring her faith. And he did admire it, greatly. He just didn't think he could go beyond admiration to the sharing of that faith. He didn't think it worked that way.

Still, Matthew owed it to Georgia not to make a pretense of the services on Friday. He would, he decided as he put the sword back into its case, make an honest attempt at participation. Out of respect for her and all the people who had been so kind to him at Grace House. And there was really only one way he could think of to do that.

He ignored the trepidation that assailed him when he walked over to the desk and picked up the Bible. He'd open it. For her. To respect her.

Since it was the fate of Jesus they would be honoring, Matthew calculated that the life of Jesus would be the story to read. Those were laid out in the four Gospels—he remembered that much from the half-dozen Sunday school lessons he'd endured. They were somewhere toward the back. He was relatively certain he'd recognize the four names when he came to them.

He laughed when he came across the first one: Matthew.

Well, if one had to pick a place to start…

Chapter Twenty-Nine

Sudden chords from the small chapel piano brought Matthew's thoughts back to the service. It was a simple, honest service. Reverend Bauers read scripture passages telling the story of Jesus's trial, crucifixion and death, interspersed by half a dozen somber hymns. Had Matthew attended such a service back in England, he would have found it dour and depressing.

His own response today surprised him. The seriousness did not seem out of place anymore, for he knew the story. In fierce detail. And now those details came upon him with such intensity that they seemed to puncture him. He'd never considered the possibility of the world—the universe itself— hanging on the outcome of a single day. It wouldn't fit into the confines of human logic.

This man, this "savior," had gone to a grisly death reserved for the lowest criminals.

And he went *by choice.* That was the part that festered in Matthew's spirit. If this Jesus really had all that power, was who He claimed to be, then why this outcome? Why not go straight to the victory everyone celebrated on Easter Sunday? It made no sense. Matthew had been angry the first time he'd read the gospel last night, thinking it all unjust torture. A waste of a good man. Why would a God as powerful as that allow such a thing to become the pivotal moment in human history?

Agitated, Matthew had stayed up later to read it all a second time. He was sure he'd somehow missed a crucial element, some key point that would let the story make sense.

But the clear choice of it, the dozens of times a mighty God could have stopped it all, had not changed. There was no other conclusion: it was Jesus's conscious choice to endure this gruesome thing. This hideous mistake that was really no mistake at all, but planned from the dawn of time.

Why? Matthew's whole being seemed to resonate with the word as the readings followed the plot to destruction.

Halfway through the service, Reverend Bauers read the passage where Jesus, in the throes of pain and suffering, gave his mother to another disciple. Matthew heard a small whimper next to him and realized Georgia was crying. His heart ached for her. For her devotion, for her acceptance, when it seemed all he could do was resist.

Then—quickly or gradually, he couldn't really tell— the resistance grew too much to bear. His heart went legions beyond aching for her and her devotion, and began aching for everything. It was as if all the details crushed down upon him, breaking his heart wide-open, in a way he didn't recognize but somehow always knew existed. And he couldn't bear to resist anymore. Because he realized it wasn't the injustice he was resisting, it was the unfathomable love behind it.

This story was never about power or justice or any of the things he'd thought before. This was a love story.

The readings went on, pushing toward the terrible end, where the final hymn hung in the air like a funeral dirge and tears shone on Georgia's cheeks. For the first time, Matthew glimpsed what it was that she saw. And he felt his heart crush. Yet it wasn't an obliteration, it was a transformation. As if his heart were crushed to burst open again. Burst open to reveal an affection. Matthew thought about what he felt for her—sorry excuse for a man that he was—and realized that it must have been only a shred of what this God would have to have felt for mankind—for *him*—to endure such a gruesome path.

There was a large hill on Matthew's property when he was a boy. Legs churning, he would run toward the top until his lungs burned, toward the place where he could see the valley on the other side. He was always running so fast, and the summit was so broad, that he never quite knew when he'd hit the top. It didn't really have a top. It was more like a shift, a realization that his churning legs were now going down, and he could see the valley. The sensation that he'd shifted sides without truly knowing when it happened.

It was like that.

He believed.

It wasn't a single moment or a great, peaking precipice, but a slow shift that altered his view. The churning of all those details, all the people newly come into his life, all the feelings surging up inside of him, had propelled him toward a summit he had almost imperceptibly reached.

And now he believed.

It was both awesome and quiet at the same time. Like a rope drawn so tight it finally snapped, but then again, not at all like that. Like a gear finally slipping into place, but not at all like that, either. As if everything made sense, but now had been turned inside out.

He realized, as the events of the past few weeks strung themselves together in his mind, that God had been propelling him up the mountain even before Matthew knew it. That the path had been there all along. Reverend Bauers, Georgia, even the boy who'd cut him—these people were placed in his life, at this time, for a reason. He was the man he was, faults and strengths, for a purpose. Unique by design. Loved beyond his comprehension. Sent.

He believed.

He found himself having to tell his body to breathe in and out, for it no longer seemed to work right. Nothing had changed, and yet everything seemed in far sharper focus. He felt as if he should run and shout, but wondered if he could move at all. It may have been minutes until the end of the service, or it might have been hours; he seemed unable to tell. He stared at the edge of the pew in front of him without seeing it. How very odd to be caught by surprise by something that hadn't sneaked up on him at all. God had, just as the reverend had said, gone "after him with both barrels blazing."

And Matthew hadn't even recognized Him until Georgia Waterhouse stared so hard at God that He came into view.

Now what?

At some point the service would come to an end and he'd need to walk out of this dear little chapel and return to the world he'd known. How would it change? Would it change at all? How would the Matthew Covington of faith be different from the Matthew Covington of before? Was it visible? It seemed both worthy of shouting from rooftops and excruciatingly private at the same time. He found himself, quite simply, at a complete loss.

The service did come to an end, and the congregation followed Reverend Bauers's instructions to file out in respectful silence. The door to the church was closed with a declarative thud. Matthew felt slightly dizzy.

Out of the corner of his eye, he caught Georgia's concerned glance. "Are you well?" she said, putting a gentle hand on his elbow. The tender touch felt as if it would knock him across a room. He wanted to take her hand and cling to it, but forced himself to tuck it into his elbow with any semblance of formality he could muster.

"May we walk?" he choked out, his voice unfamiliar.

She noticed his strange tone, and stared at him for a long moment before nodding. Somehow sensing his need for silence, she led him around the building into the mission's garden. They ended up standing in the small courtyard, where he'd been cut what seemed so long ago.

He sat down on the wide rim of the fountain facing a small fruit tree just venturing to bud. Signs of newness—something he usually never noticed—seemed to surround him. Buds, sprouts, new leaves...*ugh:* He thought it all a bit conspicuous of the universe to get so metaphorical all at once. He was not fond of poetry. Was it appropriate to hope that faith did not lead one immediately to artistic pursuits?

The sheer ridiculousness of the thought forced a laugh out of him, but it sounded far more like a sputtering cough.

Something was very wrong with Matthew. His agitation had begun somewhere during the middle of the service, and it was nearly palpable by the end. He seemed unable to talk, and yet kept growling with some kind of furor. Had he been insulted by the dark drama of the service? Had Reverend Bauers forced him to attend somehow, and angered him? He looked as though he might launch into a tirade at any moment. When his face contorted and he choked, Georgia panicked. "Goodness," she said, alarm in her voice. "Are you ill?"

He blinked at her, looking as if she'd spoken a foreign language he couldn't understand. Was he having some sort of spell? If he fell over, she'd be quite unable to stop him from toppling into the fountain. She grabbed his hand, worried that he might start swaying at any moment.

The moment she reached toward him, he clasped her hand. Hard. "Matthew," she said, as loudly as she dared, not sure he could even hear. "Gracious, what is wrong?"

He looked at her for a long moment. "I believe," he said, his voice full of surprise and concern.

It didn't make any sense. *I believe I'm going to be ill? I believe you've insulted me? I believe I'll have ham for dinner? I—*

"I believe," he repeated, clutching her hand for emphasis. "I *believe.*"

The entire world stopped and turned. Truly, it felt as if even the trees perked up and took notice. She widened her eyes. "Matthew?"

He shook his head, pulling one hand from hers to run his fingers agitatedly through his hair. "I believe. *It*. I read through that Bible three times last night and... I believe."

He seemed so shocked, so completely taken by surprise, that she couldn't think how to respond, except maybe to cry, which seemed inappropriate but rather unavoidable. Reverend Bauers always had the most wonderful things to say to someone who'd just come to faith, but every single word seemed to desert her. She felt a tear steal down her cheek, and prayed for the right words of response. Nothing came to her. She clasped his hand more tightly.

He looked up at her, bewildered. "What do I do now?"

The response came upon her immediately, and she knew where Reverend Bauers gained his insight at such moments. Surely, only God could grant such timely wisdom.

"It is Good Friday, my dear Mr. Covington. There is nothing to be done. The greatest work has just been done for us. We need only accept it."

Chapter Thirty

Reverend Bauers clasped Matthew's arm with great enthusiasm the next morning. "My son, I could not be happier to hear what you have said." He eased himself down on the fountain rim, patting the ledge beside him in an invitation for Matthew to join him.

Matthew couldn't suppress a smile as he sat beside the old man. The reverend's rampant enthusiasm for Matthew's newfound faith was as entertaining as it was heartwarming. The man was practically giddy, exclaiming that he couldn't have been more surprised. The knowing smirk behind his smile, however, hinted that he'd suspected nothing less. In fact, he looked so satisfied that Matthew hadn't wondered if Bauers himself had been beseeching God to go after him all along. He felt as if God *had* been after him from the moment he'd set foot on American soil. Bauers laughed heartily when Matthew admitted as much to him.

"I've been waiting more than a few years for the right set of hands to receive that Bible. I won't say I wasn't surprised when God said you were him—it did seem like a bit of a long shot, if you don't mind my saying.

But I've learned to trust God's vision as better than my own. He has been waiting for you, even when you could not see it. Even when *I* could not see it." The reverend folded his arms across his chest and narrowed his eyes at Matthew. "I believe God has special plans for your... how shall we say it? Your 'unique talents.'"

Matthew took the chubby hand of this man who had become so dear to him in such a short time. "You are more kind than I am talented, Reverend."

"I find myself debating whether you are going to tell Miss Waterhouse that you are the Bandit, or that you care for her. Or is it both? You do seem to be a man given to extremes."

"Reverend, I—"

Bauers waved his protest away. "Come now, do you think I cannot see it? I believe I knew it even before you did. When you brought her favorite flowers, my suspicions were only confirmed." His face grew serious. "Yesterday, I would have done my best to dissuade you. Miss Waterhouse is dear to me, and I'll not have her hurt."

"And today?" Matthew asked, still dumbfounded that Bauers knew at all. Had it been that obvious?

"And today I'll still not have her hurt, even if you now share a common faith. She's an uncommon woman. I'll not have you toying with her affections, Covington. Her heart is very tender. Don't venture where you do not mean to stay."

Matthew sighed. "That's just it, Reverend, I cannot say where I will be in a month's time. It is why I cannot declare my...affections...now."

"Then why even..." The Reverend's face darkened as Matthew pulled a white ribbon from his pocket. "Oh, you do not mean to… Covington, can you not see the wrong in that?"

"To have the Bandit declare himself as an admirer of hers? And why not? No one seems to notice all that she does. She exists only as Stuart Waterhouse's shadow. His conscience. His keeper. I cannot give her encouragement for any kind of future. But the Bandit can pay her some attention."

"What good is that? It is a fantasy, Covington." Bauers raised his hands in the air. "Does she not deserve the admiration of a real man? Would you hand her a lie?"

"I have nothing else to give her. She would no sooner join me in England than I could cut off ties and stay here." Matthew lowered his voice. "Have you seen the way she looks when she speaks of the Bandit? She admires the hero. I wouldn't be surprised if Stuart wrote the episodes just for her."

Bauers's eyebrows knit together. "She deserves better."

Matthew stood up. "She deserves far more than I can give her."

"She deserves the truth. Not more shadows. Covington, don't."

"Bauers, you should know by now I'm not much good at doing as I am told."

The air was clear and pleasant as Matthew slipped into position Saturday night and waited.

She came out onto the terrace, pulling a shawl around her shoulders against the breeze. She looked beautiful, bathed in the splash of light that came from the French doors. Her gown and hair glowed in the blue-black, moonless night. It was like something out of a

Shakespeare sonnet. He felt the urge to burst out of the bushes and declare his affections for her, to sweep her off her feet and ride into the sunset, like the fantasy she admired.

Instead, he waited until her back was to him. Then he reached into his pocket and pulled out a white ribbon tied to a small stone. In a slightly accented voice, he said, "Do not turn around, Miss Waterhouse. I mean you no harm, but you must not turn." He tossed the stone so that the white strip sailed into her view.

She gasped and gave a start, but did not turn. "Oh!" she exclaimed, pulling her shawl more tightly around her. He watched her plant her feet. "I... I shall remain where I am."

Matthew took a cautious step out of the bushes. "You think that no one sees, that no one knows the good you do, but you are wrong. I have seen. I know. You are a fine and admirable woman, Georgia Waterhouse." It was overly dramatic, but then again, this was a memory he was building, a memory to last a lifetime. If Stuart wrote such high drama to please her, then it must be high drama that she desired.

He took two more steps toward her, and with the tip of his sword he pushed the French doors closed, so that less light spilled out onto the terrace.

She heard his steps, saw the sword push the doors, and reacted. He heard her breath quicken, watched the way her body tensed. Two more steps brought him near enough. He could reach out and touch her hair, she was that close to him. He thought, as he looked at her in the moonlight, that if she turned, if he saw her eyes, there would be no hope for him. He would surrender to the overpowering urge to embrace her, to kiss her, and be lost forever.

God above, he prayed, *do not let her turn. I am not that strong.*

Chapter Thirty-One

"Who are you?" she whispered, her voice a mixture of thrill and fear.

"An admirer," he said, wanting to say much more. He had thought of a dozen things to say, a dozen heroic, romantic things, just like the Bandit would say, but they all fled his mind in the reality of the moment.

"How did you know I wrote them?" she gasped.

What? Matthew nearly stumbled in his shock. *She wrote them? Georgia wrote the Bandit stories?*

Of course Georgia wrote them. Suddenly, it all made perfect sense. How could he not have seen that? How could he not have considered it? She wrote them. She was George Towers. It seemed almost obvious now.

It was *her* words he'd read to her—that was why she'd reacted so. Her words he'd mocked, thinking they were Stuart's ploys—and that was why it hurt her so. Her hero that he impersonated. The knowledge was so intimate, so terrifying, that he had trouble thinking clearly.

"The Bandit knows many things," he finally choked out. Such a ridiculous response. Then again, he was so stunned, he was lucky to have remembered to speak in an accent at all, much less wax eloquent under the circumstances.

She wrote them. She was George.

Leave it to Georgia Waterhouse to take his surprise for her and send it back upon himself threefold.

She wrote the Bandit.

He was at a complete loss.

"Will I ever know who you are?" she asked breathlessly.

He thought his heart would split open if he stayed a second longer. He must get out of there as fast as possible. He whispered, "God bless you, Georgia Waterhouse. Good night and good Easter," and backed away.

Stuart could not have been more surprised when Georgia told him of Matthew Covington's newfound faith.

"Covington?" Stuart sputtered over his coffee as they sat in the parlor after Easter dinner. "What have you done to him, the pair of you?"

Georgia fingered the lilies from her birthday bouquet, still brilliant and fragrant in their vase by the window. "The pair of us?"

"You and Bauers. Covington's not even an American citizen. Evangelizing the tourists, are we now?"

"God is no respecter of borders," Georgia retorted, turning to face her brother. The strength in her own voice surprised her. "He'd even take you in, should you ever come to your senses."

Stuart shook his head. "I'm thinking it's Covington who needs to come to his senses."

"Stuart," she chided. Tonight she found she could no

longer endure his insults to her faith. "That's enough of that."

He looked up at her. When she stared at him, he pursed his lips and returned to his coffee without another word.

He had complied.

Normally, when Stuart went too far—which was almost always—she would swallow her feelings and silently endure. Today she stood her ground. And survived. She pulled in a deep breath of courage and pressed forward. "I've been thinking about your ball."

"*Your* ball," he corrected.

"No, it was *your* ball, Stuart. Given for me, I suppose. But I've decided to accept. I'd like you to have the ball for me, but I'd like to make a few changes."

That got her brother's complete attention.

"Such as?"

"It will be a charity ball, raising money for Grace House. The First Annual Bandit's Charity Ball. Every man who donates may come dressed as the Bandit. And you'll see to it that every man donates, won't you, Stuart?"

"A hundred Bandits? Peach, are you serious?"

She crossed her arms over her chest and went to stand before him. "Quite. It will be a sensation. You'll gain loads of press, and I'll gain enough money to ensure that Grace House never lacks for what it needs." She held out her hand. "Do we have a bargain?"

Stuart looked up. "What's gotten into you?"

"Do we have a bargain?"

He turned the idea over in his mind for a moment, looking, she was sure, for the escape clause. There wasn't one. Everyone got what they wanted in this bargain, including her. She had to admit it felt wonderful.

"I believe we do." He shook her hand.

Georgia leaned down, brought his hand to her and kissed it. "Brilliant. I'll have the list of things you need to do on your desk by tomorrow morning. How many waltzes are there in the Gilbert and Sullivan works, anyway?"

He gazed at her, mouth agape. "I don't know," he said slowly.

"Really? I was sure you would. Well, we'd best find out so we can give the list to the orchestra this week."

"Waltzes."

"Yes, Stuart, waltzes. Lots of them. They're my favorite. And red roses. Only red roses. But with white ribbons, of course. Yards and yards of white ribbons."

"Georgia," her brother said, furrowing his brow, "are you ill?"

"Not at all." She smiled back at him. "I'm just plain wonderful."

Chapter Thirty-Two

Matthew found Reverend Bauers on Grace House's front steps Monday morning, fixing the doorknob. "I need to speak with you," he said, pulling the clergyman into the mission by his elbow.

"Goodness," chuckled the reverend, who barely had enough time to put aside his tools. "Would that all my converts were so enthusiastic. But I didn't see you at Easter services."

"I had some matters to attend to." Bauers frowned, but Matthew pressed on. "Things have just become a good deal more interesting..." he lowered his voice "... in the area of my 'unique talents.'"

The reverend gave him a surprised look and ushered him into his study.

"I know the author of the Bandit episodes," Matthew declared the moment the door was shut.

"Stuart revealed himself to you? However did you accomplish that?"

Matthew sat down in one of the study chairs. "I did no such thing. Georgia told me."

The reverend settled beside him. "I'd forgotten that

you were speaking to her. Tell me, does she share your feelings?"

"Bauers, *she* writes the Bandit. Georgia is George Towers."

"Georgia?" Bauers stared at him. "*Georgia?* She admitted such to you?"

"She admitted such to *him.* I believe I startled it out of her—I don't believe she planned to tell me—him."

Reverend Bauers leaned his elbows on his knees. With a heavy sigh, he dropped his head into his hand. "Covington, can you not see the terrible folly in all this?"

"Georgia writes the Bandit."

"Georgia writes the Bandit. And you have just as much as lied to her. Despite your feelings for her, of which she knows nothing. No, instead you have directed her attentions to an imaginary man who just *happens to be you.*" The reverend looked up at him. "Yes, I am surprised. I had not known Georgia had such talents, nor did I suspect she held such sway over Stuart. But my surprise pales against my concern for what *you* are doing. Look, she is due here within the hour. I will arrange for you to be uninterrupted in the garden. Tell her, son, and do the right thing."

"I cannot."

"You could, but you will not." Bauers stood up. "You would if you really cared for her at all."

A storm brewed in the back of Matthew's throat. "I care too much for her. I care *too much* to encourage her where there is no future."

"After all you have seen this past week, how can you say that? Who knows what God has planned? And yet you would deceive her into caring for an illusion?" The clergyman pointed a finger at him. "You have poached off her imagination, that's what you have done. Can you live with that?"

Matthew would never have believed he'd need to quash the urge to punch a member of the clergy. He'd chosen an unorthodox path with Georgia, he was well aware of that. But it was his choice to make. He could not share his future with Georgia. He would not wrench her away from her home. Was the Bandit's visit deceit? Of course it was, and some part of him ached for what he had done. But it was overthrown by his ache to be near her. For that gasp she'd made when she understood the Bandit was behind her. Matthew hadn't even realized how much until that moment. But it could not be. "Now look here, Bauers…" he growled.

A knock hushed him. "Gentlemen?" Georgia's voice called from behind the study door. "Reverend Bauers?"

Bauers opened the door.

"I heard voices raised," she continued, stepping into the room. "You two arguing? What on earth could bring you to that?"

"We were…debating a course of action," the reverend said, throwing a cold glare at Matthew.

She tugged on the ribbon that held her hat, and took it off. "Who won?"

"It is as of yet undetermined," Matthew said tersely.

Matthew watched her face. He could practically read her decision to move forward despite whatever it was she thought she'd interrupted. There was a fascinating new boldness to her features. "Well, then," she said, walking farther into the study, "I shall be happy to provide a very large and pleasant diversion."

"And what would that be?" Reverend Bauers asked.

"Stuart is throwing a ball. A Bandit Ball, later this month. And I've convinced him to make it a charity event to support Grace House."

"A Bandit Ball?" Matthew repeated, the storm in his throat turning to a great lump. "This month?"

"Two weeks from Saturday. Every man who donates can come dressed as the Black Bandit. It is at once publicity, philanthropy and a chance for our newfound hero to show himself among a bevy of admirers."

"What an extraordinary idea," Reverend Bauers said, the strain in his voice almost hidden. "Miss Waterhouse, you and your brother outdo yourselves."

"It is mostly Stuart," she said. "But in this case I am delighted to help matters along."

Lord, Heavenly Father, what have I done? Matthew wondered if God had not shown up in his life at precisely the right moment. Or precisely the wrong one. "Most extraordinary," he said, at a loss for any other reply.

"Mr. Covington, please tell me you will be able to attend."

It's not as if I'll need to find a costume, Matthew thought absurdly. "I can think of nothing more intriguing." And to think he'd found sedating chickens complicated a mere week ago.

"The door! I just remembered I left my tools on the front steps. Covington, would you mind helping Miss Waterhouse transport a few boxes of material down the street to the convent storeroom? I had hoped to help her myself, but…" Bauers gave a poorly rehearsed shrug and bolted from the study.

Matthew shook his head after the less-than-subtle departure.

"You and I seem to have an odd, flight-inducing effect on people," Georgia said with a lopsided smile. "But I am glad for the chance to talk with you. Tell me, how are you? I can remember believing from my earliest years, but in some ways I envy the man or woman who comes to faith in the full awareness of adulthood. It must be an incredible experience." She gazed at Matthew. "You looked as if someone had lit a firecracker inside you Friday night."

An apt metaphor. But more like a dozen explosives. "I can't say I've sorted it out yet. Some things feel settled, others feel completely jumbled. I'm still the same man, and yet I'm not." He knew it was unsafe territory, and yet he could not resist. "And how are you? How was your Easter?"

She did not reply right away, but instead headed down the mission hallway. "I must confess I was feeling despondent of late." She glanced at Matthew for a moment. "It is not always pleasant to be the 'other Waterhouse.' One feels small and unnoticed every now and then."

I could never ignore you, Matthew thought, but said nothing.

"Several things on Easter drove me to a long time of prayer. I'll not tire you with what they were. But I was reminded of all the souls who worked in obscurity, keeping their eye on God. Whom He sees. Sister Charlotte calls it 'the audience of One.' I've come to understand her now. It's given me a strength of sorts, I suppose." Georgia shook her head. "My goodness, I think I've rambled on, when you were so kind to ask. But it has been important to me, this awareness—oh, that's not the word. But I—I'm not making any sense, am I?"

Matthew felt a pang of remorse. Here he was, thinking he could craft an affirmation for her. She, in her wisdom, had gone looking for affirmation in the place where it truly mattered. How he flattered himself to think *he'd* brought that strength to her step. How God must laugh at his idiocies today. Matthew stared at her, thinking her so far above him that he could never hope to reach her level.

"What you must think of me." She blushed.

You have no idea, Matthew mused.

Chapter Thirty-Three

Georgia was beyond distracted for the next week. The situation seemed to have gained momentum of its own accord. The Bandit had a voice now, and she could hear it when he spoke in her dialogue. How easily she could picture the tale Quinn had first told her. Had it truly happened? Had she not invented the Bandit, not crafted the legend, but merely stumbled onto it? Suddenly everything was twisting back on itself. There seemed only one way to untangle the mess: to see him again. To know who he was. And so the ball became her best opportunity. Stuart's manipulation would be turned to her own design.

That night, Georgia gave up the struggle to write a Bandit episode and wrote an open letter instead.

"To our Black Bandit:
You defend those who cannot defend themselves. You champion the cause of the oppressed and the victimized. You move among us, masked by moonlight, unseen yet not unknown. Unmet yet not unadmired. We wish to honor you. Stuart Wa-

terhouse hosts a ball in your honor on next Saturday evening. Many men will come in your guise so that you may circulate without revealing your identity, if you so choose. Each will make charitable gifts for the honor of donning your costume. Come and let a city show you its respect, and remind us that each man can share in your calling. Until April 26, I remain your humble servant, George Towers. After that night, I hope many will have the honor of calling you friend."

If Stuart resisted running the installment, well, she'd just have to find a way to convince him. But *oh, Lord, could you grant me another visit from him? Would that be too much to ask?*

Matthew waited in the terrace shadows even though he shouldn't have.

He knew he shouldn't.

God probably had tired of telling him that.

He waited anyway. He knew Stuart was out tonight—he'd been invited to the same dinner himself—and Georgia was most certainly alone. She would come. Even if the note he'd secretly sent her earlier today had asked her to travel miles in the middle of the night, she would come. A corner of his mind wondered if she would go to such lengths for Matthew Covington instead of the Bandit but he hushed his thoughts.

The latch on the French doors clicked and Georgia stepped out onto the terrace. She had dressed in darker tones tonight, a smartly cut dress with only a small bustle, in an indigo that matched the night, and a mesmerizing cascade of small pearl buttons that looked

like stars against the night sky. The shade emphasized
the luminous quality of her skin, and made her beauty
seem that much more ethereal. Had she dressed for the
meeting? Did she realize how beautiful she was, how
fragile she looked standing there clutching her wrap
about her shoulders?

"Are you there?" she called in a voice just above a
whisper.

"Yes," he replied from his place in the shadows, almost forgetting to alter his voice. She looked in his direction and he backed farther into the darkness.

"Why do you alter your voice?" she asked.

He paused a long time, struggling for an answer.
"It is for the best." He knew she expected him to drop
the pretense when she identified it, but he did not. He
could not.

"Do I know you by day?" Her voice revealed a hint of
frustration. Matthew realized she was probably insulted
that he retained his secret once she had disclosed hers.
Had she assumed that was why he had called again? In
order to show his face?

"That is not a safe question to answer," Matthew replied, admiring her persistence.

She crushed a bit of her skirt in one delicate fist. "I
wish to know who you are."

"That cannot be."

"Now or always?" she pressed. Georgia took a half
step toward him, forcing him to retreat farther into the
bushes. She was disappointed, and it was his doing.
Yet he found himself helpless to stop it. He had come
for no nobler reason than the driving need to see her
again. To hear the catch in her voice when she spoke

to the Bandit, to note the look in her eyes when she strained to see him.

"Did I create you? Or was it you that night saving Quinn from those thugs trying to steal his money?"

How on earth should he answer that? "Both," he said, opting for the strange truth.

Georgia put her hands to her forehead. "I cannot do this anymore. George Towers is a lie."

He would not have her doubt her gifts because of his cowardice. "George Towers is an act of God. Can you not see that? Can you not see the role you've been given? The gifts you have to carry it out?"

"No," she replied in almost a gasp, "I cannot. It started out as a good idea, a lark, but now... No, I thought I could see that once, but not now."

"I can. I am what you made me."

"You are more than that."

He did not answer.

"I want to know who you are. Why can you not tell me?"

Tell her, part of him cried out, his chest feeling as though it were breaking open.

You cannot. If you go to her, you will not be able to leave her, and you must *leave her. England will not disappear. Your duty will not evaporate simply because you are in love.*

And he *was* in love. For all the good it did him. The Bandit could love and be loved—even if from afar— but Matthew Covington would be prisoner to sums and tallies and England.

He turned away and ducked through the bushes.

Reverend Bauers had said the world made more sense to a man of faith. Matthew found he could not agree.

* * *

For the next few days, Matthew buried himself in the part of his life that ought to make sense. He tried to lose himself in the orderly procession of numbers, in the sheer volume of ledgers at Covington Enterprises.

The ledgers refused him any solace. Subtle discrepancies kept peeking out at him. Strange transactions. Odd numbers that seemed to fit entirely too easily into gaps created by other commerce. Produce bought too far out of season. Ships that returned to docks slightly before their voyages should have been over. Payrolls that seemed a tad too large for one ship, too small for another. Yet everything still added up—*if* one didn't look too closely. It was as if someone was poring through the books ahead of him, shifting figures, covering tracks, smoothing over clues.

"Mr. Covington, a moment?"

"Oakman." Matthew pulled his head up and rubbed his eyes.

"Everything in order, sir?"

"Yes." That wasn't a lie. Everything was in order. It was just in the wrong order, or too perfect an order... Matthew couldn't quite put his finger on it, but something in the books did not feel right to him at all. They felt tampered with, although by whom and to what end he could not yet say.

"Mrs. Oakman and I were wondering if you wouldn't care to join us for dinner tonight. Caroline says she is sure you must be tiring of hotel fare."

Matthew had planned to spend the evening going over more documents, but he did have to admit his eyes were bleary. And sleep? Sleep had become a luxury. Some nights he hadn't slept at all. On the one hand, such wakefulness offered him great chances to pore through the tattered little Bible, and he'd learned much. On the other hand, he was becoming a bit unsteady during the day. He couldn't be entirely sure that the dark doubts his mind produced were more the product of too little sleep than of suspicious bookkeeping. Matthew was long past weary. Perhaps a good sound meal was just what he needed. Besides, conversation with Oakman could only help to shed light on things—provided he asked the correct discreet questions.

"Mrs. Oakman is quite right. I should be delighted to attend. Do thank her for me."

Chapter Thirty-Four

S}he was there.

It was both a wonderful and an awful turn of events to find Georgia Waterhouse and Sister Charlotte waiting with Mrs. Oakman in the parlor when Matthew and Dexter arrived at the house. Without Stuart. At first glance, Matthew thought it best to plead fatigue and end the evening as quickly as courtesy would allow. With his wits fraying, it would be the wisest thing to do.

Propriety told him he couldn't, but he knew the real reason.

The Oakmans' daughter also played the harp, and Mr. and Mrs. Oakman had invited them all into the library after dinner to hear her play. As they walked down the hall, Matthew inquired how things were going at Grace House.

"Quinn has asked Reverend Bauers for fencing lessons," Georgia reported.

"Fencing lessons?" Matthew nearly stumbled as he entered the room.

"Evidently the combination of your victory over Ian and Michael, combined with a fascination for Black

Bandit stories, has sparked an interest in swordplay. The reverend is understandably concerned."

"Ian and Michael?"

"Oh, you know them." She smiled and touched his once-injured arm. It was a light touch, yet his entire body felt the contact. "You owe your new scar to Ian."

Matthew frowned. "In my opinion, I owe my new scar to Reverend Bauers's medical skills."

"He has a good heart," she said, lowering her voice to a whisper as Amelia Oakman took her place behind the harp.

"Would that his hand were as steady," Matthew couldn't help adding, even though he had to lean close to her to do it. She smelled of lavender and something creamy that made his head swim. He saw the momentary reaction in her shoulders, the start she gave at his nearness, the smile that lingered at the corner of her mouth when she turned her attention to the music.

He, however, could not turn his attention to the music. He faced in that direction, gave the appearance of attending to the performance, but it was all pretense. Matthew watched Georgia instead.

"I've not yet heard *you* play, Miss Waterhouse," Matthew said when the girl had finished. "Stuart tells me you are quite accomplished."

"Georgia is exquisite at the harp, Mr. Covington," Sister Charlotte declared. "A gifted musician, believe me."

"As is Amelia," Georgia added. "I see great talent in you, my dear."

"Thank you." Amelia dipped into a curtsy. "Would you like to play my harp?" Amelia asked. "I should love to hear you."

"As would I," agreed Sister Charlotte.

"And I," said Matthew.

She resisted once, but finally agreed to play, and settled herself behind the instrument. Matthew was not prepared for what he saw.

Georgia was an altogether different woman when she played. Passionate. Dramatic. Matthew watched her shoulders press into the falling notes, pull others out of the velvety depth. That spark that always hid within her eyes burst into flame when she played the harp. Everything he had suspected of Georgia, everything that made her capable of writing the Bandit, emerged. She caught his eye once and he thought his heart would stop.

As they entered the carriage to ride home, Georgia wondered if inviting Sister Charlotte had been wise. She'd appeared as if she were enjoying herself earlier in the evening, but as the night wore on the nun began to look more and more agitated. Once inside the carriage, Sister Charlotte planted herself across from Georgia and crossed her arms sharply.

"Georgia Waterhouse," she said the moment the carriage lurched into motion, "I never thought I'd have cause to say this, but you are a fool." Those violet eyes gave her a look that likely stopped any misbehaving student dead in her tracks.

"A fool?"

Her slim fingers drummed against the black sleeves of her habit. "Do not think I've missed it. I have seen you back off from our young Mr. Covington because of this…this…character. The Bandit is not real. Covington is, and he is more than taken with you."

Georgia pushed out a breath. She did not wish to get

into this just now. Her brain was atumble enough as it was. "Charlotte, you know he visited me. The Bandit *is* real. Mr. Covington and I can have no future, however pleasing he may be."

Charlotte untangled her arms. "I believe there is a man *portraying* your Bandit. He may be real. The Bandit is not. I wonder, Georgia, if you know the difference."

"Of course I do," she retorted.

Now it was Charlotte's turn to look exasperated. "Are you sure? Forget the Bandit mess for a moment. Covington. Can you not see how he looks at you? Has he not given you any encouragement in the matter?"

Georgia sighed. "Yes and no. It is a jumble in my head." She let her head fall against the carriage window. "Yes, he has been kind. Attentive, even." She looked at her friend. "But Charlotte, what does any of that matter if he is going back to England?"

Charlotte rose off her seat and came to sit on the cushion next to Georgia. "What does any of England matter if there is a chance for love?" She looked intently into her eyes. "Tell me. Is there a chance you can love this man?"

Georgia thought of the lemon cake, and the flowers, and the way he'd looked at her tonight. She thought of what she'd seen in the mission garden, and how he made her laugh so many times. Yes, of course she could love this man. Part of her already did. She just refused to admit it. "I cannot go to England," she said, in an almost whimpering tone.

Charlotte's voice grew tender. "And why not? What is it that you think is keeping you here? Certainly not Stuart. Bauers will be sorry to lose you, but far more eager to see you happy." She reached out and clasped Georgia's arm. "You think you cannot be happy anywhere but here, but I think you haven't even begun to know what your *own* life is. How happy you could be."

Her expression darkened. "Or perhaps it is something deeper. It is far safer to love a man who does not exist, isn't it? One who cannot hurt you because he isn't real? After all, I did say how much some real men pale under scrutiny, didn't I? Oh, Georgia, don't listen to my foolish words."

The carriage pulled to a stop outside of the convent. "I cannot tell you what to do," Charlotte continued. "That job belongs to God. But I can tell you to heed your heart. God has your own life prepared for you, Georgia. Don't miss it by staring at dreams and surrendering to obstacles."

Later that night, Matthew reread the open letter "George" had written to the Bandit. The intensity of the plea, the need he saw in it for Georgia to meet her Bandit, took down the last of his resistance.

She had to know. He wouldn't lie any longer, even if it cost him everything to reveal himself to her. She deserved no less.

She deserved so much more.

He would have to trust God with the consequences of that truth if he were to trust God at all. Even if all they would have would be the time before England called him home, who was he to say that would not be enough for her?

But how? Where? Part of him wanted to climb up her balustrade like Romeo and profess his identity tonight. An hour from now suddenly seemed too long.

Then again, that moment of revelation might be all they would have. After all his cowardice, he owed her a dramatic, romantic, Bandit-worthy revelation. Perhaps it was time for Matthew Covington to write a Bandit episode of his own. And the upcoming Bandit Ball seemed ideal. Providential, even.

He found himself staring at the newspaper as if it could link him to her. *I love you,* his mind shouted into the night as he pulled on his coat. *I am the Bandit, and I love you. And at the ball, you will know.*

Chapter Thirty-Five

Matthew banged on the Grace House door until someone let him in. He demanded to see Reverend Bauers and, no, he didn't care about the hour.

Bauers eased himself down into one of the chairs after letting Matthew into his study. "I'd offer you some coffee—" he yawned "—but you don't look as if you'd care to wait that long." He ran his hands down his face and squinted at Matthew. "What is it, son?"

"I love her. She needs to know everything. I see that now."

The reverend's smile was warm despite his chiding tone. "Could you not have come to this life-altering conclusion at a more decent hour?"

Matthew simply sighed.

"Of course not. Such things seem always to hit us in the middle of the night. And you, we know, are at your best by moonlight. I have gotten far less sleep since meeting you, my friend. And I didn't get much sleep before."

"You were right. It is as much as lying to her. She deserves the truth, and she deserves to know how I feel about her, no matter where it leads." Matthew shook his head. "I sound like an idiot. Talking in valentines. I don't know what's come over me."

"Love and faith in a single fortnight? It's a wonder you're still standing. A little high-minded speech can only be expected." The clergyman settled back in his chair. "How did you come to realize this? No, wait, don't tell me. I don't want the details—there's enough of it on your face. I wish love and our Lord kept more sensible hours." He yawned again, but grinned all the same. "You're going to tell her."

"At the ball."

Bauers cocked an eyebrow. "You couldn't think of someplace more private?"

"Don't you see? It will be private. I'll be hiding among a sea of Bandits. It won't have to be a rushed meeting in the middle of the night. I can be both men at once."

"May I remind you that you *always* have been both men at once? It is only *you* who've chosen to hide one side or the other." He gave Matthew a long stare. "She shares your feelings?"

Now, here was the sticky wicket. Matthew got up from the chair and paced the room. "She cares for the Bandit. I know that much."

"Matthew," Bauers replied, "do not do this only because you think it will gain you Georgia. Do it because it is the truth, and because you know she deserves as much. Do not think to trick the lady's heart." He rested his hands on the arms of the chair. "She may be angered by your deception. Have you thought of that? You told me yourself she asked the Bandit to reveal himself, and you denied her. If she does not care for you the way you think she does, she may use the truth to hurt you."

Matthew paced the floor for a moment, hands stuffed in his pockets, considering all the possible outcomes. He stopped and turned. "It comes down to one question, doesn't it, Bauers?"

"And what is that?"

"Is she worth everything?"

Matthew could not remember being more unsettled for a social occasion. Sensing his nerves, Thompson paid extra attention to his attire. Some of that, of course, may have been the personal pride of finally getting the opportunity to show off the Bandit's costume. He fussed and fidgeted until Matthew could barely endure the attention.

As he left for the ball, Matthew had the distinct impression that he had best return with a list of compliments on his attire. And whether or not he had the best Bandit costume, he would tell Thompson that had been the case. It could not be considered lying, for how could it not be the best Bandit costume, since it was the genuine thing?

He had the head-spinning, contradictory sensation of being a public secret. The room would be filled with men pretending to be the Bandit. He actually *was,* and yet no one would know. No one but him knew that the gray shirt had been patched in one sleeve thanks to a scrape from the chicken crates. Casual observers would miss the nick in his broad black hat made by Trivolatti's meat hook. And no one, not even Thompson, knew about the odd but dear little Bible tucked under the shirt over his heart.

The absurdity of the whole evening struck Matthew as he walked out of the Palace Hotel in plain sight, dressed as the Bandit right down to the whip and a pocketful of white ribbons.

And was promptly greeted by two more Bandits.

There was no doubt this would be one of the more extraordinary evenings of his life.

Knowing Stuart as he did, Matthew thought he was prepared for the extravagance that would be the Waterhouse mansion. Despite his wildest imaginings on the subject, he found he had vastly underestimated Stuart's gift for excess. It was rather hard to find the monstrous house under all the flowers and ribbons. White bunting, festooned with billows of silver-gray fabric, strung itself around the fence like cake frosting. Where the fabric paused, cascades of flowers erupted.

Every conceivable combination of the Bandit's black trousers, dark gray shirt, black hat and gray mask wandered the grounds. The efforts at mock weaponry made Matthew chuckle; some men sported riding crops instead of bullwhips, and more than a few, rusty swords that looked as if they'd been recently wrenched off living room walls. Matthew could never describe this experience to anyone who hadn't been there.

But he couldn't merely stand and gawk; there was work to be done. He had a list of people to find and engage in conversation. A few carefully placed questions, to tongues loosened with frivolity, could provide all kinds of useful information. Matthew knew that under the right circumstances, men could be induced to boast of their crimes rather than cover them. Tonight, he guessed, plied with both drink and disguise,

men might leak legions as to what was truly going on
on San Francisco's docks.

Even so, tonight was really only about one conversation: with Georgia.

What would come of it, he couldn't begin to say.
Would they have weeks together, then feel both of their
hearts break as he lugged himself back to England?
Would he uncover calamities at Covington Enterprises
that would keep him here for years? Was there a way he
could simply decide to stay? Tonight would certainly
be easier if he had answers to these questions, but there
were no answers to be had.

*If any set of circumstances could drive a man to
prayer, it'd be these,* Matthew thought, remembering
the hour he'd spent pouring his heart and his anxieties
to God earlier today. *Father, guide me. This is all so
new. I'm so far from home, from who I was. I'm trusting You have a plan in place.*

Matthew kept up a steady stream of prayer as he
wandered from room to room, from Bandit to Bandit,
working his way through his list of sources. He had
failed to find Georgia after a good half an hour of min-
gling. Nor, he realized, had he seen Stuart.

Five interviews and three frighteningly enthusiastic
Bandits later, he saw her. He had expected his heart to
skip when he saw her. He had not expected the whole
world to grind to a stop. She did not see him at first—
proof of God's grace, he decided—for it took him long
moments to recover his composure.

She wore white. A simple, exquisitely cut gown of the
most iridescent, liquid white he had ever seen. It stood
out among the riot of gown colors and black-gray Bandit costumes. Her hair was done up with a shower of

tiny yellow flowers. She wore gloves of the palest yellow, matching the ribbon trim of her dress. Around one wrist, tied in a simple bow, was a long white ribbon. It danced and fluttered as she gestured, and Matthew felt its movement beneath his skin. If there was any question that he found her the most beautiful woman God had ever created, it was put to rest now. His admiration, his affection went far deeper than her charm or grace. It was the knowledge that inside this tiny, frail-looking creature beat a heart of courage. A soul of endurance, a warrior who wielded any weapon she could against the sins of her city. A woman so busy looking to the needs of others that she could not even see her own strength.

I would change that, he thought. *I would help her see all that she is. Remind her of all the strengths she has. I would love her, even if it cannot be forever.*

And then, as she turned and caught his eye, he added, *God help me if it cannot be forever.*

Chapter Thirty-Six

She would know him.

She wasn't sure how, but the Bandit would come and she would know it was him. The knowledge steadied her steps as she descended the grand stairway into the crowd of Bandits and other revelers. *He is here and I will find him.*

Stuart made a grandiose speech, but she didn't hear a word of it. She was scanning the room, looking at the men, wondering which one had the deep, smooth voice from her terrace. Looking at the hands, wondering which ones held the whip and the sword.

She danced with many of them, thinking that would provide the opportunity for him to reveal his identity. It proved a tiresome task—for she grew impatient with each dance, as it took only moments for her to decide this man could not be her Bandit.

Her Bandit. She'd come to think of him that way, even though it was unwise to do so. Sister Charlotte's words had pounded in her head all day—how she should look to the men in her real world and not dismiss them for a man of her imagination. It made perfect sense.

It was sage advice. Georgia's heart simply refused to comply. *Once I see him,* she thought, *once I know who he is, perhaps I can settle my heart on someone else.*

She knew that for the lie it was.

There was a moment, though, where her heart skipped. She walked into the front hallway with Mrs. Oakman and caught sight of a tall man. "My dear Miss Waterhouse," he said, as his blue-black eyes danced from behind the oddly fashioned gray mask he wore. She knew at once from his accent that it was Matthew Covington. "You are the most beautiful woman in the room tonight." He took her hand and kissed it, just as he had on her birthday, and the same spark danced up her arm.

She had hoped he would come. He had dressed as the Bandit, too, which charmed her, for she wasn't sure he would. He had made the best he could as a visitor, and he had crafted a slightly tattered but very authentic-looking costume. His trousers had so many odd pockets they looked almost military, and one sleeve sported a patch. The whip coiled at his waist certainly looked far more dangerous than any of the ones carried by other "Bandits"—heaven knows where he had been forced to shop to have ended up with one so large and fierce. Other Bandits looked dashing and piratelike. Covington looked hard-edged and, well, a bit ragged. He was the only Bandit with both whip and sword. She could not deny that the overall effect was rather eye-catching. He was somehow all the more handsome for his rough-hewn attire. Truly, if any man could come close to what she felt the Bandit ought to be, it was Matthew. Given time, the two of them could have had something.

But England would call him home soon, and so it

was wise to ignore the tug she felt in her heart when he took off his hat and bowed deeply, saying, "You look stunning."

She smiled. "I see you have not quite yet fetched back your reserve."

"Tonight," he said as he gestured around the ornate hall, "seems to be a night for excess rather than reserve."

"I do not believe there is a white ribbon left in San Francisco," she mused.

"I've a few in my pocket, but I am saving them for later." He offered no further explanation when she raised her eyebrow at the comment. The orchestra started up a waltz. "I recall you are especially fond of waltzes. May I have this dance?"

"Yes." It delighted her that he remembered. "I would like that very much."

He danced well, sweeping her around the crowded floor with a fluid ease. His gaze blotted every detail out of the room until it felt as if the two of them were alone together. Which in some ways was true, for few could tell one of her Bandit partners from another for any given dance. It was a delightfully public sort of privacy.

"Bauers will be busting his buttons. You've surely raised enormous funds for Grace House."

Did he pull her half an inch closer as they rounded that turn, or did she just imagine it? "I am sorry he missed it. He'd have enjoyed it, don't you think?"

"I'm certain." Matthew continued to stare at her, hard and deliberate, as if memorizing her features. "Is it a hectic evening for you?" he inquired, and Georgia had the odd sense that it was not the question he'd intended to ask at all.

"Not as much as one would think. Stuart knows how

to get things done. The decorations, I'm afraid, are all his. I was able to wrest away some control of the other parts of the evening. I must say it took him a bit to adjust to my telling him what I wanted. You can imagine it usually goes the other way around."

Matthew grinned. "So, are you enjoying your ball?"

"It is a most extraordinary evening," she said, finding every other description too complex.

"Miss Waterhouse—"

"Please!" She interrupted on an impulse, realizing she and Matthew might never have such an occasion again. "Call me Georgia. Just for tonight."

His eyes did something she could not name, something that lit up the air between them. He let his face come near to her shoulder as he pulled her into a sweeping turn. "Georgia," he said softly, and the tone of his voice nearly made her miss a step. "Georgia, I would—"

"Peach! We've got to make an announcement of how much money has been raised. Come." Stuart snatched her efficiently from the dance floor before Matthew could say a word in protest. She was beginning to despise her brother's gift for interruption.

"Thank you all for your generosity. The funds you've donated will help so many families and improve so many lives. Tonight, you are all heroes."

Georgia stepped down off the grand staircase and accepted the congratulations of several friends. How satisfying it was to have finally redirected one of Stuart's schemes to a higher purpose. To have asserted herself at last. Months ago, she would have quietly but miserably endured the ball as Stuart's misguided idea of a gift. Now, by standing up for what she valued, she had managed to turn affairs to something that truly pleased her. And, she hoped, pleased God.

God had granted to her the one thing she most valued in her hero: courage. The most important kind—the courage to stand up for what was right. God had honored that courage, for Georgia knew that it was the first and only time many of these people had ever given money to Grace House. San Francisco was already famous for its vice. Perhaps now it could also be known for the virtue of philanthropy. She was, after all, a legendary—and now courageous—optimist.

One of the house staff approached her. "This came for you," the girl said, handing her a message. Georgia's heart stopped when she saw the rolled paper was tied with a simple strip of white cloth. She ducked into an alcove and pulled at the ribbon with shaking hands.

"George"ia—
Terrace eleven o'clock
—BB

It was him. It had to be him. Only he and Stuart knew she was George Towers. He had come, just as she knew he would. She rushed to the library to check the clock. Ten-fifty. Ten minutes! It would seem like ten years.

Foolishly, she checked her hair in the glass of the clock face. If she went through the back hallway and the kitchen, she could slip through the dining room to the terrace without having to see anyone. Georgia was quite sure she could not converse with a single soul at present. She was feeling light-headed as it was. It was best to just go now and wait on the terrace—praying the entire time, she decided.

Oh, Father, thank You. I'll accept whatever comes of this, but thank You!

Matthew was pacing the terrace like a schoolboy. He'd planned this a dozen times in his head, and suddenly every plan seemed like rubbish. Words tangled on his tongue. He surely must be sweating despite the cool of the evening. Some part of him had hoped she would realize the truth earlier, when she saw him dressed as the Bandit. He'd harbored a silly fantasy that some sort of surreal spark would fly between them and she would *know.* But she didn't.

I saw this going so much differently, he thought to himself. Now who had written a ridiculous Bandit episode? He had envisioned them sweeping around the ballroom with their grand secret, just as they had done about the Bible he hid in his pocket. They'd share a secret the whole world wanted to know, just the two of them.

He was about to give in and tell her when Stuart had plucked her from his grasp. Matthew had stood there, fuming on the dance floor for a few minutes, his great plan foiled. It was then that he came up with the idea of the note.

Surely now she'd come. This was a private part of the house, and no one from the party would be here. She'd know why the Bandit wanted to meet her. And then he could tell her. Ten long minutes from now. *Help me, Lord,* he pleaded as he pulled off his hat. *I'm twisted up enough as it is.*

He still had his hat in his hand when the French

doors opened up and she came out onto the terrace. He gulped. So much for ten minutes.

She looked even more surprised than he. "Matthew!" she blurted, sounding much less pleased than he would have liked. "I… I found I needed some air." She put her hand behind her back. "I'll be fine in a moment. Please, don't let me keep you. Surely you ought to go and enjoy yourself at the party."

She was urging him to leave. Matthew's resolve wobbled a bit when he realized she truly had no idea he was the Bandit. It stung, but not enough to stop him. "Georgia…"

"I'll be back inside momentarily," she said, trying to look around casually. She was a charmingly poor liar. "It's a grand evening. I wouldn't want you to miss any of it."

The music of another waltz flooded out through the open doors. Matthew walked around her, noting how Georgia shifted her hand out of his view as he passed. She who kept many secrets was unskilled at deceit.

Instead of leaving, as he suspected she thought he was doing, he gently shut the doors. "Were you expecting someone?"

Her face twisted up just a bit, and the sight of it tied his heart in knots. "Well, I…" She was trying to lie, but couldn't bring herself to do it.

He laid his hat on the terrace table and pulled his mask off with the other hand. Somehow, as he removed it, every shred of doubt left him. He was, in every sense of the word, unmasking himself to her. "*I* was," he said softly.

She blinked, shaking her head just a bit. Her expression was so stunned, so transparent that he could watch her think. Watch the thoughts collide in her head. "No, really, I…"

He altered his voice to the one he had used as the Bandit. "I was expecting George."

Chapter Thirty-Seven

Georgia would have sworn an earthquake had just struck her back terrace. He? Expecting George? That could only mean...no. It couldn't be. He had somehow discovered the truth and had the audacity to toy with her so. Something close to anger swept through her.

She stared at him. "You couldn't... George..." The pieces began to fall into place. It was, in fact, completely possible. He'd told her he was good with voices as a child. As a visitor, he could move unrecognized throughout many parts of the city. The first strips of cloth had always been bandages from his arm. She'd just not seen it because she was embroidering every detail with her own fantasy.

"It is me," Matthew said, his gaze so fierce she thought she'd keel over. "It has always been me."

A thousand questions, a thousand thoughts tumbled in her head. The two men who held her heart were one man. Matthew was the Bandit. The Bandit was Matthew.

"H-how?" she stammered. "Why?"

He took a step toward her. "Mostly because it pleased

you so. I saved Quinn by accident—it was happenstance that I was there. Then, when it appeared in the papers, I didn't know what to think. I didn't know you'd written the story. That first time, at Grace House, it was mostly because I knew you wished the Bandit to be true. I thought Stuart wrote about him as a gift of sorts to you. And, somehow, I knew I could make that gift come alive for you."

At first, it pained her as yet another manipulation. But looking at him, hearing his words and seeing the emotion laid bare in his eyes, she knew it truly had been a gift. "I begged you to tell me."

"It will be only a matter of weeks before I am called home. I thought it would hurt less if you did not know. If he remained unreal."

"And now?" Her voice wavered with the threat of tears. From pain or happiness, she couldn't yet say—they collided in the back of her throat.

"It hurt too much to keep deceiving you. It came to the point where even if I sailed tomorrow, I would bear it to give you one day of knowing it was me." He took another step toward her, his face suddenly dissolving into a look of vulnerability. "Can you not see it? How I care for you?" He swung his hands in a frustrated gesture. "I cannot bear to take you away from everything you love, and yet I cannot bear to stay away from you. I thought having the Bandit appear to you would solve it—that you could remain enamored of him in your mind and not suffer when I left." He stepped closer still and touched her cheek.

She brought her hand up to clasp his, and felt as if their joined hands were the only thing keeping them from spinning off the end of the world. She tried to say something, but couldn't find words.

"But I could not bear it," he continued, the pain in his face slowly melting into a look of such tenderness that she was certain her knees would give way. "And, truth be told, I was jealous of your affection for him. I am your Bandit, Georgia. For as long as I can, I will do anything to save your world and make you happy."

The night careened around her. She could not draw in a breath deep enough.

He put his other hand to her cheek, so that he held her face. He stared at her as if she were the most precious treasure in all the universe. "Please say something," he whispered.

Georgia thought of all she had wished, the hero she had dreamed of, and the man she had resisted. She thought of Sister Charlotte's call to follow her heart, and God's call to her newfound courage.

Georgia Waterhouse became something she had never been: bold. And discovered that Sister Charlotte was indeed right—a wise woman *did* know a true kiss when it came her way.

Chapter Thirty-Eight

"You," Georgia said, when at last she pulled away. He nodded with a broad smile and sparkling eyes. "You," she repeated, still trying to grasp the wild idea.

"Do you find the concept so entirely implausible?" he teased. "I should like to think I am not entirely unheroic by daylight." He had the look of a man who had shed a great weight.

"I think you are a wonderful man, armed or unarmed." She couldn't resist. "But I must admit I did think your costume below par." She ran her hand down his arm, feeling the strength of his muscle as he held her. Delighting in the fact that it was *he* who held her. She touched the fabric of his shirt with wonder, as if it would give up clues to the adventures it had seen. "How amazing to discover it is in fact the real thing."

Matthew smiled, his eyes alight. "My hat has no mere nick in it, you know. Signore Trivolatti's meat hook is a most deadly weapon." He nodded as Georgia's fingers ran across the patch on his sleeve. "That came from those dreadful chickens."

"Oh," said Georgia, her head falling against his chest

as the memory of the pandemonium made her laugh. "The chickens! Even Stuart enjoyed that chaos." She kept her head there, clinging just a bit tighter as the mention of her brother brought the world back into somber focus. "Does anyone know?" she asked, marveling when her cheek bumped up against a corner of what she knew to be Reverend Bauers's Bible.

"Bauers knows." Matthew stroked his palm down her arm, and she thought it the most soothing sensation in all the world. "He's been after me to tell you since Good Friday. He's been an accomplice of sorts." Matthew pulled back to look into her eyes. It seemed amazing to her that his could look so dark and so bright all at once. "My valet, Thompson," he said, "worked it out weeks ago, but I've no idea how. The clothing was his doing. He'd be insulted to know you found my costume inferior."

"Perhaps I should revise my comment to say it is more 'authentic.'"

Matthew smiled. "Who knows you are George?" he asked softly.

"Only Stuart. I believe most people suspect it has been Stuart all along."

"Oh, they do. I did." He fingered a stray lock of her hair, his smile broadening at the feel of it. "I imagine quite a few of them would be slack-jawed to discover the author's real identity. You would surprise quite a few people."

Which brought up the unwelcome subject of what to do now. The world had spun on its ear not half an hour ago. How would the new world turn from here? She pulled away from his embrace and walked to the edge of the terrace. "Matthew, what do we do?"

He sat down on the short wall. "I am at a loss. Other than praying for legions of divine guidance, I hadn't thought it through any further than that."

Georgia sat down on the wall beside him. "Surely, God must have some sort of reason for all this."

"I can only—"

"Peach!" Stuart's voice came from behind the French doors. "Are you out here?"

Georgia's heart leaped into her throat. She shot up off the wall and rushed to the doors as she heard a rustle behind her. "Stuart?" She kept her hands firmly on the door latch, prepared to block it from opening with her foot if need be. When she turned and looked behind her, she was alone on the terrace. Matthew had somehow disappeared, but had left his hat and mask. "I'm out here," she said, as calmly as she knew how while she tossed the items over the wall into the bushes. "I needed some air." Stuart came though the doors. "All those Bandits."

"There's about a dozen you still haven't met yet. Have you spotted him?"

Georgia dreaded the prospect of having to lie to Stuart, so she was thankful when God gave her an answer that was indeed the truth. "I thought I would know him when I saw him."

"I'm sure you will. But you won't meet him out here, that's for certain."

Oh, Stuart, you have no idea how wrong you are. "It seems you'll have more introductions to make on my behalf, then."

"Actually, Peach," Stuart said as he undid the buttons on his frock coat and checked his watch, "I've got a bit of business to attend to. Can you manage on your own for a time? I won't be but half an hour, if that."

"Business, at this hour?" Georgia frowned at her brother.

"My presses never stop. Therefore my problems arise at all hours." It was a weak maxim Stuart quoted entirely too often.

"I am all too well acquainted with the notion," she replied. "Very well, do what you must. I'll be in the parlor searching out heroes."

Her brother's face darkened slightly. "Do find him, Georgia. I need to know who he is."

"So do I." She said a quick prayer that God would keep Stuart or anyone else from finding the hat and mask before Matthew did, and left Stuart to do whatever it was that needed doing "at all hours."

Matthew was doubling back for his hat and mask when he saw that the terrace was not empty. Stuart was pacing it, and there was no sign of Matthew's belongings. Georgia must have been clever enough to whisk them from sight in the nick of time. But why was Waterhouse out here when he had a houseful of guests to attend?

Matthew hung back in the shadows, watching. Stuart snapped his watch open and shut. Twice. He was meeting someone. Someone who was late, from the looks of his impatient frown. After a moment of two, Dexter Oakman walked out onto the terrace.

"Well," barked Stuart the minute Oakman had shut the French doors behind him. "What's the matter? I'm in the middle of something, if you hadn't noticed."

"There's a problem," said Oakman, taking a handkerchief from his pocket and wiping his balding forehead. It wasn't that warm an evening, something else was making him sweat.

"Well, I *gathered* there was a problem. I doubt you pulled me out here just to compliment me on the decorations." Stuart's voice took on a snarl Matthew had not heard before.

"There's a new policeman on the force. He's the problem I told you about before. We haven't been able to find a sufficient…incentive to get his cooperation. He'll be on the docks Thursday when the shipment comes in."

Incentive? Cooperation? Was Oakman talking about bribing someone? And whose shipment? Stuart's? He had his fingers in dozens of businesses around the city—importing could easily be one of them. Or, worse yet, were they discussing one of Covington Enterprises' own shipments?

"So offer him more money," Stuart replied, as if it were as simple as that. "It's taken me months to set this up. You know I can't afford to have this one go wrong. So find his price and pay it. Covington's got boxes coming in all the time. It shouldn't pose that big a problem, Dex." Stuart stared straight at Oakman, turning his back to Matthew in the process. From the look on Oakman's face, Stuart's expression must be deadly. "Your job is the easy part," he snarled. "Three hours. In the middle of the night, for that matter. Just get the opium off the boat and get Covington markings on the crates. Everyone suspects the Chinese, so no one's even looking our way." Stuart threw down a white ribbon he was holding and swore liberally. "Even my sister could do this. Get it done or I'll find someone else who can."

"I will," Oakman promised.

"Yes, you will. You will or it'll be the last thing you do for me. Now get out of here, and I don't want to hear about any more problems." He waved Dexter Oakman away and cursed a bit more as the man fled off through the French doors. Stuart stood alone on the terrace for a minute, fuming, before he snatched up the ribbon again and left the terrace, muttering under his breath.

Matthew pushed out a breath. Dexter Oakman and Stuart Waterhouse? Trafficking? It seemed impossible to believe. He'd always assumed the men were friends, but what he saw tonight was not friendship.

It all clicked into place within seconds. The funds moving in and out of the books at odd places—they were to and from Stuart. The extra personnel hid payoffs. And for as many crates that came onto the docks under the Covington stamp, a few more, for something as small and disguisable as opium, would slip by with ease. Stuart was right—everyone assumed opium the territory of the Chinese. No one would be looking for a well-bred white man to be trafficking against their powerful smugglers. Matthew imagined the Chinese thugs called "highbinders" would be quite nasty to Stuart should they discover him muscling in on their dealings.

Covington Enterprises had been corrupted.

What's more, Covington Enterprises had been corrupted by Dex Oakman working for Stuart Waterhouse. And who knew how many other Covington employees were under Stuart's thumb? There must be more than Oakman by now. There'd be no end to the ugliness if this came to light. The weight of deceit Matthew had felt lifting off his shoulders just an hour earlier returned threefold.

His gut twisted. He'd just dispelled a lie, only to learn a far more gruesome truth.

Dear God, he cried out in the silence of his heart, *what do I do now?*

There were a dozen things he had to do. He had to get out of there and think—for a week, he guessed—about how to handle Covington Enterprises. He had to find a way to face Stuart Waterhouse calmly now that his stomach roiled in anger against the man—not to mention keep Dexter Oakman from suspecting he'd discovered something. He had to find a way to see Georgia again privately—although who knew what he'd say to her when he did. He had to go find Reverend Bauers and pray for guidance. He had to consult his father.

And all before Thursday. He sank down on his haunches at the base of a tree and shut his eyes. He'd read the story of Joshua and the walls of Jericho the other night. Another man facing an impossible challenge. *Could You please send one of those angels, Father? The army of the Lord would be rather handy right now.*

It had to start with Georgia. And it couldn't start with her unless he could see her. Bauers could arrange it more quickly than anyone. Tonight, even. Matthew hated to end tonight's happiness with such an ugly blow. Still, he had loved her enough an hour ago to give her the truth no matter the cost, and he would not stop now. She was like his Bible, he thought as he straightened up and put his hand over the book underneath his shirt. One could cut an enormous chunk out of her, and she'd still be able to do more good than most people. He just never thought he'd be the one wielding the knife.

Chapter Thirty-Nine

Reverend Bauers wandered out of his bedchamber with the look of someone growing weary of being roused by an Englishman at all hours of the night. He managed a weak grin when he saw that Matthew was still dressed as the Bandit—whip, sword and all. It was near one o'clock in the morning.

"I half suspected," Bauers said, yawning as he led Matthew into his study, "you'd come here tonight, but I thought you'd be glowing with happiness. You look dashing. And terrible." He stifled another yawn. "What has happened?"

"Everything," Matthew said, still working to keep the tidal wave of emotions from overtaking him. He slumped into a chair, planting his elbows on his knees and letting his head hang. He looked at his polished black boots and thought sourly, *I am no hero.*

Bauers pulled a chair up next to him. "I was so sure she cared for you. I am sorry."

Matthew looked up. "She does," he said, a cock-eyed smile flitting across his face. "I am in love. It is dreadful."

The reverend looked puzzled. "I'll admit you have some rather unusual circumstances, but most men do look happier when they say such things. What happened?"

"She did not believe me at first. I thought she would know, somehow, just by looking at me, but even when I told her…it took a moment."

"You are the last person she would suspect," Bauers offered. "I imagine she's never had so great a surprise."

Matthew's heart turned over in his chest when he remembered the look in her eyes. "It was wonderful." He cast his gaze over to Bauers, who still appeared confused as to why a man who has just kissed the woman he loves seemed as if he were to be hanged within the hour. "And then it all fell to pieces."

"How?"

"We were almost interrupted by Stuart, but I managed to escape while Georgia held him off. I left my hat and mask, though, so I went back a few moments later. That was where I overheard Stuart and Dexter Oakman on the terrace." Matthew scrubbed at his face, trying to wipe away the fatigue suddenly flooding him. "I've been seeing trouble in the Covington books. Signs of wrongdoing, but nothing I could put a finger on. But it's them."

"What do you mean?" Bauers asked, still confused.

"Waterhouse and Oakman. They've been collaborating. Conspiring, actually. They've got a plan to traffic opium through Covington Enterprises. I believe the first shipment is to arrive Thursday night."

Bauers's face paled. "I find that hard to believe. Opium? Even Stuart would not fall in league with that lot."

"He's not," said Matthew darkly. "He's crossing them."

"Going against the highbinders? For opium? They'll have him killed."

"He wouldn't be the first." Matthew looked gravely at Reverend Bauers. "Or the last." He voiced the thought that had driven him here in the middle of the night. "They'd harm Georgia if they thought it would be the way to Stuart."

"I wish I could say you exaggerate. But I don't think you do." Bauers sighed heavily. "What ugliness. I do not think highly of Stuart Waterhouse, but even I would think him above this."

"The shipment must already be en route. We cannot stop it now. So the question becomes what do we do when it gets here?"

Bauers's expression echoed Matthew's thoughts: there were no good choices. Every option had terrible consequences. "The *true* question is what are you going to tell Georgia?"

It felt as if all Matthew's breath ran out of his body. "I must tell her. She needs to be part of whatever is decided."

Reverend Bauers looked relieved. "I am glad you see it that way." He leaned closer. "Still, can you not also see God's timing in this? It is no mistake that you are here, now, with her. That you were the one to discover this. Can you take heart from knowing this must surely be part of God's plan?"

"I should, but I'm finding it rather difficult to get past the disaster part. I do not care for the Lord's sense of timing on this."

Bauers put his hand on Matthew's shoulder. "I have a friend who once said that what we think of as disaster and calamity is often God's prelude to a mighty victory. After all, it takes a big problem to let God show how powerful He can be."

"In that case, I believe we qualify for a miracle." Matthew looked at the reverend. "Can you get her here? Now? Under some pretense?"

"Do you not think that a little rest might give you a clearer head? The dawn will not make things worse, but it might clear your thinking. You are welcome to stay here if you like, but perhaps you might want to get out of those clothes."

Matthew pulled himself off the chair and paced the room. "I'm exhausted, but I'm too angry to sleep. He's a weasel. A thoughtless, spineless snake without a moral to his name." He turned on the reverend. "What right does he have to take the Covington name down with him? To endanger Georgia? I have never been a man prone to violence, but so help me, Bauers..."

The reverend grabbed his arm. "All the more reason to put a little time behind you before you see Georgia. You've got to have your head about you when you tell her. You owe her that much."

Georgia woke to find her inkwell still open, her pen still lying atop the journal beside her on the bed. She'd written pages upon pages after retiring last night. The remainder of the party seemed a blur of unnecessary introductions, distracted small talk and secretive glances around the room. Part of her knew Matthew would be gone after their encounter on the terrace, yet part of her still surveyed the party on the slim chance he dared to stay.

Did he feel the way she did this morning? As if the world had begun turning in a new fashion? As if everything were too wonderful? Their circumstances had not changed; all the reasons why they could have little time together were still there. Yet when she thought of him and what it had felt like to settle into his strong arms last night, the obstacles seemed smaller. She knew one thing for certain: no matter what the future held, she would not have traded last night for all the world. Even though he did not know the half of what he'd done, Stuart had given her the most marvelous present ever. The fact that she would be presenting Reverend Bauers with a generous contribution later today was just God's overabundant blessing.

You knew all along, didn't You, Father? You knew he was there, but You knew the steps I needed to take to find him. The Bandit, the ball, I accomplished those things with the gifts You gave me. You've blessed me with courage and confidence, and rewarded me with love.

Love. Did she love him? Her heart answered with a cautious, exhilarated "yes." As if it felt too new to say for certain. She had loved parts of two men, knowing the impossibility of both. Now those two men had become one, and impossibility didn't seem…well, impossible. Did everyone newly in love feel as if nothing was beyond them? As if the combination of their hearts rendered all obstacles defeated?

England was still England. California was still California. Stuart, for that matter, was still Stuart. But Matthew was the Bandit. And that changed everything.

* * *

Georgia watched Matthew pull the door shut. Reverend Bauers's study was hardly a fitting place for such a meeting, but it was the most private, and inconspicuous, place possible.

Had Matthew been this handsome before? Surely he had not changed, yet Georgia could have sworn his eyes were a deeper blue, the cut of his shoulders broader, his voice smoother than yesterday.

He took her hand and kissed it as if it were the most precious thing God ever created. She'd rehearsed what she would say to him next time they stole a moment in private, and it came tumbling out of her at his touch. "I love you, and I don't care if you have to go back to England, because last night was enough for a lifetime and I love you for letting me know the truth." It came out in a gush of words, a single babbling exhalation that made her blush so fiercely she thought even the tops of her feet must be pink.

The resulting glow in his eyes surely turned her feet scarlet. He reached up and feathered his fingers against her cheek. He planted the tenderest of kisses where his fingers had been. It made her heart drop through her stomach.

"I had meant to be more elegant than that," she added when she could finally open her eyes. "But you seem to make my sense leave me."

Matthew circled her waist with his hands. "I don't know what future God holds for us, Georgia. Especially now. But I do know that I love you. I loved you even before you were George. I love you doubly now, and I would not take last night back for anything."

She'd thought, in her daydreams, that the moment

they professed their love he would sweep her into a breathtaking kiss. She was sure of his words, but there was something dark lurking in his eyes, a tension in his face. "But what?" she said slowly, her intuition telling her all was far from well.

"But I do love you enough to offer you the truth," he continued, choosing his words carefully, "and there is something you must know. Something I only learned last night. A very hard truth, Georgia."

It seemed there should be something dramatic she should say. Something about drawing strength from love, or Paul's words about welcoming trials, but none of them fit the deeply pained way Matthew was looking at her. Something was very, very wrong.

"What is it, Matthew?" she asked, as steadily as she could.

He shifted his feet, glanced away for a second and then gazed straight into her eyes. *He's gathering courage,* she thought. *Whatever can be so awful now?*

"I have suspected for some weeks that all is not well at Covington Enterprises. Things have been...altered... for my arrival. Last night, after I left you, I discovered who has been planning crimes through Covington Enterprises and why." His hands tightened around her waist. He shook his head and groaned. "I do not know how to say this easily."

"Then simply say it," Georgia said, fighting her growing sense of fear. *He is leaving on the next ship,* she thought. *He's to be arrested within the hour. Men are plotting his murder and he needs to run for his life.* A thousand scenarios played out in her imagination. The horrible black hole in the pit of her stomach grew deeper with every look from him.

Matthew pulled in a shuddering breath. "The two men corrupting Covington Enterprises are Dexter Oakman and—and Stuart."

Chapter Forty

Georgia registered the names, but her mind would not accept the concept. "Stuart?" She stared at Matthew as he waited patiently for her to wade through the shock of what he had just told her. "Stuart?" she repeated. "He has no reason to. I don't understand."

"I came back for my hat and mask after I left you last night. Stuart was still on the terrace, evidently waiting for Oakman. I overheard their conversation. They are planning to smuggle in opium and hide it within the Covington shipments. They've been paying off port officials and policeman for some time, evidently, and that's what I've found hidden in the books."

Georgia pulled her hands from Matthew's. "Opium? The Chinamen's drug?"

"I gather there's a lot of money to be made in it. No one would suspect someone like Stuart. Or Covington Enterprises. Most consider it a purely Chinese affair."

"Stuart? Involved in something like that? No. Stuart is misguided at times, but not this. Surely you misunderstood. Why ever would Stuart get involved? He's no friend of the Chinese, and certainly not their crimes.

Those highbinders—I've heard enough about those. They…they *kill* people over far less than opium."

Matthew put his hand to his forehead. "I've no doubt they'd kill Stuart if he crossed them. Which, Georgia, is exactly what he is planning to do. Undercut the Chinese opium black market. He'd make a fortune—if he lives. Which I very much doubt he will, no matter how powerful he thinks himself to be. He's in danger, Georgia. Grave danger. Stuart's made enough enemies over the years. The highbinders would find him an easy target." He took her shoulders in his hands. "And, Georgia, you need to understand this. Listen to me. I fear they wouldn't hesitate to harm you to get to him. If Stuart fails Thursday night, he might pay for it in jail. But if he succeeds, then both of you are in danger. And Covington Enterprises is undone. Your world and mine could come apart Thursday night, and I do not know what to do about it."

It became hard to breathe. Stuart was cunning, unscrupulous, but this? This seemed beneath even him. His holdings were doing splendidly—what need did they have of more money? Such dangerous money? From such a horrible source? "It can't be true. Matthew, it cannot be."

He ran his finger down the angled edges of a pewter candlestick on the study shelf next to him. "I would give anything that it were not so." He looked at her, and she thought all the blue had fled his eyes, leaving them black and fathomless. He was afraid.

"Have you seen anything, heard anything, that might lead you to believe Stuart is up to something?" Matthew asked.

She looked at him—this man who was both a man

and a hero—and felt her own fear ignite. Stuart had been acting strangely lately, and had indeed spent a lot of time with Dexter Oakman. He'd even started locking up his papers in a safe at night—something he had never done before. Could Stuart now be some stranger she did not really know? Some man capable of things she could not fathom?

"Perhaps. What do we do if it's true?" she whispered, clutching suddenly at his shoulder. "How can we save him? Or me?"

"I don't know how yet," he said, pulling her to him. She heard the frustration in his voice, felt the urgency tightening his chest. "But I promise you, if there's a way, we will find it. We," he repeated, tilting her face up to his. "You and me together. Between the four of us— you, me, the Bandit and George, there's got to be a way."

"Six," Georgia answered shakily. "I have a feeling we can count on Reverend Bauers and God as well." She attempted a small smile, but it failed miserably. Her lips melted into a pathetic, trembling pout.

He kissed away the tear that pooled at the corner of her eye. She felt small and defenseless, unable to keep up any semblance of courage. "Just when I thought I could not love you more," he whispered into her hair as he wrapped his strong arms around her, as if to keep the whole world at bay.

"Shut down the docks? We cannot simply shut down the port of San Francisco, Covington. It can't be done." Reverend Bauers, Georgia and Matthew sat around a table in the Reverend's study, supposedly factoring the Bandit Ball donations into Grace House's bookkeeping.

"I know that, Bauers, but we must find a way to effectively do that very thing."

"Or," mused Georgia, "focus so much attention onto the docks that the shipment can't go through unnoticed. Oh," she sighed, looking pained, "I hate this. I hate every single bit of it. I just can't believe Stuart's capable of something like this." Her voice quivered as she added, "He's my brother. My only family."

Matthew grasped her hand. "You have me. And I cannot begin to understand what it must feel like to be plotting Stuart's demise. But you must bear up, Georgia. You have it in you, I know you do."

"How can I go home? How can I pretend everything is fine when I know it is all going to pieces right in front of me?"

He wanted to wrap her up in his arms all over again. "Because you are strong enough," he said. "Because if Stuart suspects something it will be all the more difficult to seize the shipment." He stared hard into her eyes, willing her to feel the strength in herself that he had seen from the first. "You *are* strong enough." After a moment, he turned his gaze to Bauers. "We've got to paralyze the docks. Or at least slow the activity down substantially."

Georgia let her head fall into her hands. "Goodness, we'll need an army to do that."

Reverend Bauers suddenly froze. "And we know just how to raise one. Glory! I hadn't even thought of that."

"Bauers?" Matthew questioned.

"An army. I was thinking we needed an army to clear the docks, but that's not it at all. We need an army to *fill* them. We've already done it once. It will be easy to do it again."

"Reverend?" Georgia said, looking as baffled as Matthew felt.

"Don't you see, Georgia? You called forth an army of Bandits for your ball. Hundreds of men dressed as the Bandit. They raised money because money *was what they had.* Now, call forth another army of Bandits for May Day, on Thursday. Call for a gathering of Bandits on the docks. They'll raise a ruckus because that's what *they* do. Think of it—the German tradition of the May-pole, all the ribbons—it's as good as if we planned it all along. If you issue an invitation through the *Herald,* the police will be primed to show up in heavy numbers. The docks will be swarmed and no will know who's who because there'll be so many Bandits."

"Are there that many German families here?" Matthew asked.

"Yes, but we don't have to stop there. You could write something to invite everyone. Irish families. Italian families. Even Chinese families. Turn it into a spontaneous May Day festival. They'll all have just finished reading about your Bandit Ball, and they're all ready to have a party of their own." Bauers reached across the table to take Georgia's hand. "You could do it, Georgia. You could write something to stir them up."

"I could very well start a riot," she replied.

"A riot might be the best weapon we have," Matthew answered. "It would both slow Stuart down and direct everyone's attention to the docks. I daresay it might work."

"How could I ever get something like that into the *Herald?* Stuart would never run it. Not only that, if I somehow got him to, he'd know in advance and divert the shipment."

"Even if he knew in advance," Matthew retorted, "he has no way of diverting the shipment until the boat is already at the dock. In which case all he can do is keep it on board and delay its off-loading. We'd still be in a position to expose him."

"This is such a hideous business." Georgia stood up, her anger rising. Matthew had expected it to eventually find its way to the surface, and she was more than entitled to her feelings. She'd held out such hopes for Stuart. Persisted in believing the best of him, only to have it ripped out from beneath her. She paced the room now, her hands flailing in frustration.

"Exposing," she said bitterly. "Rioting. Why can't we simply go to the police with what we know? Why must it be so cloak-and-dagger?"

"Because we don't know who can be trusted," replied Reverend Bauers. "If Stuart's been buying off the officials for months, we've no idea who's in his pocket and who isn't." The clergyman rose and walked over to put a hand on Georgia's shoulder. "Try to think of it this way, child. If we expose Stuart, he'll suffer time in jail. If we don't expose him and he succeeds, eventually the highbinders will catch up with him, and I doubt their treatment will be anything as kind as jail. We are not exposing Stuart so much as saving him from himself."

"I'm done saving Stuart," she retorted, boiling over. Matthew was rather amazed that she'd lasted as long as she had. "Let him hang himself with his own greed." She pulled away from Bauers's grasp. "Who knows what else he's done? Who knows what sorts of awful things have been putting food on our table or buying my clothes or paying for silly balls! I've been a fool! A naive fool."

Matthew caught her arm as she stormed past him. "You've not been a fool. You have every right to be angry. And I admit, it's tempting to leave Stuart to his own fate. But you know you don't mean that. You're tired and upset and not yourself. Deserting Stuart is not who you are, even in anger. And aside from all else, it would put you in peril. I won't have that."

She turned to him, eyes blazing. "You won't have that?" He immediately knew he'd chosen the wrong words. "Isn't this *my* peril we're discussing?" she countered. "Shouldn't that be my decision?"

"Can't you see that perhaps I *am* here to protect you?" Matthew squared off in front of her. "That God brought me here, to you, to *see you safe?*" He took her by the shoulders, almost wanting to shake her despair out of her, surprised at his own panic that she might do something rash. "That He has made you so dear to me that I will do whatever it takes?"

He felt the set of her shoulders give just a little, and he pulled her to him, feeling her soften against his chest. "You've been betrayed by someone you love, and that's a terrible shock. But you are strong and clever. You've been saving San Francisco for years—do not stop now when it's yourself you must save." Her head fell against his shoulder and he planted a kiss onto her hair. "Go home. Plead a headache. Anything to keep to your rooms. I will ask Stuart to lunch or some such thing. Keep him occupied. He is no less a snake than many in London—I will be fine, even if I would like to wring his neck at the moment."

Matthew tilted her head to look into her eyes. "This is a part I can play. The part only you can do, Georgia, is to write Thursday's episode. Raise up our army. That is your gift. And now is the time to wield it."

Chapter Forty-One

Georgia felt ill. Sad. Furious. The emotions came so quickly she couldn't sort through them. *How amusing,* she thought to herself as she sprawled across her chair by the window. *I do remember once considering my life rather uneventful.*

Here she thought she had gained such courage over the past few weeks. Now, when it really mattered, when the storm of San Francisco's corruption showed up at her own doorstep, she was weak and frightened. She knew Stuart better than anyone. She knew what a ferocious enemy he could be.

Then again, she didn't know Stuart at all, did she? She thought she knew what he was capable of—but how sadly she'd misjudged how low he could sink.

Lord, help me! What am I to do? She remembered the story of Gideon, and fingered through her Bible to the sixth chapter of Judges. How she longed for an angel of the Lord to appear to her, to call her a mighty warrior and make her feel equipped for the task ahead of her. When Gideon asked, "If the Lord is with us, why

has all this happened?" she felt as if the ancient warrior was voicing her own thoughts.

Why, if God had indeed been instrumental in all
the extraordinary things happening in her life, had it
all unraveled so quickly? Gideon pleaded weakness.
So did she. God promised to be with him, to help him
conquer with the small strength he had. Oh, how she
longed to claim that promise for herself. Gideon had
named his altar, the spot he built to mark his encounter with the Lord, "The Lord is Peace." Gideon did not
yet know how he was going to conquer his enemies.
Yet he'd built an altar named for the Lord's peace. She
could feel the words taking root in her heart. And when
she read the final detail, one most casual readers would
probably dismiss, she knew God had sent her comfort.
Gideon, it seemed, was too afraid to do his tasks in the
daylight—so he did them at night. Just like her Bandit.

Guide my pen, Lord, she prayed as she took her place
at her writing desk. *Like Gideon, I am the least in my
family and my enemies are great. My task is large. Be
my mighty God, and do not leave my side for one second until I am through this.*

She dipped her pen into the ink and took a breath.

"People of San Francisco,
Let us find the heroes among us...."

"Grand of you to have lunch with me today, Stuart."
Matthew shook his napkin open and signaled to the
waiter to deliver the first course. He'd made sure they
had the best table in the Palace dining room. Today, he
was going to pull out every stop to monopolize Stuart's
attention. In the time since he'd sent the invitation over

and received Stuart's acceptance, he'd hatched a plan. It was extreme, rather risky, but Matthew doubted the circumstances called for anything less.

"Fine of you to ask. I'd been thinking we ought to chat, you and I." Stuart picked up a fork and surveyed his food. "You've been seeing a great deal of Georgia."

Ah, so he *had* been thinking along those lines. Matthew had suspected as much when Waterhouse agreed to the last-minute luncheon. "I have," he said, keeping his voice intentionally neutral.

"She's all I have in the world," Stuart stated.

It should have sounded sentimental. Instead, it sounded to Matthew entirely too much like the opening bid in an auction. He hid the twist in his gut and smiled genially. "She's a delightful woman. I find her talented and clever and of tremendous moral character."

"Oh, yes," replied Stuart, rolling his eyes the tiniest bit, "tremendous."

They ate for a few minutes, talking cordially, testing the waters as each waited for the true nature of the conversation to surface. When the second course had arrived, Matthew cleared his throat.

"Stuart," he said, leaning in, "I find you to be a direct man. I admire that, so I shall be direct as well. I find myself exceptionally fond of Georgia. I'd like to pursue her affections. I could give her a very comfortable life."

Stuart smiled. "I'm not entirely surprised, Covington. I know my sister well enough to see when a man has caught her eye." He cut into his chicken. "But I must admit, I hadn't thought things to have already grown that serious between you."

"These things," Matthew said with a wry smile, "do

have a way of escalating." *Stuart Waterhouse, if you only knew the half of it.*

"Am I to understand you're declaring your intentions?"

"I am." Matthew reached for his glass. "I must admit, however, I've some doubts as to whether or not you'll let her go." He took a long drink, watching Stuart's reaction. "England is far away," he offered, "even with the railroad up and running."

"She's dear to me, Covington. I'll not have her hurt."

Not have her hurt? Have you given any thought to how you've placed her in danger just to stuff your coffers? It took a supreme effort of will to keep his voice cordial. "I think the world of her, Stuart. She'll want for nothing."

"Except me. I'll lose her to you. Do you deserve her?" her brother challenged.

Do you? It had been years since Matthew wanted to knock a man across a room as he wanted to this very moment. "Will you let her go with your blessing?"

Stuart wiped his mouth with his napkin, making a show of considering the offer before him. "The idea has merit. Can you prove to me she'll be well cared for?"

Matthew had anticipated this kind of thrust and parry, and he had a strategy prepared. "I'm prepared to place the San Francisco holdings of Covington Enterprises in Georgia's name as an engagement gift. I'll send for the papers tomorrow if you give me your consent to the marriage." It was just the sort of offer Stuart couldn't refuse—an importing firm in the family name. As such, it made the ideal setup for the final strike Matthew had planned.

"Does Georgia know of this?" Stuart asked, stalling

his answer with another question. The man was shrewd, Matthew gave him that.

"I believe I know Georgia's heart. But I would not approach her about this until I'd spoken with you. As a matter of honor."

Stuart waited a full minute more before extending his hand. "Very well, then, Covington, it seems we are to be family."

Matthew couldn't think of a more disturbing thought. "Covington Enterprises will be hers by the month's end. On one condition."

Stuart's brows shot up. "'Condition'? Rather unconventional, wouldn't you say?"

"You strike me as a man who understands a deal, Waterhouse."

"That depends on the deal." Stuart crossed his arms over his chest, looking intrigued and not a little annoyed.

"I know more than you think I do, Stuart." He lowered his voice. "I know, for example, who George is."

Chapter Forty-Two

Stuart went very still. He stared at Matthew before saying, "Go on."

"I value her role in that, because I value that part of her. So, if I'm to place my family holdings in her name—and within your family—I want to know you value it as well. I've declared my pledge. I only want one thing from you in return."

"Not really your place to bargain, is it, Covington?"

"It's simple, really. No effort from you at all. I just want your promise to run the Bandit episodes verbatim. Just as Georgia writes them, no editing. If she's to finish out her run as George Towers, then I want her to have the freedom to do it as she pleases. *Exactly* as she pleases."

"That's it?" Stuart balked. "That's what you want?"

"It's important to her, therefore it's important to me. I've read the latest installment, so I'll know if it's been altered in any way when it appears in print on Thursday." He held out a hand. "Have we a deal, Stuart?"

"Is this how brides are won in England?" Confound him, Stuart was stalling to the end.

"It's how *this* particular bride is *wooed.* Do we have a deal?"

Stuart shook his hand. "Done."

"I'm grateful. I'll speak to her tomorrow night, if that suits you. You'll have your papers by Monday if I can manage it."

Stuart gripped Matthew's hand a moment longer. "She's all I have in the world, Covington."

"She's worth the world to *me,* Stuart. I hope you see that."

"Believe it or not," he said, with a smile that could be described as warm—if one did not look too carefully, "I think I do."

Georgia could barely wait to get out the door with Matthew the following afternoon. The air in the house felt thick with secrets, and it seemed like hours before he came to call. Adventure and intrigue were clearly ideas best left to the printed page, and not one's own family. She'd avoided Stuart all day yesterday, and he had been looking at her oddly today. It added to her nerves when she handed him the fateful Bandit episode over lunch. Odder still, he accepted it without a single question—not reading it then, as he usually did, and as near as she could tell not reading it at all.

Sensing that an "outing" was not really suited to their moods, Matthew suggested they simply take a walk. It was a fine afternoon, and he led her to the set of benches where he had first read the Bandit to her. The slanting gold sunlight brought a deep sapphire to his eyes. He sat down opposite her, looked at her, then stood up again.

Nervous, she realized. *He's nervous.* She'd never

seen him nervous. Alarmed, yes. Agitated. But never nervous. She wondered if something had gone very wrong with his meeting with Stuart. "Matthew," she began, at the exact same moment he said her name. They both blustered a bit, and then he gestured for her to continue.

"What have you said to Stuart? He has been acting strangely all day, and he took my Bandit episode without so much as a peep. I'm not even sure he's planning on reading it before he hands it to the typesetter. How did you do it?"

"Yes, well," said Matthew, with the tone of voice one uses when starting a long speech, "I've been meaning to speak to you about that." He thrust his hands into his pockets, only to remove them again, and sat down. "Georgia, do you remember the verse you read to me? The one from Corinthians?"

"Of course," she replied.

"It speaks of having everything, but of it all coming to nothing without love."

"Yes, it does."

"I… I don't find it any accident that that was the verse you shared with me. It's had a great impact on me." He turned to look at her. "You've had a great impact on me."

She wanted to reply that he'd changed her as well, but something told her to stay silent, to let him finish whatever he needed to say.

"I have a great many things. I own more than I can ever use, I have more influence than I can ever hope to wield wisely, and—" the spark in his eyes traveled to ignite his wide smile "—I have gained faith and friends I would never have imagined. But I had not love until

I met you. I understand now what those verses mean, because all the things I have, the things I am, pale in comparison to love." He took her hand. "I have come to love you. Dearly. And yet I cannot tell you what our future will be. I find I can't even predict how the week will end."

Had he said "our future"? Georgia suddenly realized what he was doing, why his nerves were so wound up, and she fought to pull in a breath.

"Yesterday morning, I sat in my rooms and begged God to show me what to do. He did, Georgia. He gave me a plan so perfect and so impossible that I knew at once how to proceed. But here, now, is not about any plan. It is not about how useful this tactic is. It is about how I cannot see myself without you, no matter what the circumstances."

She wasn't quite sure what he meant, talking about tactics and such, but she could see an astounding intensity in his eyes.

He took her hands. "Yesterday I asked Stuart for his blessing to marry you. I want to marry you, Georgia Waterhouse, and I don't care how impossible it all sounds right now." He gave a sheepish laugh, something so out of place in his usually confident demeanor. "I don't even know how I'll manage it yet. I don't know any of the details—here or England or family or any of it." His hands tightened around hers. "But I know it is what I want. More than anything. And I think...no, I *believe*... God has a life together planned for us. If you'll have me."

Georgia understood his words. She knew what he was saying. Yet it felt as if someone had just hit her with a thousand sparks of light. "You're...you're asking me to marry you."

He pulled one hand away and raked it through his hair. "Well, I admit to being rather long-winded, but yes." He took her hands again and stared into her eyes. Oh, what the blue-black depths of them did to her. "Georgia, I am asking you to marry me. Will you?"

She had told herself over and over that it could not be. That it wasn't really what she wanted, for it might mean leaving San Francisco. She'd given herself all manner of sensible reasons why their happiness would only be a fleeting thing. Nothing to grasp at. But here, now, she wanted to grab it with both hands and hold it close forever. She wanted to be with Matthew, and the future would have to be God's problem to contend with as He chose. There wasn't even a moment's hesitation to her answer. She realized that no matter how she'd deceived her more sensible self, she'd said yes to a future with him a long time ago.

"You?" she said, knowing he'd already seen her acceptance in her eyes, "or the Black Bandit?"

He grinned. "The whole lot of us."

"Yes," she said breathlessly. "Yes, I will."

Forgetting they were in the middle of a park, he pulled her into a recklessly long kiss. "I've no ring yet," he said, when they found their wits again. "You'll have a fine one in time, but for now, I think perhaps I've found a suitable proxy." Fumbling in his pocket, he pulled out a tiny white ribbon and tied it around her ring finger, finishing off with a kiss to her hand. "A fitting token for our most unusual courtship, don't you think?"

"I don't know how on earth we'll manage it," she agreed, touching the tiny bow, "but we've managed quite a lot of the impossible so far. Perhaps we stand a chance. Goodness, if Stuart agreed and ran the Bandit without question, God must be on our side."

"Yes, well, there's something I have to tell you about that. But I needed to hear your yes first before I let you in on my agreement with your brother."

"Your agreement," she repeated, feeling a bit unsteady, "with Stuart?"

"I'll admit at first I thought it only a tactic. But I think that is purely how God got my attention. I think it might have taken me months to work up the nerve otherwise."

"Matthew, what are you talking about?"

"I told Stuart I would transfer Covington's San Francisco holdings into your name—something I knew he'd find irresistible—as an engagement gift. On the condition that he run your future Bandit episodes without any editing whatsoever. He knows I know you're George. And I told him I'd seen the present Bandit installment, so you'd best show it to me quickly so I can verify he's kept his end of the deal."

"A deal? You struck a deal with Stuart? For me?" She eyed him.

"I struck no deal for you, Georgia. I want to marry you. God just had to knock me over the head to realize it. But I'll admit to playing my present desires to our best advantage. It works beautifully. Your Bandit episode will run in the *Herald* now, and our plan stands a greater chance of succeeding. But please, know it is only a happy consequence of what I truly want—which is for us to be together."

Georgia sighed. "I cannot see how it is at all possible. One of us should have to leave everything."

"I made it here. The railroad is growing every day. Each ship built is faster than the last. Perhaps the world is not as large as it once was. I believe we will find a way. Perhaps, Georgia, God is paving the way for a new life for you. Whether it is here or in England, I don't know. We'll have to deal with that as it comes. But if Stuart is brought down, can you not see that perhaps God is clearing the way for you to go to England? Or at least granting us that possibility?"

She let out another sigh. "I don't know."

"You and the reverend won me to faith with half a Bible. You created a hero out of thin air. The Bandit has worked wonders and still no one knows who he is. I've been stabbed by an Irishman, stitched by a German, costumed by an Englishman, conspired with an Italian and loved by an American. I believe the small matter of a few continents and an ocean is well within our means."

Chapter Forty-Three

The world seemed to grind to a halt until Thursday. Georgia nearly ran to breakfast Thursday morning, eager to see the Bandit episode printed in the *Herald*. It appeared exactly as she had written it. If Stuart suspected anything or was annoyed with her call for an impromptu celebration on the docks that night, he showed none of it. As a matter of fact, he was up and at the offices long before she even woke. She laid her hand over the newsprint and prayed. *Send these words out in Your name, Father. Let Your will be done today. Raise up a throng to fill the docks, and let the police find what they need to find.*

Her heart constricted as she contemplated Stuart's fate by this time tomorrow. *Is there no way to save him from this, Lord? Turn him back from this mistake, I beg You. Can You not see Your way clear to a fate that is neither prison nor the highbinders? Can You not work a miracle?* Her soul fell upon the words she'd so long resented from Stuart: *he's all I have in the world.*

Matthew thought it would be far more difficult to locate the boxes. As head of Covington Enterprises, he found it easy to gain access to the ship's manifest when it docked. Within an hour, he'd managed to sort out a dozen or so likely crates from the legitimate cargo. Then, by discreetly watching the unloading, noting how each crate was handled and by whom, he had narrowed it down to six by the end of the day. He had his target. Matthew went home to get ready, the first part of his role done. Now it was up to Bauers to direct the crowd Georgia had summoned.

As evening fell and he pulled on his boots, Matthew took a moment to run a finger across the glossy leather. How odd that he had to hide in a sea of Bandits tonight in order to drop that persona forever. He looked up at Thompson, who seemed to understand the irony of the moment. "I won't be home tonight, Thompson. Not till daylight at best."

"I gather the Bandit is facing a great challenge this evening, sir?" There was no hint of teasing in the valet's voice.

Matthew thought of all the times throughout his life he'd kept things from Thompson, tried to outwit him. It struck him that today might be the time for a new tactic—to tell Thompson everything. To allow him to be the ally he had always quietly been. Without saying a word, Matthew got up, poured two cups of coffee from the service on the sideboard and added two sugars to one—that was how Thompson took his coffee. He offered it to him, a gesture of service to the man who had so faithfully served him.

Thompson seemed to understand what Matthew was doing, and offered a rare, wide smile. "Thank you, sir."

"Matthew. Just Matthew will be fine."

"Thank you... Matthew."

He sat down opposite the valet, and they sipped their coffee in silence. "Covington Enterprises has been corrupted," Matthew began. "Stuart Waterhouse is planning to smuggle opium into the country through our shipments, beginning tonight. Waterhouse is taking on the highbinders, powerful Chinese smugglers, and trying to undercut them. To his danger and Georgia's." He looked into Thompson's face. "I care a great deal for Georgia Waterhouse."

The valet set down his cup. "I have been waiting a long time for you to find someone, Mr. Cov... Matthew. I believe you have chosen exceptionally well."

Matthew managed a lopsided grin. "Does one really choose such things?"

"No," replied Thompson, "I suppose they come upon us—even when we would have chosen otherwise." He sighed, taking another sip of coffee. Matthew remembered that Thompson had been married once. His wife had died several years earlier. Had Matthew ever truly paid attention to his grief, or just assumed that the man's service would simply endure, at it always had?

"Waterhouse—and Covington Enterprises—will be exposed tonight. It will be an ugly evening for all of us, Stuart most of all. I doubt this division of the company will survive the month, either. I'm sorry for that."

"Your father will not be pleased," Thompson agreed. "But Covington Enterprises has many holdings. The fall of one office will not bring down so vast an empire."

"So vast an empire," Matthew echoed, the enormity of the evening pressing down upon him.

"The Bandit is a clever man. I believe he can manage it." Thompson caught his eye with a strangely confident look. "And she is worth it."

Matthew found himself sharing Thompson's smile. "Yes, she most certainly is."

While she knew it was the least dangerous, Georgia felt as though she had the most difficult task of all: keeping Stuart occupied. Even sharing the happy news of her engagement to Matthew—which provided her a bevy of small details to "pretend" the need to discuss— it was as though she and Stuart were different people. No longer the lone siblings. At first, she thought it was because Matthew had entered that very private circle, but she recognized that deceit had been the true invader.

What had come between them was not Matthew, but Stuart himself.

"What fun you shall have with new British relatives!" she said too cheerfully. "I imagine several of Matthew's family will share your love of operetta."

"They might at that," said Stuart, also grasping at conversation. He checked his watch again.

"Crisis at the presses tonight?" she inquired stiffly.

"Isn't there always?" he answered with another question—a sure sign he was on the defensive. Georgia pretended to be engrossed in her embroidery, praying for God's sovereignty with each distracted stitch. It would be so long a night.

Still, she had come to a significant realization today: this was about more than Stuart and his faults. Today— in fact for many weeks now—she was discovering how to be Georgia Waterhouse. Not merely "the other Waterhouse," or "Stuart's sister." God was granting her the gift, however painful, of becoming her own person.

Such a gift took courage of a whole other kind to receive. Not the courage of sword or whip or strength in the face of danger, but one of trust and faith and confidence. No matter what transpired tonight, none of those blessings would be taken away. Challenged, perhaps, but they were hers now, and could no longer be stolen from her. Not even by Stuart.

When she looked up from her stitches, Stuart was staring at her. "Do you love him, Peach?" he asked in a tone that tightened her throat. "Really?" The old Stuart, the wild, misguided, big-hearted child returned in his eyes.

Suddenly, for the first time ever, Georgia felt older than her brother. As though she had grown in a way he never had. Stuart had loved once—fallen madly in love—but it was always a possessive sort of craving with him. It seemed a shallow echo of what she felt for Matthew. A tinge of pity stole into the mixture of fear and anger she'd felt since she'd learned of his plans.

"Yes," she said. "Very much." And there, right there, was faith working itself out in her life. Faith giving her the strength to love when it was not deserved. Faith enabling her to love the sinner, yet hate the sin. Faith to grasp her life apart from Stuart, to release him to his fate, and yet still love him. "Thank you," she said sincerely, "for extending your blessing. It means a great deal to me."

"We're all we have in the world," he said, nearly hiding the hint of sadness in his eyes.

No, she thought, *there's where you're wrong.*

Matthew waited outside Dexter Oakman's house until the man left around ten o'clock. While Stuart would never sully his hands with the actual dirty work, Matthew had seen him apply enough pressure that he suspected Oakman would personally oversee the transfer. Sadly enough, the man who would come out the worst for all of this was Oakman. Stuart might have the finances and wit to recover one day, but Matthew doubted Oakman would ever regain any position whatsoever.

He followed Oakman's carriage down toward the docks and Covington Enterprises. The closer they got to the shipyards, the noisier the streets became. Bauers, who had always been resourceful, must have outdone himself, for the area was packed with loud, raucous people, many dressed as the Bandit. Slipping into the crowd, Matthew became instantly invisible. *Thompson, old man, I've finally mastered it,* he thought to himself, tipping his black hat in the general direction of the Palace Hotel.

Policemen were trying desperately to keep some semblance of order. If there was one thing this part of the city did well, it was raise a ruckus. Put the crowd in masks, add a generous amount of ale and inspiration, and it quickly turned into May Day chaos. In the three-block radius around Covington Enterprises, Matthew saw more policemen than he had witnessed during his entire visit.

He flattened himself against a wall as Oakman met up with two men. *Come on now, Dexter, come take your precious present home from the party.* Matthew looked around to make sure there were plenty of policemen in view. Carefully, with a few nervous glances, Oakman motioned for three of the half-dozen crates Matthew had suspected to be loaded onto a wagon.

What Oakman and his men did not know was that Matthew had loosened the bottom of each of those crates so that they would come loose when lifted. The string of curses let out when the first crate collapsed would have burned Georgia's ears. A rainbow of Oriental silks spilled out onto the street. An expensive mistake, but it confirmed Matthew's suspicion that the opium had been hidden inside something like fabric or fiber.

The mishap caught the attention of a few of the policemen, who made snide remarks about the careless nature of dockworkers.

The second crate caved in the instant it was lifted, signaling it contained more than just fabric. Sure enough, small paper parcels rolled out of their silk cocoons and sent Oakman into a panic. Now was the time.

Matthew lit the fuse on a firecracker wound with a wad of cotton he had purchased earlier, and tossed it into the center of the pile. The sound, one of many firecrackers going off in the melee, brought little attention. The flare, however, sent the cotton up in flames, which ignited the silk—a slower fire that resisted stamping out. It in turn ignited the real target by the time the police gathered. The pile began to give out the thick, musty odor every San Francisco policeman knew as opium smoke.

The scene reminded Matthew of the passage in his namesake's gospel where Christ said He would separate the sheep from the goats. Within the space of a minute, the police force divided itself squarely into men trying to cover things up and men trying to find things out. Pulling off his mask and hat, Matthew stepped into the light and headed straight for the latter.

Chapter Forty-Four

"I'm Matthew Covington," he said to the one who appeared to be in command. "I've discovered this man trying to smuggle opium into the port through my shipping, and I want him arrested along with his accomplice, immediately."

Dexter Oakman went white. The scent of opium smoke hung in the air as he stared at Matthew.

"I'm Sergeant Dickenson, Mr. Covington." The officer extended a hand. "And what do you mean by accomplice?"

Matthew pulled a roll of ledger papers—unaltered ledgers he'd managed to dig out of some back files at his office after considerable searching—from one of the pockets of his trousers. "A quick study of these should point straight to Stuart Waterhouse. You'll find him at home awaiting a report from our friend here."

Dickenson briefly riffled through the papers. "I'll have to get someone to look at these more closely, but this is a serious charge, Mr. Covington. I wouldn't make it lightly."

"Nor do I set fire to my own cargo lightly, Dickenson. This was to be the first shipment Waterhouse smuggled in, but I gather with a little digging you'll find a host set to come in behind it. I've marked the involved transactions in these ledgers here. I'm prepared to cooperate fully with your authorities and open up all of Covington's books to your perusal. But I've found many of my books to be altered. And I guarantee you, Waterhouse will disappear within the hour if you don't move quickly."

Several other policemen, the ones in obvious disagreement with Dickenson's planned course of action, came up behind them as they spoke. "I hope you know what you're saying, Covington," the sergeant warned. "Waterhouse is not a man to count among your enemies."

"I know full well what I'm saying."

Dickenson motioned to two of his colleagues. "You two, go bring in Stuart Waterhouse for questioning." They looked as though they'd been asked to wrestle a cobra with their bare hands, but they went. "You'll need to come with me, Covington. Highly unusual, what you're doing."

"You don't want to do this," snarled a burly older officer from behind Dickenson's shoulder. "You might want to think this over if you like yer job."

Dickenson caught Matthew's eye before turning to the man. "And you might want to think about what you've just said in front of a witness like Mr. Covington here. Just in case any of it might happen to be true. Which I'm not saying it is. I'm sure Mr. Waterhouse will be eager to tell us his version of the facts—" he returned his gaze to Oakman "—but for now we gotta put out this fire. Nasty smellin' stuff, it is."

Dickenson's glower put Oakman in a panic. "Matthew," he said, pulling against the pair of policemen who had just taken him by the elbows, "don't. We'll lose everything."

"I've lost nothing of real value," Matthew replied.

Dickenson glanced again at the papers, holding them up to a gaslight in the corner. "You realize what you're doing? You ready to tangle with Waterhouse? It could get just as nasty for you. We can stop at your friend here."

"I'm quite certain, Sergeant. It's a matter of some personal consequence to me."

Dickenson sighed like a man who had just resigned himself to a very nasty fight. "I been waiting for something like this to crawl its way up to Nob Hill. Like my mama used to say, it ain't just cream that rises to the top—grease does, too."

"Matthew," called Oakman, "think of your family."

"I am," he said calmly. *The one I will someday start with Georgia.*

"You've a long night of questioning ahead of you, Covington," said Sergeant Dickenson, tucking the papers into his coat pocket, "if we can carve our way through the sea of Bandits." He pointed to the full-scale calamity enjoying itself farther up the dock. "Nice Bandit costume, by the way. You must have had a good time at Waterhouse's ball, though—it looks a mite ragged around the edges."

When Matthew rang the bell, Reverend Bauers opened the front door of the Waterhouse estate. The sun was just coming up. Bauers shook his hand heartily, then led him to the front parlor, where Georgia was dozing on the settee. She held a handkerchief with the initials SW embroidered on one corner in her hand.

"He's going to be all right, Georgia," Matthew said when she opened her eyes, thinking it was what she needed to hear.

"No," she said, pulling herself upright, "he won't. But God is wise and kind, and no less God than He was yesterday." She looked at him, rumpled and dirty in his Bandit costume. Her gaze traveled to his waist. "You've lost your whip. And your hat—where is your hat?"

Matthew smiled. "I gave them to Quinn. My mask as well. I wanted to say thank-you to him. You should have seen him, stirring up the crowd. Besides, I won't be needing them anymore."

"No more Bandit adventures? Matthew, whatever shall we do now?"

"I'm afraid I haven't the foggiest idea. Can you live with that?"

She smiled. "I imagine George and I can find a way." She stood up and adjusted his collar, running her hand across the stubble on his chin. "Tell me, what do they eat for breakfast in England?"

Epilogue

London Times
"Madam Whippleton's Most Delectable Social Gossip"
May 2, 1892

London's finest were decked out in their swashbuckling best last night as Mr. and Mrs. Matthew Covington hosted what is sure to become a fixture in the spring social calendar. The First Annual May Day Bandit Ball, said to be a quaint tradition brought over by Mrs. Covington from her native California. The gala event raised funds to support the Willsbury Home for Orphaned Children, a most worthy cause that has been a focus of Mrs. Covington's since her arrival here two years ago. Festive touches such as a cascade of white ribbons and a traditional German Maypole added to the theatrical atmosphere of the evening. London's finest joined in the spirit of the costumed event, making generous philanthropic gifts for the privilege of dressing as Robin Hood, Aladdin, the Three Musketeers, Blackbeard the Pirate, or any number of legendary bandits throughout the ages. Good show, Mrs. Covington—this author, for one, delights in your spirited contribution to London's stoic social offerings.

Now, on to the loathsome qualities of Miss Edwina Dyson's gown at the opera last Thursday. Surely someone should speak to her seamstress...."

* * * * *

Widowed father Boothe Powers needs a wife in order
to retain custody of his son. Emma Spencer was sure
to see the practicality of such an arrangement.
Emma's heart yearns for marriage and children.
But she has her own secret anguish…

Read on for a sneak preview of
The Path to Her Heart *by Linda Ford*

"We don't even like each other. Why would you want to
marry me?" At the untruthfulness of her words, heat left a
spot on Emma's cheeks. She'd tried to tell herself otherwise
but she liked Boothe. Might even admit she'd grown slightly
fond of him. Okay. Truth time. She might even be a little
attracted to him. Had been since her first glimpse.

"I like you just fine."

"I'm a nurse. Have you forgotten?"

He hesitated. "Well, as nurses go, you seem to be a good
one."

She snorted in a most unladylike fashion. "I'm thrilled
to hear that."

"Surely we could work around that."

"I think not. Can you imagine how we'd disagree if I
thought one of us or—" Her cheeks burned. She'd been
about to say *one of our children*, but she couldn't say it
aloud. "If I thought someone needed medical attention?"

"I'm desperate."

"Well, thanks. I guess." Just what she'd always dreamed
of—the last pick of someone who was desperate.

"Wait. Listen to what I have to say." He pulled a battered envelope from his back pocket.

Nothing he said would change the fact they were as unsuited for each other as cat and mouse, yet she hesitated, wanting—hoping—for something to persuade her otherwise.

He waved her toward a pew and she cautiously took a seat. "This is a letter from a lawyer back in Lincoln informing me that my brother-in-law and his wife intend to adopt Jessie."

She gasped. "How can that be?"

He looked bleak. "I needed help after Alyse died and Vera offered. Only then she wanted to keep Jessie."

Emma pressed her palm to his shoulder. "Surely they don't have a chance?"

He slowly brought his gaze toward her. At the look of despair in his eyes, her throat pinched closed.

"I went to see the lawyer in town and he says the courts favor people who have money and their own home, but especially both a father and mother. My best chance is to get married."

She settled back, affronted to be no more than a means to an end, and yet, would her dreams and hopes never leave her alone? "And I was the only person you could think of?"

He shrugged. "You're fond of Jessie."

A burning mix of sympathy and annoyance shot through her. She withdrew her hand from his shoulder even though she ached to comfort him. She sat up straight, folded her hands together in her lap and forced the words from her mouth. "Yes, I'm fond of Jessie but I can't marry—not you or anyone."

Don't miss
The Parson's Christmas Gift & The Path to Her Heart
by Kerri Mountain and Linda Ford,
available December 2018.

www.LoveInspired.com

LIHEXP00672

I've got trouble, Clarabelle."

The cow didn't answer her. Bethany pitched a forkful of hay to the family's placid brown-and-white Guernsey. The bishop has decided to send Ivan to Bird-in-Hand to live with Onkel Harvey. It's not right. It's not fair. I can't bear the idea of sending my little brother away. We belong together."

Clarabelle munched a mouthful of hay as she regarded Bethany with soulful deep brown eyes.

"Advice is what I need, Clarabelle. The bishop said Ivan could stay if I had a husband. Someone to discipline and guide the boy. Any idea where I can get a husband before Christmas?"

"I doubt your cow has the answers you seek, but if she does I have a few questions for her about my own problems," a man said.

Bethany spun around. A stranger stood in the open barn door. He wore a black Amish hat pulled low on his forehead and a dark blue woolen coat with the collar turned up against the cold.

LIEXP1018

The mirth sparkling in his eyes sent a flush of hea to her cheeks. How humiliating. To be caught talkin to a cow about matrimonial prospects made her loo ridiculous.

She struggled to hide her embarrassment. "It's rude t eavesdrop on a private conversation."

"I'm not sure talking to a cow qualifies as a privat conversation, but I am sorry to intrude."

He didn't look sorry. He looked like he was strugglin; not to laugh at her.

"I'm Michael Shetler."

She considered not giving him her name. The less h knew to repeat the better.

"I am Bethany Martin," she admitted, hoping sh wasn't making a mistake.

"Nice to meet you, Bethany. Once I've had a res I'll step outside if you want to finish your privat conversation." He winked. One corner of his mouth twitched, revealing a dimple in his cheek.

"I'm glad I could supply you with some amusemen today."

"It's been a long time since I've had something to smile about."

Don't miss
An Amish Wife for Christmas *by Patricia Davids,*
available November 2018 wherever
Love Inspired® books and ebooks are sold.

www.LoveInspired.com

Inspirational Romance to Warm Your Heart and Soul

Join our social communities to connect with other readers who share your love!

Sign up for the Love Inspired newsletter at **www.LoveInspired.com** to be the first to find out about upcoming titles, special promotions and exclusive content.

CONNECT WITH US AT:

Facebook.com/groups/HarlequinConnection

 Facebook.com/LoveInspiredBooks

 Twitter.com/LoveInspiredBks

LISOCIAL2018

Reward the book lover in you!

Earn points on your purchase of new Harlequin books from participating retailers.

Turn your points into **FREE BOOKS** of your choice!

Join for FREE today at
www.HarlequinMyRewards.com.

Harlequin My Rewards is a free program (no fees) without any commitments or obligations.